UNREFINED, SUGAR

By Michael Llewellyn

Scaramouche Publishing

*"He was born with a gift of laughter
and a sense that the world was mad."*

Other Books by Michael Llewellyn

The Goat Castle Murder

"Impeccably written and rich with detail, *The Goat Castle Murder* is a provocative story of lost grandeur, peppered with elements of incest, insanity, and extreme eccentricity. What more could a reader want?"
—Celeste Berteau, *Baton Rouge Advocate*

"For the reader who likes a good historical novel, this is a must. For the reader who likes an intricate whodunit, this is also a must. For the reader who likes both, this is a gift."
—Gene Farrington, author of *The Blue Heron*

Out of Time

"In his third time travel book, Llewellyn takes his heroine, Madeleine St. Jacques, to Haiti in 1820 when it was a fanciful island kingdom under the rule of slave-turned-emperor, Henri Christophe. As with *Past Time* and *Still Time*, Llewellyn has unearthed a largely forgotten moment in history and re-imagined it with an incredible eye for detail, picaresque characters and truly compelling plot twists."
—Gregory Lindeblom, author/photographer, *Masculine Beauty*

Past Time

"The characters of *Past Time* are well-drawn and completely believable in the period of Tsarist Russia, circa 1914. I also appreciated the mysteriously referred mechanism of the time shifts and the allusions to a mystic race of time keepers. The time traveler, Madeleine, shows the proper fear of blurting out information that she should keep quiet, but I enjoyed

the little bits of modern speech she spills into the Imperial Russian household. Well-paced, satisfying ending, and a lot of fun to read."
—Richard Sutton, author of *The Red Gate*

Still Time

"*Still Time* is evocative of a new kind of historical time-travel/mystery/thriller that delights and informs the reader. Steeped in New Orleans past and present, Llewellyn creates a steamy, sultry, ultra-romantic atmosphere that will have you craving gumbo and beignets. Heroine Madeleine St. Jacques transforms quite satisfyingly from quiet librarian to cunning, action-oriented belle-of-the-ball once she is singled out by transcendent 'forces' to fulfill a critical mission in the past. Llewellyn's history is accurate and illuminating to the *nth* degree, especially in regard to the looming Civil War, which will make historical fiction readers happy, and his time-travel devices are innovative and clever, so time-slip fans will appreciate that as well. There's a fun romance thrown in for a well-rounded introduction to "Maddy" and her friends. I hope this book is the first of a long-running series."
—Mary F. Burns, author of *The Spoils of Avalon*

Communion of Sinners

"Author Michael Llewellyn has cooked up a savory literary paella inspired by the hidden history of California's Spanish missions and flavored with a touch of investigative journalism and the beauty of the Pacific coast. Mysterious deaths, long held secrets, heartbreak and wonderful descriptions of food and wine combine in this compelling new novel to create a feast of a book."
—Anne Hillerman, author of *Spider Woman's Daughter*

Creole Son

"Michael Llewellyn paints a vivid picture of time and place while chronicling the known details of French painter Edgar Degas's 1872 sojourn in New Orleans. The author's knowledge of both art history and technique enable the reader to share in Degas's creative process as does his gift for dialogue. The author's deft handling of historical detail entwined with an engrossing fictional narrative will appeal to lovers of history, lovers of art, and lovers of a good read. *Creole Son* succeeds in delivering what historical fiction should deliver. It engages, it educates, and above all, it entertains."
— *The Louisiana Advocate*

"Llewellyn captures with compelling detail Degas's artistic excitement and inspiration. I also learned a lot about 19th century New Orleans politics from the impressive research and admired the way Llewellyn met the challenge of writing a convincing novel set in the Francophone 19th century, no easy task. It's so difficult, as I've found, to write in one language while reminding readers that the characters are speaking in another. I was not surprised to learn Llewellyn had been a painter. The frenzy of the inspired eye and hand coordination rang so true that it couldn't be invented."
—James Nolan, author of *Higher Ground*

"With skill and sensitivity, Llewellyn captures the interaction of art and violence, ugliness and beauty, the transition of an artist, a man and a world."
—Barbara Hambly, author of *A Free Man of Color*

Twelfth Night

"Entertaining...a solid sense of life in antebellum New Orleans."
—*Publisher's Weekly*

"Llewellyn has a real gift for atmosphere and characterization...exploiting the rich possibilities of the Quadroon Balls, the class conflict of Mardi Gras, and the voodoo legends of Congo Square and Marie Laveau ... *Twelfth Night* will be the gilded bean in your king cake."
—*New Orleans Times-Picayune.*

"Accurately captures the atmosphere of New Orleans and Mardi Gras. The background material is well-researched, the spicy story is well-written and the pace is suspenseful."
—*The Jackson Clarion- Ledger*

Writing as Michel LaCroix

Alex in Wonderland

"Tennessee Williams meets Jackie Collins with a dash of Truman Capote ... The perfect novel to read while sipping a mint julep and fanning yourself on the veranda."
—Michael D. Craig, author of *The Ice Sculptures: A Novel of Hollywood*

"A hilarious, utterly compelling story of one man's search for identity, independence and love, at the risk of rejection and forsaking a family inheritance. A sizzling mix of fast-paced storytelling and lyrical sexuality."
—Durell Owens, author of *The Song of a Manchild*

"Richly entertaining. Celebrates New Orleans in fine style. Loaded with plot, heart and rainbow-colored characters. Everything you could want is present and accounted for."
—*Edge Boston*

UNREFINED, SUGAR

In memory of Fountain City, Tennessee,
and Harper Lee, who got me thinkin'…

You won't find Meander or Calhoun County, Tennessee, on the map. They're as ephemeral as the flicker of lightning bugs, the crunch of fried okra and scent of magnolias, but they live in Southern hearts everywhere.

"The Southerner's Kook-in-the-Attic Syndrome invariably astounds those outside the fold; cutting a wide swath through life -no matter how- is dear to the Southern heart because it is dashing, and that, too, is a sign of aristocracy."

—Florence King, *Southern Ladies and Gentlemen*

~1957~

1

Folks here say what happened at the new S & H Green Stamp Redemption Center was the biggest news since the Tennessee River changed course in 1807 and prompted early settlers to name the place Meander. Workers clearing away the kudzu jungle on the ridge behind the center exposed a home-made cross proclaiming "Jesus Saves!" Since those crosses are rampant in East Tennessee, no one batted an eye until motorists making the southbound curve on Main Street noticed the juxtaposition of signs announcing that Jesus Saves S&H Green Stamps. Although everybody with a Kodak Brownie rushed to record the moment for posterity, it was Earl Tipton's cleverly angled photograph that appeared in Life Magazine's Miscellaneous section. After that, people drove from as far away as Chattanooga to take their own pictures of the phenomenon. A handful of pious churchgoers carped that it was sacrilegious, but most folks thought it was pretty funny and local store owners enjoyed a sweet boom with tourists loading up on Krispy Kremes, Kodak film and Krystal hamburgers. The ever-enterprising Earl stenciled a bunch of white Fruit of the Loom tee shirts to read "Meander with Jesus" and did a right brisk business until the cross mysteriously vanished in the middle of the night. No one knew who'd killed the tourist boom, but the Southern Baptists were suspected after Ralph Hickman delivered a blistering sermon about being puffed up, worshipping Mammon and taking God's name in vain.

Sylvianne McNeil had no doubt that the preacher was to blame and wasn't shy about saying so when she arrived at Anrita Harrington's house for their regular Saturday afternoon canasta game.

"Reverend Hickman's getting too big for his pulpit again," she declared, joining her hostess and Cassandra Maddox on the screened side porch. "That goofy coincidence was bringing a lot of tourists to town."

Anrita doubted the preacher's guilt. "I'll bet some mischievous kids took it down."

Sylvianne rolled her eyes. "Good heavens, Anrita. Were you born to play devil's advocate?"

"Somebody has to."

"Well, I for one think Sylvianne's right," Cassandra interjected. "Reverend Hickman's trying to carve Meander a deeper notch on the Bible Belt and stick the Holy Scriptures where they don't belong. Remember last year when he preached against teaching evolution in public schools? I guess he'd forgotten we had that debate over thirty years ago with the Scopes Monkey Trial over in Dayton and how stupid we Tennesseans looked to the rest of the country. I see nothing wrong with giving students the tools to make their own decisions about evolution, and everything else for that matter."

"Spoken like an enlightened English teacher."

"I may teach English, but I don't know how enlightened I am."

Sylvianne patted her friend's arm. "You are as far as I'm concerned. I'm still proud of you for making *Catcher in the Rye* required reading."

"I did no such thing!" Cassandra insisted. "I'd be run out of town on a rail if I had."

"Exactly what did you do then?"

"I told the kids in my college-bound class that I didn't dare recommend that book, but that it would be included in their final exams."

Sylvianne said, "I admire anyone who knows how to work the system."

Cassandra turned to Anrita. "This coming from a woman who had four husbands before she was forty and got huge alimony settlements from each one."

"Is it my fault those four men were as unfaithful as they were rich?"

"For once I'm speechless."

"I wish you'd give Laverne lessons. I've never met a woman who talks so much."

Anrita said, "She gets it from her mother. Aunt Mabel was such a motor-mouth that I think it was a matter of survival for Laverne."

"Look, Anrita. I know she's your first cousin, but I truly wish we could find somebody else to play cards with." Sylvianne glanced at her watch. "In addition to talking nonstop, she always cons you into making those tacky pear salads."

Anrita ignored the jibe. "Speaking of tacky, did y'all get invitations to my Tacky Party? It's the eighteenth, a week from next Saturday."

"Don't try to change the subject. Laverne's always late too."

"Oh, you know her motto. If a lady can dress and do her hair and make-up in under an hour, she should probably stay home."

"In which case, half the women in this town should stay home," Sylvianne said. "Starting with Fern Abernathy."

"Amen," Cassandra said.

"Why're you two picking on Fern this morning?" Anrita asked.

"Because she's as trashy as her husband, that's why. Lord, every time I think about Junkin Abernathy being the new mayor and Fern being the first lady of Meander, I get so mad I could scream. If you'd get your head out of that vat of chicken salad once in a while, you'd know what I'm talking about."

"Now, don't you go making fun of my little homegrown business," Anrita teased.

"Four cartons to four million in four years is hardly a little business, darlin', homegrown or otherwise."

"Calvin and I've been blessed, that's all."

"That's the second biggest understatement I ever heard," Cassandra said.

"What's the first?"

"You ever hear what people down in Charleston call the Civil War?"

"No, I haven't."

"They call it 'that recent inconvenience.' "

2

Four years ago, Anrita was a typical American homemaker until she paid attention to friends raving about her homemade chicken salad and put four cartons of the stuff in Pratt's Grocery Store where they disappeared in less than half an hour. The more she made, the more the public wanted, and when her kitchen grew too cramped to meet the demand, Anrita turned the garage into an industrial kitchen. When that also became obsolete, her husband Calvin quit driving a delivery truck for Swan's Bakery to oversee the burgeoning enterprise and the building of a large plant on the edge of town. With the addition of ham salad, pimiento cheese and coleslaw to the line, Anrita's Home-Style Salads flew off the shelves of grocery chains across Tennessee. By the time plants opened in Nashville and Memphis, the Harringtons were millionaires, and Anrita was the envy of all Southern housewives who wished they'd gotten there first.

"To tell y'all the truth, sometimes I think I'll wake up and find it's all a dream."

"You wouldn't think like that if you got out of this cracker box and build a big house up on the bluff."

"I grew up in this house, Sylvianne, and I love this old neighborhood. For heaven's sake, you live here too."

"I only meant that you should have a place that better reflects your high-falutin' position in this town. Plus, it would drive Fern Abernathy crazy. Your success sticks in her craw like a piece of gravel."

"I can't imagine why."

"Because being the mayor's wife and having the biggest, newest house in Meander isn't enough for somebody like that," Cassandra said. "And because she's the most hateful woman on three legs."

"Three legs?"

"Yeah. The usual two, plus the one stuck up her—"

"Cassie!"

"I'm sorry, Anrita, but I'll be damned if I know why you defend that witch. You're as bad as Melanie sticking up for Scarlett."

Anrita demurred. "I was objecting to your language, not defending Fern. Besides, Melanie Wilkes was nobody's fool."

"Maybe not, but I'll bet things would've been mighty different if Scarlett had tried to steal Melanie's husband *and* her chicken salad recipe."

"Good one, Cassie!"

"Thanks."

Sylvianne continued. "Fern's also got her drawers in a twist because nobody outside Meander's ever heard of her, whereas Anrita's pretty puss is in grocery stores all over the state."

Cassandra blinked. "Did you really say whereas?"

"You're not the only one with the five-dollar words, honey. Now shush and let me finish. Anrita is rich and famous, and little Miss Fern can't stand it, but envy's far from her worst sin."

"What do you mean?" Anrita asked.

"Fern Abernathy is white trash by choice," Sylvianne declared. "In my book that's about the worst crime a Southern gal can commit."

"Sylvianne's right," Cassandra added. "Fern's a bad seed like the child murderess in that movie. She comes from a perfectly respectable family over in Seesaw, but from Day One she dated hoods and wore clothes two sizes too small. Showed her bra straps, even in church, and slept around so much that the Salvation Army refused to accept her old mattress." When Anrita glared over the rims of her glasses, Cassandra said, "Okay, I made up that last part. Truth is, Fern's nothing more to me than a passing Piggly Wiggly acquaintance."

"Then how do you know so much about her?" Anrita

asked. Cassandra pointed to Sylvianne. "It figures."

"It sure didn't surprise me when she set her cap for Junkin Abernathy," Sylvianne continued. "Then again, what woman can resist a man who comes from such a long, unbroken line of ne'er-do-wells selling fireworks, used tires and bootlegged whiskey?"

"Not to mention buying mayoral elections."

"Is that true or gossip?" Anrita asked.

"You wouldn't be asking that if you'd seen how many drunks were at the polls, all of them courtesy of Junkin's free hooch."

"That's awful, but surely Fern isn't as bad as he is."

"Oh, yes, she is," Sylvianne insisted. "Those two are a match made in redneck heaven. That fake French provincial monstrosity of a house says it all."

"And that god-awful yard art!"

"I've never seen either one," Anrita confessed.

"Lucky you. I think Fern must've raided every roadside souvenir store between here and Gatlinburg for that tacky horde of gnomes and ducks and birdbaths, and not one but three wishing wells. Not to mention the vegetable garden by the driveway filled with plywood cutouts complete with slogans."

"I didn't see those," Cassandra said.

"Then you missed the old woman bent over with her fanny sticking in the air and her bloomers showing and a slogan that reads, 'Don't bend over in the garden, granny. You know them taters have eyes.' "

Anrita and Cassandra groaned in unison.

"Brace yourselves. The house is even worse."

"How would you know?"

Sylvianne huffed on her fingernails and pretended to buff them on her shoulder. "Because, sweetie pie, I have been inside!"

"No!"

"Yes, ma-am, and you'd better believe that I saw some serious Hillbilly High Baroque."

Anrita was stunned. "What on earth were you doing there?"

"Madam Fern's grand opening. It was purportedly an open house, but I've seen used car lots promoted with less fanfare."

"So, you actually went on purpose?"

"Morbid curiosity is a powerful thing."

Cassandra leaned forward. "Details, honey. Details!"

"Well, Fern not only chose the worst, most vulgar fake French provincial furniture imaginable but left it covered in the plastic it came in. Chairs, sofas, lampshades, even the throw pillows."

"That's got to be a real treat in summer with everybody sticking to the plastic and making rude noises when they got up or sat down."

Anrita ignored Cassandra's inference. "What else?"

"Anything that escaped plastic was gilded. In the gold department, that house of horrors is right up there with Fort Knox. And of course, Fern's idea of fine art is paint-by-numbers she did herself and, as God is my witness, bullfighters painted on velvet and the Eiffel Tower and...oh, Anrita, stop looking at me like that. I am *not* making this up!"

"That's what I was afraid of."

"What're the bedrooms like?"

"I was too scared to peek, especially after going to the powder room."

"I hate to ask."

"Suit yourself."

"Don't you dare clam up now!" Cassandra ordered.

"Alrighty. Since you asked, there were plastic gold fixtures and a plastic marble sink and a plastic statue of the Venus de Milo."

"You sure it wasn't plaster of Paris?"

"Plaster doesn't glow from the inside."

Anrita and Cassandra exchanged puzzled looks.

"It was a lamp, ladies. Complete with a gold shade, fringed of course. Frankly, I don't know why Fern didn't see that it clashed with the furry pink toilet seat cover and the Southern belle doll with a roll of surplus toilet paper rammed up her—" She caught Anrita's frown. "Hoopskirt."

Anrita changed the subject. "How was the food?"

"If you're asking if she served your chicken salad, the answer is no. She picked up some broasted chicken at Archie's Drive-In, but tried to make it look home-made by putting canned gravy in a gravy boat and sticking a berry spoon in the mashed potatoes."

"I don't suppose she used crystal?"

"Try glasses that come in boxes of Duz."

"Dare I ask about the silver?"

"Absolutely. It was right between the Melamine plates and paper napkins."

"That girl does love to mix and match," Cassandra observed.

"Did you recognize the pattern?" Anrita asked.

"What pattern? This stuff was so cheap-looking I could tell the knives had hollow handles without picking them up."

"I can't hear any more," Cassandra insisted. "Is it possible to go blind from mental imagery?"

"Don't you want to know about the toilet paper?"

"You didn't look under the doll's dress, did you?"

"Of course not. I'm talking about the performing roll hanging by the commode."

"Performing? You mean it had pictures?"

"Nothing so mundane, my dear. When you pull on the roll, there's a gizmo inside that plays Dixie!"

"Oh, no!" Cassandra cried. "Did you stand up!"

"That's enough, you two!" Anrita said.

Sylvianne couldn't stop. "Lord help me! I almost forgot the gravy boat."

"Don't tell me that was plastic too."

"Far from it. It was a gen-you-wine French antique."

"At least Fern was trying." Anrita said.

"A little too hard I'm afraid." Sylvianne's eyes gleamed with mischief. "It wasn't really a gravy boat."

"What're you talking about?"

"Uh-oh," Cassandra muttered. "Don't tell me it was a—?"

Sylvianne struggled to keep her composure. "It was ... it was—"

Anrita urged her on. "What are you trying to say, Sylvianne?"

"It was a bourdaloue!"

"A what?!"

When Cassandra exploded with laughter, Anrita stared in confusion. "What's so funny, and what in the world is a ... a boordaloo?"

Sylvianne deferred to Cassandra. "You tell her, teach. I'm too embarrassed."

"To put it as politely as possible," Cassandra explained, "it's something ladies used in the late eighteenth century when skirts were so long and cumbersome, going to the bathroom could be a chore."

Anrita was aghast. "You don't mean they—?"

"Yes, ma-am. I'm afraid some long ago French lady peed in Fern's gravy boat."

Sylvianne mused. "I just thought of what that radio announcer said when he saw the Hindenburg explode."

" 'Oh, the humanity!' " Cassie cried.

"Yes!"

All three were wiping away tears of mirth when Anrita's maid, Lou Johnson, appeared with a pitcher of iced tea and a glass of Coca Cola for Sylvianne. She'd seen them giggling like schoolgirls before and knew better than to ask what was so funny.

"I know Miss Laverne's not here yet," she said, "but I thought y'all might be thirsty."

"You thought right," Sylvianne said, reaching for the Coke. "Thanks, Lou. I'm so dry I'm spittin' cotton."

"You're welcome." Lou turned to her employer. "You

about ready for me to set out those pear salads, Miss Anrita?"

"Not yet. They'll wilt in this sticky heat."

Lou turned to go, but Sylvianne stopped her. "Tell me something, Lou. I know your sister Zanna works for Fern Abernathy. Does she ever talk about her employer?"

"She talks about her alright, but it's none of my business."

"It's none of Sylvianne's business either," Cassandra said, "but that never stopped her before."

Lou wasn't swayed. "I ain't one to kiss and tell, Miss Sylvianne. You wanna know what Zanna thinks about things, you'd best ask Zanna."

"You're no fun," Sylvianne brooded.

"No, ma-am, I ain't. Now I got a pie in the oven needs checking on."

"Be sure and make a pear salad for yourself," Anrita called after her.

Lou called over her shoulder, "No, thank you, ma-am. Not when I can have some of your chicken salad."

"She's no fool," Sylvianne said.

"She sure isn't," Anrita said. "In fact, Calvin and I are looking for a new plant manager and are thinking about Lou for the job. She's smart and efficient as the day is long and should be more than a maid. Thing is, I don't think I could get her to quit Miss Sugar."

"If I were you, I'd talk to Miss Sugar. She might surprise you." Through the porch screen, Cassandra watched a plump figure waddle up the walk. "Oh, joy. Here comes Miss Just."

"I wish you wouldn't call Laverne that. One of these days you're gonna slip up and say it to her face."

Cassandra ignored the reprimand. "I think I'll count how many times she says the word."

"I don't know if I can count that high," Sylvia lamented.

"So sorry I'm late, girls!" Laverne Richardson called, bursting into the room with her usual breathless zeal. She was so animated she was like a one-woman crowd scene, especially since she babbled in run-on sentences "I would've been on time but I just ran into Clyde Hill who just moved here from Johnson City and just joined our church and is just the sweetest man and is the brand-new projectionist over at the Tower movie theater and he was just telling me all about the new films coming to town and guess what?"

Cassandra looked at Sylvianne and announced her tally. "Five."

"Really? I must've missed one."

"Lucky you."

"Five what?" Laverne asked.

"Nothing," Anrita said quickly. "What did Mr. Hill tell you?"

"They're going to show Island in the Sun in just a couple of weeks." When she got three blank stares, Laverne said, "That's Joan Fontaine's new movie and y'all know I just fell in love with her in Jane Eyre and just adored Letter from an Unknown Woman and Ivanhoe and Born to Be Bad and she's just my absolute favorite movie star of all time and if you ask me she's just a whole lot better actress than her sister Olivia de Havilland and did you know those two are sworn enemies and just simply stopped talking to each other years ago?"

"Six," Sylvianne breathed. "What's the movie about?"

"Just let me catch my breath and I'll tell you. Lord, it's so hot today I can hardly reach for my fan!" Laverne collapsed onto Anrita's wicker divan and rummaged for the fan tucked inside her purse. She waved it feverishly, blowing her bangs in all directions as she continued. "Mr. Hill says he's not sure but he thinks it's a romance set on some tropical Caribbean island that he says is just beautiful in the previews and that James Mason is in it too and some colored actor named Harry Something-or-other and, oh, my, I'm just absolutely parched and would just love some of that iced tea."

"Help yourself and bring it to the table," Anrita said when Lou, ever vigilant, reappeared with a tray of salads. "Lunch is ready."

Laverne waved at Lou. "Hey, there. I hope you made

those wonderful pear salads with mayonnaise and maraschino cherries and grated cheddar cheese. I just can't get enough of them."

"You're in luck, Mrs. Richardson," Lou said, tone dry as the Gobi.

Laverne rattled on as she and Cassandra took their seats while Anrita lingered to watch Sylvianne grab a flask from her purse and dump a shot of bourbon in her Coke. Sylvianne enjoyed a healthy swig before confiding in Anrita as they headed for the dining room.

"I'm telling you, if my four husbands hadn't already driven me to drink, Laverne would sure be in the driver's seat." She took another slug. "And I ain't *just* whistling Dixie!"

3

Eulalie Victoria Crockett Saunders was Meander's undisputed social queen and the very definition of the Southern *grande dame*. When she sat, her spine never touched the chair back, and people knew instinctively to rise when she entered a room. Tall and slender with a head of pewter waves, she was sharp as a tack at seventy-two and as formidable as she was genteel, especially when provoked by bad manners. Any number of ill-bred locals had felt her sting, and she'd enjoyed more than one Yankee for breakfast. Eulalie's clothes came from Regenstein's in Atlanta, and she rarely appeared in public without her trademark Chanel and pearls, a fashion statement lost on most everyone but for Anrita, Sylvianne and Cassandra. She adored entertaining, whether a single friend for tea or a barbecue for forty on the lawn of Blufftop, her home overlooking Meander from high above the river. It was built by her grandfather, William Talmadge Crockett, and named because that's where it was situated and because he loathed pretentious house monikers like Bagatelle and Belle Caro. The original log cabin constructed by his own father had expanded along with the family, and in 1848 it received a dozen more rooms and a handsome Greek revival facade making it appear far grander than it actually was. Eulalie's late husband's extensive real estate holdings and dairy farms, and her own family fortune, had made her the third richest woman in East Tennessee, and Blufftop was her pride and joy.

"It's an illusion," she was fond of saying about the place. "Rather like the Old South itself." People were never sure what she meant, but no one ever mustered the courage to ask.

Eulalie had other idiosyncrasies, including one that disarmed people meeting her for the first time. If she liked them well enough, she instructed them to call her "Miss Sugar." She insisted it was because she called everyone "sugar," but it was, in fact, a charming ruse. Eulalie, like many Southern women of a certain age, could recite entire genealogies of the local deceased, but she rarely remembered the live ones and addressed only a handful of people by name. They included her beloved late husband, Edward Thomas Saunders, dead of a heart attack in 1931, and their only child, Geoffrey, killed on Iwo Jima when he was twenty-four. The only living soul whose name she never forgot, and the only one allowed to call her Eulalie, was Lou Johnson, who had been in her employ for twenty years, well before she went to work for Anrita Harrington.

Despite her fondness for entertaining, Eulalie was less than enthusiastic about the caller due that pretty May morning. She was honored that Ida Turnbull, the town librarian and chief historian, asked her to head the Entertainment Committee for Meander's Labor Day Sesquicentennial, but less than thrilled to learn the entire celebration would be presided over by Fern Abernathy. She'd never met the woman but had noted her from a distance, not a difficult achievement since Fern's gaudy clothes were louder than a sonic boom. And, of course. she knew Fern was married to Junkin Abernathy, the newly elected mayor whom Eulalie detested and avoided like the plague. Once when she had filled in at Anrita's canasta club, Eulalie learned that Fern was "a trashy, social climbing bulldozer" (Sylvianne) who "smiled incessantly" (Anrita) and was "as insincere as the day is long" (Cassandra). As far as Eulalie was concerned, the woman's social fate was sealed when Sylvianne added that Fern chewed gum while taking her wedding vows and teased her hair so high that it once snagged a ceiling fan in the church fellowship hall.

Feeling that Blufftop was under siege, Eulalie slapped on her best Elizabeth Arden war paint, along with a favorite Chanel suit, and went downstairs to await the enemy. She found Lou in the parlor setting up the silver tea service. An arrangement of peachy pink Antoine Rivoire roses, so freshly picked they were flecked with dew, gleamed on the coffee table alongside a luscious array of petits fours. Eulalie clasped her hands in silent applause

"It's perfect." Eulalie leaned down to smell the roses. "Tell me something."

"Yes, ma-am?"

"What do you know about Fern Abernathy?"

"Hmmm. That's the second time in as many days I've been asked about that woman. Why's she so important all of a sudden?"

"Who else was asking?"

"Sylvianne McNeil over at Miss Anrita's canasta party. She asked me if Zanna had said anything about her."

"What did you say?"

"I told her to ask Zanna, not me."

"So, you don't know anything?"

"Nothing nice, if that's what you mean." Lou paused. "And I imagine it is."

Eulalie chuckled. "You know me too well."

Lou thought a moment. "I don't mind telling you things because I know it won't go no further. All Zanna ever says is that the Abernathys are mighty peculiar, and that if she could find other work in this town that she'd quit them in a flash."

"Is Mrs. Abernathy unkind?"

"Hateful is more like it. Zanna says some days she's mean as a snake."

Lou left to answer the doorbell before Eulalie could pursue that remark. Girding for battle, Eulalie retreated to a Queen Anne wing chair, her favorite perch because it faced the foyer and afforded her time to size up whoever approached. With Fern, however, this assessment was instantaneous, and Eulalie found herself wishing her bifocals were sunglasses.

In addition to an ear-to-ear grin, Fern sported a cotton candy mop of teased, hennaed hair and a bright green off-the-shoulder blouse stuffed into a pair of matching Capri pants a size too small. To her horror, Eulalie realized their sparkly harlequin pattern came from tiny mirrors. A wide silver Concho belt emphasized Fern's lumpy, dumpy figure, and her fat little feet were crammed into sandals with frighteningly high heels. The ensemble swarmed with silver earrings, rings, bracelets and the largest, most vulgar turquoise necklace Eulalie had ever seen. It was so heavy Fern listed forward as she clacked her way across the marble foyer floor.

My Lord, Eulalie thought. The woman is an exploding piñata. She got another shock when she realized Fern was wearing neither gloves nor girdle.

"You must be—"

"Fern Abernathy, Miz. Saunders." Her vigorous handshake begged for a pump handle. "It's real nice to meet you after all this time.

Eulalie did not invite Fern to call her Miss Sugar. "Thank you."

Assaulted by a pungent perfume cloud, Eulalie waved her lacy handkerchief, grateful when the ever-vigilant Lou threw open French doors to the terrace. Neither gesture was lost on Fern.

"I hope I'm not wearing too much perfume," she said, still smiling. "My husband, Junkin—" She paused dramatically before adding, "He's the mayor, you know." Another pause. "He gave me oodles of Joy for Christmas. I love it so much I guess I get carried away."

"Is that right?"

"Did you know it's the most expensive perfume in the world? Why, it's high as a cat's back!"

"How fascinating." Eulalie indicated a downwind chair. "Won't you sit down?"

"Thanks." Fern sat and dabbed her damp brow with a Kleenex. "Something wrong, Mrs. Saunders?"

"Forgive me for staring, but I've never seen anything quite like that necklace."

Fern beamed. "Lots of people stare at my jewelry, especially when they see it for the first time." Realizing one turquoise strand had looped under her right boob, Fern rearranged it with a loud clatter. "Junkin took me out to Santa Fe last fall. It's in New Mexico, you know. Not old Mexico."

"So I understand."

"Anyhoo, we went to this cute little Indian reservation where the natives were selling scads of this turquoise stuff, and when I saw this thing I just had to have it." Eulalie winced at another annoying clatter when Fern fiddled with the necklace again. "You know, the Navahos or Arapahos or whatever they are make such pretty jewelry. I don't know why our Cherokees don't do something like that. Seems like everything they sell is made in Japan."

"Perhaps because they don't have turquoise and silver to work with."

"Mmmm. I guess I never thought about it. Indians are pretty much Indians as far as I'm concerned. You know what I mean?"

"I do indeed, my dear." Knowing this was a dead-end conversation, Eulalie picked up a teacup and saucer. "Suppose I pour and we get down to business, Mrs. Abernathy."

"You mean hot tea?"

"Why, yes."

"Don't suppose you have any iced tea, do you?"

"I'm sure I can have some made." Eulalie caught Lou's eye before she exited for the kitchen, a step ahead as usual.

"Oh, goodie!"

While waiting for the iced tea, Fern loaded up on petits fours and, between mouthfuls, recited a nonstop list of her plans for the Sesquicentennial celebration. Eulalie struggled to keep still as she heard one horror story after another. Meander history, as interpreted by Fern Abernathy, was a wildly overbaked salute to the long-lost Confederacy.

"The parade down Main Street will end at Crockett Park where I think we should kick things off with the band playing Dixie, don't you?" Fern didn't wait for a response, nor did Eulalie offer one. The woman's party planning techniques could've been applied to a demolition derby. "Everyone will stand of course, and once they're seated we'll have a concert of Southern music, showcasing the Tennessee Waltz naturally, which will accompany the Cavalcade of Confederate Cavaliers and Beautiful Belles, which is my personal favorite event and promises to be a surefire crowd pleaser what with all the pretty costumes and everything. Next up is a very moving re-enactment of the Inauguration of President Jefferson Davis, and I'm tickled pink that Junkin has agreed to portray President Davis. Isn't that wonderful?" Eulalie's mind was almost numb from this breathless, mindless recitation. "After that we'll have a slide show on the glorious history of the South, but I think we should stop with the firing on Fort Sumter, don't you? And to wrap things up, by then it'll be dark you see, we'll have a candlelight eulogy honoring some of our more illustrious citizens who have passed on, and of course our fallen heroes in gray." Fern dabbed a mock tear with her handkerchief before popping another tea cake into her maw. "It leaves you speechless, don't it?" she expelled between chews. To her dismay, Eulalie couldn't help envisioning Fern chomping gum as a bride.

"Indeed, it does, Mrs. Abernathy," she managed finally. Eulalie realized she'd been so mesmerized by Fern's run-on recitation that she'd let her tea grow cold. She poured a fresh cup, spiced it with lemon and stirred while attempting to sort sense from what she'd heard. "You certainly seem to have thought of everything, but isn't there a bit too much emphasis on the old South and not enough on the new Tennessee? After all, Meander has made great strides since the Civil War and has important ties to both the Tennessee Valley Authority and Oak Ridge which are famous all over the world and—"

Fern waved her Kleenex dismissively. "Oh, I know all

that, but those old dams and atomic bombs aren't nearly as much fun as girls dressed up like Southern belles, and heaven knows they're not as pretty." She leaned forward as though whispering a confidence despite talking loud enough for Lou to hear in the kitchen. "My Lurleen has already ordered her dress, and let me tell you those crinolines and pantalets are the cutest things you've ever seen."

"Might I assume Lurleen is your daughter?"

"Why, yes, and if I have anything to say about it she'll be Queen of the Sequincentennial."

"Sesquicentennial," Eulalie corrected with an internal shudder. "You didn't mention there was to be a queen."

"Why, I thought it was a given. I can't hardly imagine a Southern celebration without a beauty queen and her court, can you? Good heavens! The very idea gives me the fantods!"

Eulalie was drowning in a sea of crinolines, tiaras and rebel flags. "So there's to be a beauty contest too?"

"Sure enough," Fern announced proudly, as though she was the first to think of such a thing. "The night before the sequincentennial."

Eulalie didn't bother correcting her this time as she realized sequincentennial might be a more appropriate name, at least in the flashy World According To Fern. "Will there be a talent competition?"

"Certainly. And swimsuits too."

"Who will the judges be?"

"Oh, Junkin and I haven't picked them yet, but they'll all be prominent folks. You know. Pillars of the community and maybe some preachers and … well, like that."

Lurleen is definitely the new queen, Eulalie thought grimly.

"I see."

"It's the queen who'll lead the Cavalcade of Confederate Cavaliers and their Beautiful Belles, which is the royal court of course. After they parade through the crowd on a special red carpet, they'll take their seats alongside Junkin and the other local dignitaries." Fern paused long enough to conjure false modesty from the same source as her crocodile tears. "Since I'm chairman of this whole shebang, I probably shouldn't be a judge, but the mayor has to be up there, don-cha know, and, as Meander's First Lady, I really don't have no choice."

Apparently, neither does anyone else, Eulalie thought. "I see." She did a little math. "This sounds like quite a production. Do you know where to get a dais big enough to hold a dozen ladies in hoopskirts?"

Fern's forehead wrinkled. "Day-us?"

"A platform."

"Oh, I thought we'd grab some of those collapsible bleachers from the high school football field and put them up in Crockett Park." Fern jumped like she was stung when an idea bloomed under her beehive. "I swan! How could I have been such a ninny?"

Eulalie didn't know where to begin. "I beg your pardon."

"Davy Crockett of course. He's got to be Tennessee's most famous native son. I mean they made that movie about him and everything and that song was on Your Hit Parade forever and ... oh, how could I have forgotten, especially since we'll be in a park named after him!"

Eulalie was once again blind-sided by the woman's stultifying stupidity. "The park is named after my grandfather, William Talmadge Crockett."

Fern looked peeved. "Are you sure?"

"Quite sure," Eulalie said, certain that poor Davy Crockett would want no part of this unholy mess. Nor would her grandfather, for that matter.

"Hmmm. Maybe it's just as well that I don't have to plan another tribute. It's only a little over three months before Labor Day and I've about run out of ideas."

"Heaven forfend."

"I know. Wouldn't that be awful?"

"Ghastly."

"Here's your iced tea, ma-am."

Fern had ignored Lou when she answered the door and gasped when she saw her for the first time. "Lordy! You're sure a dead ringer for the girl who works for me!"

"Lou and Zanna are twins," Eulalie offered.

"Well, she sure gave me a start!" Fern fanned a fresh tissue and unleashed another potent Joy cloud. "My word!"

While Fern sipped, Eulalie struggled to salvage something from the impending disaster. She began as genteelly as possible. "Mrs. Abernathy, you've obviously put a lot of thought and effort into this ... this production, but would you mind if I made a suggestion?"

Fern's smile flickered and faded before the idling bulldozer roared back to life. "You don't wanna change something, do ya?"

"Why, no, but since I'm a member of the town's oldest family and the slide show is about history, I'd like to help with that if I may."

Fern cocked her head, beehive tilting precariously. "You mean you want to operate the slide projector?"

That was hardly what Eulalie meant, but she capitulated out of sheer desperation. "If you wouldn't mind."

Fern looked relieved. "Why, sure!"

Emboldened, Eulalie pushed her luck. "I'd like to narrate too if that would be alright."

"Uh, okay." The treacly smile rebloomed, bigger than ever as Fern shuffled through her papers. "I've got the history speech in here somewhere."

"I thought you might."

"Aha. Here's that little booger. I finished writing it last night, and if I do say so myself it's a dilly."

"I'm sure it is."

"Why, thank you!" Fern cocked her head the other way, and the beehive caromed again. "You know something, Mrs. Saunders? When I came here today I was worried that you might give me a hard time."

"Why would you think that?"

"Oh, you know how folks talk. Some say you're the high-and-mighty type, but I don't think you could've been nicer."

"Thank you."

"In fact, I think I'll let you in on a little secret. Junkin and I got something planned that's gonna be a big surprise. You'll never guess it in a million years."

"Then perhaps I'd better not try."

Oblivious to any innuendo, Fern actually giggled. "Why, I didn't really want you to guess, Mrs. Saunders."

"I'm so relieved."

"All I can say is that Junkin and I are going to ride in the parade in a very, very special new convertible. He's had it on order for months and is getting it before anybody else in the whole state of Tennessee because—" She dropped her voice to a conspiratorial whisper. "Between us gals, he knows some mighty important folks."

"I'm quite sure he does."

Fern started to say something, but instead, to Eulalie's surprise, stood to go. "Darn! I just remembered Junkin made me promise not to tell the name of the car. Don't you hate people who start stories and don't finish them?" The red beehive teetered yet again. "Shame on me."

And then some, Eulalie thought.

4

Junkin Abernathy cut a lumpish figure in a rumpled seersucker suit, stained Panama hat and suspenders working overtime to contain a watermelon-size belly. His physique, overbearing personality and loud, grating drawl were so cartoonish that Cassandra had nicknamed him Foghorn Leghorn.

"Damned heat!" He tugged a damp handkerchief from his jacket and mopped his forehead again. "Not even ten o'clock, and already hot as the hinges of hell!"

Junkin waddled into his City Hall office, hung up his hat and jacket and switched on the overhead fan. It hummed and crackled but refused to budge. He called down the hall for his secretary. "Coralee, did you call somebody about fixing this confounded fan?"

"Yes, sir. I talked to Eustace Miller yesterday afternoon, and he promised to send someone out first thing this morning. Want me to call him again?"

"Damned right I do! Call him and then hustle your sweet behind in here with my coffee and doughnuts."

"Yes, Mr. Mayor."

Junkin eased onto the inner tube cushion in his chair and tossed the damp handkerchief aside. After Fern told him he had no business sweating like a field hand now that he was mayor, Junkin kept a fresh supply of hankies in a desk drawer. He wiped the back of his neck and checked his desk calendar for the morning agenda. He was thinking he'd never get through the day in this sticky heat when Coralee appeared with his coffee.

"Eustace said he was sorry but that he had a family emergency." Coralee set down the coffee and doughnuts. "Something about car trouble."

"More likely he stayed at Big Shots all night and is too

hung-over to work."

"He promised to be here directly." Before Junkin could comment, Coralee added, "Sonny Hull's here to see you."

"What the devil's the postman want at this time of day?"

"He didn't say, sir."

"Tell him I'm not here."

Coralee tilted her head toward the big glass pane in the wooden door. "Mr. Hull can see you, sir."

Junkin muttered to himself as he dismissed Coralee and motioned Sonny into his office. There were few things that annoyed him more than having his morning coffee interrupted, and his mood didn't improve when Sonny eyed the box of doughnuts.

"You gonna eat all those?"

"Damned right I am." Junkin took a greedy bite and ignored the glob of grape jelly oozing onto his chin. "What you think I was gonna do with them?"

"I was just asking." Sonny was over six feet tall and weighed 135 pounds soaking wet. Nobody understood why the man was so thin because he had an appetite like a junkyard dog and was the Kiwanis Club's nemesis at their all-you-can-eat pancake breakfasts. He could also sulk like a ten-year-old girl, and when he pulled a face, Junkin tossed him a plain doughnut. "Hey, thanks, boss!"

Junkin gobbled the rest of his doughnut. "You've got exactly ten minutes to speak your piece, boy."

"What's the rush?"

"Reverend Hickman, that's the rush. I sure as hell ain't looking forward to seeing him. He may be my preacher, but he's been high on my shit list ever since he started preaching on the evils of whiskey. Some of my best customers are in that congregation, and it's damned bad for business."

"What's he wanna see you about?"

"Said somebody's dog's been crapping on the parsonage lawn." Junkin shook his head. "I'm telling you, Sonny. Being mayor ain't as grand as you might think."

"Whose dog is it?"

"Never mind about that. Tell me why you're here."

"I checked up on that movie you asked about."

Junkin stopped chewing. Maybe this was important after all. "Yeah?"

"It's opening at the Tower Theater two weeks from Wednesday."

"Then we'll hit it right about dark on opening night. You'll spread the word, huh?"

"Yes, siree. Reckon we could enlist some boys from Lenoir City?"

"Screw Lenoir City. I want Knoxville backing us up on this one. This'll be our first appearance in Meander, and it's gotta be a big one. I wanna get people talking."

Sonny inhaled his doughnut and looked longingly back at the plate. When he was ignored, he got back to business. "Last time we got together, four of the boys said they needed new robes, so I looked around and found a widow woman over in Seesaw who says she'll make 'em up for us."

"You sure she can keep her mouth shut? There'll be lots of people asking questions after we hit the Tower, and I don't wanna leave a trail."

"She's okay. In fact, when I explained what we needed, she said she'd give us a discount because she's a true believer herself. I told her that was mighty white of her."

"Be sure she makes the eyeholes big enough and keeps the hems high. Don't want nobody tripping like Doyle Richardson that time down in Ooltewah. Poor fool coulda broke his neck."

"I'll tell her."

"We can't afford to take any chances." Junkin helped himself to another doughnut and chewed thoughtfully. "Not after Ronny Lay printed our flyers and threatened to blab if we didn't pay him extra."

"Speaking of printers, the grammar school's bought itself a brand new mimeograph machine, so I got them to give me the old one. It's not the best but it's good enough for what we need."

Junkin was pleased. "You're on the ball, boy. Here. Grab yourself a chocolate one."

"I reckon we all need to be on the ball with what's going on up these days. New battles to be fought and all."

"Which means we're gonna have to raise a bigger army."

"Think we ought to have a membership drive this summer?"

"Damned right I do. This business at the Tower ought to win us some new blood." Junkin looked nostalgic. "I sure wish I could join you fellows. I feel like a different man when I get dressed up, don't you?"

"Sure do." Sonny wolfed down the chocolate doughnut. "Why can't you be there, boss?"

"I told you a million times I may be Exalted Cyclops but I gotta watch my step now that I'm mayor. I'll support you all I can, but we can't have any more initiations on that land behind my house, and I sure can't risk being seen in my robe." Junkin checked his watch. "Okay, boy. You better scoot before the preacher gets here. Tell that woman in Seesaw to put a rush on those robes. I've decided to call an emergency meeting for the weekend."

"Yes, sir!"

Sonny was barely out the door before Coralee announced Reverend Hickman. Junkin swallowed his loathing and stood as the minister entered the office. "Hey, there, Reverend!" he boomed. "Good to see you this fine morning. And you know what they say. Punctuality is the politeness of kings."

The preacher shook hands and gave the idle overhead fan a dirty look. "Why isn't that fan running? The heat in here is un-Christian."

"It's temporarily out of order, like most everything else in city hall. I've got my work cut out for me."

"I'm sure you do." Hickman looked through the window behind Junkin's desk. "What say we go outside and talk at

one of those picnic tables? It's stifling in here, and besides—"
He nodded at Coralee. "It's more private."

"You need privacy to talk about dog shit?"

"There's no dog. Your secretary asked about the nature of my business, so I had to tell her something. Heaven forgive me for lying, but dog-do was all I could think of on the spur of the moment." He lowered his voice. "I have something important to discuss, Mr. Mayor. Something very, very important."

Junkin jerked his head toward the windows. "Alright. Let's go."

As he and the minister faced each other across a warped wooden picnic table, Junkin conceded coming outside was a good idea. There was abundant shade from an ancient grove of butternut trees, and because city hall backed up to the river, a cool breeze stirred the heavy humidity. He even stopped sweating.

"What's on your mind, preacher?"

The minister gave Junkin a penetrating look before propping his elbows on the table, tenting his hands and closing his eyes. "Let us pray."

Junkin obeyed, but paid no attention to the intonation of "Thees" and "Thous" which, despite the awful heat, sent a chill to his heart. He'd dealt with Hickman before, and he knew this long-winded prayer was a prelude to bad news. He waited edgily for an "Amen!" and watched the preacher fold arms across his chest and assumed the authoritarian tone reserved for the pulpit.

"I've heard some distressing things these past few days, Mayor Abernathy."

"Oh?"

"Yes, indeed. Some mighty distressing things indeed. I've prayed long and hard about them, and when God didn't advise me, I decided to come to you."

"Well, I'm always willing to play second fiddle to the Almighty." He knew Hickman's wide-flung spy network reported everything that happened in Meander and felt another chill when he wondered if Ronny Lay had blabbed after all. If that was the case, he'd have the guy's Grapenuts for breakfast.

"As you surely know, having power is a mighty big responsibility," the minister continued, "because it can be used for evil as well as good. The people I'm referring to fall into the former category."

Junkin's patience was running out. "Look here, reverend. I'm a very busy man, so suppose you stop dancing the Tennessee waltz and get to the point. Is this about Cassandra Maddox teaching filth in our schools or the Jesus Saves sign that got stolen or Eugene Proctor peeping in windows? If it's one of those things. I'll handle it personally and pronto."

Maddox leveled his gaze. "It's about that mysterious fire out Old Quarry Road."

When Junkin's stomach turned over, he swallowed hard and told himself too much was at stake to lose his cool, much less all those jelly doughnuts. "What about it?"

"It damaged quite a bit of private property, and, well—" Hickman drawled the word into three syllables. "Certain people suspect it involved some sort of initiation ceremony and that you had a hand in it."

Junkin's fear was trumped by sudden anger. "What the hell you talking about?"

"Please watch your language, Mr. Abernathy. I'm a man of the cloth."

"I don't give a rat's ass if you're the fucking pope! Where do you get off blaming me for that damned fire?"

The minister raised a silencing hand which Junkin, to his surprise, obeyed. "I never said I blamed you, Mr. Mayor. Only that certain people had some suspicions."

"So why are you here?"

"Because as Mayor of Meander, you need to know folks say there was a witness to that unfortunate conflagration." When Hickman put his elbows back on the table and laced his fingers, Junkin expected another prayer, but he was wrong. "Don't you see I'm here to help?"

"I'm not sure what I see, reverend. Not yet anyway." Junkin began to sweat again. "I don't suppose you can identify this mystery person."

"For now, I prefer to keep the witness's confidence a secret." Hickman paused before adding. "Especially from Sheriff Kirkendol."

Junkin glowered. "Chuck Kirkendol won't make a move without me, so you needn't worry about him."

"I still maintain that silence is golden, and with your help I can and will keep things quiet, for the time being anyway."

"My help, huh?"

"Yes, sir."

Here it comes, Junkin thought.

"How much is this going to cost me, reverend?"

Hickman appeared affronted. "Why, I said nothing about money, Mr. Mayor."

"Then how come I'm getting the message loud and clear?"

"If that's what you choose to believe, I won't dispute your words."

"Then I reckon you better tell me how much you want to keep some guy's mouth shut."

The preacher looked up into the butternut trees when a couple of squirrels stopped chasing each other and perched on a limb, tails twitching frantically. "God certainly created some wondrous creatures, didn't He?"

"He created some assholes too. Now get to the damned point."

"Language, please."

"How much, preacher?"

"I'll leave that up to you, Mr. Mayor." Reverend Hickman drew a collection envelope from his black coat, slid it across the picnic table and stood. "As you know, our church is in desperate need of a new organ which is, I'm afraid, quite expensive."

The back of Junkin's neck burned as the extortion plot was finally revealed. He stared at the envelope a long moment before rising to glower at the minister. "You'll get your money, preacher, but if you don't get the hell out of my sight your church won't be all that needs a new organ. Do you hear me?"

"Why, yes, I do. Shall we have another prayer before I run along?"

"I'm pretty much prayed out for the moment, but maybe you can answer a question for me."

"I'll be happy to try, my brother."

"How come preachers and vultures both wear black?"

5

Anrita checked her reflection in the dressing room mirror. Over her shoulder, she watched her husband adjust his Windsor knot and splash Old Spice on his face. Tall and distinguished with thick black hair silvering at the temples, Calvin Harrington was, she thought, as handsome as when they met in high school. He caught her looking at him.

"I sure enjoyed myself last night, sweetheart."

Anrita and Calvin had been married twenty-one years, but she still got flustered when her husband alluded to sex. "You make me blush, Mr. Harrington."

"Good." He pretended to sneak across the room to buss her neck. "I like making you blush."

Anrita let him nuzzle for a moment before pulling away. "Don't mess up my hair, honey. I spent three hours at the beauty parlor yesterday."

Calvin retreated. "I think it would take a baseball bat to move all that Spray-Net."

"All the same, I like to look my best in church."

"You always look good to me, honey." He gave her a quick kiss. "And you know I have a weakness for rich women."

"Which I wouldn't be without you."

"Nah. If you hadn't cooked up that first batch of chicken salad, I'd still be driving a bread truck."

"And if you hadn't quit driving that truck to manage the business, we wouldn't be where we are today. We're a team, sugar pie. Always have been. Always will be."

"That's sweet of you to say so, but the truth is, I like pretending I'm a kept man."

"Calvin Harrington, how do you come up with such foolishness? You're a real caution, you know that?"

"I sure hope so."

Anrita stood and smoothed her skirts. "My seams straight?"

"Lady, if your legs looked any better we'd never make it to church." Calvin gave her a playful swat on her behind. "You ready?"

"Almost." She reached for the red rosebud on the dressing table. "I need my Mother's Day rose. Your white one is in the refrigerator."

"Do I have to wear it?"

Calvin's beloved mother Virginia had died only two months ago, and Anrita knew he dreaded this reminder.

"Not if you don't want to."

"Won't people think it's disrespectful?"

"No one who matters." Anrita pecked his cheek. "Why don't you run on over to the church and spend a few private minutes in the cemetery? I'll be along directly."

"You don't mind?"

" 'Course not. Sylvianne's due any minute. We'll walk over together."

"Alright. I'll meet you in front of the church."

Alone again, Anrita gave her make-up a final inspection and pinned the rosebud on the lapel of her blue suit jacket. She was tugging on white gloves when Sylvianne yoo-hooed at the front door.

"Anybody home?"

"I'm in the bedroom!" Anrita was adjusting her corsage when Sylvianne bustled in wearing a white lace dress with a plunging neckline. "My goodness! Are you going to church or a cocktail party?"

"Oh, I know it's a bit much, but I felt like rattling some cages this morning."

Anrita tut-tutted. "I'd say spring isn't the only thing that's busting out all over."

"So much for my unassailable fashion sense."

"That's not what you should worry about being assailed."

"Never mind. I need to raid your rose garden."

"What's the matter with yours?"

"The red ones are all bloomed out, and there's not a bud to be had." Sylvianne pulled a handkerchief from her cleavage and dabbed her throat. "Gonna be another scorcher."

"The weatherman on Channel Ten said this was the hottest May on record."

"He'll get no argument from me. Whew!" Sylvianne shook the front of her dress and unleashed the scent of White Shoulders tempered with Jack Daniels. Anrita wondered which was more recently applied. "Whose idea is this anyway?"

"What idea?"

"Wearing rosebuds to church on Mother's Day?"

"I don't know, but if we don't get moving we're going to be late. Calvin's meeting us at the church."

"I'll hurry!" With Anrita close behind, Sylvianne rushed into the back yard and inspected a cluster of red rose bushes in the corner. She searched closely before coming up empty-handed. "You'd think there would be one damned bud in all these bushes."

"I must've gotten the last one." Anrita watched Sylvianne head across the yard and rifle through her prized Duchesse de Bourbon roses. "You can't use those."

Sylvianne's response was a triumphant, "Aha!" She broke off a large bud and held it against her shoulder. "What do you think?"

"I think you're color blind, that's what."

"So it's a little pink."

"A *little* pink? It's almost cerise!"

"So what?"

Anrita was horrified. "You know good and well that you wear a red bud if your mother's living and white if she's deceased. What will people think if you march down the aisle wearing bright pink?"

"Maybe they'll think Mama's got one foot in the grave. Lord knows I wish she did!"

"What an awful thing to say about Miss Mamie, especially on Mother's Day."

"She's the mama from hell, Anrita, and you know it."

"It's still an awful thing to say."

"About a woman who could give Medea lessons on child-rearing?"

Anrita didn't argue further. Everyone knew Sylvianne's mother, Mamie Freels, had devoted her adult life to making her husband Ralph and their children miserable. Decades ago Ralph found escape in a floating crap game that kept him up in Knoxville most of the time, and Sylvianne's younger brother Jack went out to get a pack of cigarettes when he was eighteen and joined the merchant marines instead of coming home. Sylvianne fled the house by getting married, and when her first husband didn't work out, she found three more.

"Last time I visited, Mama took out those awful false teeth and threw them at me!"

"Why?"

"I guess the dentist wasn't handy."

Anrita quickly changed the subject. "Let's go back inside so I can fix your corsage."

In her sewing room, Anrita rifled through a box of ribbons and quickly fashioned an elegant bow. She pinned the rosebud to Sylvianne's dress and looked pleased.

"Not bad if I say so myself."

"It's gorgeous!" Sylvianne said. "I swan, Anrita. Is there anything you can't do?"

"Mama taught me how to make corsages. Remember she had a little greenhouse out back where she grew camellias and orchids."

"Of course I remember. You had the most beautiful corsages in high school. The other girls couldn't wait to see what you'd wear to the dance, and we all hated you because your corsages made ours look cheap."

"I think some of those boys asked me to dances because

they knew I came with a free corsage. That's when I realized how special Calvin was."

"What do you mean?"

"He told Mama he didn't feel right not paying for my flowers, and, after that, he could do no wrong in her book. Mine either for that matter." Anrita steered Sylvianne outside and through the front gate. "That was the moment I fell in love with the guy."

"What a sweet story." Sylvianne took Anrita's arm as they strolled a sidewalk shaded by huge oaks and elms and a scattering of dogwood and redbud trees. "You'll never know how much I wish I could find a man like Calvin."

"Don't think I don't know how lucky I am to have him."

Both enjoyed the splendid May morning as they walked the six short blocks to the First Methodist Church. Its bells merged with those of other churches calling people to worship, and Anrita embraced the sweet moment. Sylvianne was less than enthralled. Their rapid pace and the heat prompted her to pull an antique Japanese fan from her purse and snap it open. She waved it furiously and tugged Anrita's arm.

"If we don't slow down I'm going to break a sweat."

"You know what they say, Sylvianne. Horses sweat, gentlemen perspire and ladies glisten."

"Honey, if my deodorant fails, there's gonna be a whole lotta glistenin' going on by the time I get to the church." She tapped her watch. "We've still got time."

"You're right." Anrita slowed down and glanced at Sylvianne's fan. "I don't remember seeing that fan before. Is it new?"

"Jack sent it to me from Indo-China. Do you like it?"

"It's lovely."

"Thanks. I can't abide those hideous church fans in the pew racks. They always have ads for funeral homes on the back."

"And Christ praying in the Garden of Gethsemane on the front."

"Yes, and it's always bothered me that I can switch from Christianity to crass commercialism with the wave of a hand."

6

Eulalie had a restless night punctuated by nightmares of smirking girls in grotesquely oversized hoopskirts whirling through Crockett Park while her great-great grandfather shouted curses from a showboat. She was relieved when she woke up to her familiar morning routine. Promptly at seven, Lou appeared with a breakfast tray and opened portieres to flood the room with morning light. That done, she helped Eulalie into a lacy bed jacket and set the tray across her lap. It contained a silver pot of coffee, two china cups and saucers, a vase with a fresh sprig of whatever was blooming in Blufftop's vast gardens and a copy of the *Knoxville Journal.*

Lou frowned. "You look like you didn't sleep much."

"I didn't, and you don't want to know why."

"Fine with me. I've heard that tone before."

"But I will say that this Labor Day event is going to be a fiasco of epic proportions."

"Why's that?"

Eulalie poured two cups of coffee and passed one to Lou. For the past thirteen years, the two women took their morning coffee together, a formal ritual that would have scandalized the Abernathys and their ilk who believed that colored folks had no business eating or drinking with white people. That made the custom all the sweeter for Eulalie who savored the moment along with the pungent aroma of coffee. She drank nothing but Café du Monde brand because she and Edward spent their honeymoon in New Orleans where she learned to love the tang of chicory.

After a sip, she said, "For starters, the event is supposed to celebrate our town's history which is something Fern Abernathy is making up as she goes along."

"I didn't think people knew much about Meander's history before the courthouse burned down."

"They don't, but to hear Fern tell it, Meander was the heart and soul of the Old South and everything it stood for."

"Hmmm. Don't like the sound of that."

"I didn't think you would, and neither do I. The woman wants to dress girls up in pantaloons and hoop skirts, stage a beauty pageant and crown a queen of the Sesquicentennial and, dear Lord, it's going to be tacky beyond words."

"I thought you were head of the entertainment committee."

"So did I, but Fern's in charge of the whole thing and has decided to do my job and, as best I can determine, everybody else's too. We might as well call it Fern's Follies. Or maybe the Meander Monkey Trial."

"Sure doesn't sound like something I want to see."

"Or anyone else for that matter."

"From what Zanna tells me, Miss Fern's not the kind of lady who's willing to reason."

"You ever tried reasoning with a steamroller?"

"No, thank you." Lou sipped thoughtfully. "Nothing you can do?"

"I'm in charge of the slide show because Fern thought all I wanted to do was change the slides. She agreed to let me narrate, but announced she'd already written the script."

"Have you read it?"

"Yes, and ye gods! It's not only full of typos and grammatical errors, but includes every stale stereotype and cliché about the Old South you can think of." Eulalie's eyes narrowed. "Why do you have such a strange look on your face?"

"Because I'm wondering if those stereotypes include white folks in black face."

"No, thank goodness. I expected a minstrel show every time I turned another awful page, but somehow, she overlooked it. If she hadn't ... well, I would've had to take steps."

"You talking about the scorched earth kind of steps?"

"Yes, ma-am, I am."

"Hmmm. Sure hope I still got the fire in my belly when

I'm your age."

"You will. I can feel it in these old bones." Eulalie squeezed Lou's arm. "I knew you had something special the day I got you out of that shack and into my house."

"I appreciate you saying that, lady, and you know something else? I remember that morning like it was yesterday."

"Twenty years ago this December." Eulalie embraced the nostalgic memory. "And I'll never forget what you said when I asked if I could call you Lou."

Looking for help hadn't been on Eulalie's mind that winter day in 1937 when she drove into Knoxville to buy Christmas presents at Miller's Department Store. While enjoying a cigarette in the ladies' lounge, she ran into Suzanne Jernigan, a classmate and old friend from Sullins College up in Bristol. Suzanne had married a wealthy tobacco planter and insisted Eulalie come see their home an hour west of town. Eulalie happily accepted and rode with Suzanne in her Daimler New Fifteen. It was a pleasant ride filled with reminiscing until they drove through some entrance gates and Eulalie spotted a row of ramshackle cabins. They were such a common sight during the Great Depression that she rarely noticed them, but that day they caught her eye.

"Are those cabins on your land?"

"Why, yes. Those people work for us."

"They look like a good wind would flatten them."

"I ... I guess I never noticed."

Eulalie quickly apologized. "I'm certainly not one to point fingers. Did you see that woman begging money outside Miller's? She looked like she hadn't eaten in days. Shame on me for not giving her a little something."

"Shame on both of us." Suzanne lamented. "I'll say something to Stewart about fixing up those shacks."

"Good for you." Eulalie continued peering through the car window. "Stop for a minute, would you please?"

"What for?"

"Those colored girls over there, the ones carrying fire-wood. Do you know them?"

Suzanne stopped the car and studied two raggedy figures silhouetted against the white wintry sky. "They're the John-son twins. They're the oldest of eight children. Their Daddy works for Stewart."

"Are they in school?"

"There are no colored schools this far out in the country." When Eulalie seemed lost in thought, Suzanne said, "They've done some housework for me, but their mother died last summer and they stay busy taking care of their brothers and sisters."

"I want to talk to them."

"About what?"

"I'm not sure. Back this thing up, will you?"

Somewhat reluctantly, Suzanne threw the car into reverse and parked in front of a dilapidated wooden shack with smoke rising from the chimney. The girls eyed the fancy car before dumping their wood into a box by the front door. Eulalie called to them before they went inside to get warm.

"Hello there!" She got out of the car. "May I talk to you for a moment?" The twins watched warily as she approached along with a mystified Suzanne. "I'm Eulalie Saunders, an old friend of Mrs. Jernigan. May I ask your names?"

The girls exchanged looks before one answered. "I'm Hal-lelujah Johnson, and this here's my sister, Hosanna."

"What lovely names."

"Thank you, ma-am."

"How old are you girls?"

"Seventeen."

Eulalie took quick inventory, noting the heavily patched woolen coats that did little to keep out the winter cold, and battered shoes that were likewise reworked. The girls' hair was wild and unkempt, and when Eulalie got closer she real-ized they hadn't bathed in some time. Recognizing diamonds in the rough, she had an idea.

"Mrs. Jernigan says you've done housework for her." Both girls nodded. "I live a couple of hours away in Meander. How would one of you like to come work for me?"

"Eulalie!" Suzanne cried.

"I know I should've asked you first, Suzanne, but I need a new girl." She turned back to the twins. "Well?"

The twins whispered to each other before Hosanna disappeared into the house, leaving her sister to face Eulalie alone. Hallelujah gave the white woman a frank look. "Where would I stay?"

"You'd have your own room and bath, and I'll pay you ten dollars a month." Suzanne's gasp announced her shock at the generous wage, but Hallelujah had no visible reaction.

"I reckon I'd be alright with that."

"Good. Now which one are you again?"

"Hallelujah."

"Would you mind if I call you Lou?"

"Ma-am, you treat me right and you can call me whatever you want." Hallelujah drew herself up. "But I got a question first."

"Yes?"

"When I clear the table, are you quality folk or do you stack?"

* * *

Two old friends collapsed with laughter at their shared memory. "I knew right then and there that I was getting myself a handful," Eulalie said.

"You know what, lady?" Lou wiped away a mirthful tear. "So did I."

7

Junkin Abernathy had his fingers in lots of Meander pies, and the Big Shots Saloon was his biggest and dirtiest. Lurking at the end of a nameless gravel road in a kudzu-infested woods called the Devil's Claw, it was nothing more than a badly rusted Quonset hut, but the parking lot was almost always packed. No mystery there. Big Shots was the only public place to get a drink in a dry county. Never shy about bending the law, Junkin got around the alcohol ban by selling memberships, making Big Shots a private club. Never mind that membership cost fifty cents and was deducted from the price of the first drink, or that the booze was brought in by Junkin's bootleggers. He also stocked moonshine from stills buried deep in the Cumberland Mountains and delivered by daredevils driving souped-up cars with back seats ripped out and trunks reconfigured to hold "moontanks" of white lightning. They haunted a highway from Harlan, Kentucky, through the Cumberland Gap to Knoxville, and because of their reckless speed and roaring engines, that twisty stretch of asphalt was nicknamed Thunder Road.

Another reason for the place's popularity was the Kitty Korner, a smaller, even rustier Quonset hut stashed deeper in the woods and offering services exclusively to Big Shots' male patrons. A Knoxville madam called Miss Lola had staffed it with a half dozen working girls from the Cincinnati-Atlanta circuit. Her regular-as-clockwork protection payments to Sheriff Kirkendol meant the place was never raided.

Junkin dropped by Big Shots daily to check up on things. A brass plaque by the cash register announced his personal bar stool where he parked his oversized posterior and oversaw his raunchy little enterprise. This particular happy hour he sat sipping a bourbon while watching the wiggle on the new cocktail waitress hired last week. He'd forgotten her name already but decided she did mighty fine justice to the short shorts and halter tops required for his girls. Junkin turned to Sonny, perched on an adjacent bar stool.

"She's got some caboose, don't she?"

"Damned right." Sonny watched the girl lean over to distribute drinks in a booth. "Don't look like she's wearing panties neither." Junkin spun around so fast he grabbed the sticky bar to keep from toppling over. "Careful, Mr. Mayor. What would you tell the doctor if you hurt yourself?"

"How about 'Fell down sneaking a peek at poontang?' "

"That reminds me. Did you ever hear what happened to the Widow Griffin? The poor old soul was pulling on her granny panties and got her ankle caught in the leg hole and fell over and hit her head on the dresser."

"Is that true?"

"Ask Sheriff Kirkendol. He was first on the scene. I always wondered what he put down for cause of death."

"Maybe it was panty tangle." When the men finished guffawing, Junkin turned serious. "Tell me something, Sonny. Working for the post office, you pretty much see everybody and hear all sorts of things, don't you?"

"I reckon."

"When Reverend Hickman came in the other day, he had no more interest in dog shit than the man in the moon. He wanted to talk about that damned fire."

"How much does he know?"

"He says he's got a witness, but I couldn't pin the bastard down. Since people gossip like crazy in this town, I wondered if you've heard anything."

"No, sir. Not a word. You know I'd come straight to you if I did."

"Well, you keep your ear to the ground just the same, and for now I want you to drive out Old Quarry Road and talk to that hermit living out there. Find out if he saw anything the night of the fire."

"Like what?"

"Like a burning cross, fool! I just told you somebody shot their mouth off to Reverend Hickman and I need to know who it is."

"Okay, boss."

"Alright." Junkin took another slug of bourbon. "Now there's something else I'm worried about. Calvin Harrington was in Eustace Miller's electrical shop the other day asking about wiring something onto his station wagon. You know. That beat-up old Nash he bought over at Dan's Used Cars."

"What's he wiring?"

"Some kind of dummy, that's what. He wants Eustace to fix the thing so it lights up and flashes lights and stuff."

"What's he doing that for?"

"The guy's such a bleeding heart, who the hell knows? One time it was rescuing stray dogs and another time it was putting seat belts in cars. I know damned good and well that Harrington's up to something that ain't in my best interest."

"Haven't heard nothing about that neither."

"Then I better get the sheriff on it." Junkin downed his bourbon and belched. "Hey, the boys will be here for a meeting in a few minutes. Come with me while I check the proof on my new shipment. Last batch was watered down bad."

"Right behind you, boss."

A small shed behind the Kitty Korner was stacked with bottles of freshly decanted moonshine. Junkin grabbed one at random and gave it a vigorous shake. As he hoped, big beads appeared and quickly disappeared, indicating a high alcoholic content. Smaller bubbles that took a while to dissipate warned that the product had been diluted.

"Looks good." He unscrewed the bottle. "Let's see how pure it is. Hold up that spoon."

Sonny steadied a scorched spoon while Junkin filled it, struck a match and lit the liquid. Both studied the color of the flame. Blue indicated the purest possible, but a yellow burn announced that it was tainted. A red flame was worse because it meant that the moonshine had been distilled with a radiator condenser coil, leaving the product full of lead. There was truth in the old hillbilly adage, "Lead burns red and makes you dead."

Junkin watched with satisfaction when the flame glowed bright blue, then blew it out. "Looks like Virgil and Rufus did okay with this stuff."

"Yes, indeed," Sonny said. "Think we oughta have a little snort?"

"Maybe after the meeting." Junkin screwed the lid back in place and returned the bottle to the shelf. "C'mon."

The nine men gathered in Miss Lola's parlor weren't there for the women and listened closely as Junkin explained the impromptu meeting.

"Alright, boys. Now you may or may not have heard that the Tower Theater's gonna show something called Island in the Sun in a couple of weeks. It's another piece of crap from the Hollywood race-mixers, but this time they've gone too far."

"What's it about?" someone asked.

"Same garbage those communists are shoving down our throats." Junkin's face darkened with revulsion. "White women mixing with colored men, dancing and carrying on and God knows what else, and they want to put that up on a movie screen right here in Meander. I'm telling you it's a damned outrage." Rumbles of disgust and angry obscenities arose as this registered with the men. Junkin waited until the grumbling died down. "What we'll do is show up right before the movie opens at eight. It'll be getting dark by then, so everyone remember to bring their torches. For those who need new robes, we've got a woman over in Seesaw working on them so they'll be ready in time. They'll be in the shed out back of here as usual."

There were more mutterings before another man spoke up. "What about pamphlets?"

Junkin pointed at Sonny. "Y'all can thank Sonny here for

finding us a free mimeo machine. Miss Lola's gonna let us hook it up in her garage so we can print our materials over there. I did the drawing myself this time." He pulled a sheet of paper from his shirt pocket, unfolded it and handed it to the closest man. "Y'all pass that around and let me know what you think. I'm mighty proud of it."

Junkin's sketch was a crude caricature of a humpbacked black man looking more like a gorilla than a human being. Naked except for a raggedy loin cloth, his legs were bowed and his fingers dragged the ground. He bore a ferocious expression and stood beneath a headline reading, "The Downfall of Mankind!" Below the hideous sketch was a list of civilizations supposedly undermined by the Negro race, everything from Pharaonic Egypt and classical Greece to Renaissance Italy and of course the Confederate States of America. It was immaterial that this was totally bogus history. What mattered was that this gathering of uneducated bigots bought into it, and, to a man, they did.

"Great drawing, boss"

"Time somebody told the truth about those apes!"

"Sure ought to stir up some shit!"

Junkin took a few minutes to bask in their praise before giving his final instructions. "Okay, boys. Y'all gather here at the shed at seven fifteen, get dressed and head out at seven thirty. The movie theater's five minutes away, so that'll give you plenty of time to get there and get organized. Some of you should line up around the parking lot and pass out flyers when people pull in. I'm sure they don't have no idea what that movie's about, so I'll write up another flyer explaining it."

"Have you seen it?"

"Hell, no! I wouldn't waste my hard-earned money on shit like that."

Nobody bothered asking Junkin to explain something he didn't know anything about. This was standard operating procedure for the Meander chapter of the Invisible Empire.

8

Andy Jenkins was in his workroom at Belle Fleur, Meander's only flower shop, busy with an assignment for Anrita's Tacky Party. It was the first time in his sixteen years as a florist that he'd been asked to create an intentionally ugly arrangement. He'd laughed out loud when he heard Anrita's instructions.

"The tackier, the better."

Andy's solution was cheap plastic flowers purchased from Edith's Variety Store a couple doors down. He added insult to injury by spraying the fake tulips and calla lilies with glue and showering them with purple glitter. He was mixing unharmonious varieties and ignoring all thoughts of symmetry and balance when the front door bell announced a customer. Good spirits evaporated when a flash of clashing colors announced Fern Abernathy, along with her shadow, Myrna Riddick, in tow. Fern wore a lemon-lime striped sleeveless blouse and an orange pencil skirt made of some tawdry new stretch fabric. The besieged skirt was under such stress Andy prayed it wouldn't snap and take out the gold FDS figure of Mercury on his counter. After talking to some of the other Main Street merchants, Andy had been expecting this visit. He put on his game face and marched into the lion's den.

"Good morning, ladies," he called cheerily. "What can I do for you today?"

"Oh, we're not here to buy anything." Fern flashed a brassy grin and drummed pudgy fingers on his counter. "I need to talk to you about the upcoming sequincentennial. You know. On Labor Day weekend."

Andy knew exactly where this conversation was going. "Yes, ma-am?"

"You surely know that, as the mayor's wife, I'm in charge of the entire event, so I'm going around town asking shopkeepers for contributions making it the biggest and best celebration Meander's ever had."

Andy's smile remained pasted in place. "So you'll be wanting some flowers."

"Why, yes I do. I need especially fancy arrangements for the dais." Fern puffed up a little, proud that she'd used Eulalie's big word for platform. As if Andy needed further explanation, she added, "That's where the mayor and I and other local dignitaries will be seated, you know."

Andy could barely keep from rolling his eyes. "How big is the dais?"

"Let's see." Fern yanked a notebook from her purse and flipped some pages. "Like I said, there will be the mayor and me, his wife."

Andy wondered how often she was going to remind him she was Mrs. Mayor.

"The Reverend Hickman and his wife and some of the city councilmen and the presidents of Kiwanis and the Lion's Club and Masons and Rotary and their wives." Fern took a few more seconds to come up with a total of eighteen.

"Goodness, Mrs. Abernathy. A dais that big large will require quite a lot of—"

Fern bulldozed on. "I plan on extending the platform ... uh, the dais with collapsible bleachers. That's for the queen and her court and their escorts, which adds another twenty-four."

Andy gulped as he did the math. "Forty-two people?!"

"Not counting the queen's bouquet." Fern stopped tapping and fixed him with a hard look. "Well?"

"What sort of flowers are you thinking about?"

Fern wasted no time reeling off her demands. "Roses and lilies are my favorites, and I guess you can throw in some potted palms and ferns and use smilax for the garlands."

"Garlands?"

"For the bleachers." When Andy gave her a blank stare, she huffed, "Young man, we can hardly have our queen and her court looking like they're at a football game, can we?"

Andy came back to reality when he ran guesstimates in his head. "That's an enormous order, Mrs. Abernathy."

"Sure it is! It's for a once-in-a-lifetime celebration."

"You've got me there. Very few people live to a hundred and fifty." When Fern's glare warned she was not amused, he said, "I hate to tell you this, ma-am, but Belle Fleur is simply not equipped for a job that size. To begin with, I don't have refrigeration space for that many flowers."

The fingers resumed drumming. "So what are you saying?"

"I'm saying that for something that elaborate you'll need a Knoxville florist."

"Is that right?" Fern's notebook slapped shut. "You know, Mr. Jenkins, the mayor and I expect every business in town to contribute because it's a real community effort. Each and every one who helps out will get a free advertisement in the Official Sequincentennial Guide, and the size of those ads will be based on the amount of goods and/or services they contribute. I would sure hate to see that program go to press without a single mention of Belle Fleur."

Andy ignored the effrontery. "Oh, I'm sure you would."

"I knew you'd understand," Fern said, oblivious as Andy's barb flew over her beehive. "Then we can count on you to decorate the platform, correct?"

"I'll do the best I can, ma-am."

"Wonderful!" Fern's smile returned full force as she reopened her notebook and checked off the florist's name with an exaggerated flourish. "Flowers, done!"

"But Mrs. Abernathy," Andy protested. "Please understand I may not be able to provide everything you—"

Fern heard only her own voice. "Now let's see. I still have Shorty's Garage and the Rivoli restaurant and Klovia's dress shop to call on this morning, so we'd better be on our way. If we get a move on, I think we can knock off ... Myrna, why are your eyes all bugged out?" Myrna pointed toward the doorway to Andy's workroom and the hideous glittered arrangement. "What in the world is that?!"

Andy thought fast. "Just something frivolous."

Fern's saccharine demeanor was rekindled. "Who's it for?"

Client anonymity was usually the rule at Belle Fleur, but owing to Fern's attempt to extort hundreds of dollars' worth of flowers, Andy made an exception. It was no secret that she disliked Anrita, and he couldn't resist a little revenge.

"Anrita Harrington."

"But that's the craziest looking flower arrangement I've ever seen," Myrna said, opening her mouth for the first time.

"It's supposed to be that way, Mrs. Riddick. It's for Mrs. Harrington's Tacky Party, and shame on me for not keeping her secret." His face was the picture of innocence as he twisted the knife. "I hope you ladies will pretend to be surprised when you see it tonight."

"What makes you think we'll see it?" Fern asked tartly.

"Why wouldn't you?"

"Because we weren't invited!"

Andy feigned embarrassment. "Why, I never dreamed that the mayor's wife wouldn't be … oh, how careless of me. Please forgive me, ladies."

To his surprise, Fern grew calm and waved a hand dismissively. "I couldn't care less about that silly party, Mr. Jenkins. My day is filled with official duties of the most important kind. In fact, I shouldn't be wasting any more time on such nonsense. Come along, Myrna."

The bell jangled wildly when Fern yanked the door open and strong-armed her startled friend onto the sidewalk. When they got to her Chrysler Imperial, Fern slung her purse onto the front seat with such force Myrna was surprised it didn't explode.

"How dare Anrita Harrington not invite me!" Fern snarled.

"I'm sure it was an oversight, honey." Myrna had barely scrambled into the passenger's seat when Fern threw the car into reverse and backed into Main Street. "I ... I wasn't invited either."

"That's hardly the same thing!" Fern blustered. "I'm the goddamned mayor's wife for heaven's sake!"

"Oh!" Myrna was as unnerved by Fern's anger as she was the profanity. She was all too familiar with her best friend's temper and knew to keep still until the storm passed. Fern's next words warned it might be a while.

"The devil with calling on the rest of these stores. I'm too upset to pretend politeness all over town." She turned hard left and nearly collided with a delivery truck, enraged all over again when she saw Anrita's Home-Style Salads emblazoned on the side. "And the devil with Anrita Harrington too. I'm sick to death of her and Sylvianne McNeil. Those two are thick as thieves. I still can't believe that witch Sylvianne came to my open house unannounced!"

"I thought the notice in the church bulletin said everyone was invited," Myrna blurted, regretting her mistake too late.

"That's not the point, you nitwit!" Fern yanked the steering wheel the other way and swerved off Main Street onto River Road. Myrna grabbed the arm rest and held on for dear life as they sped along the Tennessee River, willow trees and oaks a blur through the window. Her heart continued racing until they turned into the Abernathy driveway and screeched to a halt. She watched, horrified, as Fern leapt out of the car and walked over to the wooden figure of the old lady bent over the garden and kicked it in the behind.

Hearing the screaming tires, Zanna stopped hanging laundry in the back yard and peeked over the fence in time to see the wooden granny sail across the lawn.

"Mmmm-mmm. Looks like the lady of the house is home."

9

Calvin and Anrita's only child, John, was a senior at Meander High School where he made good grades, was a star on the basketball team and, to his parents' delight, went steady with a sweet, respectable girl named Dottisue Davis. John was one of those rare teenagers who gave his parents almost no trouble, although Calvin was fond of saying, "Still waters run deep."

John found his father in the garage, bent over his workbench. "Hey, Daddy. Mama says you're looking for me."

Calvin was flushed with excitement. "That's right, boy. I want to show you my latest project." He stepped away from his work bench to reveal a white-faced male dummy dressed in a black suit. It clutched a funereal spray of plastic calla lilies to its chest.

"What the heck is that?"

"Part of my new campaign. Between squiring Dottisue around and working at the drug store, you're too busy to see what I've been up to. Take a look at what's parked out back."

John trailed his father to a black 1951 Nash Rambler Airflyte station wagon that had definitely seen better days. "Where'd you find this old heap?"

"Over at Dan Hatcher's lot. He had it stuck way in the back because he didn't think anybody would want it." Calvin caressed a heavily dented front fender. "It looks pretty ratty but it's perfect for what I need."

John could only wonder at his father's latest eccentric scheme. His favorite so far was a kid's space helmet made from red plastic mixing bowls that fit over the head and ears. The yellow plastic salt shaker on top was for receiving intergalactic messages which could be answered with a blue mouthpiece made from a rubber dish sprayer. Somehow Calvin managed to sell the product to Woolworth's and McClellan's. Like all his inventions, it lost money, but that didn't keep him from pursuing other dreams.

"Okay. I give. What're you up to with this old clunker and that crazy corpse?"

Calvin pointed. "The dummy is going up there on top, right beside a flashing sign that reads 'Moonshine Kills!' "

"Anything in particular prompt this?"

"That Fountain City boy who died last winter after drinking bad moonshine."

"Yeah. That was awful."

"That's only part of it. When I was growing up in Scott County, people were always dying from drinking that rotgut. A lot of them were poor ignorant hillbillies who never suspected shine could be distilled with mothballs or ammonia."

"That's pretty scary."

"It's more than scary, John. It's downright criminal. This is 1957, for heaven's sake, and there's no reason to drink something not regulated by the government. For that matter, there's no reason alcohol should stay illegal. I enjoy an occasional shot of good Tennessee bourbon, and I hate that someone wanting a drink has to go to bootleggers or that awful dive Junkin Abernathy runs out in the Devil's Claw. That place is a disgrace to the community. For that matter, so's Junkin Abernathy."

"I guess."

"There's no guessing about it. When Meander elected that man mayor, it was the darkest day in this town's history."

Like all teenagers, John wasn't much on politics and changed the subject by peering inside the station wagon. "So you're gonna drive this thing around town, huh, Daddy?"

"Yes, I am, and I know you and your mama will be highly embarrassed, but she knew I was full of harebrained schemes when she married me."

"None of your harebrained schemes ever embarrassed me." John paused. "Except—"

"The space helmet made out of plastic bowls?"

"Uh, yeah. Maybe a little."

"In hindsight, I guess it wasn't such a hot idea."

"You were trying, Daddy, and that's what mattered."

"What on earth did I ever do to deserve such a respectful son?"

"Maybe it's that five bucks you slip me every so often."

"You mean on top of the five you mooch off your mother?"

John didn't see that coming. "She promised not to tell you!"

"She didn't." Calvin nudged his son in the ribs. "I was guessing."

"Darn! Tricked again!"

"I may have taught you everything you know, son, but I didn't teach you everything *I* know." When John looked alarmed, his father said, "Don't worry. I'll keep your secret. A few fives here and there aren't going to break the bank, not with the family business booming."

"Is it really doing that well?"

"So well that you don't have to work at the drug store this summer. After all, you graduate next month and start college this fall, and your mother and I want you to enjoy your last months of freedom. I've worked since I was twelve years old, but that doesn't mean you have to."

"I appreciate that, Daddy, but I think I'll work anyway."

Calvin was surprised. "Why?"

"Because I enjoy working for Dr. Rochelle, and because it's an ongoing education."

"What do you mean?"

John was usually honest with his parents, but there were times, like now, when little white lies were in order. His duties at Rochelle Drugs involved everything from jerking sodas to driving a delivery jeep, and while he enjoyed both, the latter was especially rewarding. He discovered that his very first week on the job when he delivered aspirin, Massengill Powder and Band-Aids to Mrs. Dianne Glass out on Kingston

Pike. She was a pretty young widow whose husband Bud had been killed in the Korean War, and when she answered the door in a red silk Japanese robe with nothing underneath, John realized his job had hidden benefits. Like any polite six-teen-year-old, John graciously accepted her offer to come in for an Orange Crush, and when she explained how sad and lonely she was, he realized he would be delivering more than aspirin that summer. While some young men would consider it cheating on their girlfriend, John decided it was his patriot-ic duty to comfort the Widow Glass.

John thought fast. "The other day a colored couple came in for sundaes. It was the first time it had happened, but Dr. Rochelle had told us boys what to do if it did."

"What did he say?"

"He said we should always polite to coloreds and always make their food to-go."

"How do you manage that?"

"They get the message when I put the sundaes in paper cups instead of glasses."

"So they won't sit down at those little ice cream tables by the soda fountain?"

"Yes, sir. I guess so."

"Is that what happened?"

"Not exactly. When I gave the girl the sundae, she looked at it and then looked at the table and then at me. I pretended not to notice and stayed busy making her boyfriend's sundae. I guess I was hoping nothing would happen, but when the boy got his and paid for it, they went right over to one of the tables and sat down."

"What did you do?"

"Nothing. I knew I was supposed to tell them to take their food outside, but ... oh, I don't know. You and Mama and I have never talked about segregation but—"

"You let them sit there?"

"Yes, sir."

"So they could enjoy their sundaes like everyone else?"

"Yes, sir."

"Did Dr. Rochelle say anything?"

"He was filling prescriptions in the back of the store, so he didn't see what happened. That couple finished their sundaes and the girl thanked me and the boy said it was the best sundae he'd ever had and they left."

"Had you seen them before?"

"No, sir."

"Then it might have been a test case."

"What do you mean?"

"Colored people have started quietly challenging those ugly Jim Crow laws dictating separate facilities for the races. Those laws have been on the books for years, and I believe they've worn out their welcome." He paused. "Not that they ever deserved one."

"Are you saying I broke the law?"

"Yes, John, you did." Calvin put an arm around his son's shoulders as they walked toward the house. "And I want you to go inside and repeat that story for your mother."

"Why?"

"Because I want her to be as proud of you as I am."

10

Fern slammed the front door and glared at Myrna. "It would serve Anrita right if I put on something tacky and crashed her party like Sylvianne crashed mine."

"What on earth would you wear?"

"That's the problem," she said, flipping a wayward bra strap back into place and gesturing at her outfit, unmindful that it hugged every wrong curve of her body. "Where could I find something tacky this late in the game?"

"You're right." Myrna followed Fern into the den and watched as she rested a hand atop the television. "What are you doing, honey?"

Fern looked surprised. "Didn't anybody teach you how to keep tabs on the maid when you're out of the house?"

"Why, no. Are you checking for dust?"

"Nope. Checking the temperature. If the TV's warm, it would mean Zanna's been watching soap operas. Hmmm. No heat. I reckon she was telling the truth when she said she doesn't watch them, but that Eleanora! I used to catch her all the time, and even though the TV felt hot as a firecracker, she'd deny having it on."

"That why you fired her?"

"That was just part of it. That woman was drinking us out of house and home. I swear she even swilled the damned vanilla!"

"You think Zanna's gonna work out?"

"Too soon to tell. She's only been here a month." She leaned close. "These days you have to keep a close eye on these people. They're starting to act up everywhere, even right here in Meander. When Junkin picked up the new yard man last week, that fool opened the front door like he was going to ride right up front. Can you imagine?!"

Myrna was aghast. "Our yard man would never dream of

doing that, and my Sallie's a jewel."

"She was with your mama, wasn't she?"

"My grandmama, too."

"She must be getting up there."

Myrna giggled. "She does such good work that I never thought to ask how old she is."

"Well, you sure better hang on to her because good maids are real hard to find these days. Junkin and I've gone through seven in the last two years."

"My goodness!"

"What else can we do? I wouldn't know what to do with white help." Fern headed for the back door. "I better go check on Zanna. If she's doing like I told her, she's hanging the wash."

Myrna trailed Fern outside where Zanna was filling the clothes line with damp laundry. "I'm back, Zanna!" Fern called. "Everything alright?"

"Yes, ma-am."

"Any phone calls?"

"Phone rang a couple of times but I was out here and couldn't get to it in time."

"I sure wish you had. It might've been important."

"I reckon if it's important they'll call back."

Fern was trying to figure out if she'd been sassed when Myrna began praising Zanna's handiwork. "I see you're careful to hang the sheets on the outside lines so people can't see Miss Fern's unmentionables."

"Yes, ma-am. It's how I was taught."

"You were sure taught right. We can't be too careful these days, not with that crazy Eugene Proctor roaming around peeping in windows and everything. And look there. The socks are hanging by the toes, not the tops. You're every bit as neat as my Sallie."

Zanna frowned. "You talking about Sallie Harmon?"

"I sure am." She watched approvingly as Zanna picked up a rag and wiped the clothesline clean before hanging more wash. "Do you know her?"

"She goes to my church, but I haven't seen her in such a long time I been wondering if she was sick. You mean to say she's still working for you?"

"Why, yes. She's worked for my family for years."

Zanna gave Myrna a hard look. "That woman's eighty-three years old!"

"Is she?" Myrna retreated a couple of steps, uneasy with Zanna's tone. "I wouldn't know."

"Good Lord! She ought to have somebody waiting on her, not the other way around."

Fern scowled. "That's none of your business, Zanna."

"I reckon it's anybody's business who doesn't like seeing a poor old soul worked to death. Even mules get put out to pasture when they reach a certain age."

"That's enough, girl!"

Knowing Fern was in a foul mood, Zanna went back to the clothes line.

"By the way," Fern continued, "I was over at Eulalie Saunders' house a couple days ago and saw your sister, Lou." Zanna didn't respond. "How come you never told me you had an identical twin?"

"Why would I tell you that, Miz Abernathy? We don't never talk about our families."

"You needn't get huffy, Zanna. I just asked a question."

"And I just answered it."

Fern bristled. "Are you trying to sass me, girl?"

"Oh, no, ma-am." Zanna insisted. "I reckon I'm trying *not* to sass you."

"That's better." Fern said, oblivious as ever. "Did you make iced tea like I told you?"

"In the refrigerator."

"Sweetened?"

"Sweet as can be."

"C'mon, Myrna. Let's go have us some tea." Once inside, Fern said, "There's something peculiar about that girl that I can't put my finger on."

"What do you mean?"

"Sometimes I think she's being uppity, but I'm never quite sure." She thought a moment. "There's something peculiar about Andy Jenkins too, but I can't figure that out either."

"I wouldn't waste time thinking on it, Fern. You've got more important things to do."

"You're right." Happy to be distracted, Fern poured two glasses of iced tea and went into the den where she flopped onto a La-Z-Boy. "I don't know why I got myself so upset over that silly Tacky Party. Anrita and Sylvianne are nothing but a bunch of snobs with their canasta clubs and fancy buffet dinners and all. So is their schoolteacher friend. What's her name?"

"Cassandra Maddox."

"Oh, yeah. She's one of Lurleen's teachers. Lurleen says she's a free-thinker or something."

"What does that mean?"

"That she's free to think about anything she wants to think about, I guess. Sounds pretty stupid if you ask me." Fern took an overly ambitious slug of iced tea and sloshed some on her blouse. "Oh, well. The good thing about wearing so many patterns is that you can't tell where you've spilled something." She and Myrna were still laughing when a soft voice interrupted from the kitchen.

"What're y'all laughing at?"

Myrna waved. "Hey, Lurleen!"

"Come give your mama a hug," Fern called. Lurleen obeyed and perched demurely on a nearby ottoman. The mere sight of her only child made Fern forget about being mad. "Isn't she the prettiest thing you ever saw, Myrna?"

"Pretty as a picture, and as sweet as she is pretty."

It was no exaggeration. More than once Cassandra had remarked to Anrita that it was one of God's miracles that Junkin and Fern Abernathy had produced something as exquisite as Lurleen. The girl was bright, attractive, soft-spoken and genteel, in short everything her parents were not. She looked especially fetching that morning in a pale blue sundress with a smocked empire waist and spaghetti straps.

"Y'all hush now." Lurleen stared at her feet. "You're gonna make me blush."

"Which is what proper young Southern ladies are supposed to do, aren't they, Myrna?"

"Yes, indeed," Myrna said, relieved that Fern's ugly mood was gone. "Are you still dating that good-looking Millsaps boy?"

"Yes, ma-am. In fact, Rocky's picking me up any minute."

"How come you're not in school today?"

"It's something Miss Maddox suggested," Lurleen explained. "We seniors with a certain point average can take a half day off every week between now and graduation. I thought Wednesday was a good idea because it makes the week go faster."

"Honey, at your age, you don't want to speed up time. You want to savor every waking moment."

"Oh, I do, Mrs. Riddick. That's why Rocky and I are riding up to the Smokies this afternoon. They're so beautiful in the spring." She jumped up when the doorbell rang. "There's my beau!"

A few minutes later, after Rocky Millsaps came in to pay his respects, Lurleen was gone. "He's such a polite young man," Myrna said. "They make a darlin' couple, don't they?"

"Yes, indeed." Fern sipped her tea. "They've been going steady for over a year, so I think they're serious. I can't tell you how relieved I am."

"You mean because the Millsaps are such fine people?"

"No. I mean because Lurleen got a crush on John Harrington her junior year."

"Uh-oh."

"Uh-oh is right. I put a stop to that right away, let me tell you. I don't care how rich the Harringtons are, no daughter of mine is going to marry into that bunch of snooty McSnoots." She took another sip. "Hell, girl. They're not even Baptists."

11

Lou opened the front door and gaped at the plastic flower arrangement in Andy Jenkins's arms.

"Have mercy, Mr. Andy! What in the world's all that foolishness?"

"I believe it's the centerpiece for tonight's party."

Lou motioned him inside. "You white folks got some mighty peculiar ways."

"I think the word you're looking for is 'goofy.' " Andy carried the flowers into the dining room and centered them on the table. It was his turn to gape when he saw the buffet's splendid array of china, silverware, crystal goblets and damask napkins. "Talk about goofy!"

Lou was affronted since she had arranged things herself. "What do you mean?"

"I mean that this buffet looks like something right out of House Beautiful. I think Princess Margaret herself would approve."

"Too fancy for a Tacky Party, huh?"

"Absolutely! Mrs. Abernathy would be using paper plates and napkins and Dixie cups and plastic forks."

"I wish I'd thought of that," Anrita said from the doorway.

"Oh, hi, Mrs. Harrington. Looks like this is going to be quite the to-do."

"I never realized being tacky was such hard work."

Andy sniffed the air. "What am I smelling?"

"I've got a ham in the oven," Anrita said.

"Much too fancy. You should be serving pork rinds and Vienna sausages and Jell-O cake and definitely Velveeta. You need to keep the tacky theme going."

Anrita smiled. "You know what, Andy? You ought to open up a party planning business. There's nothing like it in Meander, and you could run it right out of your florist shop."

"The truth is I'd like to go into the landscaping business. That's what I'm best at."

"Then why don't you?"

Andy's face lit up but quickly darkened. "Because new businesses take money, and right now I'm what you'd call financially embarrassed. The flower business isn't exactly booming in our little burg."

Anrita turned to Lou. "Would you check the ham, please? I think it's about ready to come out of the oven." With Lou gone, Anrita took Andy's arm and ushered him into the living room. "I wonder if you'd do a couple of favors for me."

"Yes, ma-am?"

"First off, I want you to call me Anrita. You're only a few years younger, you know."

"Alright. Anrita, it is."

"Good. Now the second thing I want to ask is that you let Calvin and me give you a little something to get your landscaping business started. We could even call it seed money, if you'll pardon the pun."

"Mrs. Harring … Anrita, I can't do that."

She ignored his protest. "Now you know I've been blessed with my salad business. Quite frankly, Calvin and I are making more money than we know what to do with, and we enjoy giving back into the community that gave us our start. We've invested in a number of Meander businesses, and I'd like to add you to the list. You can sit down with Calvin some time and figure out how much you need. Now before you protest any further and say you're worried about a new business failing, this will be a gift, not a loan. You're not required to pay it back."

Andy was deeply moved. "I … I don't know what to say."

Anrita squeezed his arm. "Say that you'll at least think about it."

"Of course, I'll think about it," Andy said, spirits soaring as he delivered a comic drawl. "My Mama didn't raise no dumb children."

"No, she didn't. Miss Alberta was a good woman, and all three of you children turned out fine."

"I know she'd appreciate you saying that. Now I'd better be going. I've got a couple more deliveries to make, including a big order over at the mayor's house."

"Is that right?" she asked as they walked to the door.

"Yes, ma-am. It's the strangest thing. Fern Abernathy was in the shop earlier today soliciting contributions for the Labor Day festivities. She came back later and ordered every flower I had left and said she wanted them delivered as soon as possible. Apparently, she's throwing some kind of last-minute barbecue party."

"Wonder what prompted that?"

"It's my fault." Andy pointed to the dining room centerpiece. "She saw that in the store and asked who it was for, and I'm afraid I let the cat out of the bag."

"It doesn't matter, Andy. This is such a small town she would've found out about my party anyway, but I still don't get the connection."

"I think this is her way of getting even." He thought a moment. "You know Mrs. Abernathy a lot better than I do. Do you know why she's got such a bee in her bonnet?"

"Maybe that poor little bee's trying to find some honey where there is none."

"Coming from you, those are mighty strong words."

"If you're late with that delivery I suspect you'll be hearing much stronger ones from Mrs. Abernathy. You sure don't want that."

"No, ma-am, I don't. And thanks again for your kind offer."

"Call Calvin when you're ready to talk." Anrita waved good-bye and went into the kitchen. She found Lou up to her elbows in dishwater. She got a pitcher of iced tea from the refrigerator and filled two glasses before sitting at the kitchen table. "Take off those rubber gloves and sit down a few minutes. Those dishes can wait."

"You sure we got enough time before the party?"

Anrita glanced at the clock over the sink. "We're in good shape, and besides I need to talk to you."

Lou stripped off the gloves and sat. "You got your serious face on, Miss Anrita."

"Because I want to have a serious conversation." She dropped a tablet of saccharin into her glass and stirred it with a tea spoon. "I've been watching you for a lot of years, Lou, and you're one of the smartest, most responsible women I know."

Lou was surprised. "Why, thank you."

"The fact is, you're so well qualified that Mr. Harrington and I would like you to come work for us at the plant. In an administrative position, mind you, not making chicken salad. Now, I know how loyal you are to Eulalie Saunders and I wouldn't dream of trying to hire you away, but my offer is something I wish you'd discuss with her. Eulalie's a mighty fine woman and a fair one too. She might agree that this is a good thing for everyone concerned."

"I'm mighty flattered, Miss Anrita, but I've been with that woman way too many years and I ain't about to leave now."

"You don't even want to discuss it with her?"

"No, ma-am, because she might say yes."

"I don't understand."

"And I'm not sure I can explain myself either. Eulalie's been looking out for me for a long time, and some day I'm gonna be returning the favor. I don't even want to think about somebody else trying to take care of that old lady. It wouldn't be right."

"Well, I have to say I'm disappointed but not surprised at your loyalty. Calvin said you'd say no, but I had to ask because we desperately need somebody in that plant."

"You said an administrative position, didn't you?" Anrita nodded. "I know somebody who might work out."

"Anyone I know?"

"No, ma-am. A cousin of mine who lives up in Knoxville.

She's not my blood cousin, but never mind about all that. Her name's Mary Fox. She and her husband just got divorced, and I know she's looking for another job."

"What does she do now?"

"She supervises the cafeteria at Booker T. Washington High School."

"Hmmm. I like that she's in food services. How long has she been there?"

"Twelve years."

"Why is she looking for something else?"

"Because Tennessee public schools don't pay much, especially the colored ones." The comment didn't surprise or embarrass Anrita. Over the years she and Lou had had some heart-to-heart talks about race relations and a host of other delicate subjects. "Mary's also tired of living in the city. She's been down here to visit me in Meander and knows how much I like it and—"

"Do you, Lou? Like it here I mean."

"I can tell you it's a sight better than that shack where Miss Eulalie found me. I got myself steady work and a nice little house over on Vine Street and my church. I never even dreamed about those things when I was little." She shrugged. "I reckon I'm one of those people who dreams small."

"There's something to be said for that." Anrita thought a moment. "When do you suppose Mary could get down here for an interview?"

"I'll drop her a line tomorrow and find out."

Anrita pointed to the phone. "Why not call her right now?"

"Alright. I'll get my little phone book." Lou stood and paused. "I appreciate this and I know Mary will too."

"Lou, if she's half as industrious and dependable as you, she should work out fine."

"I promise you she's a real ball of fire. Shoot, she's been shaking up things as long as I can remember."

"Maybe that's what this town needs," Anrita said.

12

"You and John are officially banished from five thirty until nine." Anrita dropped a slip over her head and let it shimmy over her bra and panty girdle. "Maybe you could go see that new movie at the Tower. It's called Twelve Angry Men, and Henry Fonda's in it. I know he's your favorite."

"Exactly what are your two angry men supposed to do for supper?"

Anrita sat at her dressing table and began brushing her hair. "Grab something at Louis's Pizza Parlor or get a hamburger at Archie's."

"I want some of that ham that's smelling up the house."

"I'll fix you some tomorrow. I'm sure there will be plenty left over."

"Fine thing. A man works hard, and all he gets are leftovers."

Anrita hummed, "My Heart Cries for You."

"What's the occasion for this latest hen gathering?"

"It's a Tacky Party, and they're all the rage."

Calvin pretended to pout. "Since you're throwing me out, I'm not going to tell you about my trip out of town."

"What trip?"

"I said I'm not going to tell you."

"Since when do we have secrets?"

"Since now." Calvin sat on the edge of the bed and watched Anrita roll her hair in curlers. "What in Sam Hill are you doing?"

Anrita forgot about his trip. "What's it look like, boy of mine?"

"Like you're going to bed instead of hosting a party."

"This is how I'm greeting my guests. At Tacky Parties, whoever looks the tackiest wins a prize."

"I should've known better than to ask."

"If you want to see what I'm wearing, it's hanging on the back of the closet door."

Anrita watched the mirror for her husband's reaction, and as she expected, Calvin let out a yelp. "What the heck is this?"

"It's a chenille bathrobe, that's what. Sylvianne and I drove halfway to Pigeon Forge before I found what I wanted. It was hanging on a clothesline outside that model of Jerusalem made out of old tires."

"Couldn't you just buy one downtown?"

"Heavens, no. They only sell them at roadside attractions. Look at the back, Calvin, and tell me that's not the most beautiful thing you've ever seen."

Calvin turned the bright scarlet robe around and saw a peacock with its tail unfurled. Each feathery eye was a different color. "It looks like a tv test pattern."

Anrita teased him further. "Gorgeous, don't you think?"

"What I think is that I need to grab my son and get out of this madhouse."

"But you haven't seen what color I'm going to paint my nails."

"Believe me, madam, I've seen more than enough."

"Remember you can't come back until after nine."

"Sweetie pie, you'll be lucky if I come back at all."

Anrita blew him a kiss before he bolted. She was finishing the last curler when Lou appeared to announce that Mary Fox would call Monday morning about an appointment.

"Wonderful. I look forward to meeting her." She reached under the dressing table for a roll of toilet tissue and began wrapping it around her head. "Honestly. The price we women pay for beauty."

"Hmmm. I never thought of toilet paper as a beauty aid."

"Tonight, it's an anti-beauty aid."

"I think I'll stick to my relaxers." When Lou saw Anrita struggling with the toilet paper turban, she went to her rescue. "Who taught you how to do this?"

"Cassie, but don't ask me how she knows."

"Miss Cassandra's a lady who just naturally knows things," Lou said. "I've been aware of that for quite some time."

Anrita opened some bilious pink nail polish and went to work on her fingernails. "The kitchen under control?"

"Yes, ma-am. Ham's sliced and arranged on a platter, and the side dishes are on the counter. Everything's covered in foil."

"Good."

"You sure you don't need me to help clean up after the party?"

"I'm positive. You've been on your feet all day."

"Alright then. Good night."

"Good night. And thanks again for putting me in touch with Mary."

"You're welcome."

Alone again, Anrita studied herself in the dressing room mirror before deciding to go without make-up. She retrieved the chenille robe and slipped into it. She found it surprisingly comfortable and soft against her skin.

"Not bad."

Anrita opened the closet and studied her reflection in the long mirror on the back of the door. She froze, heart racing when she saw a shadowy figure over her shoulder, then re-laxed when she guessed who it was. She marched over to the open window, leaned out and, even though she didn't see an-yone, called out anyway.

"You go on home now, Eugene Proctor!"

Anrita yanked down the shade and was immediately ashamed of yelling. She knew Eugene was harmless. His par-ents had died in a car wreck when he was twelve, and a spin-ster aunt had moved in to take care of him. He'd kept to him-self in high school, and when his aunt died right after gradu-ation, he was all alone in the world. He spent most of his time in his parents' little clapboard house on the edge of town. He didn't have a job, but everyone knew Sonny Hull put a check in Eugene's mailbox the first of every month without fail. No one knew who sent it because the return address was a post office box in Memphis. Eugene ventured out only to tend to his vegetable garden, pick up groceries or take a nightly stroll. He was polite enough when someone spoke to him, but when his walks got later and longer, folks figured he wanted to be left alone. He would occasionally cut through people's yards, and although no one actually saw him looking in anyone's window, gossip was that Eugene was a Peeping Tom. Rumors also circulated that a young divorcee named Lucinda Poteet routinely put on shows for Eugene. Maggie Buchanan, Lucinda's spinster neighbor, claimed that whenever Lucinda wanted an audience she'd hang a pair of pink panties on the clothesline, but after staring at Lucinda's drawn window shade for hours, plenty of frustrated teen-aged boys disputed Maggie's claim. Only Eugene knew the truth, that it was really Maggie doing the spying, but like everything else, he kept it to himself. Anrita considered him a lonely, harmless soul and often included him in her prayers.

Anrita forgot about Eugene and went into the kitchen for a last-minute look around. As Lou said, everything was in order and the only things missing were the party guests. Per usual, Sylvianne was the first to arrive. One reason was because she lived next door, and the other was because she liked to stash her bourbon behind Anrita's Aunt Jemima cookie jar. Anrita never served anything stronger than Grapette at her parties, but she indulged Sylvianne because she was an old friend, and since Sylvianne never appeared drunk or got behind the wheel of a car, Anrita let her be.

"Shoot!" Sylvianne cried when she saw Anrita's outfit. "The toilet paper and those pin curls are the perfect touch. Why didn't I think of that?"

"Because it would've been overkill, honey. Your get-up is already one for the record books."

Sylvianne's ensemble, if it could be called that, was a raggedy mop cap and a sleeveless housedress made from a flour sack, badly faded but with the White Lily Flour label still visible. Shapeless and sad, its lopsided hemline hit right below the knee, drawing attention to Sylvianne's stockings. One was wadded around her ankle, and the other was full of runs. Her feet were shoved into worn-out brown flats. Both bra straps were conspicuously draped on her shoulders, and at least three inches of slip were visible at the bottom of her skirt.

Anrita pointed at the hemline and said, "It's snowing down South."

"I sure hope so." Sylvianne she pulled a pint of Jack Black from her dress pocket and headed for the kitchen. "It took me forever to get the thing pinned wrong."

13

In all the years they'd been married, Calvin and Anrita had never been apart more than twenty-four hours. Since his upcoming trip required an overnight stay, he knew he had to stop playing coy and tell the truth over breakfast.

"Remember my old army buddy, Grady Fletcher?"

"Maybe a thing or two," Anrita teased, refilling his coffee cup. "You were on Guadalcanal together, and he went on to become a big Hollywood stuntman, right?"

"Uh, right." Calvin looked a little hangdog. "Do I talk about him too much?"

"No. I'm just getting back at you for being so mysterious about going out of town. I couldn't stop thinking about it during the party."

"That reminds me. Who won the big prize?"

"Believe it or not, Cassandra. She's such a bookish soul I never expected her to take the competition seriously. Goodness gracious, was *I* wrong!"

"What did she do?"

"She came as Moonbeam McSwine."

Calvin's eyes widened. "That va-va-voom gal from the Li'l Abner funnies?"

"The one and only. She came in a tattered black swimsuit with dirt smeared all over the place and a stuffed pig under her arm." Anrita helped herself to more grits. "Once she started teaching school, none of us saw Cassie with her hair down or wearing anything but schoolmarm clothes, and let me tell you, she has a knockout figure. Everyone was so surprised the vote was almost unanimous."

"I hope somebody took pictures."

"Laverne brought her Brownie, but Cassie said no photos. She was worried about losing her job in case the wrong people saw her in that crazy get-up."

"With a strait-laced principal like Daniel Warren, she's right to worry." Calvin glanced at the kitchen clock and gulped the last of his coffee. "I'd better hit the road."

"Hold the phone, bud. You still haven't told me where you're going."

"Asheville. Grady's working on a movie over there and asked if I wanted to watch him film a couple of scenes."

"You're visiting a real-live movie set and not taking me?!"

"Sorry, sweetheart. Grady said they're having trouble with gawkers and need to keep crowds to a minimum."

"I understand, but I'm still disappointed."

"That's my girl." Calvin reached across the table and squeezed her hand. "You know I'd take you if I could."

"Yes, I do, and that's why I'm letting you off the hook." She dropped a couple slices of dietetic Hollywood bread into the toaster and pushed the button. "Should I wait supper?"

"No. Grady and I haven't seen each other in almost eight years, and he wants me to stay over so we can catch up. Now before you say anything, I know we've not spent a night apart since we got married, but I hope you don't mind."

"No, honey. John will keep me company, but I do need the name and number of your motel."

"On the pad by the phone."

"I swan. You think of everything."

"Except the name of the movie Grady's working on. All I know is that Robert Mitchum's in it. And Keely Smith of all people."

"Keely Smith?! Don't you know she and Dinah Shore are my two favorite singers? Are you sure I can't tag along? I promise not to gawk, and I'll be quiet as a mouse."

"Grady's doing some kind of a car chase scene, so I doubt if Miss Keely's involved. I'll be sure to ask Grady if she's around though."

Anrita raced to the den, back in a flash with a record album. "Here's her new record with Louis Prima. On the off chance that you see her—"

"I promise I'll get her to autograph it."

She bussed his cheek. "You're my hero."

Calvin put on his sunglasses and struck a pose. "Do you think anyone will mistake me for a movie star?"

Anrita indicated her waistline before reaching for the Hollywood toast. "Sure, baby doll. The same people who think I have a figure like Moonbeam McSwine."

Calvin had never been around movie folks before, and although he tried to remain blasé his insides were jelly by the time he found his old friend in a parking lot cluttered with trailers and film equipment and bustling with activity. Grady was leaning against a 1951 Ford and talking to an assistant director.

"Hey, buddy!"

"You old dog!" Grady gave him a bear hug. "How long's it been?"

"Too long." Calvin was a little embarrassed by the hug but figured that was how they did things in movieland. He returned Grady's backslaps, and took quick inventory. Grady was thirty- six, three years younger than himself, and looked impressively fit in blue jeans and denim shirt. His brown hair was much longer than Calvin's and hung carelessly over his forehead. "Looking good, man. Hollywood obviously agrees with you."

"You wouldn't say that if you saw me in my skivvies. I got more scars from flipping cars than from fighting the damned Japs."

"You flip cars?!"

"It's not as insane as it sounds, if you know what you're doing. Sometimes we use cages so it looks lots more dangerous than it is." He nudged Calvin's side and pointed. "See that fellow over there? That's Carey Wagner. He's the best special effects guy in the business."

"Yeah?"

"He worked on Rebel Without a Cause and The Wild Ones. Told me all about hanging out with Marlon Brando."

Calvin wondered if he might get some movie stories for Anrita. "Brando? Really?"

"Yeah. He said Brando's a little weird but not like the bad boys he plays on screen."

"What about Robert Mitchum?"

"Coolest cat I ever met. You wanna talk about bad boys? He wrote the book." Grady threw an arm around Calvin's shoulders and walked him through the labyrinth of trailers. "Bob's a real character."

"You're on a first name basis with him?"

"Sure. Carey and I've gone out drinking with him a couple of times. The man likes his whiskey, but he likes something else better." Grady lowered his voice and whispered. "Pot."

Calvin was shocked. "You mean marijuana?"

"Yup. Bob got busted ten years ago and went to jail. Don't you read the papers?"

"Guess that story didn't make it into the Meander News-Sentinel."

"Hell, buddy. It got his films banned from the White House. President Eisenhower says he won't show movies starring drug addicts. And I'll tell you something else. When Bob was a kid, he got arrested in Georgia for vagrancy and worked on a chain gang. The man's our age, but he's sure been around. What I like best is that he's a regular guy and makes no apologies for his past."

"For Pete's sake." All Calvin could think about was what a kick Anrita would get out of this gossip. "Have you met Keely Smith too?"

"Nah. Her work's all studio stuff back in L.A."

"You'll have to forgive me, but I've forgotten the name of the movie."

"Thunder Road. It's about a guy whose family runs

moonshine. Didn't you tell me you grew up around stills and bootleggers?"

Calvin guffawed. "I think it's safe to say most everybody in East Tennessee did."

"So Bob plays this guy who comes home from the Korean War and finds out the syndicate's trying to muscle in on his daddy's moonshine business. While he's dealing with them and dodging the law, he romances Keely Smith and does some fast driving. That's where I come in and what you're gonna see this afternoon."

"Who's the audience supposed to root for?"

"Mitchum, of course."

"But he's a moonshiner."

"Yeah, but his character won a Purple Heart in Korea and he's a folk hero who represents the independent spirit of these mountain people. It's based on a true story about some poor devil who crashed his car outside Knoxville about five years ago. Bob heard the story from some screenwriter named James Agee and that's why we're all here."

"The bad guy pays for his crimes, eh?"

"I'd say he's more an anti-hero than a bad guy. I like the character, and Bob's damned good in the part. His son Jim's in it too, playing his younger brother of all things. Part was written for Elvis Presley but his manager wanted way too much money, so Bob suggested Jim." Grady grabbed the Lucky Strike tucked over his left ear and fired up. "Okay, that's enough shop talk. How're Anrita and your boy, and what've you been doing besides running that big salad empire?"

"The family's fine, thanks." Calvin quickly brought his friend up to speed, ending with his plans to launch an anti-moonshine campaign. Grady listened closely as Calvin explained the dangers of white lightning and how determined he was to keep it away from naive and reckless young people. "I don't want any more kids dying from that rotgut."

"I grew up in Kansas so I didn't know anything about

moonshine until this movie came along. Hollywood thinks it's a Hillbilly phenomenon."

"I wish that were the case, but that poison's made all over the country, including Kansas, and it needs to be stopped."

"You sound pretty passionate about it, buddy."

"Reckon I am at that."

"I don't know how much success you're gonna have driving around town in a car with a fake corpse on top. You might want to think on a bigger scale." Grady turned his head and exhaled a long stream of smoke. "Hey. I've got an idea."

"What do you mean?"

"Let's talk about it at dinner." He looked up when his name came blasting through a bullhorn. "Sounds like they're ready for me. C'mon. I'll show you where to watch from."

"You gonna flip any cars?"

"Not today. Just some fancy fish-tailing on that stretch of asphalt over there."

Calvin followed Grady to a roadside spot blocked off with saw-horses and joined some crew and other invited spectators, heart racing when his old friend climbed into the Ford and revved the engine. Two hours later, after Grady had done half a dozen wild spinouts, Calvin was bathed in sweat and bursting with pride. He turned to a tall man in a battered jacket who'd appeared a few minutes earlier.

"These guys sure earn their money, don't they?"

The man looked back with heavily lidded eyes. "Damned sure do."

Calvin stared and continued staring when Robert Mitchum nodded politely and walked away.

14

The home plant of Anrita's Home-Style Salads was a neatly landscaped, one-story brick building that didn't look like much from the road, but a loading dock in the rear boasted a steady stream of trucks transporting thousands of salad cartons to grocery stores across the South. The small lobby was also unpretentious. A sofa and a pair of comfortable wing-chairs in a floral print announced a woman's touch, and panoramic color photos of the Great Smoky Mountains graced pale peach walls. Four offices held space for Anrita, Calvin, the plant manager and their shared secretary, Barbara Steele, and behind that was an industrial kitchen buzzing like a beehive. Visitors always remarked on the bright cleanliness of the place and the tantalizing aromas of roasting chicken, home-made mayonnaise and sweet pickle relish.

Anrita's appointment with Mary Fox was at ten o'clock. She didn't know what she expected, but it wasn't this tall, slender woman in a two-piece navy suit with matching purse and shoes, white gloves and a smart straw hat. She radiated confidence as she strode into the room with an outstretched hand.

"Hello, Mrs. Harrington. I'm Mary Fox."

"How do you do."

Anrita didn't realize until they both sat down that this was the first time she'd shaken hands with a colored person. She and Lou had hugged on occasion, but they had never shaken hands. She was annoyed with herself for even thinking about it.

"My husband Calvin and are very impressed with your resume, Mrs. Fox. I've known Lou for years and she speaks very highly of you."

"She's an old friend and a good one."

"And someone whose opinion I value highly, so highly in

fact that if you want the job it's yours. Your pay would be ninety dollars a week, but there will be periodic raises after you prove yourself."

Mary's eyes widened at the quickness of Anrita's decision and a salary beyond her wildest dreams. "You mean you're hiring me, just like that?!"

"Qualified people in the food business are hard to come by, especially those with administrative capabilities. Your references checked out fine, and since our manager left last week I need someone right away. Why beat around the bush?"

Mary smiled for the first time. "After years of fighting red tape in the public school system, I'd sure enjoy working for somebody who makes quick decisions."

"Thank you, Mrs. Fox, but we're not done yet. After I explain your considerable responsibilities and give you a tour of the plant, you may not want the job."

"Somehow I doubt that."

Fifteen minutes later, after meeting the twelve women and three men who transformed raw poultry and condiments into Anrita's famous chicken salad, Mary took the job. Anrita showed her the rest of the plant and paused at the doorway to Calvin's empty office. "He's due back this afternoon from Asheville."

"I look forward to meeting him."

"You'll find he's an easy man to work for. He and I both believe in treating our employees well, which is why every one of the people you met have been with us since the business started four years ago."

Mary looked impressed. "That certainly says something about employee loyalty."

"We like to think so." Anrita walked behind Calvin's desk and rearranged some papers on top. "Do you have any more questions?"

"One big one."

"Oh?"

"May I speak frankly, Mrs. Harrington?"

"Call me Anrita and, yes, you may."

"Lou told me your former plant manager was a white man, so I can't help wondering why you're hiring a colored woman for the job."

"Why not?"

"Two words. Colored and woman. It's not the sort of thing that happens every day."

"No, I suppose not. The truth is, Calvin and I discussed that very thing after Lou told us about you. We know people will talk about us putting you in such a big position, but that's their problem. As far as we're concerned you're more than qualified to ... now that's strange."

"Ma-am?"

Anrita leaned down and pulled out a drawer at the bottom of Calvin's desk. She flipped briefly through the files and stood up. "That drawer is supposed to stay locked when Calvin's out of the office."

"Maybe he forgot."

"Calvin's too organized to forget something like this, especially since there are some important documents in here."

"Is anything missing?"

"I don't think so." Anrita sat in Calvin's chair and took a closer look. "But the files look disorderly, like someone was looking for something." She looked at Mary. "I suppose now's a good time to tell you something. Please have a seat."

"You look a little pale, Mrs. Harrington."

"Anrita."

"Should I get you some water?"

"No, no. I'm a little upset is all." Anrita grabbed a tissue and dabbed her moist upper lip. "Not long after we became successful, people joked about stealing our secret recipe. We never thought anything about it until last winter. Right after Christmas, a man came by here claiming to be a state health inspector. His credentials looked official enough, and I was about to turn him loose in the kitchen when Calvin walked in and asked him to wait in the lobby while he called Nashville to verify the man's claims. Before Calvin could finish the call, the man hightailed it out of here."

"And you think he was after the recipe?"

"It's common knowledge that we keep no money here, so I can't think of another reason why he wanted access to our kitchen. We give tours to school children and church groups all the time, so it's not like the place is forbidden territory. We keep an eye on them to make sure nobody wanders off, but that's because kitchens, as I'm sure you know, can be dangerous places."

"Indeed, they can."

Anrita was puzzled. "I may be jumping to conclusions but this business with the drawer worries me."

"What about that plant manager who left?"

"Fred Kinser?" Anrita waved a hand. "He's a long-time family friend who's retiring because of a bad heart. We trust him implicitly."

"I assume your recipe is in a safe place."

"The basic recipe was posted on a wall here in the plant kitchen, but after that fake inspector showed up, Calvin took it down and put it in a safe place."

"By 'basic,' do you mean the complete recipe wasn't posted?"

"Correct. My kitchen workers know all the ingredients except the spices. I mix them myself and put them in jars. Calvin's alone with me when I do it. All my crew does is open the jars and dump the contents into the vats of chicken."

"Sounds foolproof."

"I hope so. Even if someone took my chicken salad to a chemist to be analyzed, there's one ingredient he'd never find."

"I'm not foolish enough to ask what it is."

"Another reason why I believe I've made the right choice." Anrita stood and ushered Mary into the lobby. "How soon can you start work?"

"School's out in another week. I can start right after that."

"Why don't you take a few days to get settled? That way you won't be rushed."

"Thank you. I could sure use the time."

Anrita shook Mary's hand again. "I hope you'll be with us a long time."

"So do I, Anrita. Please let me say how much I appreciate this opportunity. I promise you won't regret hiring me."

"I'm sure I won't." Anrita watched Mary leave and went back to her office. Barbara was right behind her. "What is it, dear?"

"Is that woman really gonna be Mr. Kinser's replacement?"

Anrita didn't like Barbara's tone. "Yes, she is."

The secretary looked crestfallen. "I ... well, I don't know if I can work for her."

"Why is that?"

Barbara's face flushed. "You already know why, Mrs. Harrington."

Of course Anrita knew, but she wanted Barbara to put it into words. She sat behind her desk and turned serious. "Tell me."

"Because I can't be taking orders from a colored person."

"Why not?"

"Because, I can't, that's all. What would my friends say?"

"If they're friends, they won't say anything. It's only a job, for heaven's sake. Mrs. Fox will be asking you to take dictation and make appointments, not clean her house."

Barbara was clearly conflicted. "You know I need this job, Mrs. Harrington."

"And we want you to keep it, Barbara. You're very competent."

"But when I started, you never said anything about putting a colored person over me."

"It was never my intention, until now anyway," Anrita said patiently. "But here's the situation. Mrs. Fox is eminently qualified for the job and we need her right away. We'd hate to lose you, but to be perfectly frank, it's a lot easier to find a secretary than a plant manager. I'm sorry you feel the way you do, but those are the cold, hard facts."

"Oh, Mrs. Harrington!" To Anrita's utter surprise, Barbara burst into tears and buried her face in her hands. "It's not me! It's not me!"

"What are you talking about?"

"It's Jarmon I'm worried about," Barbara sobbed.

"What's your husband got to do with this?"

"He'd knock me winding before he'd let me work for a colored."

"You don't mean he'd actually hit you?!" Anrita couldn't imagine mild-mannered Jarmon Steele harming a fly. He was a polite, gentle soul who married his high school sweetheart and worked hard as an auto mechanic to take care of her and their four children.

"No, ma-am. I was exaggerating, but he'd sure never let me come back to work here."

When Barbara started blubbering again, Anrita gave her a hug. "Shhh. Hush now. I know what we'll do."

"Wha … what?" Barbara asked between sobs.

"As far as Jarmon and anybody else is concerned, you're working for me, not for Mrs. Fox. If she asks you to type a letter or make a phone call, you're doing it for Anrita's Home-Style Salads, not for her. Do you understand, Barbara?"

"I … I guess so."

"You don't personally have a problem working for Mrs. Fox, do you?"

"No, ma-am. She seems real nice."

"She certainly is, and all of us are going to get along fine. You'll see." She touched Barbara's chin and tilted her head back. "Now go fix your mascara, young lady. You look like a raccoon."

"Yes, ma-am. Thank you, ma-am."

Barbara hurried to the rest room, leaving Anrita wondering what she had gotten herself into.

15

Sylvianne sucked in her tummy, wriggled into her brand-new Esther Williams swimsuit, slathered Coppertone on her face and shoulders and dabbed zinc oxide on her nose. After putting a couple of Mantovani records on the hi-fi, she went into the kitchen and rummaged through her gadget drawer until she found a bottle opener. She popped open a Coke and, as usual, checked the bottom to see where it was bottled.

"Cincinnati, huh? Nuts."

When Sylvianne was in Smithwood Grammar School, the kids stopped at the Sweet Shop on the way home and played something called "Far Away," meaning whoever's Coke was bottled farthest from Meander won the game. She'd never forgotten the day she got one from Cairo, Egypt, and marveled at the strange Arabic lettering. She washed and dried it carefully and stashed it in her box of personal treasures in her closet. It stayed there until her hateful mother Mamie found it and gave it to the family maid to use for sprinkling clothes on ironing day. It was one of the few things Sylvianne took with her when she married her first husband and moved out for good. To this day it held a place of nostalgic honor on her kitchen shelf, and after she poured the Cincinnati Coke over ice and gave it a robust shot of bourbon, Sylvianne raised her glass.

"Here's to Cairo."

She took a quick sip, dragged the telephone with the long extension cord to the backyard patio, spread a beach towel over a lounge chair and stretched out. She made sure to leave a window open so she could hear Mantovani and was soon humming along with "Charmaine." The warm sun and heavenly music combined with the booze made her content. She licked her Blistex-smeared lips and sighed.

"Now all I need is a man." She closed her eyes and drifted

with the moment, so relaxed she fell asleep. The telephone jangled her reverie. "Hello."

"Hi, sweetie."

"Cassie?" Sylvianne glanced at her watch. "What're you doing calling me this time of day? Aren't you in school?"

"Yes, but I have to talk to somebody, and Anrita's in a meeting."

"So I'm second choice, huh?"

"Oh, hush. Do you want to hear this or not?"

"Of course, I do." Sylvianne sat up and took a swig of bourbon. "Fire away."

"The principal called an emergency faculty meeting after lunch and told us about an anonymous phone call warning him against race-mixing."

"I don't get it."

"Neither did Mr. Warren. All he heard was a muffled warning that something was about to happen to expose the race-mixers in town. He asked if any of us teachers had received similar calls."

"Have you?"

"No, thank goodness, but the idea has everyone on edge."

"Maybe it was a crank call."

"Who would make a crank call about something like that? This is serious." Sylvianne sipped and waited in silence. "That's not all."

"I'm listening."

"My students have been gossiping all week, but every time I try to overhear they get quiet. Apparently all sorts of rumors are flying around."

"Rumors about what?"

"That's just it. I don't know."

Sylvianne feigned annoyance. "You called to tell me about anonymous phone calls and vague rumors? You're the worst gossip ever. I need details!"

"Can you hear me now?"

"Not very well. What happened?"

"I'm in the closet in my office. I couldn't talk before."

"Aright, missy. What the devil's going on?"

"I'm worried, that's what."

"I'm worried too." Sylvianne gulped her drink. "My best friend's talking to me from a closet."

"I heard those ice cubes. How much have you had to drink?"

"Not nearly enough for this kind of foolishness."

"Listen to me, Sylvianne. Haven't you ever been in a situation when your gut told you something awful was going to happen?"

"At least four times."

"Seriously?"

"Sure. Right after my four sets of wedding vows."

Cassandra laughed in spite of herself. "Dear Lord!"

"So what the heck is going on?"

"I'm not sure. It's like I'm on the verge of something but I don't know what."

"Honey, I can't help you if I don't know what the problem is."

"I know. And I know I sound crazy, but I needed to hear a familiar voice."

Sylvianne was suddenly sympathetic. "Why don't you drop by after school? I'll call Anrita and get her to join us, and the three of us can have a hen-fest. Who knows? Maybe she's heard something too."

"Sounds good. I'll see you in little while."

"Bye, sweetie."

Sylvianne hung up and drained her glass. When a clump of ice cubes banged her nose, she chortled at her clumsiness and went inside for a fresh drink. She was fighting a stubborn ice tray when something outside the kitchen window caught her eye. She figured it was probably Eugene Proctor but was too nearsighted to be sure. She retrieved her glasses and saw two people locked in an embrace.

"I'll be damned!"

Underneath a pecan tree not twenty feet away were Anrita's son John and Lurleen Abernathy. Their hands were all over each other, making it plain to Sylvianne that this was not their first encounter. She was glued to the kitchen window until the lusty young couple disappeared inside the house.

"Uh-oh! I sure hope Anrita doesn't come home early today."

Two more drinks and three Mantovani LPs later, Sylvianne was still lazing on the patio. She sat up and called out when she heard the doorbell. "I'm back here, Cassie!"

"Hey, you!" Cassandra called from the kitchen. "May I make myself a vodka and tonic?"

"Help yourself. You know where everything is." She offered her cheek for a kiss when Cassandra joined her. "Do you have any real news this time?"

"Sort of, but first things first." She sipped her vodka and listened to the music a moment. "You know what, milady? You've sure got the life."

Sylvianne managed a cock-eyed glance. "Believe me I've paid for it. I don't give a hoot what that song says. The best things in life are definitely not free."

"Maybe not."

"Never mind about that. Tell me what you know."

"It's worse than I thought. One of my girls is pregnant."

"Anybody I know?"

"Don't know yet. I only overheard a snippet."

"I guess we'll find out when the stork comes in for a landing."

"I guess."

Sylvianne's mind was a little foggy from the bourbon but she suddenly remembered what she'd seen next door. "If you want some real juice, I saw something this afternoon that you won't believe."

"Oh?"

"Before I tell you, you have to promise not to breathe a

word to anyone." She gave Cassandra a mischievous look over the rim of her glass. "Especially Anrita."

"Since when do we have secrets from her?"

"Since now."

"Uh-oh." Cassandra sipped her vodka while listening to Sylvianne relate what she'd seen. When Sylvianne finished, Cassandra took a big gulp and said, "Damn!"

"My thoughts exactly."

"Did John and Lurleen look that serious?"

"If they'd gotten any more serious, that stork would already be circling. I can't keep up with these damned kids. I thought John was going steady with Dottisue Davis."

"And Lurleen's supposed to be going steady with Rocky Millsaps." Cassandra thought a moment, as though weighing what to say next. Sylvianne had seen that look before.

"C'mon, girl. Spit it out."

"Lurleen's one of my favorite students. She's sweet and smart and, as I've told Anrita, absolutely nothing like her parents. We've gotten pretty close these past few months, and she's come to me several times for advice."

"About what?"

"The usual teen angst and self-esteem issues but she's also very unhappy with her parents. She'd deny it, but I know she's ashamed of them and with good reason. Her grades are excellent, but the Abernathys are discouraging college. In fact, Junkin wants her to work for him after graduation."

"Doing what? Bagging bootlegged booze or waiting tables at Big Shots?"

"God knows, but the larger issue is that Lurleen confessed to having a big crush on John Harrington. She didn't say anything about pursuing it, only that she was forbidden to date him because the Abernathys despise the Harringtons."

"I think the word is envy, not despise."

"Or both." Cassandra sipped again. "It's like the Capulets and Montagues."

"More like the Hatfields and McCoys."

"I was trying to keep things on a classical plain."

"Either way, poor Lurleen."

"I want to help her and I'd never have betrayed her confidence if you hadn't seen her with John. Those two better be careful or the whole town's gonna find out. Then the you-know-what will really hit the fan!"

"Sounds like little Lurleen's got a mind of her own. Good for her!"

"There's something else, Sylvianne. Since Rocky is John's best buddy and Lurleen and Dottisue are best friends and since I know from Anrita that they double date all the time—"

Sylvianne leaned forward when the truth dawned. "Those four scamps! They've cooked up a scheme to make it look like it's the other way around!"

"Exactly."

"God, I feel like Miss Marple."

"And I feel like I'm watching a French farce."

"Kids," Sylvianne muttered. "Who can keep up with them these days?"

"A more important question is what we're going to tell Anrita. Truth is best, you know."

"I agree, but what're we going to tell Anrita?"

"Tell me about what?"

Sylvianne and Cassandra were so engrossed that they didn't hear the gate swing open or see Anrita standing on the patio. She enjoyed the awkward silence as her friends struggled to respond, and then put them out of their misery.

"It's alright, girls. When I overheard your voices, I decided to join the fun."

"Uh, how much did you hear?"

"Let's say I heard enough."

"Oh, dear." Sylvianne motioned her over. "Do you want a drink, honey?"

"No, thanks. Actually, I'm not surprised to hear about my son and Lurleen."

"No?"

"Not at all. I've seen those four together a million times and I've seen how John looks at Lurleen and vice versa. The same with Rocky and Dottisue. I don't know how serious they are, but I think Lurleen's a fine young lady."

"Pedigree notwithstanding."

"Lurleen can't help who her parents are."

"Touché."

Cassandra jumped back in. "Does Calvin suspect anything? We all know what he thinks of our illustrious mayor."

"I doubt it. He's not around the kids that much, but I'm not sure it's something a man would notice. Either way, I'd appreciate it if you kept this between us."

"Of course, we will."

"Calvin especially doesn't need to know right now. Somebody called him at the office this afternoon and left an ugly message with Barbara about race-mixing. The poor little thing was so upset."

Cassandra groaned. "Uh-oh. Here we go again."

"What do you mean?"

"Daniel Warren got a call too. This afternoon at the school."

Anrita looked puzzled. "I don't get the connection."

"What connection?"

"I assumed Calvin got the call because I hired a colored woman this morning to be plant manager. I wondered how somebody could've found out and acted so fast."

"I think it was coincidence," Cassandra said. "I'd be willing to bet that some bigoted bastard, pardon my French, Anrita, was making random calls. I'll also bet people all over town got them."

"What an awful thought," Sylvianne said. A sudden breeze stirred a nearby weeping willow, shimmering its graceful branches in the late afternoon sunshine and bathing everyone in the scent of honeysuckle. "And on such a beautiful afternoon."

Cassandra sipped. "My dear, it just goes to show you how deceiving appearances can be."

16

One of the first things Eulalie did after inviting Lou into her home was teach her how to read and write. Lou had learned the ABCs from her mother and could decipher a few basic words, but Eulalie soon discovered the girl was starved for knowledge. Once the genie was out of the bottle, Lou buried her nose in a book whenever she found time, and when she was listless in the morning Eulalie knew she had read into the wee hours. It was clear that the girl belonged in school, but with the closest one for colored children way up in Knoxville, it wasn't feasible. She felt better about the predicament when Lou insisted she liked the status quo.

"I can get all the learning I need right here, Miss Eulalie. All I ask is that you keep those books coming."

"How about a subscription to Reader's Digest Condensed Books? They're not as rich as the originals, but you can read more in less time."

"Fine with me. I reckon I'm a gal in a hurry."

Eulalie had been pleased. "So I see."

By the time she was twenty-one, Lou had lost count of how many novels she'd devoured. Reading remained her passion, and she was lost in Harriet Arnow's *The Dollmaker* when a car parked in front of her little house. She set the book aside and peered through the screen door to see Mary coming up the flagstone walk. Her old friend had taken a day off from work to look for a place to live in Meander.

"Get in this house!" Lou called. "I'm so happy to see you."

Mary gave her a hug. "Pretty soon you're going to be seeing lots more of me."

"I can't wait." They sat in the living room where, Lou noted, Mary took inventory. "You like my little place?"

"It looks fine."

"How about the neighborhood?"

"It looks fine, too. I love those old oak trees."

"Good. I've been asking around and found something you might like. It's the rent you want to pay and best of all it's on the next block. We can visit whenever we like."

"When can I see it? That car belongs to a friend of mine, and I promised to get it back to Knoxville by this afternoon."

"Can't you at least stay for lunch?"

"Not today, but we'll have plenty of time for that after I move here." As they stood to go, Mary looked at Lou's novel. "You read those condensed books, huh?"

"Miss Eulalie gave me a subscription a long time ago."

"Hmmm. Too bad she couldn't give you whole books."

Lou ignored the implication. "She knows how much I love to read, and these sure speed up the process."

"I see." Mary gave the book a disdainful look. "Ready to go?"

"Yes, indeed."

The apartment was smaller than Mary wanted, but because it was on the bus-line and she needed it right away, she signed a lease. On the walk back, she asked Lou if she had a boyfriend.

"Not right now."

"How do you spend your free time?"

"I have my church activities over at AME Zion and I love to babysit Zanna's children. Obviously, I read a lot and I have a little vegetable garden out behind the house. You know. Tomatoes, squash, pole beans. Miss Eulalie gave me some hydrangea and peonies so I have those to take care of too."

"Don't you go to meetings?"

"What kind of meetings?"

Mary glanced around and lowered her voice. "Civil rights meetings."

"No, I don't."

"Why not?"

"I guess I never thought about them. Besides, as far as I know there aren't any around here."

"There should be."

"Is this something you've taken up?"

"There are a couple of groups in Knoxville. I went to see what they were all about after my marriage fell apart."

"What did you find out?" Lou looked away when a passing car slowed and someone called out.

"Hey, Lou!"

"Hey, John!"

"Tell your Mama I'll see her in the morning."

"Okay." John Harrington waved and sped down the street.

"Who's that?"

"Your new boss's son. You'll like him. Nice young man."

"Mmmm." They walked the rest of the way in silence. When they got to Mary's borrowed car, she said, "Do me a favor, will you?"

"If I can."

"Ask around and find out if there are any meetings. I'd like to attend some after I get settled."

"I wouldn't know who to ask."

"Church is a good place to start. You know how church folks like to gossip. If there's something going on, you'll find out about it sooner or later."

"I guess so, but—"

"But what?"

Lou gave Mary a long look. "I'm not sure I want to do that."

"Why not?"

"This isn't Knoxville, Mary. It's a small town. Everybody knows everybody's business, and if I start asking about civil rights meetings, everybody's gonna know about it before the day's out."

"So what? People in Knoxville know I'm involved and—"

Lou repeated herself, firmly this time. "Like I said, this isn't Knoxville."

"I know that, but aren't there things here in Meander you want to change?"

"Like what?"

Mary was dumbfounded. "For somebody who reads all the time, you sure sound out of touch. I'm talking about segregation, girl."

"I knew that, but I was hoping it was something else."

Mary's eyes narrowed. "Why?"

"I don't know. I guess I don't mind things the way they are. Fact is, separate facilities don't bother me because I don't ever use them."

Mary was aghast. "How's that possible? They're all over the place. Water fountains. Movie theaters. Restrooms. Restaurants."

"I don't go out."

"Not even to the movies?"

"I don't care much about movies."

"Maybe you'd go more often if you didn't have to sit up in nigger heaven."

"Mary!"

"I figured you for a smart girl, but maybe you're not as smart as I thought."

Lou was annoyed and upset by her friend's abrasive tone. "Because I'm not ready to jump on your civil rights band wagon doesn't mean I'm dumb, Mary. It might even mean I'm smart."

"What do you mean?"

"I mean that my life suits me fine." Mary started to speak, but Lou talked over her. "You're one of my oldest friends, Mary Fox, and I've got a lot of respect for you and I'm mighty glad you're moving to Meander, but folks here do things a certain way. Do whatever you want, but don't expect me to turn my life upside down because of your high falutin', big city ideas."

"They're not big city ideas, Lou. They're about equality and dignity for colored people and—" Mary retreated when she realized now was not the time for this particular talk. "I'm sorry, Lou. It's just me and my big mouth. I've got no business coming down here and telling you what to do, especially after all you've done to help me. I have a lot on my mind these days, what with divorcing Jesse and changing jobs and towns and all and … oh, I reckon that's no real excuse. Please say you're not mad." She squeezed Lou's hand. "Please."

"The only reason I'm not mad is that I've seen you act like this before. Long as I can remember, you've stirred the pot one way or another. I already told Miss Anrita you're probably gonna shake things up once you get here."

"Maybe so, and then again maybe I'm a little full of myself what with the new job and all. From what you've said, I'm thinking maybe Meander isn't ready for meetings. Not yet anyway."

"Probably not. People here get along well enough, but in my heart I pray that change is down the road. I know about the awful things happening in Alabama and Mississippi, but that's the Deep South."

"You saying there's not room for improvement in Tennessee?"

"Heavens, no!"

"Good. Prayer is fine, but I'm here to tell you change will come. Want to know how I know?"

"I'm listening."

"Because a minute ago you said you weren't ready to jump on my bandwagon, and now you admitted you're praying for change. You'll eventually come around, and a whole lot of other folks will too."

"Don't hold your breath, Miss Firecracker." Lou chuckled. "And don't tell me you don't have time for a chicken salad sandwich before you head back to Knoxville."

"Sure, I do." Mary gave Lou a hug before they went inside the house. "You remember how much I love chicken salad, huh?"

"Have you had Miss Anrita's before?"

"I've never had store-bought chicken salad in my life. In

fact, we use my preacher's wife's recipe at the school. Hmmm. I better not let my new boss know I've not tried her product."

"Girl, we're gonna fix that right now. Come in the kitchen." Lou crumpled fresh mint into the iced tea glasses, gave it a stir, opened a loaf of Swan's white bread and set about making chicken salad sandwiches. "One of the advantages of working for Miss Anrita is that I get all the chicken salad I want, and I'm sure you will too. Shoot! I go through this stuff like Sherman through Georgia. Here. Take a bite."

Mary took a bite. "I hate to say it, but this is the best I've ever had."

"It's no wonder Miss Anrita sells so much."

"I wonder what's in it."

"I suspect nobody knows except her and maybe her husband," Lou said.

"Somebody's sure trying to find out."

"What do you mean?" Mary related the story about Calvin's desk and the imposter claiming to be a health inspector. "That's awful."

"Yeah, but you know how people are. Soon as somebody comes up with a money-making idea, everybody else wants a piece of the pie." She took another bite. "Or a chunk of the chicken salad."

"I'd sure like to know who's the culprit." Lou chewed thoughtfully. "On second thought, maybe not."

"I'm just so excited I can hardly stand it!" Laverne gushed, scrambling into the back seat of Calvin's Continental Mark II. "I've been waiting weeks just to see this movie."

"I hope you're not disappointed," Anrita said as Calvin backed out of the driveway. "I haven't heard much about it."

"I don't much care just as long as Joan Fontaine's in it."

"When did you become such a big fan?"

"Gosh, Anrita. I've just loved her as long as I can remember. I guess everyone has to have a favorite and Joan Fontaine is mine. I also like Joan Crawford and Barbara Stanwyck and I just love Bette Davis too, only you never know whether she's gonna kill her men or just kiss 'em."

"I guess that's one way of looking at it." Anrita thought about Cassie when she heard Laverne's ongoing tally of "justs."

"Well, the way I see it, Miss Bette just can't—"

Anrita and Calvin exchanged helpless looks as Laverne launched into another interminable run-on sentence. Anrita had long ago learned how to tune her out, but Calvin wasn't so successful. He was a man with remarkable fortitude, but Laverne's incessant babbling wore his patience wafer-thin. He was trying to think of a diplomatic way to interrupt and change the subject when he turned onto Main Street and spotted something that hurtled gentlemanly manners out the window. He glanced into the rear-view mirror and caught Laverne's eye.

"Laverne, I want you to shut your mouth and keep it shut!"

"Calvin!" Anrita was appalled. "Why would you say such a—?"

"You keep still too!"

Too stunned to speak, Anrita was so upset she almost

cried, but her tears were stillborn when she saw what triggered her husband's harsh edict.

"Sweet baby Jesus!" she breathed.

Strange glows appeared beneath the marquee of the Tower Theater a block away. Movie traffic had begun backing up, and as Calvin slowed the Continental, Anrita saw torches blazing against the deepening dusk. As they ventured closer, more torches appeared alongside the ticket booth and throughout the parking lot. Calvin didn't need to see the shadowy, hooded figures holding torches to know who they were.

"It's the damned Ku Klux Klan."

"Calvin, no!" Anrita whispered.

He turned, features grim, voice determined. "I meant what I said. I don't want you two to say a word. These men are itching for trouble, but we're not gonna give it to them." Anrita fell silent and Laverne whimpered softly as the car inched toward the parking lot. Two large men, torches crackling in the soft Southern night, flanked the entrance, and the stench of burning pine knots enveloped the car. Anrita coughed and put a handkerchief to her nose when one of the men leaned toward Calvin's open window.

"Going to the movie, friend?"

"Yes, we are."

"Know what it's about?"

Calvin focused on the eye slits in the Klansman's hood, wondering if he knew who was inside. "Can't say that I do."

"Then read this!" The man threw a flyer through the car window. "By the way, we're keeping track of who goes into the theater tonight."

The man stepped back as the car ahead moved into a parking space. As Calvin nosed the Continental alongside it, Anrita grabbed his arm.

"Please, Calvin!" she pleaded. "Let's go home."

"Not on your life," he growled. "We came to see the movie, and by God no bunch of hooded cobras is gonna stop us!"

Anrita tightened her grip, "What is it, honey?"

"Do you really think it's wise to get out of the car?"

"Wise or not, it's what we're going to do."

Anrita glanced down at the Klan flyer. "Good Lord! This drawing looks more like a gorilla than a colored man."

"Leave that filth where it is," Calvin ordered. "Now come on. You too, Laverne."

Calvin offered an arm to each woman and ushered them through the eerie figures in white robes and peaked hoods. Flickering torchlight intensified the atmosphere of menace and fear which was, Calvin knew, exactly what these thugs intended. He noticed that a few cars entering the parking lot turned around and left, but was relieved and pleased to see most people parked and headed for the theater.

"Hey, Doris," he called into the ticket booth. He'd known Doris Lowe for years but had never seen her so pale and nervous. "Three, please."

"Hello, Mr. Harrington," she managed in a shaky voice. "How're y'all doing?"

"We're fine." He leaned closer to the booth. "You alright in there?"

"Mr. Reed told me something like this might happen, but I guess I'm not as prepared as I thought."

"Did he call Sheriff Kirkendol?"

"He told me he was going to call if these men showed up, but far as I know he's still in his office." Doris took Calvin's money and slid three tickets underneath the glass partition. "I can't imagine why the sheriff's not here."

"Me either, but I'm sure everything will be fine." He tried hard to sound reassuring. "These hoodlums are just trying to throw a scare into folks."

"I sure hope you're right, Mr. Harrington." Doris managed a nervous smile. "Y'all enjoy the movie."

"We will."

As Calvin steered Anrita and Laverne through the turnstile, one of the Klansmen leaned over the railing. "We see you, Mr. Harrington."

Calvin glowered. "Who the hell are you?"

"You don't know me, but I know you."

Calvin's temper flared, and it took all his self-control to keep from yanking off the man's hood. "You're one cowardly son of a bitch, you know that?"

Beery breath oozed from beneath the hood. "We're merely exercising our freedom to assemble, friend."

"I'm no friend of yours. You can all go to hell!"

The man muttered something unintelligible and stepped back as Calvin steered Anrita and Laverne into the theater lobby. He told them to find seats and stay put. "I'll be right back."

"Where are you going?" Anrita asked.

"To see a man about a dog."

It was a lie and she knew it, but Anrita said nothing as Calvin went looking for the manager. He found Ken Reed in his office, talking animatedly on the telephone. He motioned for Calvin to take a seat and talked another couple of minutes before hanging up.

"That was Chuck Kirkendol."

Calvin made a face. "Where the devil is he?"

"Heading back from the old Carlisle place."

"About time."

"It's not his fault, Mr. Harrington. Somebody sent him and Buzzy out there on a wild goose chase."

"Not hard to figure out who."

"And it's not hard to figure out who's been sending us hate mail ever since we announced Island in the Sun. We've been getting nasty calls about race-mixing too. Poor Doris is almost too scared to answer the phone."

"You're not the only one getting phone calls. I got one, and so did George Collignon and several of my Kiwanis brothers. I'm gonna round up a bunch of men tomorrow and have a meeting about this. You want to join us?"

"Damned right. I don't need those troublemakers messing

with my business." Reed grabbed his manager jacket from a hook by the door. "I better get out there and do what I can do to keep order."

"Want me to go with you?"

"Thanks, buddy, but all I need is for people to get in their seats so we can start the movie." He clapped Calvin on the shoulder before rushing into the lobby. "Call me when you're ready for that meeting."

"Will do."

Calvin went back into the theater and found his seat as the lights went down and previews began for a new Elvis Presley film called Jailhouse Rock. He barely saw the screen. All he could think about was the evil lurking outside the theater. Because this was not the first time he had encountered the Ku Klux Klan, Calvin knew their most insidious weapon was secrecy. He couldn't help wondering if some of the men he would invite to his meeting tomorrow were among those wearing hoods.

Most of all he wondered about the man who called his name. Where had he heard that voice before?

18

"Come on in!"

Lou had barely tapped the bedroom door when she heard Eulalie's voice. She found her employer sitting up in bed, fussing with her bed jacket and looking mad as a wet hen. Lou had seen that look before.

"Maybe I'd better leave the coffee and come back later this morning."

"You'll do no such thing, young lady! You'll sit down and we'll have our coffee as usual, only this time I'll be doing a little ranting and raving."

Lou slid the breakfast tray in place. "'Bout anything or anybody I know?"

"We'll see soon enough." As she had hundreds of times, Eulalie poured two cups of coffee and passed one to Lou. She took her first sip and waited for the strong rich taste to yield the jolt she wanted. "I don't suppose you were at the Tower Theater last night."

"You know I don't go to picture shows."

"Neither do I, but the real show was apparently not on the movie screen."

Lou sipped. "You mean the Ku Kluxers?"

Eulalie was caught off-guard. "You already know what happened?"

"I'd say every colored person in Calhoun County knows when the Klan shows up, usually within the hour. How'd you find out?"

"Anrita Harrington called me last night. I've never heard her so upset and for good reason. She was at the Tower and said Mr. Harrington had words with one of those men."

"You sure don't want to be messing with those people."

"Please don't tell me you ever had a run-in with them."

"No, but Mama and Daddy warned us about them when

we were little, told us all about white men who dressed in robes and hoods and how they burned crosses and killed innocent black folks. They said if we ever saw them to run hide as quick as we could."

"Were your parents speaking from personal experience?"

"Not that I know of. Just said it was something all colored people knew about and told their children to watch out for."

"I've lived in Meander all my life, and that miserable lot of humanity has never showed themselves here. What I want to know is why they're doing it now."

"The movie, that's why. I guess it's got some race-mixing in it."

"Then why didn't they show up six years ago when the Tower played Showboat? Ava Gardener played a black girl with a white husband. If that's not race-mixing, I don't know what is."

"The difference is that Miss Ava's a white actress pretending to be black. If Lena Horne had played that part, it would've been a whole other story."

Eulalie pursed her lips. "Mmmm. I should've thought of that." She gave Lou a self-effacing look. "I'm embarrassed to say there are lots of things I should've been thinking about. I've behaved like an ostrich with its head in the sand."

"What do you mean?"

"I mean that, like a lot of white folks in this town, I've ignored injustice and lied to myself that our separate-but-equal system was exactly that, when I've known in my heart that it wasn't." For the first time in their many years together, Eulalie wept in front of Lou. "I'm ashamed of myself, Lou. Very, very ashamed."

Lou was deeply moved. "It's alright, Eulalie. Things have been this way so long folks got used to them. I know you're a good woman with love in your heart. I've known that since you brought me into this house and taught me how to read and write and treated me like family. I don't know any other colored folks around here who have it as good as I do."

"That's exactly the point, Lou. Most of them aren't treated like they ought to be, and it's not right. People need to wake up, black and white both."

"I reckon so, and I guess now's a good time to tell you about my good friend Mary Fox. She's moving here from Knoxville to be Miss Anrita's plant manager."

Eulalie brightened. "Good for Anrita. That's certainly a step in the right direction."

"Yes, ma-am. Mary was here last week, and she said we're probably gonna be seeing a lot more of the Klan."

"Oh?"

"She said colored folks are tired of being treated like dogs, and that what's gonna happen has to happen 'cause it's been festering since 1952 when the government said segregated schools were against the law. Obviously saying and doing are two different things."

"Because schools in the South are still segregated."

"Along with everything else." Lou sipped her coffee. "Mary also said colored people up in Knoxville are fed up with waiting for the law to be enforced, and when they start making noise about it, so does the Klan. I never thought there was much we could do, but she's got me thinking maybe that's not so."

"That makes three of us." Eulalie set aside her coffee cup. "Are you looking to get involved with civil rights work?"

"I don't know, but Mary wants me to, and I guess I've been thinking about it."

Eulalie brightened. "My, my! This morning's bursting with surprises, isn't it?"

"You're not upset with me, are you?"

"Heavens, no! Why would you even ask such a thing? You're a grown woman, Lou Johnson, and you should be able to do anything and go anywhere you want."

Lou gave her a funny look. "To tell you the truth, I wouldn't mind eating lunch at the S&W Cafeteria up in Knoxville."

Eulalie looked surprised. "Why that particular place?"

"Because there's something that's bothered me for a long time about that restaurant and other places in Knoxville too. You know how foreigners come from all over the world to study the Tennessee Valley Authority and learn how the government dammed the river to control it and build all those plants to make electricity?"

"Yes."

"Some of those folks are from Africa, and I know if they go out to dinner with the T.V.A folks and wear their native costumes, they can get served. White people running those restaurants let them in because they're foreign coloreds."

"Something else I never thought about."

"I suspect most white people haven't because they think chances are slim that they'll run into that situation. Or maybe they think it's okay to sit next to a colored person if they're from the Belgian Congo but not if they're from across town."

"That's a very interesting point, Lou."

"I'll tell you something else. I was making up my bed the other day and thought to myself that I could wrap that striped bedspread around me and put a turban on my head and sandals on my bare feet and get me some big old gold hoop earrings and walk right into the S&W with some white folks and nobody would bat an eye."

"Hmmm. I'll bet you could at that."

"'Course I'd be scared to death to try it."

"Maybe you wouldn't be frightened if you had a friend giving you moral support."

"Miss Eulalie, you are one crazy white lady."

"Mind you, it's something to think about."

Lou was far from convinced. "Don't you think I see those wheels spinning? Don't you think I know you're gonna call one of Mr. Sugar's big mucky-mucks at the T.V.A. and concoct a plan to take your colored maid to the S&W?"

"Sometimes I think you're a mind-reader."

"No, I'm not, but I know you better than anybody, so I'm on to your shenanigans."

"Regardless of all that, you've given me a couple of good ideas."

"Me and my big mouth."

"Suzanne Jernigan's daughter Ann writes for the Knox-ville Journal, and I'll bet she'd be interested in an exclusive story. She could even have photographers there to—"

Lou was floored. "Are you serious?"

"I wasn't at first, but now I think I am. What better way to get some publicity and expose the local hypocrisy in segrega-tion?"

"Uh-oh!" Lou cupped a hand to her ear. "Did you hear that noise?"

"What noise?"

"'Bout a hundred of your Confederate ancestors just rolled over in their graves."

"Maybe they weren't resting so peacefully after all. In fact, maybe they've been waiting for me to do something like this so they can get a good night's sleep. It sure makes *me* feel better."

"Me too. I didn't sleep much after hearing about what went on down at the Tower." Lou drained her cup and stood. "You about ready for some breakfast?"

"Yes, indeed. My appetite's back, but I don't want break-fast in bed. It's such a pretty morning I'll eat on the back ve-randa and I want you to join me."

"Hmmm. This wouldn't have anything to do with more of your white guilt, would it?"

"No, smarty pants. It's because I want you to fix us eggs Benedict, so it's a bribe, plain and simple."

Lou's retort was lost when the telephone rang. "Who in the world is calling this early?" She picked up Eulalie's phone. "Saunders residence . . . . Who? … Oh, yes, ma-am. I'll see if she's up yet." Lou silently mouthed the name. "Fern Abernathy."

Eulalie crossed her forefingers like she was warding off evil and shook her head no.

"I'm sorry, ma-am, but she's still asleep ... Yes, I'll take a message ... extreme pageant emergency ... yes, ma-am ... I'll have her call." Lou hung up. "You heard all that?"

"Unfortunately, yes. Extreme pageant emergency, eh? Probably something earth-shattering like a shortage of hoop-skirts."

19

The morning after his run-in with the KKK, Calvin hurriedly organized a meeting for that night. His first calls were to Ken Reed and George Collignon who helped round up over thirty men. Because he was a past president of Kiwanis and member in good standing, Calvin had no trouble securing their clubhouse, and by six that night he faced a sea of concerned faces. Sheriff Chuck Kirkendol stood in a far corner, hands behind his back, and wore a no-nonsense scowl.

"Sheriff Kirkendol?" Calvin called. "Do you know where our mayor is?"

"Said he had important business down in Sweetwater."

"Those are some mighty peculiar priorities. What could be important than this?" Calvin didn't know if Kirkendol recognized a rhetorical question but didn't wait for an answer. "I'm sure everyone present knows what happened last night at the Tower Theater, but for those who weren't there, Ken Reed and I will give you first-person accounts."

For the next ten minutes, a rapt audience listened to Calvin describe his ugly encounter with a Klansmen and heard Ken describe how business had been scared off and that his ticket seller had been frightened half to death. They also discussed the threatening phone calls and learned several men in the audience had also received them. The only sounds other than the occasional nervous cough and cleared throat were striking matches as cigars, cigarettes and pipes were lit. By the time Calvin finished, a grey cloud hovered in the small hall.

"Before I open the floor to discussion, I have a personal story to tell. I purposely excluded ladies from attending tonight because I didn't want them to hear this." Calvin glanced around the room. "Most of you know I was born in up in Oneida in 1905. In those days, Scott County was like the Wild West with a lot of men carrying guns, my daddy in-cluded. There were no colored people living there, and I learned why when I was nine. A couple of black hobos rode the rails through town on an L&N freight train. Somebody spotted them and pulled them out of their box car, and some men started shooting at their feet to make them dance. Somebody aimed too high and shot one of those poor souls in the chest. Killed him instantly." A few in the audience muttered and shifted uneasily. "The corpse was thrown into a boxcar, and the man who survived was told to spread the word that coloreds weren't welcome in Scott County. That memory haunts me to this day, and so does knowing that those killers were Klansmen." He waited for murmurs and whispers to die down. "If you've had run-ins with these char-acters before, you know they mean business, which is why their appearance at the Tower is serious cause for alarm. We need to get the word out pronto that they're not welcome, and that their bigotry won't be tolerated. Any comments?" He saw a hand go up. "Andy Jenkins."

"I saw them once when I was down in Atlanta. They burned a cross on the lawn of some rabbi. It's not only col-ored people that they hate. It's Jews. Catholics too."

"And Communists," someone added.

Calvin chuckled. "I'm not too fond of commies myself, but I'd hate to think I have anything in common with the damned Klan."

A few more men added similar stories, and by the time Calvin took back the floor, the room was rumbling with de-mands to prevent the Klan from making a reappearance. "Any suggestions on how we get started?" He saw another hand. "Dave Mearns."

"Y'all know I'm editor of the News-Sentinel. I'd be happy to write an editorial about the incident and run a series of ar-ticles on the history of Klan and their evil work."

"Excellent! Who else has ideas?"

"We could put posters in our stores saying the Klan isn't

welcome," Andy said.

George Collignon stood up. "I'll be glad to put a sign in front of my store."

A number of others spoke out, and the hall rumbled with voices as ideas were exchanged and vows made to keep the Klan out of Meander. Their excitement was interrupted by a shrill whistle from Kirkendol.

"Y'all hold on a minute." Everyone grew quiet as the sheriff approached the podium and Calvin stepped aside. "Newspaper stories and signs are fine as far as they go, but they're not going to keep these guys from popping up again."

"If they come back, I say we arrest them," George said.

"On what charge?"

"How about disturbing the peace?"

"They conducted a peaceful demonstration at the movie theater, Mr. Collignon, and under the constitution, everybody is allowed freedom of assembly."

"Even if they're assembling to preach hatred?" Andy asked.

"Correct."

"I'm sure that's not what our Founding Fathers had in mind," Calvin countered.

"That's beside the point, sir, and you know it."

"In that case, since we can't amend the Constitution how about we amend the laws here in Meander? I say we ban those hooligans outright. If they can't be here, they can't assemble."

"That won't work either," the sheriff insisted. "The Constitution also guarantees people the right to join any association they choose."

"Then I say the heck with the Constitution. I say we pass a law saying the Ku Klux Klan is illegal in Meander, and if they want to challenge us in a higher court, so be it."

"What makes you think they won't?"

"Because they'd have to take off their hoods to file a lawsuit, and we all know they're too cowardly to do that. Men who hide behind masks and belong to something called the Invisible Empire obviously want to keep their identity secret."

"Excellent idea," said Ray Dillon, chairman of the Meander Town Council. "I'll get to work drafting a bill and propose it at the next session."

"Should we be there to support the agenda?"

"I believe I can say without reservation that the other four members will support such a bill. Who in their right mind wouldn't?"

The hall burst into spontaneous applause at the first real positive news of the evening. Sheriff Kirkendol remained skeptical. "I assume you'll want the mayor's input on this matter."

"Our meeting is open to the public," Dillon said icily. He had lost the recent mayoral election to Junkin Abernathy, and everyone knew they were bitter enemies. "He's welcome to say whatever he likes about the new bill."

"What if he vetoes it?" Kirkendol pressed.

Dillon looked smug. "I'm happy to say our town charter enables city council to override a mayoral veto. Either way, as crazy as Abernathy is, I doubt he'd veto something this emotionally charged. Then again, he thought nothing about greasing palms to get himself elected."

Everyone but the sheriff roared with approval. "You're using pretty strong words, Mr. Dillon."

"Like the people who elected Abernathy used pretty strong drink," Dillon shot back.

Kirkendol retreated, but a stony glare announced that he wasn't pleased. He moved to the side of the dais, folded his arms across his chest and stayed quiet. Calvin moved back to the podium and asked if anyone had further comments or questions.

"I have one," came a voice from the back of the crowd. "Why wasn't I invited to this august gathering of prominent citizenry?"

"Uh-oh," Calvin mumbled when Reverend Hickman

headed in his direction. "Here comes trouble."

The preacher wore his usual possum grin as he made his way through the crowd, glad-handing as he went and calling everyone "brother." By the time he reached Calvin, his face looked as though it might crack from smiling.

"May I say a few words?"

"Of course, Reverend. But we were about to adjourn."

"I'll only take a moment." He slipped behind the podium. "I heard about your meeting, and even though I was not invited here, I came to deliver important and pertinent news." No one in the crowd belonged to Hickman's congregation, but everyone knew about his holier-than-thou proselytizing and fondness for preaching outside the pulpit. "Even as I stand here speaking to you, a group of coloreds are picketing the Lookout Cafeteria down in Chattanooga and demanding to eat alongside white patrons." He waited for his news to sink in. "How long do you suppose it will be before the coloreds right here in Meander try to get served at Louis's Pizza Parlor?"

Calvin's hackles rose. He and Anrita both considered Hickman deceitful and unctuous, never more so than right now. "What does that have to do with this meeting?"

"Why, everything, Mr. Harrington. Don't you see that this proposed bill will throw a roadblock in front of the very group that can help you stop such an eventuality?"

"You can't be serious, Reverend Hickman. The Klan has been killing innocent people for decades!"

"I'm quite aware of the Klan's activities, and I believe if you look at these incidents closely you'll see that the people who were … uh, removed were a menace to society and civilization as we know it."

Calvin knew the man to be a pious, ignorant fool, but this convoluted logic was beyond comprehension. "So you, a man of the cloth, condone racial bigotry?"

"I said no such thing, Mr. Harrington," Hickman retorted, swelling with self-righteous indignation. "I'm merely suggesting that sometimes steps must be taken to keep us on a Christian path. After all, the Bible says 'an eye for an eye.' "

"It also says 'Thou shalt not kill,' " Calvin shot back. "Look, reverend. With all due respect, we're not interested in your views on unjustifiable homicide or the Klan or civil rights in Chattanooga. We're interested in keeping bigotry and violence out of our hometown."

The minister puffed up like a toad. "You wouldn't care if a colored person sat beside you in a public restaurant?"

"Considering that my wife and I often eat lunch with the colored employees in our plant kitchen, I'd say that's a moot point."

Reverend Hickman bristled. "I'm sure there are others here who don't feel that way."

"If they did, they wouldn't be here, and frankly I don't care how anybody else feels," Calvin said, temper flaring. "The truth is, preacher, that I'd rather break bread with our yard man Elijah than a hate-spewing Southern Baptist hypocrite."

The minister was livid. "How dare you speak to me like that?!"

Calvin hitched his shoulders. "Actually it came pretty easily. In fact, it felt damned good."

"You—!" Hickman sputtered helplessly.

Calvin's gavel crashed onto the podium. "Meeting adjourned." He stepped down from the dais and waded into the crowd, pausing when men clapped him on the shoulder and praised his courage. He enjoyed his moment of triumph until he glanced over his shoulder and saw Hickman in deep conversation with Sheriff Kirkendol. "It figures," he muttered.

The battle lines were being drawn.

20

Junkin finished his regular Saturday afternoon rounds at Big Shots and the Kitty Korner and went home to find Fern in the kitchen, slathering Blue Plate mayonnaise on white bread. "I reckon you heard about that business at the Kiwanis Club last night."

"Myrna said something, but I didn't pay much attention." She looked up. "What's in the package?"

"Uh, some work I brought home."

"Looks like a lot of work."

"Nothing I can't handle."

"Want a bologna sandwich?"

"Thought we were going out for pizza."

"We are, honey. I'm just having a little snack."

Junkin glanced at the overhang on the waist of Fern's aqua stretch pants. "You sure you ought to be eating that before we—?"

Fern poked his big belly. "Glass houses, Junkin."

"Sorry." He grabbed a Pabst bottle from the refrigerator and rummaged through the junk drawer. "Where's the church key?"

"Don't you remember I had an opener installed on the end of the cabinet there?"

"Oh, yeah." He popped open the beer, took a swig and belched contentedly. "You think of everything, Little Bit."

"I try." Fern took a big bite of her sandwich and giggled when a big glob of mayonnaise oozed onto her chin. "Tell me about the meeting."

Junkin sipped again. "Calvin Harrington got a bunch of men together to talk about what happened at the Tower a couple nights ago."

"Is that right?" Fern munched thoughtfully. "I swear, he and his wife are forever messing in other people's business."

"I was thinking the same thing. In fact, it's something I want to talk to you about."

"Me? Why?"

"Because ever since I got elected mayor, the Harringtons have been a big pain in my ass." Junkin frowned. "What the devil are you grinning at?"

"I'm grinning at the word 'elected,' that's what. I don't think there's a soul in this town, except maybe for Crazy Nadine, who doesn't know you bought that election."

"What are you belly-aching about? It made you First Lady of Meander, didn't it?"

"Oh, I'm not complaining, honey." Fern knew better than to rile his notorious temper. "You've made me the happiest lady in Tennessee, and I love you more every day." She stood on her tiptoes and gave him a greasy kiss.

"In that case, I want you to do a little something for me."

"Anything you want, sweetie pie."

"I want you to make friends with Anrita Harrington."

"What?!"

"You heard me. I need to know what my enemies are up to, and the best way to do that is to get close to them. Anrita's one, and so is her husband."

"So, are you planning on getting buddy-buddy with him?"

"Don't be ridiculous. Chuck Kirkendol's keeping an eye on things."

"Why do you think I'd get anywhere with that snob Anrita?" A derisive snort shot mayonnaise up her nose, making her cough and clear her throat. "She and her snooty friends have snubbed me for years, and even if I wanted to get chummy, I don't know if I could. Anrita would be mighty polite and all but—"

"Then let me remind you that you're the First Lady of Meander and nobody would dare slam a door in your face. For God's sake, Fern. You've been in Eulalie Saunders's house, and everybody knows she's the grandest dame in town."

"What does that prove?"

"She's working with you on this Labor Day thing, isn't she?"

Fern harrumphed. "All that old lady's doing is running the silly slide projector."

"That's something at least. If Miss Sugar's on your team, I don't see how Anrita Harrington could turn you down."

"You want me to ask Anrita to work on the celebration with me?"

"Sylvianne McNeil too, since you're always talking about them and their little canasta club."

Fern stopped chewing and made a confession. "I guess maybe I've secretly wanted an excuse to have them over. This might be the ticket."

"Sure it would."

"And I could sure use some more help on the sequincentennial."

"Wonderful!" Junkin was relieved that Fern hadn't given him much argument. He slugged away half his beer and said, "You just might get a sweet surprise for helping me out."

Fern melted on cue when a present was in sight. "Really?"

"Really." Junkin spread his arms, inviting Fern for a hug. She giggled when they rubbed bellies. "That's my girl."

Fern gave him another oily smooch and went back to her sandwich. "I'll finish this and we'll be on our way."

"Take your time, Little Bit. I need to make a few phone calls and change clothes. I smell like a smoky bar."

"Don't dawdle!" she chirped.

The sun was setting when Junkin went into the bedroom and set his package aside. He sank into an easy chair by the open window and enjoyed a breeze as he dialed the sheriff. "Chuck, this is Junkin. I want you to put Buzzy on the Harrington house tonight. Tell him to keep a record of where Calvin goes and who he talks to."

"Yes, sir. Anything else?"

"Keep an eye on the newspaper office too. I hear tell Dave Mearns is about to run an editorial that's not in our best interest."

"Yes, sir." The sheriff listened to dead air for a long moment. "You still there, Mr. Mayor?"

"Yeah. I was wondering if the newspaper office might accidentally catch fire."

"Like that property out Old Quarry Road?"

"What's that got to do with anything?" Junkin barked, temper flaring.

"Well, sir. I was thinking—"

"You ain't paid to think! You're paid to do as you're told, and you'd be smart to forget thinking I had something to do with that damned fire. Far as I'm concerned, it was started by lightning."

"Yes, sir."

Junkin hung up and dialed again. "That you, Sonny?"

"Yeah, boss. What's up?"

"Got a little job for you. Get over to the shed where our robes are stashed. The city council's gonna propose a bill outlawing the Klan tonight. That's sure to get people riled up, and I don't want nothing found on my property."

"You know Sheriff Kirkendol wouldn't—?"

"Not Kirkendol. I'm talking about Eugene Proctor or somebody Calvin Harrington might put up to snooping around. You hear me?"

"Yes, sir. You want me to put them out at the old Boruff place? I reckon we're the only people who go out there anymore."

"Good idea. Wrap 'em in dry cleaning bags and stick 'em up the farmhouse chimney."

"Anything else?"

"Yeah. Do it right now. I know you'll be heading over to Big Shots later tonight, and I want those robes off the premises before you get a snoot full."

Sonny gave him no argument. "Right away, boss."

Junkin hung up, closed the bedroom door and shucked off everything but his BVDs and shoes. He tore open his package and admired the contents.

"Man, oh, man! When the boys see this, they'll be jealous as all hell."

He slipped the robe over his head and gave himself a long look in the mirror. The Seesaw seamstress had done a fine job, and the fit was perfect. He was especially pleased with the hem which, as he specified, hit at the ankle. He turned around and looked over his shoulder.

"Junkin Abernathy, you old dog! If you ain't looking at a future Grand Dragon, I miss my guess!" He shed the robe and retrieved something else special from the envelope. He held it up to his bare chest and checked the mirror again, cheeks flushed with excitement when he saw his reflection. He continued admiring himself until Fern called down the hall. "You 'bout ready, Junkin? I think my sandwich's wearing off."

"Coming, Little Bit!"

Junkin hastily stuffed everything back in the envelope and hid it on the top shelf of his closet where Fern wouldn't see it. He ignored the usual twinge of guilt when he remembered he and Fern had promised never to keep secrets from one other.

That brown paper package was just the beginning.

21

"We'd gotta start being more careful, sweetheart."

"We're okay." Lurleen squeezed John's hand as they strolled alongside the moonlit river. "These old willow woods are thick, and nobody ever comes down here because the property belongs to Daddy."

Close behind were Rocky Millsaps and Dottisue Davis. Because their fathers were rival car dealers and bitter enemies, they were also forbidden to date, so double dating was the ideal ruse. John came calling for Dottisue while Rocky picked up Lurleen. When they were out of sight from prying eyes, the couples switched to their real partners.

"That's not what I meant. Sylvianne McNeil may have seen us last Tuesday."

"Where?" Lurleen asked, alarmed.

"On my parents' back porch. When we were smooching, I think I saw her looking out of her kitchen window."

"Maybe she didn't see you," Dottisue said. "Gossip says she drinks like a fish."

Rocky sipped his Bud. "Nothing wrong with a short snort every now and then."

"You keep that up and you'll have a beer belly before you're twenty," she teased.

"Drinking or not, I like Mrs. McNeil," Lurleen said. "I don't know her very well, but we had a nice long talk when she came to Mama and Daddy's open house. She's very sweet and funny and, golly, she's a real clothes horse."

"I'll say," Dottisue chimed. "We both go to Meander Methodist, and between you and me, I go to see what she's wearing as much as I do to hear the sermon. She wore a sack dress one Sunday last spring, and looked fantabulous. You should've seen the stares she got."

"Good for her," Lurleen said.

"John's right though." Rocky nuzzled Dottisue's ear as he steered talk away from fashion. "You two better be careful because if you get caught, we're all caught."

"And we sure don't want to do that with graduation two weeks away," Dottisue said.

"I agree," Lurleen said. "I'm looking forward to the senior prom and baccalaureate and graduation and signing yearbooks. If Mama and Daddy found out I was dating John, they'd ground me for the rest of the summer."

"My parents would ground me too," Dottisue lamented. "I'm counting the days until we elope."

"You two still running off to Ringgold?"

"Sure are," Rocky said. "That's where everybody goes. You can get a blood test and a wedding license and get married all in the same day."

"Have y'all set a date?"

"Right after my eighteenth birthday, which is June seventeenth." Dottisue gave Rocky a playful swat on his bottom. "Which means you'll be in double trouble if you forget those dates."

Rocky nuzzled her again. "I won't forget, sweetie,"

Dottisue giggled. "I think it's so cute the way that little Georgia town calls itself Ringgold. I mean, it's the perfect place to get married, isn't it?" She drawled the words, "Ring gold."

Dottisue was the prettiest girl in school, but not the brightest. When Rocky teased her about a bad test grade, Dottisue, who was nobody's fool and wasn't nicknamed Dottie the Body for nothing, sweetly reminded him that he wasn't screwing her brains.

"Actually," John said, "it was named after Sam Ringgold. He was a hero in the Mexican-American War."

Dottisue stuck out her tongue. "And how do you know so much, Mr. Smarty Pants?"

"I found out when Lurleen and I—" He stopped when he got an elbow in the ribs.

Dottisue didn't miss a thing. "When you and Lurleen were what?"

"When Lurleen and I were reading about the place," John said, thinking fast.

"Bull hockey!" Dottisue hurried to block their path. "You two are planning to elope too, aren't you?"

"Don't be ridiculous."

Dottisue wouldn't be put off. "Lurleen Abernathy, you look me right in the eye and tell me you aren't going to elope."

"We're not going to elope."

"You're looking at my forehead." Dottisue giggled again. "Now tell me the truth."

"Okay. We plan to sneak off sometime this summer, before we start college at U.T. They've got some nice housing for married students."

"Son of a gun!" Rocky clapped his old friend on the back while the girls embraced. "That's great, Johnny boy!"

"It might not be so great once Lurleen's parents find out. I think Mama and Daddy will be okay with it, but not the Abernathys."

"Do you think they'll try to get it annulled?"

"Lurleen and I are both eighteen, so it'd be perfectly legal." John glanced at Rocky. "And I don't think a marriage can be annulled once it's consummated, and since we've already—"

"John!" Lurleen cried. "Be still!"

Dottisue nudged her. "Don't be a hypocrite, Lurleen." Dottisue danced away, not to be stopped. "You boys think you're so smart with your locker room bragging. Well, we girls talk too, and Lurleen and I have been comparing notes ever since we lost our cherries. Don't tell me you boys haven't done the same thing."

"Certainly not!" John protested with exaggerated drama. "Men believe in honor and chivalry. We would never discuss such things."

Rocky was about to explode. "Come on, buddy. Even I'm not buying that load of crap."

The four old friends roared with laughter, pleased and relieved that they had aired intimate secrets. They were so lost in the moment that they didn't notice they weren't alone until Rocky spotted a suspicious shadow behind a weeping willow.

"We've got company, y'all."

The girls hurried behind the boys, but fear evaporated when a familiar figure crept into the moonlight.

Lurleen smiled and waved. "Hey, Eugene! How're you doing?"

"I'm okay. How're y'all tonight?"

"We're fine."

Eugene wore his usual summer uniform, a pair of jeans and a tee shirt and a Knoxville Smokies baseball cap. Rocky noticed a transistor radio hanging from his belt and a cord running to an ear piece.

"You listening to the Smokies' game, Eugene?"

"Yeah. They're losing again."

"They're having a real bad season."

"I reckon."

"It's a beautiful night, isn't it?" Dottisue said after an awkward silence. "I've never seen so many lightning bugs."

Lurleen pointed toward the river. "Did y'all see over there? It looks like they're blinking off and on at the same time. Did you see that, Eugene?"

"I reckon I don't miss much on my nightly ramblings."

"You see some pretty crazy stuff?" Rocky asked.

"I see crazy alright. I see some sick stuff, too."

"What do you mean?"

Eugene ignored the question. "Y'all shouldn't be down here this time of night."

"Why not?" John asked.

"Just shouldn't. That's all."

"In that case, we better be on our way. Thanks for warning us, Eugene."

"Sure thing." Eugene adjusted his baseball cap. "'Night, everybody."

"Good night."

The four watched Eugene disappear into the woods like a will-o'-the-wisp.

"That's one of God's stranger children," Rocky said. "I don't know about y'all, but that's by far the most conversation I've ever had with the guy."

"I think he's sweet," Lurleen said.

"Kind of sad too," Dottisue added.

"Nice that he's looking out for us," John said. "C'mon, everybody. Let's go."

As they walked back to the car, Rocky said, "After Eugene's comment, I guess we'd better find a new place to smooch."

"What kind of sick stuff do you think he saw?"

"No idea, but the way he gets around, I'll bet he knows Meander better than anybody. If he says he saw something bad, I believe him."

"Me too," Lurleen said, "but something is bothering me."

John draped a protective arm around her shoulders. "What's that, honey?"

"Eugene gave me a strange look before saying he saw sick things." She shuddered. "It was almost like he was warning me."

"About what?"

"I've no idea, but there's something else too."

"Oh?"

"When we first saw him, he was coming from the direction of my parents' house."

22

Anrita was pleased but not surprised when Mary showed up fifteen minutes early her first day of work. She welcomed her with an appreciative look. "Good morning."

"Good morning, Anrita."

"Did you enjoy your weekend?"

"I don't think 'enjoy' is the right word." When Anrita looked perplexed, Mary said, "I moved down from Knoxville last Friday and been unpacking ever since. If it hadn't been for Lou, I might've given up the ghost."

"Calvin and I would've been happy to lend a hand."

"I appreciate that, but it wouldn't seem right asking my boss for help before I even started my job."

"We wouldn't have minded." Anrita directed Mary into her office. "You'll find we're like one big family here."

Mary lit up when she saw an enormous flower arrangement on her desk. "They're beautiful. Are they from your garden?"

"I wish they were. I grow a few roses but have absolutely no talent when it comes to arranging them. These are from Belle Fleur on Main Street. Andy Jenkins runs it. He's a good friend of ours."

"Lou and I walked by there last Saturday. The florist was putting a big sign in the window."

Anrita knew she shouldn't be embarrassed but she was. "About the K.K.K. not being welcome in Meander?"

"Yes, ma-am."

"I guess you heard what happened last weekend."

"Lou told me about it."

"I don't want you to get the wrong impression, Mary. This is a very peaceful little community where everyone gets along. Nothing like that's ever happened here before, and my husband and some other businessmen are working with the city council to see that it doesn't happen again."

"I sure hope they figure it out."

Eager to change the subject, Anrita said, "Hang your hat over there and we'll get to work. By the way, I appreciate you coming in early, but it's not necessary."

"Well, the truth is, I was making a trial run to see how long the bus would take."

"Don't you have a car?"

"I never could afford one, but I'm hoping this job will change that."

"Maybe it will."

"Do the busses pretty much run on schedule?"

Anrita was embarrassed again. "I don't know. I've never … ridden one."

"No reason why you should, I guess." Mary hung up her hat. "Looks like we're getting off to an awkward start. Maybe we should clear the air a little."

"Good idea."

Both women sat.

"Lou tells me she's worked for you a lot of years and that you've always treated her right. Now that you've hired me, it's only fair that I tell you a few things about myself. If you're not happy with them, then I can walk right out that door and forget we ever knew each other."

"You sound serious."

"I'm very serious. For starters, I'm probably not like the other colored people in Meander. I don't mean that because I'm from Knoxville I've got big city ways or anything, but I've been going to some civil rights meetings and I can tell you we're gonna stir things up all across the South." She paused, waiting for a reaction.

"Go on," Anrita urged. "Please."

"I know you're a bright lady or you wouldn't be running a multi-million-dollar business, and Lou says y'all have talked about civil rights before."

"A little."

"The way you looked embarrassed when you mentioned the Klan and said you'd never ridden the bus, I know you're a sensitive soul. Most white folks don't see what's right under their noses."

Anrita looked down at her hands and absently twirled her wedding ring. "Anybody with an ounce of Christianity and a lick of sense knows segregation is wrong. It was all over the country in the beginning, but the South got stuck with it, like pirates stuck us with slavery."

Mary looked surprised. "Pirates?"

"English pirates captured a Portuguese slave ship in sixteen-nineteen and brought nineteen slaves to Virginia. That's why I can remember it. Nineteen in sixteen-nineteen."

"I didn't know that."

"Did you know that one of the first slave owners in the Colonies was a colored man named Anthony Johnson."

Mary's jaw dropped. "How come you know that?"

"Because I love history and read a lot in my spare time. My friend Cassandra Maddox knows lots more than I do. She teaches English at the local high school, and I've learned a lot from her. I agree that we need change, but I'm afraid it's going to bring out the worst in people."

"I'm afraid, period, but that shouldn't keep us from trying."

"No, it shouldn't. And we should look to each other for support. I hope we can do that."

"I hope so too." Mary eyed the stack of paper on her desk. "Good heavens. It looks like I've got a lot of work to do."

Anrita stood. "Yes, you do. There's a little kitchen with a coffee maker through that door there. Get yourself a cup and look over that paperwork and I'll be back in a jiffy to help you get started. Your two most important duties are keeping our inventory stocked and our orders filled and billed. It sounds simple but it requires a lot of attention to detail."

"Yes, ma-am."

"Calvin's at a prayer breakfast this morning, but I'll introduce you as soon as he gets here. You'll be reporting directly to him, not me."

"Yes, ma-am," Mary said again.

"Good luck and welcome aboard."

Anrita went into her office and closed the door. Although it was only 9:15, she was already tired and as she sat down she knew why. She propped her elbows on her desk, folded her hands and closed her eyes.

"Dear Lord," she prayed, "I'm feeling a little lost. Please help me understand this good woman and to do the right thing by her." She sighed the last word. "Amen."

23

Eulalie was in high spirits as she walked into the Meander Public Library and waved at Ida Turnbull. Ida was somewhere in her sixties and pretty much the spitting image of an old maid librarian. Tall and thin, with hair pulled into a tight bun, she wore high-necked blouses with an old timey lapel watch, and skirts hitting way below the knee. Her smile softened an otherwise severe appearance and reminded those who knew her that Ida was once a very pretty girl.

"Hello, Miss Sugar," she said softly when Eulalie got within hearing distance. She was not one to raise her voice, unless undisciplined children demanded she intervene. "How're you doing?"

"I'm fine, sugar. How about you?"

"Fine, thank you. You looking for anything special today?"

"Gardening books. I'm going to redo my back yard and need some landscaping ideas."

Ida pulled a pencil from her bun and aimed it toward a far corner. "The gardening books are to the left of that rubber plant. There's an oversized edition on English gardens you might find particularly helpful."

"Thank you."

"You might also see if Andy Jenkins has some ideas. He's at a table over there by the stacks. I remember him studying landscape architecture at U.T." When Eulalie gave her a blank look, Ida knew the man's name didn't ring a bell. "He owns the florist shop on Main Street. Belle Fleur."

"Oh, yes. Andy Jenkins. Thank you again."

Eulalie turned left at the rubber plant and found two books of interest, plus the big one recommended by the librarian. It was perched on a shelf slightly out of reach, and when she looked around for a step stool she caught Andy's eye.

"Looks like you could use a little help. Andy Jenkins at your service."

"Thank you, young man," she said as he retrieved the book and put it on his table. "The librarian told me you were over here. Might I have a word?"

"Why, sure. About what?"

"Landscaping. I'm thinking of making some changes at my home."

"Really? It's lovely just the way it was."

As she often did when flummoxed, Eulalie fiddled with her pearl necklace. "You've been to Blufftop?"

"A friend took me there to her church picnic once. There were a couple hundred people there, so you and I never met."

"I'm so sorry."

"I am too, but at least I got to see the grounds. They're spectacular, especially the rear lawn. I'd wager you have the only formal parterres and espaliered trees in town, not to mention a boxwood maze and a pagoda with tinkling bells."

"You're very sweet," Eulalie said, "but what needs work is beyond the pagoda."

"What's there now?"

"Nothing but a dilapidated slave cabin that's been locked up as long as I can remember. I don't want to tear it down because it has historical value, what with it being one of the oldest buildings in town."

Andy pulled out a chair, and Eulalie lowered her voice as she sat and continued. Everyone in town knew Ida Turnbull had very keen hearing. Calvin once shocked Anrita by saying Miss Ida could hear a bat poop on top of Old Smoky in the middle of a thunderstorm.

"The cabin's practically covered with kudzu, but once that's peeled away, I'd like to restore it and bank the place with azaleas. Perhaps plant some dogwoods and redbuds."

"Excellent choices."

"Do you have some experience in this area?"

"I studied landscape architecture for several years but never completed my degree."

"Oh?"

"I had to drop out of school and never got around to going back."

"Your tone of voice says not to ask why, so I won't."

"Thank you."

"Did you at least learn enough to design a space like the one I described?"

"Absolutely. It doesn't sound difficult at all, but I'd have to see it first."

"When might you be available to drop by?" Before Andy could answer, Eulalie's eye wandered to the book he had been reading. *Life's Picture History of World War II.* It was open to the section on Iwo Jima. "Why in the world are you reading this?"

"Personal reasons."

"Were you in the war?"

"No, ma-am. I have flat feet and a heart murmur."

Eulalie was silent a few moments. "Did you know almost seven thousand of our boys died on that Godforsaken rock?"

"Yes, ma-am, I did. One was a very close friend."

"I'm sorry to hear that. Was he from here?"

"No, ma-am. Jefferson City. Name was Clark Foster."

"Clark Foster. My husband did business with some Jefferson City Fosters. Some rather tough customers if I recall correctly."

"Could be the same family. Clark never got along with his father. When he enlisted, I think it was as much to get away from his family as it was to fight the Nazis and Japs."

Eulalie's voice turned reverent. "I lost someone on Iwo Jima too. My son Geoffrey."

"I remember someone telling me that, Miss Sugar. I'm sorry for your loss."

"Thank you." Eulalie's fingertips brushed the photo of

amphibious craft streaming toward the beaches below Mount Suribachi. "He was only twenty-four."

"That was Clark's age when he died too."

Eulalie marveled at the coincidence. "Two boys from little East Tennessee towns dying on an island half a world away at age twenty-four. What are the odds?"

"Bad enough I guess."

"I guess." Both were lost in thought until Eulalie broke the silence. "You remind me of Geoffrey a bit. Not so much physically, although you both have sandy red hair and blue eyes. No, it's something else. Your manner or maybe your voice. He's been gone so long I've almost forgotten what he sounded like." She picked up her purse and rummaged for a handkerchief, then quickly pushed the purse aside. "No, I am not going to cry right here in the middle of the public library." She straightened in her chair. "I don't mean to interrupt what you're doing, but would you like to come home with me and look at my yard?"

"Right now?"

"Right now."

"I'd like nothing better, Miss Sugar." He closed the book. "I could use a break from this."

"I thought you might."

Andy followed Eulalie's Packard Patrician in his Ford delivery truck, and fifteen minutes later he was wandering Blufftop's grounds and admiring a bird's eye view of the town and river down below. It was even more stunning than he remembered, and as he strolled toward the pagoda it was hard to believe he was still in East Tennessee. A yard man was busy trimming the hedges.

"Hey, there, Elijah!" Eulalie waved. "He's been taking care of Meander yards over twenty years, you know. He's the best gardener in town."

"I'd have to agree. I don't see a dead leaf or weed anywhere."

"The slave cabin is over there."

The two walked past the pagoda through a stand of bamboo to a clearing dominated by a small cabin on a stone foundation. The roof, chimney and three sides swarmed with kudzu, but the exposed front porch revealed mortar chinked between the logs and two small windows with blurry glass panes. Andy climbed the steps and peered inside.

"My word! There's furniture in there!"

"I know. My older brothers and I begged Daddy to let us use the place as a playhouse, but he wouldn't hear of it. The front door was padlocked, so there was no way we could get inside. Those bad boys almost convinced me to let them lower me down the chimney, but I had enough sense to refuse. I'm sure I was afraid of getting stuck."

Andy eyed the rusted padlock. "I wonder why your father kept it locked."

"He probably thought it was dangerous. His word was law, so that was the end of it. I pretty much forgot about it once this bamboo grew up and concealed it." She gave him a funny look. "How peculiar. All of a sudden I'm dying to get inside."

"I don't suppose you have a key."

"Heavens, no."

"I'll bet Elijah has something to cut it off."

Sure enough, the yard man succeeded in sawing through the ancient lock and pushing the door open. He coughed and stepped back. "Whew!"

"Does the air smell bad?" Eulalie asked.

"It's just old and dead," the gardener replied.

"I guess that's no surprise since the cabin's been closed up almost a century." She thanked Elijah and sent him on his way before turning to Andy. "Ready?"

"Ladies first."

"Not this time, sugar, and please watch your step. For all we know, those old floorboards have rotted right through."

"If this porch is still intact, it's a good sign the inside flooring is in good shape too."

"I still want you to be careful."

"I will."

Eulalie watched Andy enter the cabin and use the heel of his shoe to tap the floor for weak spots. As he predicted, the floor was solid, so he motioned Eulalie to follow. He unhooked the windows and creaked them open, pleased when a breeze flooded the stagnant space with fresh air. He pointed to the hearth.

"Look at that old iron kettle." He continued taking inventory. "A table and chairs too. Even a pair of beds."

Eulalie touched the table top and inspected a blackened fingertip. "Covered in dust that's old as the hills."

"Once we get that kudzu stripped away, it won't take much to clean up the inside. I'd be happy to take care of it. In fact, I'll make you a deal. If you contract me to do the landscaping, I'll include clean-up for the cabin in the price."

"That's nothing but housework," Eulalie protested.

"Not for me, ma-am." Andy glanced around a room lost in time. "This is pure archaeology."

"Then you have yourself a deal. My housekeeper would probably quit on the spot if I asked her to tidy up out here, and I wouldn't blame her." Eulalie watched Andy bend over a wooden box between the beds and look behind it. "Anything there?"

"This thing is turned around so that the back is facing the front." He tilted it forward and looked behind it. "Well what do you know?"

"What is it?"

"It has shelves and a drawer with a rawhide pull." He gave the rawhide a tug and it came off in his hand. "So much for that."

"Can you get the drawer open?"

"It's tight as a tick." He picked up the little stand and shook it. "There's something rattling around inside."

"Can't you wiggle the drawer open?"

"There's nothing to grab hold of. Is there a screwdriver

around?"

"The tool shed's behind the garage. Elijah will show you"

"Be right back."

Left alone in the musty slave cabin, Eulalie was over-whelmed by a sense of history, family and déjà vu. It began with a humming in her head that grew so loud she sat on one of the dusty chairs until it passed. She was still there when Andy returned with the screwdriver.

"You alright, Miss Sugar?"

"A little dizzy is all. I think it's the stale air."

"Let me help you outside, and then I'll try to get this drawer open."

"No, no. I'm fine right here. I want to see what's in there."

"Alright." It took Andy a few minutes to inch the drawer open enough to slip fingers inside and pull it all the way out.

"Find anything?"

"Books."

"Be careful. They'll probably fall apart if you pick them up."

"They look like they're in pretty good shape. I guess that stuck drawer kept the mice out. Well, what do you know!"

"What is it?"

"It looked like several books, but it's only one. The binding has rotted apart." Andy found the cover and dusted it off. "I'll be darned!"

"What is it?"

"It's the Crockett family Bible!"

"How peculiar." Eulalie was flummoxed. "Daddy always said it had been lost."

"Maybe this is where it was lost."

"But he'd been out here many times and was the one who installed the padlock."

"Maybe he forgot," Andy suggested.

"Maybe and maybe not. You know what they say."

"Ma-am?"

"Some things are lost on purpose."

24

Sylvianne fidgeted in her seat. "Are you absolutely sure about this, Anrita?"

With someone right on her car's rear end, Anrita hung out her arm to signal a left turn into the Abernathy driveway. "It won't be that bad, for heaven's sake."

"I swear I'd rather go to the dentist. Tell me again how you got roped into helping Fern with this Labor Day shindig."

"She said she was short-handed and asked very politely if I would help out. I have the time, and it's for a good cause, so why not?"

"What does Calvin think about this little venture?"

"He's all for it." Anrita parked the car and killed the engine. "So were you when I first mentioned it."

"Was I buzzed?"

"I've no idea, but you're not buzzed now and we're here, so let's make the best of it. Besides, I have a confession to make."

Sylvianne perked up. "I'm all ears."

"After what you told Cassie and me about this house, I've been dying to see it for myself."

"You'll be sorry, honey. I had nightmares for weeks, and I'm worried that some new horrors have been added since I was here." She flipped open her compact and touched up her Hazel Bishop no-smear lipstick. "How do I look?"

"I have yet to meet a woman who doesn't know when she looks good, now stop stalling and come on."

"Oh, alright."

Both women got out and gave their girdles a discreet tug before climbing the steps to the Abernathys' front door. "Brace yourself." Sylvianne pushed the doorbell and unleashed an off-key version of the Doxology.

Anrita gasped. "Oh, my Lord! I thought you were pulling my leg about that."

"No need to kid when the truth is better than anything you can make up."

After a moment, Zanna opened the door. "Hello, ladies."

"How are you, Zanna?" Seeing the woman's grimace, Anrita said, "Is Mrs. Abernathy giving you a hard time today?"

"Today and every day." Knowing Lou had told Anrita how irascible Fern could be, Zanna dropped a comical curtsey. "Madam Queen's waiting for y'all out on the patio."

"Careful," Sylvianne warned. "I'm betting Fern would fire you for saying that."

"God works in strange ways."

"If she's that awful, why don't you quit?"

"Because my husband and I got two babies to feed, and there aren't any other jobs in town right now." Zanna lowered her voice to a whisper as Anrita walked by. "You sure you don't want to fire my sister and hire me? I'm a much better worker, and I'm the prettier twin too." She batted her eyelashes in her best burlesque style.

"Now, you know I can't do that, Zanna, and I don't think Lou would agree that you're prettier. I've never been able to tell you two apart, although I think you might be funnier."

"See there? I could entertain you while I'm working. And I can sing too. I'll bet I already know your favorite hymn."

"You're hilarious!" Sylvianne said.

"Yeah. I'm Moms Mabley with teeth."

Anrita could barely stop laughing. "You'd better stop before you get us in trouble."

"Can't blame a girl for trying." Zanna pointed toward the patio. "Y'all go on out."

Fern heard laughter in the vestibule and was heading to investigate when she spotted Sylvianne pointing at the living room. By the time she got close enough to hear what they were saying, Anrita's eye caught the chartreuse and cerise print blouse and yellow slacks and quickly talked over Sylvianne's scathing dissection of the plastic-covered furniture.

"It's lovely!" she announced loudly before pretending to see Fern. "Hello, there."

"Hi, Anrita. Hey, Sylvianne." Fern delivered her usual pump-handle handshake along with a fixed grin while reminding herself of Junkin's dictate to play up to these women. "I've got everything all set up by the pool, so let's go on out."

"We're right behind you." As they trailed Fern, Sylvianne whispered in Anrita's ear. "I didn't know they made clothes in Technicolor and Stereophonic Sound."

"Be still. She'll hear you."

"I don't care. I'm on Zanna's team." Anrita's disapproving look hushed her up. "Alright. I'll behave."

Sylvianne meant what she said, but her determination was hard pressed when they reached the newly decorated patio. A fence surrounding the pool was covered with fake fishing nets dangling fake buoys, oars, sea shells, tiki gods and even a rubber shark. Pink plastic flamingos dotted the lawn, and a thatched hut behind the diving board boasted two signs. One designated "Junkin's Hooch Hut" while the other proclaimed the dos and don'ts for using the Abernathy pool. It included the usual safety rules about not running or diving in the shallow end, but when she read further, Sylvianne stopped dead in her tracks.

"What on earth—?"

"Something wrong?" Fern asked.

"Your sign," Sylvianne managed.

"Isn't that the cutest thing you ever saw? Junkin saw it somewhere and insisted we get one when we put in the pool."

"What are y'all talking about?" Anrita asked, fumbling in her purse. "I must've left my glasses in the car."

"Don't worry, hon." Sylvianne turned to Fern. "May I do the honors?"

"Why, sure."

"The Abernathys have a cute list of rules for using the

pool," Sylvianne explained, "and this last one is the best. It says, 'We don't swim in your toilet, so please don't pee in our pool.' Isn't that adorable?"

Literally at a loss for words, Anrita was grateful when Fern quickly took up the slack. "I'm telling you, the mayor thinks of everything. It was also his idea to do the Hawaiian theme with all the tiki lights and the thatched hut and everything. He's got some lava lamps on order too." When Fern met two blank stares, she added, "You know. Because Hawaii has all those volcanoes. I was watching the Arthur Godfrey Show last winter and heard Haleloke talking about them. You know. Mona Key and Mona Loa and all."

"Don't forget Mona Lisa and Mona Freeman," Sylvianne added.

Fern giggled. "You're such a cut-up, Sylvianne,"

"That's what they tell me."

Fern was still smiling as they sat around a frosted glass-top table with three stacks of paper. "I made copies of my plans for the celebration, so why don't y'all go ahead and leaf through them while I go tell Zanna to get us some tea."

"Fine." Anrita and Sylvianne began flipping through the folder, horror growing with each page. When she got to the part about the Cavalcade of Cavaliers, Anrita hissed, "This is even worse than I expected."

Sylvianne was even more appalled. "Meander's gonna be the laughingstock of Calhoun County."

"Try the whole state of Tennessee."

"What are we going to do?"

"What can we do? Fern's the head of the whole sesquicentennial and, as we're constantly reminded, the mayor's wife too. I don't think we have any choice except to play along."

"I wonder what she needs us for."

"Maybe we can work on the profiles of prominent citizens. That's the only part of this mess that makes any sense." When Sylvianne looked lost, Anrita said, "It's on the last page."

"So what do y'all think of my little extravaganza?" Fern chirped, reappearing with Zanna in tow. "Put the glasses there and fetch us some of those little sandwiches you made this morning." She oozed smugness when she added, "With Anrita's Home-Style Chicken Salad, I want you to know."

"How thoughtful," Anrita said.

"Did you remember to cut the crusts off the white bread, Zanna?"

"Yes, Miss Fern," Zanna said tiredly. "I think I managed to remember that."

"Good. Now you run on." Before Zanna was out of earshot, Fern said, "I don't know what to do about her. I can't quite put my finger on it, but I don't think she's as respectful as she oughta be." When the others made no comment, she said, "I'd sure like to find a new girl. I don't suppose y'all know of anybody."

"No, I don't," Anrita and Sylvianne chorused.

"No? Oh, well. Now this tea's already sweetened, so y'all help yourself to the lemon and tell me what you think about my plans for the sequincentennial."

Anrita's toe nudged Sylvianne's shin before she could correct Fern's pronunciation.

"I must say it's certainly an ambitious undertaking," Anrita said. "Are you sure you can pull all this together in such a short time?"

"Why, sure. Especially if I have ladies like you helping out."

"What exactly is it you want us to do?"

"Let's see." Fern licked her fingers and started flipping pages. "I need a couple more judges for the Sunday night beauty pageant and I could use some help making the pantaloons for the queen and her court. They'll be in hoop skirts, you know."

"Oh, dear," Sylvianne lamented. "Anrita and I don't sew."

"That's alright. Junkin told me about a widow woman over in Seesaw who's a real whiz." Fern flipped more pages and ran her finger down a list. "The float for Swan's Bakery is going to be the biggest, and I'm sure they need helpers to stuff the chicken wire with crepe paper and whatever else they stuff it with." The grin reached alarming proportions as she turned to Anrita. "Doesn't your husband drive a truck for Swan's?"

"He used to," Anrita replied sweetly, ignoring the implication.

"Yeah, Calvin Harrington's quite a guy," Sylvianne said, going where she knew Anrita wouldn't. "He came from a dirt-poor family up in Scott County and look at him now. The richest man in Meander." She gave her tea a vigorous stir. "By far."

"Is that right?" Fern's grin withered. "How about I put y'all down as float workers?"

"I think Sylvianne and I are a little old to fool around with chicken wire," Anrita said, "but maybe we could help with the profiles."

"I think those are fine the way they are, but we still need signs."

"What signs?"

"The ones we're gonna put up all over Calhoun County to advertise the event. I want them on more barns than those for Rock City and Ruby Falls. Y'all know how to use a hammer and nails, don't you?" Before Anrita could respond, Fern said, "Good. Here comes Zanna with the sandwiches."

Anrita was boiling mad at being offered such demeaning work and needed a moment to cool off and collect herself. "Would you tell me where I might find the powder room?"

"Come with me, Miss Anrita," Zanna said. "I'll show you."

"Don't stand up when you hear Dixie!" Sylvianne called.

Fern was lost. "How in the world did you ... oh, I'd forgotten you were here before."

"Oh, my, yes." Sylvianne reached for a sandwich. "Some things you just don't forget."

25

Cassandra was looking forward to the last day of class, and not just because it meant summer vacation. At his request, she had a two o'clock appointment with John Harrington and was bursting with curiosity because she was so fond of him. This was partly because John was one of her best students and partly because he was Anrita's and Calvin's son. A few minutes before two, there was a knock at the door.

"Come in, John."

To her surprise, it was Donna Moon, the assistant principal. She held out a manila envelope with Cassandra's name printed on it. "Someone slipped this under my office door while we were at lunch."

"Wonder why they didn't put it in my mailbox."

"No idea. Peculiar, isn't it?"

"Yes, it is." Cassandra thanked Donna and slipped a fingernail under the flap to rip open the envelope. She felt a sharp shudder when she found a crude drawing of Moonbeam McSwine. "Uh-oh."

At the bottom of the drawing was a message made of words cut from magazines, like ransom notes in the movies. Cassandra felt a second chill when she read aloud.

"Stop teaching smut or you will fall like Troy."

The crude warning was disturbing on a number of levels. It meant the sender knew about the racy costume she wore to Anrita's Tacky Party and was smart enough to know the original Cassandra was the prophetess daughter of King Priam of Troy.

"Who on earth could've—?" She hastily shoved the drawing under a folder atop her desk when she heard another knock. "Come in."

"Hi, Miss Maddox." John's youthful energy made her momentarily forget the threatening message. "Happy last day of school."

"You too, young man. What can I do for you at this late date?"

"Just wanted to talk a little, if that's okay."

"Of course. Have a seat and tell me what's on your mind."

"Well, like most seniors, I've been thinking a lot about what I want to do after graduation."

"Don't tell me you've changed your mind about an engineering major?"

"No. It's ... it's—" Suddenly shy, John looked at his hands and fumbled for words. "I'm not sure how to explain it."

"It might help if you stopped jiggling your leg. Everything on my desk is shaking."

"Uh, sorry. Mama says I jiggle my leg when I'm nervous."

"A lot of people do, but there's no reason to be nervous. I've known you since you were a baby, and your mother is my best friend. You've earned some of the best grades in my class, and once you get that diploma tomorrow, as far as I'm concerned, you'll be my equal. You can even start calling me Cassie if you like."

John demurred. "Oh, I don't think I'm ready to do that yet."

"Alright, but I want you to calm down and tell me what's bothering you."

John obeyed, and when he regained his composure he blurted the truth. "I'm in love with Lurleen Abernathy and I want to marry her."

"That's wonderful, John. Especially since the feeling's mutual."

"She sure says so, but ... wait a minute." John's eyes widened. "How would you know?"

"Because she sat in that very chair several weeks ago and said the same thing."

"She didn't tell me that."

"And I suspect you didn't tell her you were coming here today, either."

John looked sheepish. "No, ma-am."

"Do you see a lesson there somewhere?"

"I guess it means that people in love don't tell each other everything."

"Which is pure human nature." Cassandra gave him a moment to register that bit of advice. "And since we're being honest, I knew about your romance from another source. Y'all were a little careless in your back yard a couple of weeks ago."

John's face reddened. "I guess Mrs. McNeil saw us, huh?"

"She and I discussed it. We were trying to decide if we should tell your mother when she said she already knew."

"She did?!"

"Well, she at least had her suspicions. Now, unless I miss my guess, the real reason you're here is because you want me to act as an intermediary with your parents."

"Boy, you're smart!"

"Simple deductive reasoning, John. I've seen you and Lurleen five days a week for the

last nine months, and I know you better than you might think. Just because I'm middle-aged doesn't mean I don't remember my first big love."

"Wow!"

"Good heavens, John. You sound like I just gave you Marilyn Monroe's phone number."

"Sorry, Miss Maddox."

"Never mind. Now, you don't need me to intercede because your mother thinks very highly of Lurleen and would be happy to have her as a daughter-in-law. Your father doesn't know anything yet, but Anrita thinks he'll be fine with it too."

John looked deeply relieved. "That's sure a load off my mind."

Cassandra grew serious. "But you know Lurleen's folks will be a different story."

"Yes, ma-am. We've talked about it and decided there's no point in arguing with them."

"Meaning?" Cassandra asked slowly.

"We're going to get married this summer and go on to U. T."

"I didn't think Lurleen was going to college."

"Her parents don't want her to, but she's determined to go anyway."

"Good for her. She's too smart not to do something with her life."

John brightened. "That's exactly what I told her. She says her folks will throw her out and cut her off, but I know we can manage. Daddy said he'd pay for my college if I worked every summer, and I've kept my end of the bargain. If he won't pay for Lurleen, we'll get jobs and work our way through school."

"I'm sure it won't come to that. Tuition to U.T. isn't that much, and certainly your parents can afford it." Good Lord, she thought. The Harringtons could afford Princeton without batting an eye. "It sounds like you and Lurleen have thought things through. Now is there anything else you want to discuss?"

"No, ma-am. I feel a lot better now." When John stood to go, he bumped the desk hard and knocked the drawing onto the floor. Before Cassandra could react, he picked it up and read the nasty warning. He frowned. "What in the world is this?"

"I don't know, John. I wish I did."

"Who sent it?"

"Don't know. Mrs. Moon found it shoved under her office door."

"But why would anyone—? Hey, wait a minute. I remember Mama said something about you coming to her Tacky Party dressed as Moonbeam McSwine."

"I did, but nobody was supposed to see me except the ladies at the party."

"You think one of them sent this?"

"I think it's more likely that one of them told somebody about my costume and that particular somebody sent this ugly message."

John's frowned deepened. "Why would anybody think you were teaching smut?"

"Because I let those of you in my advanced class read *Catcher in the Rye* and told you to read cheap dime novels so you'd know what bad writing is and to study Tennessee Williams's plays so you could intelligently discuss adult issues like alcoholism and drug addiction. I assure you teachers have been fired for much, much less."

"Gosh, Miss Maddox. The kids didn't realize that. We just thought you were cool."

"I'm happy to hear that, but not everyone would agree." She nodded at the drawing. "Either somebody in your class told their parents what they've been studying or somebody else figured it out."

"You mean a faculty member?"

"Possibly, but I don't think deductive reasoning applies here. There are some peculiar things going on in this town, and they're making me very uneasy."

"Like the Ku Klux Klan at the Tower theater?"

"For one."

"Man, that was so stupid. Lurleen and I saw that movie and thought it was kind of silly. Who cares if white and colored people dance together on some Caribbean island?"

"The Klan cares because they think it'll make people believe that sort of behavior is acceptable everywhere, which it should be of course."

"Yeah, I know. Daddy and I've talked about the K.K.K. and integration and stuff. He told me he got an ugly phone call at work. About race-mixing."

"Principal Warren got one too. The day the Klan showed up at the Tower."

"For real?"

"For real."

John sucked his teeth. "Kinda makes you wonder who your friends and neighbors really are, doesn't it?"

"Yes, it does," Cassandra said. "Sometimes I think our pretty little Norman Rockwell village is a powder keg with a lit fuse."

26

Junkin furled the latest copy of the Meander News-Sentinel and slapped it against the palm of his hand as he paced his Big Shots office. After a few minutes, he poked his head out the door and scanned the noisy Saturday night crowd. He spotted Sonny at the bar and bellowed over the juke box blasting Hank Williams' Hey, Good Lookin'!

"Hey, Sonny! Get your skinny butt in here!"

Sonny knew that tone of voice meant to grab his Pabst and get a move on. "What's up, boss?"

"Close the door." Junkin continued pacing and slapping the paper before getting to the point. "That damned Mearns is starting to get on my nerves."

"You mean that thing he put in the paper about the Klan?"

"What else, you nincompoop?" Junkin shoved the paper in Sonny's face. "That damned editorial two weeks ago was only the beginning. Now he's started a series on the history of the Klan, going all the way back to our founding over in Pulaski in 1865."

Sonny scanned the paper, thrilled by an old engraving of a hooded Klansman on a rearing horse. "Wow! Looks pretty fierce, don't it?"

Junkin was seething. "Forget the damned picture and look at the headline." Sonny's lips moved as he read, an annoying habit that worsened Junkin's already foul mood. "Well?"

Sonny's eyes widened. "I sure didn't know that *kuklos* was a Greek word that means brotherhood, did you?"

Junkin fought to curb his temper. "Did you read that headline or not?"

"Yes, sir. I reckon calling the Klan the spawn of the devil ain't exactly a bouquet of roses."

"No, I reckon it ain't. And you can be damned sure the rest of Mearns's articles will be as bad if not worse. Have you seen those signs in those shops on Main Street saying we're not welcome in Meander?"

"Yes, sir. Some folks got signs in their yards too."

"We gotta do something about this, Sonny. We can't sit here like a bunch of scared sissies while this town tramples on our constitutional rights as American citizens."

"No, sir. We sure can't." Sonny watched Junkin resume his pacing. "Uh, so what're we gonna do?"

"A meeting for starters. Make some phone calls and round up everybody. Tell them to gather out at the Boruff place tomorrow night after church. I want everybody there, no exceptions. It won't kill nobody to miss an episode of Country Music Jubilee."

"You got it, boss."

"You stashed those robes out there, didn't you?"

"In brown bags shoved up the chimney like you told me. Your new one, too."

"Good. Did you ever track down that hermit out Old Quarry Road?"

"The guy that might've seen the fire? No. I been out there a couple times but he's never around."

"Then you keep looking 'cause I need to know if he's Reverend Hickman's spy. That damned preacher's bleeding me dry."

"I'll head out first thing tomorrow morning."

"Good. Now go make those phone calls and tell Virgil and Rufus to get in here. I need to talk to them too."

"Yes, sir."

Junkin grabbed the bottle of Jim Beam and refilled his shot glass. He downed it in one gulp and relished the sweet throat burn while waiting for the most daring moonshine runners in the state. He didn't trust either one as far as he could throw them, but he ran the risk because their high quality white lightning brought top dollar. He was enjoying another belt when he heard a knock at the door.

"Come on in, gentlemen, and make yourselves at home."

Smelly and unkempt in greasy tee shirts and overalls, Virgil Turner and Rufus Farley were mountain men of action and few words. They helped themselves to the whiskey before sprawling in chairs facing Junkin's desk. They sipped noisily and waited.

"I'm sure y'all have heard that the revenuers are planning a crackdown on you fellas." Virgil's smug snort announced it was old news. "So what're you gonna do about it? I got a lot of customers who don't want an interruption in their supply."

"Ain't nobody gonna find our new stills," Rufus said.

"What about supply routes?" Junkin pursued. "The feds are big on throwing up roadblocks."

"We got some back roads those boys don't know about."

"You don't see any problem?"

Rufus glanced at Virgil. "Looks to me like you're the one with problems, mayor. We been reading all about you in the newspapers."

"We're not here to talk about that," Junkin growled. "I got enough trouble with that business out Quarry Road. There's a preacher here in town that's been sniffing around and thinks I had something to do with it."

"Pretty savvy preacher sounds like to me."

"You better watch your mouth, boy. You two are in this as damned deep as I am. In fact, I've been thinking about asking all y'all to kick in on the hush money that minister's bilking me out of."

"It'll be a cold day in hell 'fore that happens. Me and Virgil both got alibis putting us nowhere near that fire."

"Says who?"

"Says a couple of Lola's girls, that's who."

"What the hell!?" Junkin was livid. "You got no cause to drag my other enterprises into this."

"Too late. We've already paid them gals and they've rehearsed what to say if anybody asks."

"This is unbelievable!" Junkin roared as new worries piled atop those already crawling in his brain. "Fucking unbelievable!"

Rufus leaned forward and rested his elbows on Junkin's desk. "I'll tell you what's unbelievable, Mr. Mayor, and that's the fact that you didn't think to cover your tracks like we did. If you're thinking me and Virgil are a couple of half-witted hillbillies who can't do nothing but make shine and drive fast cars, you better think again."

Junkin muttered under his breath. He didn't like the way this was going one bit.

"And I'll tell you something else. You're the one the preacher came to about the fire, not us. I think that says one helluva lot about who's smart and who ain't."

Junkin reached for a handkerchief when his brow went slick with sweat. Then he held up his hands. "Alright. Alright. You've made your point."

"The big question is why the preacher got suspicious," Virgil said, piping up for the first time.

"Damned if I know."

Rufus leaned back and pursed his lips. "Since you're mayor of this town, I suggest you call in some favors and find out."

"I've already asked around and come up empty-handed."

"Then you better ask around some more."

"Can't y'all help out? I mean, you know plenty of folks in this county."

"Maybe." Rufus tossed down his drink and looked at his cohort. "What do you think, Virge?"

"I think it's probably not worth our time."

"I'll make it worth your time," Junkin said, seeing a glimmer of hope for his predicament. "Starting with a free night at the Kitty Korner."

"Paulette still working over there?"

"Far as I know."

Virgil brightened. "Then I say we get over there and get

busy."

Rufus took a while to answer. "I'm in, but I ain't promising nothing."

"I'll take my chances," Junkin said. "Now you boys run on. I'll call Lola and tell her to take good care of you. Like I said, the whole evening's on me."

Junkin closed the door behind them and picked up the newspaper again. As he studied the old engraving, the Klansman on the horse seemed to be looking back at him, as though challenging him to make a move. Tomorrow night's meeting was a start, but what if nobody came up with a solution for overcoming the town's resistance? He decided to check with the neighboring Klaverns and ask if they'd confronted this same issue. He reached for the phone but decided to make the call from home. He'd already had a snort too many and needed a clear head for tomorrow's meeting, not to mention driving home.

He locked his office door and climbed into his car. As he swerved from the gravel drive onto River Road, he misjudged the distance and nearly collided with an oncoming vehicle. At the sound of the other driver's horn, Junkin yanked the steering wheel and fishtailed until the dangerous moment passed. Heart pounding, he slowed down to collect himself until he checked the rearview mirror and saw the other vehicle turning around. In no mood for confrontation, he floored the Eldorado, throwing grit and burning rubber for a good twenty feet before speeding down River Road. The car behind him shrank in the mirror, but by the time Junkin reached home, it was close enough for its driver to see him turn into his driveway. Junkin watched nervously as a station wagon with a dummy corpse on the roof stopped at the foot of his driveway.

"Aw, shit!" When it became clear that Calvin wasn't going anywhere, Junkin got out of the Eldorado and walked over to the station wagon. "Sorry about our close call, Harrington."

"Reckless driving and speeding, Mr. Mayor. Not exactly

setting a good example, are you?"

"I said I was sorry," Junkin said, annoyance growing. "What more do you want?"

"I want you to take a breathalyzer test, that's what."

"What the hell are you talking about?"

"If that wasn't a drunken swerve when you peeled out of your saloon, I don't know what is. Plus, I can smell whiskey all the way over here."

"I had a drink at Big Shots. So what?"

"Why don't we get Sheriff Kirkendol's opinion?"

"Fat chance!"

"What are you afraid of, Mr. Mayor? Your constituents finding out you're not the upright citizen you pretend to be?"

"I'm not afraid of anything!" Junkin shot back. "And I've got only one thing to say to you before I go inside."

"What's that?"

"I'll take a DUI test when my butt learns how to chew Krispy Kremes."

Junkin hawked and spat before turning around and waddling unsteadily up the driveway. His neck burned when he heard Calvin's loud laugh.

"Looks to me like it already has, Mr. Mayor."

27

Anrita sounded bubbly as she, Cassandra and Sylvianne left the First Methodist Church. "I do believe that was one of Reverend Brooks more powerful sermons."

"Me too. I didn't think anybody could put a new spin on the Golden Rule, but he made his point beautifully."

"I sure didn't expect him to speak out so strongly against the Klan," Cassandra added. "He really made me proud."

"I wonder if any of the other ministers in town are addressing the issue."

"Not that gasbag, Farnsworth. I wouldn't put it past him to be a Klansman."

"What a dreadful thought!"

"But not out of the realm of possibility given what's going on in Meander these days."

Sylvianne's mind had already drifted elsewhere. "Never mind about all that. Did y'all see what Cookie Darden was wearing?"

"No, but I know what you're going to say," Cassandra replied.

"What?"

"It's too tight, too short and too low-cut for morning church."

"Give the little lady a kewpie doll!"

"How did you know what she was going to say?" Anrita asked.

Cassandra sighed wistfully. "Because I cherish consistency in a world filled with inconsistency, and I can always count on Sylvianne to be consistent. Cookie, too, unfortunately."

"Like when she wears a bra that makes her boobs look like sno-cones or walks down the aisle with half her dress in her butt crack?" Sylvianne snickered. "One of these days somebody's going to yell, 'Lady, you're eating your skirt!' ”

Anrita was horrified. "Y'all are awful!"

Sylvianne nudged Cassandra. "Wanna go to the next plateau?"

"Sure."

"What did Cookie's hair look like?"

"A stump full of granddaddy longlegs."

"Two out of three. Want to go for the $64,000 question?"

"Lay it on me, girl."

"What color was it?"

"Hostess black."

"And we have another winner!"

Anrita was lost. "Are you talking about airline hostesses?"

"Restaurant hostesses, honey. Haven't you noticed most them dye their hair dead black?"

"No, but thanks to you, I'm sure I will now."

Sylvianne wasn't about to give up the juicy topic. "And Cookie's poor daughters, all named after country music queens. Patsy and Kitty are alright, but who names a girl Maybelle in this day and age?"

"Someone who brags about being Ramp Queen a hundred years ago. That's who."

Anrita said, "I've heard about ramps all my life but I've no idea what they are."

Cassandra rolled her eyes. "And I thought you were the food expert in the group. Ramps are wild onions that reek to high heavens when they're cooked. For reasons known only to the Almighty, the folks over in Cosby see fit to honor them with a festival, a cook-out and a queen. I hear you can smell the celebration for miles around."

"One might even say," Sylvianne drawled, "that being Ramp Queen stinks."

"One might indeed. You know what though? I don't care if Cookie wants to look like she's going trick or treating. It's her holier-than-thou attitude that gets my goat. She talks about Jesus like they're joined at the hip."

"Isn't that the truth. She's forever saying things like 'I know Jesus was with me when I baked my Scripture Cake.' Or 'He helped me pick out my new hat for prayer meeting.' Last summer when we were looking for ways to raise money for the church mission, Cookie suggested a cookbook called Praise the Lard."

"Lard help us!"

"All I know is that *my* Jesus has lots better taste."

"What's happened to you two?" Anrita chided. "You used to be such nice girls."

"May I defer to Mae West?" Cassandra asked.

Sylvianne eagerly egged her on. "By all means, please do!"

" 'I was Snow White, but I drifted.' "

All three were still laughing when they reached Anrita's front gate. "Calvin and some of the men are having a word with the minister," she said, "so Sunday dinner is going to be a little late. Anybody want to come in for some iced tea?"

"Thanks, hon, but I've got to scoot," Sylvianne said.

"What's the rush?"

"I have a lunch date in Gatlinburg."

"Not so fast," Cassandra said, instantly on alert. "Who're you lunching with?"

"None of your bee's wax, honey child."

"Anyone we know?" Anrita asked.

Sylvianne pretended to lock her lips and throw away the key.

Cassandra snorted. "Go ahead and play your little games. We'll find out. We always do."

"Maybe so, but at least let me enjoy my fleeting moment of mystery and romance."

"Have fun," Anrita said.

"That goes double for me," Cassandra added.

Sylvianne blew kisses and hurried home.

"I hope her mystery man is nice," Anrita said as she and Cassandra went inside. "I worry about her living alone."

"It's her drinking that worries me."

"Me too, Cassie. I try not to think about it because I get so upset." Anrita took off her hat and gloves and smoothed her hair. She spoke over her shoulder as Cassandra followed her into the kitchen. "It's just as well that Sylvianne left because I want to talk to you about something."

"Sounds ominous."

"It is." Anrita slipped sweat sleeves on two tall glasses and retrieved a pitcher from the refrigerator. She filled the glasses with ice and tea and brought them to the kitchen table along with tea spoons and some mint sprigs. "Calvin had a run-in last night with Junkin Abernathy."

"Uh-oh."

"Calvin was driving his moonshine station wagon out River Road when a car swerved out of that driveway to Big Shots and ran him off the road. When Calvin recognized Junkin's Cadillac, he turned around and went after him. He said Junkin hit over a hundred going home and was all over the road. He caught up with him in the Abernathy driveway and said Junkin smelled like a distillery."

"That road's so winding I'm surprised he didn't kill somebody."

"I know." Anrita sipped her tea. "They had words of course, and Calvin wanted to call Chuck Kirkendol and make Junkin take a sobriety test. Junkin said that would never happen, which goes to show how deep Junkin's got the sheriff in his pocket."

"Seems to be no end to Abernathy's sorry deeds."

"Which surely include Buzzy McMillan constantly cruising up and down our street. I feel like we're being watched by Big Brother."

"You're not the only one."

"What do you mean?" Cassandra told her about the threatening Moonbeam McSwine letter. "Good heavens! I hope you took it straight to Mr. Warren!"

"No, I didn't."

"But that's a serious threat, Cassie."

"It's not the first time," Cassandra admitted wearily. "After I discussed Darwin's Theory in class, I got phone calls from outraged parents. They were all church-going folks, so I wasn't surprised."

"What did you tell them?"

"That their kids were old enough to look at both sides of the evolutionary coin and make up their own minds. As you can imagine, that didn't sit well with the hard-shell Baptists, so they promptly called Mr. Warren who promptly called me on the carpet and promptly told me to shape up. You might say it was a very prompt chain of events."

"What did he tell you?"

"To stop talking about evolution in the classroom."

"Did you stop?"

"Sort of."

"How can you sort of stop talking about something?"

"I stopped in all my classes except the special one your son is in. Those young people have a real hunger for knowledge. They're what teachers like myself long for, and I'm not about to deny them anything. In fact, I made a deal with them after the Darwin fiasco."

"Oh?"

"I explained the situation and told them if they didn't want to learn about evolution or read *Catcher in the Rye* that I would abide by their wishes. When I put it to a vote, I'm happy to say it was a unanimous triumph over censorship."

"That's wonderful!"

"But it came with a caveat. I made them promise not to tell their parents, and I figured I was safe when several said they were sure their folks had never even heard of J.D. Salinger."

"John never said a word, although whatever you teach is fine with Calvin and me."

"Far as I know, none of the other kids blabbed either. They jumped at the chance to get something extra in their education, and that's why I cherish them."

"So who could be behind this Moonbeam McSwine thing?"

"Who knows? Any one of those women at the Tacky Party could've said something, especially after I won the prize, but I can't figure a connection between that and my teaching agenda."

"Neither can I." Anrita glanced at the clock and realized it was time to turn off her pressure cooker. "I better check on my roast."

"And I better get going."

"Won't you stay for Sunday dinner?"

"I was hoping you'd ask." Cassandra inhaled the kitchen aroma. "You make the best roast in town."

"Thank you, my dear. Now I have another question for you."

"Okay."

"Who do you suppose Sylvianne's mystery man is?"

28

Situated some eleven miles outside Meander, Cas Boruff's farm was abandoned in 1953 when he was killed in a tractor accident. Vandals ignored the No Trespassing sign posted by Sheriff Kirkendol and picked the place clean, but its isolation made it a perfect place for Junkin to gather his fellow Klansmen. When he announced it was to be an informal meeting without robes, Doyle Richardson and Dub Hutchison insisted that they at least have a cross burning.

"Hell, Junkin," Dub complained. "It's only a little one me and Doyle nailed together this afternoon. Let us have some fun."

"It'd be right good for morale," Doyle added.

Junkin agreed but ordered them to keep a close eye on things. "For God's sake, we don't need a repeat of that last damned fire."

"Don't worry, chief. We know what we're doing."

Junkin wasn't in the best of moods after last night's run-in with Calvin Harrington, but he felt better as he watched his men set up the cross, douse it with kerosene and strike a match. The thing ignited with a loud whoosh triggering cheers and applause from the gathering of sixteen Klansmen. Junkin let them enjoy the sight for a few minutes before stepping onto the front porch of the dilapidated farm house and calling for order.

"Okay, boys. I got important business to discuss, so gather around and listen up."

He waited while everyone jockeyed for places to sit, lean or stand. The steamy Tennessee heat was made worse by the burning cross, but Junkin found it invigorating because it reminded him of his spiritual calling. As the flames crackled and popped, he welcomed the sweat streaking his face while he scanned the faces of his loyal flock.

"First off, I want to commend everyone who participated in our show of strength at the Tower Theater a couple of weeks ago, but I gotta say I'm disappointed that we didn't generate much support from the townsfolk and I ain't too happy about those newspaper articles and signs saying we're not welcome in Meander. Just this morning, Reverend Brooks condemned us over there at First Methodist."

Junkin waited for the expected muttering and obscenities to die down.

"Boys, I'm here to tell you if these people think signs and sermons and newspaper stories are gonna to keep us from our divine mission, they're sadly mistaken."

As Junkin hoped, he was rewarded with applause and whistles.

"Now I've been in touch with our brother Klaverns over in Nashville and down in Charlotte, and they suggested a number of options I wanna discuss. Under the United States Constitution, all citizens have rights to free speech and assembly. That means we can have public gatherings any time we want, but rumor has it that, thanks to that meddling bastard Calvin Harrington, City Council is working on legislation to thwart that." When Junkin saw Doyle's quizzical expression, he added, "That means they want to stop us." Doyle looked relieved.

"You're the mayor, Junkin!" someone called. "Can't you veto that kinda stuff?"

"Sure, I can, but the damned City Council can override my veto. The good news is that any bill has to have a public referendum, and I think I know a little something about winning at the polls. If by chance it passes, we'll challenge it in the courts. All we need is one man to represent us, and I nominate Dub Hutchison for that honor." As Junkin expected, Dub looked around and preened at the mention of his name. "Stand up and take a bow, Dub. Let's have a round of applause, gentlemen."

Junkin knew Dub had no idea what he was volunteering

for, that such a deed meant going public with his membership in the Klan. As he watched Dub enjoy the attention, he wondered if all sacrificial lambs had such idiotic grins. He raised his hands and quieted the applause.

"Y'all all know Meander has a big birthday celebration coming up on Labor Day. The festivities will be held in Crockett Park, and I'm sure you'll agree that we need to make our presence known at that event. I have to oversee the ceremonies, but I'll sure be with you in spirit and wishing I were in my sacred robes." After a moment of basking in his own magnanimity, Junkin delivered his potent parting shot. "There's no place on earth I'd rather be!"

Junkin enjoyed more applause before announcing that the meeting was over. The accolades dissolved into individual conversations as the men got revved up over a public appearance on Labor Day. Sonny took a few men inside the empty farmhouse and retrieved their new robes from the chimney. They went back outside to show them off, and after a few more moments of perverse camaraderie the group began to disperse. Junkin shouted to Dub and Doyle and pointed at the cross, now a sacrilegious silhouette of glowing embers.

"Y'all make double sure that fire's out, you hear?"

"Okay, boss."

The two Klansmen scattered the charred wood and stomped it until the embers were gone and all smoke had dissipated. They kicked dirt on the remains of the cross so no signs of scorched earth remained. Within minutes, all cars and trucks were all gone, and the Boruff farm was once again deserted.

Except for the two people in the hayloft.

Rocky and Dottisue huddled together, still trembling after what they'd witnessed. Anticipating a couple of hours of privacy, they'd been dropped off by John and Lurleen only moments before the first Klansmen arrived. Rocky had been spreading a blanket on the creaky floor when Dottisue heard cars down below. One look at the intruders sent them scurrying into a dark corner where they watched through cracks in the rotting wood walls. What they witnessed chilled them to the bone.

"It was like a real-life horror movie," Dottisue said when the last pair of red taillights disappeared into the night. "I was never so scared in my life."

"Me, too," Rocky confessed. "That was really creepy."

"Thank goodness they left before John came back to pick us up. I hate to think what they would've done if they'd caught us up here."

"They'd probably threaten us not to tell anybody what we saw, but I sure don't like the idea of them knowing that we know who they are."

"I can't believe some of the men down there," Dottisue said, sadness and disappointment in her voice. "Glenn Tapp and Donald Gryder go to our church."

"Did you see Dan Hatcher?"

"He goes to our church too, and his mother's in Mama's church circle." Dottisue was mystified. "What in the world is he doing with that awful bunch?"

"I reckon he hates colored people and Jews and Catholics like the rest of them."

Dottisue pressed against him, encouraging him to put his arms around her. "I'm scared, Rocky."

"It's alright, honey. They're gone."

"That's not what I mean." The air in the loft, dusty with stale hay motes, prompted a sneeze. She grabbed a Kleenex from her purse. "Now I'm wondering about other awful stuff we don't know about."

"I only counted sixteen men, so maybe it's not as bad as we think."

"That's sixteen too many, Rocky, especially when you consider that our mayor is the damned ringleader."

Rocky was surprised by her language. "I've never seen you so upset."

"I don't know whether I'm upset or just plain scared, but I sure wish John and Lurleen would get here with the car."

"What're we going to tell them?"

"We have to tell them everything. We can't keep something like this a secret."

"You're right, but it's gonna be pretty rough for Lurleen to hear that her daddy's head of the Ku Klux Klan."

"And his plans for the Sesquicentennial, what with her mother being head of it and all. Lord, Rocky. This is so awful I don't even want to think about it."

Rocky pulled her closer. "I know something that'll take your mind off of it."

"Forget about it, Rocky Millsaps," she said, slapping his hand away. "Sex is the last thing I want right now."

Rocky feigned shame. "I'm sorry. It's just that you look so hot when you're all riled up."

"You behave yourself or I'll give you something else to get riled about."

Rocky leaned away and held up his hands. "I surrender."

"Look!" Dottisue whispered. "Here comes another car."

"I hope to God it's John."

"Me too." Dottisue hastily crossed herself.

"What's that for? You're not Catholic."

"I know. I'm just covering all the bases."

"Somebody's been watching too much Bishop Sheen."

29

The library at Blufftop had been Eulalie's favorite room since she was a little girl, mainly because it was the original log cabin built by her great-grandfather, James William Crockett. Her grandfather, the Colonel, incorporated the cabin when he expanded the house, and her father Randolph converted it into a library, lining the chinked logs with cabinets for an impressive collection of guns as well as books. The guns were under lock and key, but the books were always Eulalie's to explore. Both her parents were avid readers who encouraged her to pursue their passion and bought a special little chair so she could read alongside them. When it became apparent that Eulalie preferred books to playing outside, her frustrated father picked her up, chair and all, and set her underneath a chinaberry tree.

"At least," he told his wife Vera, "she'll get some fresh air."

When Eulalie wasn't planning parties or traveling abroad, she was most often in her father's overstuffed chair, nose buried in a book. In winter, she'd have Lou build a fire in the fireplace once used for cooking. In summers, the room stayed surprisingly cool, especially on days like today when river breezes scaled the bluff. This particular morning, she was seated at her father's old roll-top desk, poring over the newly discovered Crockett family Bible when Lou showed Andy into the library.

"Good morning."

"Good morning, Miss Sugar." Andy had never seen the room before and was obviously impressed. "This is really something."

"I'm glad you like it. It's the oldest part of the house."

"It's so unexpected."

"Yes, I suppose it is." She watched him inspect the gun

cabinets. "Especially that big elephant gun."

"I was about to ask what that was for."

"My Daddy loved to hunt and kept our freezer full of venison and quail. One winter he decided to go on African safari. I was horrified because every year he would take me to the Ringling Brothers Circus and I'd fall in love with the elephants. I was relieved when he confessed that he'd never used the elephant gun because he found no sport in shooting an animal with something that powerful."

"They can penetrate tanks, you know. In fact, that's how they were used in the First World War."

"You're such a bright young man, Andy." She cocked her head. "Goodness! Why do you look so startled?"

"Because you've never used my name before."

"Oh, I know everyone thinks I can't remember names, but I'm making an exception in your case." She indicated the Bible. "Names have suddenly taken on great importance, you see."

"Sounds like you've made some interesting discoveries."

"My dear, you have no idea. To begin with, this thing dates back to the late eighteenth century."

"My word!"

Eulalie rested a hand on the Bible. "What you stumbled onto in that old slave cabin is much more than a chronicle of births, marriages and deaths in my family. It's a history of this town before it was called Meander." She gently turned some fragile pages and pointed to the margins. "According to this, my great-grandfather James William Crockett brought this Bible from England and was just nineteen when his ship landed at New Bern, North Carolina in seventeen-ninety-three. He made his way west across the Smoky Mountains to Knoxville when it was the capital of the Southwest Territory and formed a party of settlers looking to found their own town." Eulalie waved a hand. "They ended up here in seventeen-ninety-six."

"The year Tennessee entered the Union."

"Exactly. Even at such a young age, James was apparently someone to be reckoned with because the original settlement was named Crockett after him. It stayed that way until the river moved eleven years later and they changed the name to Meander."

"That's all in there?"

"That and much more. It's our history from the founding to a courthouse fire in eighteen-sixty-three that destroyed all historical records. Meander's missing link, if you will."

"Did the Yankees burn it?"

Eulalie chuckled. "Oh, nothing as mundane as that. Judge Roland Petree and some floozy were carrying on in his chambers one night, turned over a gas lamp and burned the place up and themselves with it."

"Wow!"

"Until now, no one knew what happened in those early years, not even Miss Ida."

"I'm listening."

"For starters there's the terminology that sent me straight to the dictionary. James used words like 'mudsills' and 'grum', which is apparently a combination of grim and glum."

"What's a mudsill?"

"Someone that was uneducated, of the working class. What Edward George Bulwer-Lytton called the 'great un-washed.' There are other things I can't decipher, like ab-squatulate and exfluncticate."

"I'll bet Miss Ida can help with those, but what else have you found?"

"A lot of information about the weather, no surprise since these people were farmers. What I find most interesting is the account of the river shifting. According to James, there had been a series of earth tremors in the weeks before and a very strong earthquake the day the river jumped its banks. I believe him because four years later, an earthquake in west Tennessee made the Mississippi River flow backwards and pour into open land to form Reelfoot Lake."

"It must've been some quake for the river to move around the bluff the way it did."

"Which leads me to believe the bluff was originally an island, and that the river merely shifted back to an old channel."

"Either way it's fascinating." He watched Lou deliver tall glasses of iced tea and say she'd be back with some peanut butter cookies. "Tell me more."

"The strangest entries have to do with legislation," Eulalie continued. "It was against the law to sell hollow logs, for example, or to catch fish with a lasso, of all things. Stealing a horse was punishable by hanging, and if more than six women occupied a house it was considered a brothel."

"And I thought we lived in a weird world."

"You haven't heard my favorites," Eulalie continued. "Frogs were prohibited to croak after midnight, and men were not allowed to wear more than two items of women's clothing in public." She peered at Andy over the tops of her glasses. "Sounds to me like those early Tennesseans were smoking something besides tobacco."

When Lou returned with the cookies, Eulalie and Andy were howling with laughter. "If y'all are studying that old Bible, I think I've been going to the wrong church."

"It's Bible studies alright, but not the sort you think." When Lou looked bemused, Eulalie added, "People made all sorts of entries in their family Bibles and some of them are choice."

"Such as?" Lou snorted when Eulalie repeated what she told Andy about frogs and men wearing men's clothing. "No wonder Tennessee's in such a fix."

Once Lou was gone, Eulalie turned serious. "Andy, I need your opinion on something, but our discussion will have to be confidential along with everything I've told you about the Crockett Family Bible."

"Aren't you going to make that information public? It

fills in a big chunk of Meander's missing history, and what could be timelier with the sesquicentennial coming up?"

"I agree, but I don't know how to do it. Fern Abernathy's in charge of the whole shebang, and she's planned everything down to the last twirling parasol."

"You don't think she'd make room for something this important?"

Eulalie's eyes narrowed. "How much have you been around Fern?"

Andy remembered Fern's infantile reaction to Anrita's Tacky Party. "Enough, I guess."

Eulalie rose to slowly pace the small room. "She and I had a meeting about the celebration a while back. Vainglorious soul that I am, I foolishly assumed she'd want me to do some sort of reading, but it turns out I'm operating the slide projector."

"Oh, my."

"That's not the worst part. This slide presentation is about the history of the Old South. Meander's hardly mentioned."

"Why would she do that?"

"Because Fern thinks she's Scarlett O'Hara, and this whole production is *Gone with the Wind* revisited. At least before Fort Sumter."

"That's ridiculous. Someone needs to stop her."

"I agree, but it won't be me. Whatever influence I might have had disappeared with the last administration. Who can stand up to a mayor's wife who's with an ego the size of all outdoors? Fern wouldn't hear me out, much less listen to reason. Either you play by her rules, or she takes her toys and goes home."

Andy thought a moment. "When did you see the slide show?"

"Over a month ago when she brought it over with the projector."

"Is it still here?"

"In that closet over there. The script too."

"Script?"

"Yes, script. It's loaded with big asterisks which are my cue to change to the next slide while Fern narrates."

"So, on the day of the celebration, you're supposed to bring everything to the park and follow Fern's bouncing ball?"

"Yes."

"And she won't see the slides again until then?"

"No, and she made me promise not to show them to anyone because she wants the town to be surprised."

"For once I agree with Fern."

Eulalie stopped pacing. "What are you thinking, young man?"

"You should grab this chance to write an appropriate script and replace the slides with material about Meander. By the time Miss Fern learns what you've done, it will be too late to do anything about it."

"But that would be underhanded and disrespectful."

"Yes, I suppose it would."

Eulalie feigned shock. "Horror of horrors! Fern Abernathy would never speak to me again."

"A reward if I ever heard one. Look, Miss Sugar. I don't know you very well, but—"

Eulalie's eyes crinkled with merriment as she dropped the pretense. "Au contraire, my dear. You know me very well indeed."

"Shall we get busy?"

"Indeed, we should, my dear." She headed for the closet. "There's not a moment to lose."

30

"I appreciate you inviting me over, Zanna." Mary looked around the modest living room. "Lou said you had a right pretty little place, and she was right."

"Thank you. We could use some extra room since the babies came, but Luther and me have been happy here and that's what matters."

"Mmm-hmm."

"Now you and Lou make yourself comfortable while I go check on lunch. It'll be ready in a jiffy."

Mary looked at Lou as soon as Zanna was out of earshot. "How on earth does she live in this cracker box with a husband and two kids?"

"She manages." Lou didn't appreciate the dig about her sister's small home. "Frankly I'd be happy too if I had a husband like Luther and two sweet babies."

If Mary realized her comment was rude, she gave no indication. "I used to think I wanted those things, but not anymore."

"Was the divorce from Jesse that awful?"

"Worse than awful. I guarantee you I won't get a nickel out of that deadbeat, and after he cheated on me too."

"How'd you find out?"

Mary glowered. "His girlfriend told me, that's how! Called me at the high school, I want you to know. I was so upset I almost had to go home, and after that it was one nasty scene after another. Sometimes I think my friend Lorraine has the right idea."

"What's that?"

"Got herself a sugar daddy to take care of her, that's what."

"Is he married?"

"Aren't they all? He's a white guy too. He got her a nice

little apartment and pays her bills and treats her fine."

"How'd she meet him?"

"She's a manicurist at the Andrew Johnson Hotel in Knoxville. He came in one day to get a haircut and I guess sparks flew. I don't know why because I've seen his picture, and he's sure nothing to write home about. Lorraine calls him Bubbles. She never said why, and I for sure don't want to know. Anyway, they've been together six or seven years now, but I think things are starting to cool down."

"Why's that?"

Mary hitched her shoulders. "Lorraine thinks there's something to that seven-year-itch business. Remember that movie with Marilyn Monroe?"

"Only the title."

"Married folks supposedly get a romantic itch for somebody new after seven years, and I'm here to tell you Lorraine's got the itch big-time."

"What's she gonna do about it?"

"There's no 'gonna' about it. Last month she got herself a black man on the side. That white guy only comes to town every few weeks, so I reckon it's working out."

"Sounds like she's got her cake and is eating it too."

"Just like her sugar daddy, and why not? Why should men have all the fun?"

"I guess so, but that juggling act would frazzle my nerves."

"Mine too. It sounded like fun when Lorraine talked about it, but I know it's lots more work than play. I wouldn't be surprised if she dumped both men before long."

"I wouldn't mind a man taking care of me," Lou said, "but I never found one worth putting up with. Know what I mean?"

"Sure do."

"I told Zanna if Luther had an identical twin brother that I'd be all over him. Men like that don't come along every day."

"You talking about my sugar pie?" Zanna called from the kitchen.

"Yes, I am, little sister!" Lou called her that because Zanna was all of ten minutes younger.

Zanna leaned around the corner. "I'm here to tell you they broke the mold when they made Luther Tyson. No matter how rough his day's been, he's happy to see me when he gets home."

"That's not as good as it sounds," Lou told Mary. "The man's an undertaker over in Seesaw and is around dead people all day."

"Very funny." Zanna looked at Mary. "Lou's been telling that tired old joke ever since Luther and me got married."

"It's true," Lou confessed. "And it works every time."

Zanna stuck out her tongue like they were children again and motioned them to the kitchen table. "Y'all come sit. Everything's ready. Hope you like catfish and collards, Mary. This corn's right out of Lou's garden."

"Fresh and sweet," Lou said.

"Y'all are making my mouth water."

"Good." Once the blessing was said and everybody started eating, Zanna asked, "How's your new job working out?"

"Fine. Only been there a couple of weeks but I've already got the hang of it. It's mostly accounting and clerical. The sort of stuff I've been doing for years."

"Mrs. Harrington's a good boss. I've worked for her a long time."

"And I've helped out with parties at her house," Zanna added. "She's real nice."

"It'll be alright I guess."

"What do you mean you guess?"

"She's fine, but her employees are a bunch of Uncle Toms."

Lou was surprised. "Mary!"

"I can't help it. She told me to call her Anrita, but they all call her Mrs. Harrington."

"She's only showing professional courtesy. You're management, and they're labor."

"It's more than that." Mary continued between bites of cornbread. "Y'all know the kind of colored folks I'm talking about. Too much Steppin' Fetchit and yes ma'aming for me."

"Nothing wrong with being polite to the boss lady," Zanna said. "As long as she deserves it, and I'm sure Anrita does. Now my boss lady, on the other hand, is a witch with a capital B."

"Zanna's never liked cuss words," Lou laughed.

"Who're you talking about?" Mary asked.

"I clean house for Fern Abernathy. She's the new mayor's wife and the meanest thing on two wheels."

"Why don't you quit?"

"I wish everybody would stop asking me that. I'd quit in a flash if I could, but Luther and I need the money."

"Don't you think dignity is more important than money?" Mary admonished.

Uh-oh, Lou thought. Here we go again.

"I think putting food in my babies' mouths is more important than either one," Zanna replied curtly.

"I appreciate that, but it seems to me—"

"It seems to me you're trying to get back on your civil rights soap box," Lou interrupted.

"Talking about problems is the first step toward solving them."

"I know that's right, but each problem is different."

"So what are you saying?"

"I'm saying that you're a good friend, Mary, and I'm glad you're living close by, but like I said before, you can't come down here half-cocked and expect everyone to hop on your band wagon."

"You're saying you want things to stay the same because you're scared of ruffling old Confederate feathers."

"That's not what I mean at all."

"Then why are you so loyal to that old white woman?"

Lou's temper stirred. "You talking about Eulalie Saunders?"

"Is that the one Anrita calls Miss Sugar?"

"Yes, and I call her Eulalie because she asked me too," Lou replied tartly. "And I'll tell you something else. If it hadn't been for her—"

Mary waved her fork. "I know. I know. You and Zanna would still be in some sharecropper's cabin in the middle of nowhere. You've told me that story before."

"Sounds to me like it never sunk in."

"Listen, Lou. I think that's mighty fine that this old cracker helped you out, but no matter how you look at it, you're still a maid."

Lou bristled. "Girl, you got no business calling that lady a cracker, and I'll tell you something else. I'm paid three times what maids get around here and would a sight rather polish silver in a mansion than work in the damned fields!"

"Amen to that," Zanna said.

"But don't you want more out of life?" Mary pushed. "If not for yourself, for those brothers and sisters who will come later?"

"Thanks to Eulalie Saunders I've already got more," Lou insisted. "She taught me how to read and write and she pays me plenty and gives me clothes and—"

"Cast-offs, no doubt."

"That's all you know. I'm talking about Coco Chanel, lady. Clothes that never go out of style."

Mary sniffed. "And I suppose you've got someplace to wear such finery."

"I can tell you she looks mighty fine in church," Zanna said, coming to her twin's defense.

Mary remained dismissive. "You two are trapped in another century. You've got to stop accepting things as they are and put an end to Jim Crow."

That struck a nerve when Lou remembered what she told Anrita about dreaming small. She was about to respond when her sister spoke up.

"What are you suggesting?"

Mary looked at Lou. "I take it you haven't found out anything about local civil rights activity."

"No."

"I'm going up to Knoxville next weekend for a meeting. Why don't y'all come with me?"

Lou and Zanna exchanged looks. "I'm not sure Luther would want me to do that."

"Since when do you need his permission?"

"That's not the point, Mary."

"Why would he object to you going to meetings?"

"Because Lou's right. Not everybody wants to get mixed up in all that."

"Because you're afraid some Ku Kluxers gonna come after you?"

"Maybe you don't know they were here only a few weeks ago."

Mary was shocked. "The Klan was here in Meander?"

"At the Tower movie theater." Lou explained what had happened. "I'm proud to say most of the white folks didn't approve. In fact, a lot of downtown stores have signs saying the Klan's not welcome. They're in people's yards too."

"And?"

"And things have been quiet ever since."

"But for how long?" Mary demanded. "I swear you two just don't get it. I'm so frustrated!"

"It's frustrating for us too," Lou said pointedly.

"Maybe we shouldn't talk about it anymore," Zanna suggested. "I'm so upset I'm about to lose my appetite for that peach pie cooling on the windowsill."

"Alright then. If y'all don't want to help your brothers and sisters, there's nothing I can do about it."

"Now you hold on a minute," Lou said. "Before you ask us to write Abraham Lincoln thank-you notes and think we're stuck in another damned century, I've got something to say."

Mary was surprised by her tone. "Go right ahead."

Lou reiterated what she and Eulalie had discussed about her going to Knoxville and passing herself off as African. By the time she finished, Zanna was half in shock and Mary was energized all over again.

"That's brilliant!" she cried. "You absolutely have to go to the S&W and do this. Is Mrs. Saunders sure her reporter friend will do a story?"

Lou couldn't help twisting the knife. "You mean that old cracker woman?" Mary looked sheepish. "That's what I meant about you going off half-cocked."

"You're right, Lou. I apologize."

"Apology accepted."

Zanna looked at her twin. "You really going to do that crazy thing at the S&W?"

Until that moment, Lou had been bluffing but she drew courage from a new and alien thrill coursing through her. "Yes, little sister. I believe I am. You want to come along?"

"Not me, honey, but I'll sure help make your outfit."

Mary put down her fork and grabbed each sister by the hand. "Do you ladies realize what happened here?" She squeezed their hands. "In our own little way, we've had ourselves a civil rights meeting."

31

Sylvianne poured vodkas for herself and Cassandra and a Seven-Up for Anrita and took them to the patio where her friends were lazing in the late afternoon heat. She settled into her lounge chair and lifted her glass toward the stereo music. "Here's to Duke Ellington."

"Is that his new album?" Anrita asked.

"Yes. It's called April in Paris." She hummed along with the title track. "Isn't it divine?"

"It's divine alright, but we're not here to talk about that." Cassandra took a long pull on her drink. "It's been a week. Time to 'fess up."

Sylvianne feigned ignorance. "I'm sure I don't have the faintest idea what you're talking about."

"Then I'll give you a hint. Your Sunday lunch in Gatlinburg."

"Oh, that."

"Yes, that. We're dying to know about your mystery man."

"How do you know it was a man?"

"Because Anrita and I saw you get in your car before you left. You were wearing that little white sundress with the cherry blossom print."

"So?"

"So, it's skin tight and cut down to Chattanooga with a hemline up to Knoxville. You were *not* dressed to lunch with another woman."

"I swear, Cassie. You know more than Eugene Proctor! Do I really have to tell?"

"Yes!" they chorused.

"I'm not allowed a few secrets?"

"No!"

"Promise you won't tell anyone and that you won't make fun?"

"Yes," Anrita said.

"Yes and no," Cassandra said.

"Cassie!"

"How else can I keep my promise when I have no idea what crazy rabbit Sylvianne's going to pull out of her hat? Remember that carpet salesman from Sweetwater?"

"He had a great sense of humor," Sylvianne insisted. "You know I love men with a sense of humor."

"You also loved the discount he gave you on wall-to-wall carpeting."

"Myron was a generous and thoughtful gentleman."

"What about that Cuban fellow? The roofer?"

"He didn't give me a discount, but he did teach me how to rumba."

Cassie smirked. "I've never heard it called *that* before."

"That's enough, you two," Anrita asserted. "Now tell us about your mystery man."

"Well, he's somebody I've known a long time, and when he asked me to lunch at the Hotel Blackstone, I accepted."

"The Blackstone, eh? At least we know the man has taste."

Cassandra leaned forward. "Is he local?" Sylvianne nodded. "Somebody we know?" She nodded again. "For heaven's sake, you're not going to keep us guessing, are you?"

"No, but I don't want to hear any mean comments that I can do better or that he's beneath me."

Cassandra gnawed her lower lip at the last remark. "I pass."

Sylvianne sipped her drink. "It's Mr. Hatcher."

"Not Dan 'I'm-Your-Man' Hatcher, the Used Car Czar! Oh, my Lord! Did he wear that big fake Russian crown like in his ads?"

"I knew you'd make jokes," Sylvianne sulked.

"Who's making jokes?" Cassandra said. "Dan's a fine-looking man, and besides—"

"Besides what?"

"I bet he'll give you a good deal on that old beat-up Studebaker you've been wanting to unload." Cassandra stopped teasing when Sylvianne glared over the rim of her glass. "Sorry, honey."

"Do you have it out of your system now?"

"I said I was sorry."

"Dan's a very nice young man," Anrita said, smoothing troubled waters as usual.

"I think 'young' is the secret word, Groucho."

"He's in his thirties and I'm forty-six," Sylvianne said. "What's the big deal?"

Cassandra wasn't buying it. "He was one of my English students eleven years ago, sweetie pie. That makes him all of twenty-nine."

Sylvianne tossed her head. "So I'm robbing the cradle. Excuse me for living."

"Are you kidding? I say good for you."

Sylvianne brightened. "You do?"

"Sure. I read the Kinsey Reports and I agree that anything is permissible between consenting adults."

"Did they actually say that?"

"Not in so many words, but it pretty much sums up my philosophy."

Anrita snapped open her fan and stirred the air. "Did you actually read that thing?"

"Skimmed is more like it."

"Why?"

"Why did I skim it or why did I read it?"

"Either one."

"Reading is what English teachers do, honey. There's all kinds of new material we're obliged to keep up on. Some of the things I've read would curl your hair."

"Mine's curly enough, thank you," Anrita said, absently fluffing her bangs. "But I want to know more about Dan Hatcher. What did y'all talk about?"

Sylvianne suddenly turned coquettish. "What made you think we talked?"

"Sylvianne!"

"C'mon, Anrita. If I slip off to a hotel with a man a few years my junior, can't you connect the dots?"

Cassandra sighed. "Anrita may be the only woman in Tennessee who hasn't read Peyton Place."

Anrita took umbrage. "What I read is my business."

"You're too old to pout, sweetheart." Cassandra turned back to Sylvianne. "You know what I've figured out about you, Sylvianne? You have a genuine preference for screwing the proletariat."

Anrita's fan went into overdrive.

"What's wrong with that? We all know I've been married and divorced four times from four very different men, and, frankly, what these gents lacked in class they compensated for in concupiscence." She blew on her fingernails and buffed them on her shoulder. "How'd you like *that* secret word, Groucho?"

"Very impressive. Okay, then. We can skip the gory details, but is Dan 'I'm Your Man' the man for you?"

Sylvianne's mood darkened. "I'm sorry to say he's not. Oh, he has charm to burn and is sure easy on the eyes, but—"

"But what? Stop beating around the bush and get to the point."

"He's got a crimson collar."

"And all that that implies?"

"And then some, as I just learned."

"What a shame."

"What on earth are you two talking about?" Anrita asked.

" 'Crimson collar' is code for 'redneck,' " Cassandra explained. "What tipped you off, Sylvianne?"

"Some colored people came into the dining room while we were waiting for our table. Dan turned right around and told them the Blackstone was segregated and that they'd better not make any trouble if they knew what was good for them."

"No!"

"It happened so fast I barely realized what happened. I wanted to tell Dan to be still, but he had such a hateful look on his face I kept my mouth shut. It was awful. For a few seconds, he didn't even look like himself."

"I'm sorry to hear that," Anrita said. "He's so polite I'd never have imagined him behaving that way."

"I'm a lot more disappointed than you are." Sylvianne sipped her drink. "What's even stranger was the table of Cherokee Indians with darker skin than the colored couple."

"What a world we live in," Anrita lamented.

"That reminds me," Cassandra interjected. "What's going on with Calvin and the city council? Are they ever going to pass that ordinance against the Klan? It's been three weeks."

"Calvin believes they'll eventually get it through but there's been a lot more discussion than he expected."

"I for one hope they get off their fannies and get it passed. Everyone I've talked to thinks it's a great idea."

"Calvin and I do, too, but suddenly we've got other problems on our hands."

"Like what?"

"Like someone ransacking our plant kitchen two nights ago."

"What?!"

"Nothing was taken but the place had been turned inside out. Calvin's sure it was someone else looking for my recipe. Why else would they ignore all that expensive kitchen equipment, not to mention delivery truck keys hanging in plain sight?"

"How'd they get in?"

"Sheriff Kirkendol doesn't have a clue because there were no broken windows or jimmied locks or anything. It's like someone walked right in."

"Who has keys besides you and Calvin?"

"Only Barbara Steele. Sometimes she gets there early to open up."

"You don't think she—?"

"Heavens, no! Barbara's been with us from day one, and I trust her implicitly. Besides, she knows the secret spices aren't written down anywhere, so it wouldn't make sense." Anrita thought a moment. "Speaking of crimson collars, I recently found out something awful about Barbara's husband, Jarmon."

"Uh-oh."

"She got real upset when I hired Mary Fox. Said Jarmon would make her quit if he knew she had a colored boss."

Sylvianne said, "That's even more surprising than Dan. I always thought Jarmon was a peach."

Cassandra made a face. "With this Moonbeam McSwine threat and those bigots and would-be recipe thieves, I'm beginning to wonder who's who and what's what in this crazy town."

"What's Moonbeam McSwine got to do with anything?" Sylvianne asked.

"I guess I forgot to tell you somebody's out to get me fired."

"What? Why?"

Cassandra drained her drink and rattled her ice cubes to announce she needed a refill. "I'll tell you when I get back. Yours need freshening up?"

Sylvianne gave her the glass. "Absolutely."

"How's that Seven-Up, Anrita?"

"Considering all I've just heard, it could use a shot of vodka."

Sylvianne slapped her shoulder. "Atta, girl!"

32

Anrita was pouring her second cup of coffee when Calvin breezed in from the back yard. "That thunderstorm last night sure cooled things off, didn't it?"

"Yes, thank goodness. I can't remember a hotter summer."

"Know what? It's so nice I think I'll take Klem out for a spin. He hasn't been out in a while, poor guy."

"Whatever inspired you to name that moonshine dummy Klem?"

"After Mr. Kadiddlehopper of course." Calvin grabbed his car keys from a hook by the kitchen door. "I won't be gone long."

"If you're in the neighborhood, pick up a dozen eggs at Pratt's. I'm thinking about making a chess pie for dinner."

"In that case I'll definitely be in the neighborhood!" He kissed the back of her neck. "Be back in an hour or so."

"You and Klem have fun."

It appeared to Calvin that everybody in town was enjoying the cool, refreshing morning as he drove down Main Street. He was waiting for the light to change at the corner of Main and Magnolia when he spotted the sheriff's patrol car in his rear-view mirror. He waved politely, but instead of returning the hospitality, Kirkendol turned on his spinning red light and motioned for Calvin to pull over. Calvin obeyed and watched, mystified, as the sheriff parked and walked over, scowling all the way.

"Hey, Chuck!" Calvin called. "Something wrong?"

Kirkendol braced a hand on the station wagon's roof and leaned down. "You need to come to the police station."

"What for?"

"Do as you're told and there won't be a problem."

"Is that left rear tail light out again? It was on the fritz last week, but I thought I had it fixed."

"Taillight's fine. Follow me please."

Calvin waited for the patrol car to pull ahead and trailed it down Main Street. With so many people watching and pointing, he felt like he'd been caught robbing the Park National Bank. It was only six blocks to the police station, but it seemed forever before he wheeled into the visitor parking space and went into the station house.

"Wait here," Kirkendol said.

Calvin's annoyance was growing fast as he watched the sheriff write out a citation, tear it off and hand it to the cop behind the counter. "For Pete's sake, Chuck. When are you going to tell me what this is about?"

Kirkendol pointed. "Step into my office, please."

"I'm not moving a step until you explain why I'm here."

Kirkendol indicated the front counter. "Maybe you'd rather be fingerprinted and booked and spend the night in jail." He waited for Calvin to process the bizarre ultimatum. "Well?"

"Alright. You win."

Inside his office, Kirkendol hung his Stetson on a hook, lowered the blinds on his door and yanked them shut. He sat behind his desk and told Calvin to take a chair as he explained the charges.

"You're in violation of a city ordinance prohibiting the promotion of alcoholic beverages."

Calvin's mouth dropped. "What the devil are you talking about?"

Kirkendol licked his thumb and flipped through a stack of papers. He found what he was looking for and slid it across his desk. Calvin scanned the legal gobbledygook until he found a line underlined in red. He read it out loud.

"Citizens of the town of Meander, Calhoun County, Tennessee, are prohibited to engage in the production, transport, sale or promotion of alcoholic beverages." He read further. "This is dated January, 17, 1920 for God's sake. This is prohibition stuff."

"Correct."

"In case you haven't heard, prohibition was repealed over twenty years ago."

"So?"

"So this law is seriously outdated."

"Outdated or not, it's still on the books, and that means it's still in effect."

"This is ridiculous, Chuck, and you know it."

"It's all there in black and white, and, prohibition or not, I'll thank you to remember that Calhoun is a dry county."

"Alright, alright. I hear you." Calvin struggled to hold his temper and present his argument calmly. "Let's slow down and review the situation. My intent, and that of my sign, is not to promote alcohol but to warn against its dangers."

"Regardless of intent, do you deny the sign promotes an alcoholic beverage?"

"That's not promotion. It's damnation."

"Even so."

Calvin was so stunned by the sheriff's cold, illogical response he thought his head would explode. Despite his outrage, he easily rationalized what was happening. He stood and angrily glared at Kirkendol.

"This is Junkin Abernathy's doing, isn't it? He's still pissed off because I caught him driving drunk."

"I don't know what you're talking about."

"The hell you don't!"

"I'm only doing my job," Kirkendol said heavily. "I noticed that old station wagon weeks ago, but I'm a busy man and didn't get around to doing something until I saw you just now."

"You're saying you already knew about this absurd law?"

"I'm Sheriff of Calhoun County. It's my business to know the law."

"Even one this antiquated?"

"The law's the law."

Calvin sat back down. "In that case, how come nothing's being done about the moonshiners driving Thunder Road? What about our mayor's bootlegging operation and the prostitutes at the Kitty Korner? How come those are wide-open criminal operations and an honest citizen like myself can't warn our children about the dangers of moonshine?"

Kirkendol made a tent of his hands and studied his thumbs. "Do you have proof of these activities?"

"Who needs proof, for God's sake? Everyone knows about the dirty dealings in this town, just like they know our new mayor has a hand in every one of them."

"You didn't answer my question, Calvin. Can you provide proof to back up these allegations?"

"I'd say the runner who flipped his car and burned up a hundred gallons of white lightning on Thunder Road is pretty good proof that the moonshine business is alive and well in these parts."

"That was a lotta years ago."

"Are you saying moonshine traffic has stopped?"

"I said nothing of the sort."

Calvin's frustration was reaching the breaking point. "Alright then. Forget about moonshine. Suppose we drive over to the Kitty Korner and see what's going on."

"Like I said, I'm a very busy man and don't have time for some wild goose chase—"

Calvin had heard enough. "Cut the crap, Chuck. It's more than obvious that you're avoiding the real issues and carrying out Abernathy's orders. Half the town suspects he has you in his pocket. Up until today I didn't want to believe it, but I guess they're right."

The sheriff's face went red. "I've heard enough, Mr. Harrington." He stood and opened the office door. "Go over to that counter and pay your fine."

"Fine?!"

"You broke the law, and you must face the consequences."

"You can't be serious, Chuck. I mean, come on. You and I

go way back and—"

The sheriff's tone warned that he meant business. "You'll pay the fine and you'll drive that station wagon straight home. If I see it on the street again, I'll impound it and you with it. Now get out of my office!"

Calvin only vaguely heard blinds clattering as the sheriff's door slammed. He remained in a daze as he paid the outrageous twenty-five-dollar fine and walked back outside. He was climbing into the driver's seat when someone called his name. He saw Andy Jenkins striding across the parking lot, a determined look on his face.

"Hey, Andy."

"Morning, Calvin." Andy looked across the street. "My store's right over there, and I couldn't miss seeing Sheriff Kirkendol escort you into the parking lot. Mind if I ask what this is about?"

"Why not? It'll probably be all over town before I get home anyway."

"Unless I miss my guess, it already is."

"I'm sure you're right." Calvin gave Andy a quick rundown of his crime. "Can you believe this?"

"I'm afraid so."

"What do you mean?"

"I mean the other day; Buzzy McMillan came into my shop and gave me a ticket for littering."

"What?!"

"Sure enough. I do the altar flowers for most of the churches, and when I was delivering snapdragons and glads to the Presbyterians, I dropped some stalks in the parking lot. It's happened before, but their janitor, Leroy, always sweeps them up. Obviously, McMillan got there first because by the time I finished putting those flowers on the altar, he was waiting with a ten-dollar citation."

"You got off better than I did. I got socked for twenty-five."

"We're not the only ones. Almost everybody with a store

on Main Street has been cited for one thing or another. McMillan got Edith's Variety Store for operating after hours, and I happen to know Miss Edith stayed open late because Belinda Beck was in serious need of some purple rickrack. Floyd Rochelle over at the drug store got flagged for some trumped up health violation concerning his soda fountain."

"I don't get it, Andy. What's with all the fines?"

"We can't figure it out. It's like Kirkendol and McMillan have nothing better to do than watch and wait for the most exaggerated infraction of the law."

"Maybe that explains why McMillan was watching our house."

"He what?!"

"Never mind," Calvin muttered. "Something just occurred to me. All the merchants who've been fined have signs in their shop windows protesting the Klan."

"I noticed that too. Hellfire, Calvin. I've no doubt Chuck and Buzzy are acting under Abernathy's orders. You think maybe the three of them are in the Klan?"

"It wouldn't surprise me, but even if they aren't, their actions suggest they're Klan sympathizers, and to my way of thinking, that's just as bad." Calvin glanced at his watch and squeezed Andy's shoulder before starting the engine. "I appreciate you telling me all this. I've gotta scoot."

"Where are you off to?"

"I'm gonna pay a quick visit to the News-Sentinel. I believe what's happened to us has the makings for one of Dave Mearns's fine editorials."

"Mind if I come along? I might be able to add some pertinent details."

"Alrighty then!" Calvin pointed to the roof of the station wagon. "Say hello to Klem and climb in!"

33

Fern was her usual bundle of misbegotten energy as she trailed Eulalie into the living room at Blufftop. "I sure appreciate you letting me drop in like this, Miz Saunders. What with it being such short notice and all."

"It's quite alright."

Eulalie could only wonder what sort of new lunacy had cropped up. The last crisis involved posters promoting the sesquicentennial which Fern had ordered hammered onto barns, fences and telephone poles throughout the county. The poster's inclusion of an unauthorized photo from *Gone with the Wind* prompted a cease-and-desist order from M-G-M. Studios, and a demand for the posters' immediate removal. Fern was thrilled when Eulalie not only offered to pay for new posters but provided a free photo of Bluffop's pillared façade to replace that of Tara. Only Andy knew that Eulalie's generosity was rooted in guilt for anonymously informing the studio lawyers about the misused Tara photo. She knew he would keep her secret since it was his idea in the first place, and they concurred that their actions were strictly in the interest of historical accuracy. Sort of. Eulalie hoped this latest hitch was less calamitous since she expected another visitor any minute.

"Since you said this would only take a minute, I hope you don't mind if we dispense with tea."

"Not at all." Fern eyed the gleaming tea service already set up. "My, my, how pretty!" she chirped. "You expecting more company?"

"Yes, I am."

When Eulalie offered no further information, Fern resigned herself to the business at hand. She pulled a sheaf of papers from her oversized bag and thrust them in her hostess's direction.

"I got to thinking about how much time this production needs, and you know what? It's running way too long."

No kidding, Eulalie thought.

"I can't have people falling asleep or sneaking off, so we need to scale things back. I thought you could look over the program and make some suggestions. I've underlined the parts that could be shortened."

Eulalie scanned the program and made a hurried decision. "In addition to what you've marked, I suggest cutting the concert altogether and limiting the band to the Tennessee Waltz."

Fern was aghast. "You want to cut Dixie?!"

"I see here that Dixie is being played four times. Before and after the skit with Jefferson Davis, during the promenade of the Cavaliers and after the tribute to the Confederate dead."

"Well, maybe you're right. I reckon I got carried away since Dixie's one of my favorite songs, right up there with You Are My Sunshine and of course Tara's Theme. You know, I'm still racking my brain to figure out who coulda blabbed to the movie people about my posters."

"It's quite the mystery," Eulalie demurely offered.

"You can say that again."

After a weighty silence with Fern's eyes returning to the tea service, Eulalie handed the program back and stood. "Will there be anything else?"

"No, I guess not." Fern rose slowly and put the program back in her bag. "Thanks so much for helping out."

"Not at all, but I'd like to make one more teeny suggestion."

"Sure."

"If possible, I'd like to handle future problems by telephone. It will save you the trouble of driving all the way up here." When Eulalie saw resentment on Fern's pudgy pink face, she hastily added, "What with you being so busy with all these important responsibilities."

"Oh, okay," Fern said, feathers smoothed. "I guess you're right."

Eulalie opened the front door and ushered Fern onto the veranda. Burning to know who was coming to tea, Fern paused to point at Andy's truck. "Is Andy Jenkins doing work for you?"

"Why, yes, he is. 'Bye, now." While Fern stared in disbelief, Eulalie waved, spun around, slipped inside the house and closed the door in a single deliciously fluid whirl. "Thank God I watch The Loretta Young Show." She caught her breath. "Lou? Where are you?"

"In here, putting out the canapés. Mary here yet?"

"No, thank goodness. I was scared to death she'd arrive while I was pushing Fern Abernathy out the front door." Eulalie heard Lou's cackle all the way from the living room. "What's so funny?"

"You are, lady. Letting Mrs. Abernathy come over here when you're expecting Mary Fox."

"I guess I do live a little dangerously some times." Eulalie smiled at her reflection in the foyer mirror and smoothed a wayward silver curl before joining Lou. "I don't know what I would've done if their paths had crossed."

"I know what I'd have done."

"What's that?"

"Sold tickets. Maybe some popcorn too!"

"You'd probably make a fortune." Eulalie sank tiredly into her favorite chair. "I guess I'm feeling my age today."

"Probably because of what you're about to do."

"You think so?"

"Yes, ma-am, I do." Lou sat on the couch and took Eulalie's hand. "We been together a long time, and despite what you say I know it's hard for you to welcome a colored woman in this house as a guest."

"But it shouldn't be, especially since deep in my heart I knew the moment would come. Mr. Sugar and I even talked about it."

Lou's eyebrows rose. "What did he say?"

"That the lot of the poor Negro troubled his soul, and he was sitting right where you are when he said it. Remembering his words, more than anything, helped me take this first step." She sighed again and looked at Lou. "Why am I so nervous?"

"Because you're breaking centuries-old taboos and that takes a lot of gumption. Nobody knows that better than me."

"Better than I," Eulalie corrected good-naturedly.

"You know I have trouble with pronouns and don't change the subject."

"Sorry. Force of habit. Anyway, this whole business is really your idea. Once you told me about those Knoxville women hosting dinner parties for African visitors, I decided if they could do it, why couldn't I?"

Lou squeezed Eulalie's hand. "That's wonderful."

"I appreciate that, but what you don't know is that I made a few phone calls and found out how to get on that Knoxville hostess list, and this winter I'll be welcoming visitors from the Belgian Congo."

"What makes you think I don't know that?"

"Sometimes I forget what big ears you have."

"And sometimes you forget how loud you get on the telephone. When are you gonna get your hearing checked?"

"Never mind about that. I've been thinking about you wearing that African get-up in Knoxville and decided we should have a dress rehearsal first."

"What do you mean?"

"I'll explain once Mary gets here."

"How come you're remembering people's names so easy these days?"

"The rules have changed, that's how come." Eulalie looked toward the foyer when the doorbell rang and gripped Lou's hand when she started to get up. "I'll answer it."

"That's my job."

"Not today, it isn't."

"In that case, I think I'll help myself to some of them canapés."

" 'Those' canapés," Eulalie corrected good-naturedly. "And don't push your luck, Prissy!"

Eulalie waited for Lou to stop cackling before she opened the door. Like Anrita, she was pleased with what she saw. Mary sported a tailored beige suit with white cuffs and collar, white gloves and matching brown heels and purse. Eulalie extended her hand.

"Hello, Mrs. Fox. I'm Eulalie Saunders."

Eulalie noticed a slight hesitation before Mary took her hand. "How do you do."

"Very well, thank you. And you?"

"Fine, thank you."

Eulalie stepped aside. "Won't you come in?"

"Thank you."

Mary had never been inside such a grand house and did her best not to appear awed. She noted the gleaming chandelier, oriental carpets and damask draperies puddling on parquet floors.

"Lou said you had a lovely home. She certainly didn't exaggerate."

"Thank you, Mrs. Fox. Please come this way. We'll have tea in the parlor."

"Thank you."

Hmmm, Eulalie thought. We're about to drown in thank-yous. When she saw that Lou had vanished to give her privacy, she picked up the old elephant bell her mother brought from India and gave it a shake.

"I'd like Lou to participate in our conversation. After all, she's the reason I asked you here this afternoon."

"Well, I have to admit I was very interested when she told me about your plan to dress her like an African and have dinner at the S&W up in Knoxville. Did she tell you I'm happy to help out?"

"She did. And I hope you'll be interested in another plan

along those lines." She looked toward the dining room. "Ah, here she is." After Lou and Marry exchanged pleasantries, Eulalie said, "My idea is to have a dress rehearsal right here, and if it goes as planned, we can take our little show to a bigger stage."

"I don't understand."

"Because this is such an important and risky undertaking, I think we'd be wise to be letter-perfect in our parts." When Mary looked skeptical, Eulalie added, "Think of it as an out-of-town tryout before a show moves to Broadway."

"I'm not sure I know what that means, but I can probably figure it out."

"Excellent." Eulalie filled a china cup with tea, passed it to Mary and did the same for Lou before pouring for herself. She missed Mary's dubious frown, but Lou didn't.

"Mary, did I tell you Eulalie and I have had morning coffee together for over twenty years?"

"No, you didn't." Mary sipped her tea and relaxed. "This is delicious."

"I'm glad you like it." Eulalie passed a plate of tea sandwiches and continued the conversation. "My thinking is that I'll have a garden party here at Blufftop and invite some of our more prominent citizens."

Lou cleared her throat. "I hope by 'prominent,' you don't mean the mayor."

"I do indeed, dear, now let me finish. The invitations will announce that the guest of honor is a foreign visitor. I'll make up a name of course. Once everyone arrives, that guest will make her entrance in full African regalia and will, hopefully, be welcomed by everyone present." She looked at Lou. "Especially the mayor and his wife."

"Don't look at me like that. I can't be playing Halloween dress-up for folks who already know me."

"Which means we'll have to cast someone else in the starring role." She looked at Mary. "It's a part you were born to play."

Mary was flabbergasted. "Me?!"

"Why not? I watched when you came in, and you have a fine way of carrying yourself. We should put that to use. In fact, I think we should make you an African princess."

"And I think you've lost your marbles," Lou chided. "This whole stunt is already crazy. We don't need to make it down-right insane."

"Maybe you're right," Eulalie conceded. "Maybe a princess is a bit much."

"Oh, I don't know." Mary finally showed a sense of humor. "Sounds good to me!"

Everyone laughed before Eulalie turned serious again. "I think we'd be better off saying you're the wife of an engineer from the Gold Coast."

"It's called Ghana now," Mary amended. "It declared independence last March."

"Is that right? I've been researching at the library, but obviously their books aren't up-to-date." Eulalie continued her plot. "Alright then. We'll say your husband is here to study T.V.A. and learn how its operation might apply to building the Akosombo Dam on the Volta River."

"Say what?"

"I'll explain more later. Once we discuss things, you'll know exactly how to play your part and be convincing if someone asks questions. It will help Lou prepare for what she might encounter in Knoxville. If the manager at the S&W figures out she's local, he'll turn her away. Remember, our first goal is to get seated in the restaurant. The second will be exposing the hypocrisy involved, along with its unfairness, of course. To succeed, you must both be perfect in your parts."

Mary turned serious. "Does my story have to be so detailed?"

"This is not some high school play we're talking about, Mrs. Fox. This is real life and, as Lou said, it's potentially dangerous business. To make sure things don't blow up in our faces, I want to have a dress rehearsal here at Blufftop. I'm sure the Meander paper will do a story because I intend to invite Dave Mearns. He's the editor and can be an eyewitness. I've also invited Anne Jernigan. She's the daughter of a friend of mine and a journalist for the Knoxville Journal, so we should get stories for both the Meander and Knoxville papers."

"Oh, you'll get a story alright," Lou said. "Everybody knows Abernathy's a bigot, and his wife's mean as a junkyard dog. You wouldn't believe some of the tales Zanna's told me."

"After meeting Fern, I probably would."

Mary piped up. "Is my picture gonna be in the paper?"

"Of course, but don't worry about anyone in Knoxville recognizing you. Mr. Mearns and Miss Jernigan will support what we're doing, and I'm sure they can arrange a photo that's provocative without being too recognizable."

Mary remained skeptical. "I think we should forget this masquerade party and take Lou on up to Knoxville."

Eulalie drew herself up. "You're free to do as you like, Mrs. Fox, but since Meander is now your home, I'd hope you'd be more interested in muddying the waters here rather than elsewhere."

Mary looked a bit sheepish. "You have a point, Mrs. Saunders. I guess I've been thinking this way because I was born in Knoxville and still think of it as home."

"Well, it's not," Lou said pointedly.

"You're right."

"There's more to all this than attacking segregation," Eulalie continued. "Some ugly things are happening in our little town, and I like to think this is a step toward stopping them."

"You talking about the Klan?"

"Among other things." Eulalie sounded deliberately vague because she knew she had to keep her findings in the family Bible a secret. "Let's just say that when Labor Day comes around, people are going to see Meander, Tennessee in a whole different light." She smiled sweetly. "More tea, Mrs. Fox?"

Mary held out her cup. "Please call me Mary."

"And you must call me Eulalie."

34

"You listen to me, Junkin!" Fern snapped. "I'm telling you that colored woman was bold as all get-out, walked right up on Mrs. Saunders' veranda like she owned the place!"

Junkin popped open another beer. "What do you care about some cleaning woman?"

"This was no maid, honey. No, siree! She had on a hat and heels and even gloves!"

"You didn't recognize her?"

"I was pulling away when she got out, so I didn't see her face."

"What kind of car was she driving?"

"She was in that Black Pearl taxi. You know. The one her people use."

"Hmmm. That is a little odd."

"It's more than a little odd, and I'll tell you why. That high-faluting Eulalie Saunders was all set up for a fancy tea, and I'll bet you dollars to doughnuts she was serving it to that uppity Negress! Why, you should've heard her." Fern delivered an atrocious imitation of Eulalie's aristocratic drawl. " 'I hope you don't mind if we dispense with tea.' The gall!"

Junkin had heard these tirades before. "Now, don't go getting yourself all worked up, Little Bit."

"Whose side are you on?!" Fern yelled.

"I'm on your side, but I want you to calm down."

"I won't calm down! Not when I'm the mayor's wife and some high society dame shows preference to a colored woman over me. She even said I should phone her next time I had pageant questions and not come over there. If that's not a slap in the face, I don't know what is." Fern was so angry she was shaking. "Do you know what'll happen to my reputation if this gets out?"

"I hardly think Miss Sugar's gonna go around town telling people about you coming to call, much less some colored woman."

"Since when do you call her 'Miss Sugar'?"

"Everyone calls her that, for Pete's sake, and I'll tell you something else. We need to stay on good terms with the old bat. You know what they say. 'Keep your friends close and your enemies closer.' "

"Oh, don't start spouting all that political nonsense. It makes my head swim."

"Then why don't you get busy putting out some Velveeta and Saltines and maybe some Slim Jims? Chuck Kirkendol's coming over tonight. He's been working real hard and deserves special treatment."

"What's he want?"

"He doesn't want anything. I asked him over because I need to talk to him."

"About what?"

"Men's stuff, that's what."

"Why didn't you talk to him at your office?"

Junkin's temper was eroding fast. "Because I want to have a damned beer and sit by my damned swimming pool and talk to my damned sheriff, if you don't mind. Now stop asking so many questions and put out some snacks."

Whenever Fern and Junkin fought, she retaliated by giving him the silent treatment, at least verbally. When he heard the kitchen drawers and cabinet doors slamming, Junkin retreated to the patio. On the way, he grabbed the telephone with the extra-long extension cord and went to the far side of the pool. He stretched out in a lounge chair and called long distance. After listening to the number ring twelve times, the operator told him there was no answer. He hung up, temper riled again.

"Where the hell is she on a Thursday night?" He looked at his watch. "At six o'clock too." He picked up the receiver again and called Sonny Hull. "You boys all set for the Fourth of July?"

"Sure thing, boss. You done any more thinking about where you want us to put it?"

"That's why I'm calling. I want it on that ledge overlooking the river and Crockett Park."

"Near the Saunders' house?"

"As close to her property as possible," Junkin said, knowing this would please Fern. "I want her to be able to see it real good."

"By the time we're done, she'll have to be blind to miss it."

"Alright then. I also want people in the park to get a good view, and I want it lit right before the fireworks."

"I'll tell Dub and Doyle."

"Excellent." Junkin waved at Chuck Kirkendol when he appeared across the pool. "Gotta go. Sheriff's here." Junkin hung up and motioned his visitor over. "How you doing, buddy?"

"I'm okay, Mr. Mayor. What did you want to see me about?"

"I see you're empty-handed. Didn't Fern offer you a beer?"

"She did, but I'm still on duty."

"You're not gonna let a little thing like that stop you, are you?"

"Yes, sir, I am."

"Suit yourself." Junkin pointed to a chair. "Go ahead. Take a load off."

"I'm fine standing."

Junkin was annoyed. "Why the bad mood?"

"I'm not in bad mood. Just got a lot on my mind."

"No doubt you do, what with all that's been going on lately." Junkin took a slug of beer. "Which is what I want to talk to you about."

"Yes, sir?"

"Before I get started, I want to commend you and Deputy McMillan for the fine job you're doing. Every merchant I wanted targeted has been fined, and you did an especially good job nailing Calvin Harrington. Sure wish I'd been there when you hauled him into the station house. I'll bet he was hopping mad, huh?"

"He wasn't happy."

"Too damned bad. These folks have got to learn they can't take the law into their own hands, which brings me to something else. You sure you don't wanna sit?"

"Been sitting all day. No thanks."

"Alright. I've been in touch with some of the other mayors in the county, and most agree that we need a master plan in place in case the coloreds start acting up again and trying to get into places they don't belong. You know. Restaurants, hotels and motels, movie houses, churches and swimming pools. Especially pools. Ugh! Makes my skin crawl to think about it."

Fern appeared with a paper plate piled high with chunks of Velveeta cheese and some Vienna sausages. "I can get you some mayonnaise if you want to dip your sausages, Chuck." She sat at the patio table and picked at the food. "Y'all don't mind if I join you, do you?"

Junkin glowered. "I told you this was men's talk."

Fern knew not to push her luck. "Okay, honey, but I heard what y'all were talking about and wanna put in my two cents worth before I go back inside."

Junkin gave her an indulgent look. "Go ahead, Little Bit."

"Myrna Riddick said she was visiting a girlfriend in Ducktown and found out that some coloreds tried to invade the bowling alley down there." When the men didn't comment, Fern said, "I didn't hear you mention bowling alleys and thought you should include them in your plan."

"Don't worry. We will."

Kirkendol picked up a small piece of Velveeta. "Thanks for the treats, Mrs. Abernathy."

"Sure enough, honey. Eat what you like and I'll put the rest back in the fridge. Velveeta keeps forever, you know."

When they were alone again, Junkin said, "I've made a list of rules and regulations if the coloreds try anything in Meander. Coralee typed it up for me, and I'll send her over with mimeographed copies tomorrow so you can distribute them to your staff. In the meantime, you and your officers stay on alert in case you need to step in somewhere. Some of these trouble-makers are real sneaky and you gotta keep a sharp eye out to make sure the wrong people don't get served. Know what I mean?"

Kirkendol pursed his lips. "Not sure I do."

"The coloreds who try to pass for white, mister! I fully intend for Meander to adhere to the 'one drop' rule. Just one drop of colored blood means they're all black. No service, no exceptions."

"Yes, sir."

Junkin's rant continued. "Race mixin' makes me downright sick, and it ain't natural. Like I always say, if you put manure on a vanilla sundae it might help the manure, but it sure as hell ruins the sundae."

Chuck shifted his weight from one foot to another. "Anything else, sheriff?"

"You sure are antsy tonight, Chuck. I'm not sure I like it."

"Like it or not, I've got a lot to do, and I need to get back to work."

"Alright, then. Don't want to keep a man from doing his job, especially my sheriff."

"Good night, Mr. Mayor."

Junkin was peeved. When he inherited Kirkendol from the previous administration, he was pleased when the man did as he was told without asking questions. In fact, Kirkendol's performance was exemplary, but lately something had gotten under his skin. Junkin didn't know what, but he was determined to find out. Nobody in his administration was allowed to have secrets, except for himself of course.

He looked toward the kitchen when he heard Fern banging pots and pans as she started dinner. Obviously she was still mad at him, but that was fine because he had other fish to fry. He reached for the phone and dialed the long-distance operator again. His bad mood worsened when there was still no answer.

"Okay, Missy," he muttered to himself. "You better have a damned good excuse for not being home when you know I'm gonna call."

Other people's secrets weren't allowed in Mayor Junkin Abernathy's dark little world. No, siree, Bob!

35

Eulalie was comfortably ensconced in the library, enjoying a book along with the late afternoon sunshine, when Andy burst in. He was out of breath, face flushed with excitement as he held something close to his chest. His face and hands were smeared with ashes and soot.

"Good heavens! Look at you!"

"Sorry I'm such a mess, Miss Sugar, but I've made another big discovery. Take a look at this."

"What on earth?" she said as he put a small metal box in her hands.

"I was cleaning up the fireplace when I noticed one of the big stones was loose."

"Don't tell me this was—"

"Tucked behind it," Andy interrupted, still catching his breath. "I was so anxious to show you, I barely took time to wipe it off."

Eulalie turned the box around and noted the padlock. "What are the odds of finding a key to this thing?"

"Zero, so I came prepared." Andy reached into the hip pocket of his jeans for a pair of wire cutters. "If you don't mind destroying that little lock, these should to the trick."

Eulalie handed the box back. "Be my guest, young man."

The lock proved to be sturdier than Andy anticipated, but after a few minutes and lots of elbow grease, it cracked. He set the unopened box on Eulalie's desk.

"Would you like some privacy, it being a family thing and all?"

"You're sweet, but heavens no. You found the thing and should be here for the grand opening." She touched her throat. "I feel like Howard Carter opening Tut's tomb, on a very, very small scale of course."

Andy grinned. "I told you cleaning up that cabin was archaeology."

"You were right."

Eulalie lifted the metal top, and both peered inside at another old book and some yellowed letters tied with a black ribbon. There was also a gold locket and a rabbit's foot on a thin silver chain.

"My stars! What a treasure trove!" She examined each item in turn before handing the book to Andy. "It's an old law book."

He carefully raised the cover. "It's dated eighteen-fifty-eight and belonged to that Judge Petree you told me about."

"That's interesting. He and my grandfather fought together in the Mexican-American War and were lifelong friends until the judge died in that fire." Eulalie opened the locket and studied a nineteenth century face. "For heaven's sake. It's the Colonel!" She pointed at the mantle. "Look at that old daguerreotype and see for yourself."

Andy inspected the picture. "Sure enough. Is this your grandmother with him?"

"Yes, indeed. Miss Rosalie Virginia Carpenter Crockett."

"She's a pretty lady but she looks so sad."

"Family lore has it that Grandmamma Rosalie suffered from melancholia and liked her laudanum a little too much."

"Laudanum contains opium, doesn't it?"

"Loaded with it. I guarantee it wasn't just heat and tight stays that made those Southern belles swoon." Eulalie set the locket aside and inspected the packet of letters. "I'll read those tonight after dinner. Anything interesting in that law book?"

"I don't know yet." Andy carefully turned some pages. "But here's that crazy law again about frogs being forbidden to croak after midnight."

"I wonder if anyone told the frogs," Eulalie offered, eyes twinkling.

"And here's the one about not lassoing fish. It looks like this whole section pertains to animals. This one says it's illegal to carry a chicken by its feet down Main Street on Sunday and that it's against the law to put a donkey in a bathtub."

"Ah, yes. The good old days."

"Up until now I was wondering if those things in your family Bible were a joke, but since this is a real law book I guess not."

"I guess not," Eulalie echoed. She picked up the rabbit's foot and sat back in her chair. "I sure would like to know why these things were hidden in that old cabin."

"Who do you suppose put them there?"

"My first guess is the Colonel since they're from his era. Then again it could have been my father, which could be another reason he padlocked the cabin and forbade us from going inside."

"Maybe the answers are in that packet of letters."

"I hope so. If nothing else they should make for interesting reading."

"I'm sure." Andy stretched until his neck popped. "I better go lock up the cabin and head home."

"I'd appreciate it if you'd stay and talk a few minutes."

"Like this? I'm filthy."

"Well, you do look you've been through a dozen Ash Wednesdays," Eulalie teased. "Why don't you duck into the powder room and wash up."

"Alright." While Andy was gone, Eulalie retrieved the letters and untied the black ribbon. There were nine letters in all, each written by her grandfather at Blufftop and addressed to one Bessie Winters in Knoxville. She was racking her brain to remember if she'd heard that name when Andy returned with a clean face and a fresh shirt retrieved from his truck.

"Better?"

"You look fine, my dear," Eulalie said as he sat on an ottoman beside the gun cabinet. "I'm sure you'll think I'm a silly old woman, but Lou's working over at Anrita Harrington's today, and I suddenly didn't want to be all alone. Would you like a glass of sherry or something a little more substantial? It's after five, not that that matters of course."

"No, thank you."

"I probably shouldn't have anything either. Spirits tend to make me nostalgic, and seeing that daguerreotype and these letters has already made me reflective."

"About anything in particular?"

"My husband. I've been a widow for … what? Twenty-six years. There are times when it seems as if Edward's been gone forever, and other times when I think he'll bring my morning coffee instead of Lou. He did that, you know, every day. It was a ritual he started the morning after our honeymoon night, and the only time he missed was when he had his heart attack."

"Is that what took him?"

"He was only fifty-one."

"That's much too soon."

"Yes, it was. Oh, I wish you could've known Edward. He was a true gentleman and a genuine bon vivant. He took me to New Orleans on our honeymoon, and from there we caught a ship to Havana. I still have a soft spot in my heart for both cities and other places Edward took me. Paris, Vienna, Venice. Even Saint Petersburg where, believe it or not, we caught a glimpse of the tsar."

"Wow!"

"But as glamorous as those places were for a girl who'd never been out of Tennessee, my favorite times were spent right here. Especially springtime when it seems like the whole world is in bloom. There were so many white dogwoods the hillsides looked like they were covered in snow." Eulalie closed her eyes a moment to conjure a memory. "When we were first courting, Edward took me up to the Cumberland Mountains to see a moonbow."

"A what?"

"Moonbow. It appears when moonlight reflects off spray from a waterfall. If there's no color, it's called a white rainbow. I'd love to see one again but … no, that's not true. I should leave the memory alone."

"I know what you mean."

"Do you?"

Andy hesitated, as though, Eulalie thought, carefully weighing an answer. "I felt like that about someone once. We shared special memories I wouldn't dream of sullying by re-visiting a place."

"I like your choice of words, Andy. Sullying. It suggests something was pure and clean, and that's exactly what those memories were."

"Yes, ma-am."

"You talk as though that person is no longer in your life."

"That's right. They're not."

"May I ask what happened?"

"I'm … I'm not sure I can talk about it."

"Do forgive me," Eulalie said quickly. "I didn't mean to pry."

"You're not prying. It's just that I've never talked about it before. With anyone."

"Please don't feel obliged because I've been waxing nos-talgic."

After a heavy silence, Andy said, "I think I'd like a bour-bon after all."

"The bar's over there. Shall I get it for you?"

"I'll get it, thank you. You sure you don't want some-thing?"

"A sherry would be lovely. Edward told me to never to let him drink alone."

"I think I would've like Edward."

"He would've liked you too. If you need ice, there's a small refrigerator under the bar sink."

Andy poured drinks and the two clinked glasses in a si-lent toast. He downed a shot of Jack Daniels and, when he didn't say anything, Eulalie knew to keep still. After a while he helped himself to another shot, set the glass aside and perched on the arm of her chair. She was surprised but pleased with the unexpected familiarity and looked up as he broke his silence.

"You're an intelligent, worldly woman, Eulalie Saunders. I wouldn't be at all surprised to learn you've guessed my secret."

"I think you overestimate me."

"I'm thirty-six and have never been married. I have no family and I live alone and I don't date. I—"

The rest of Andy's words were lost as Eulalie's intuition catapulted her back to the day she found him in the library, reading a book about the Second World War. The truth hit like a thunderbolt.

"Your friend who died on Iwo Jima—?"

"Clark and I met in 1939 when we were freshmen at the University of Tennessee. We knew the moment we saw each other that we belonged together, and, being young, of course we believed it would last forever."

"I see." Eulalie took a deep breath. "Andy, perhaps you'll be more at ease if I tell you Edward and I saw things in the Montmartre in Paris and Weimar Berlin that … well, let's say I don't shock easily. What's more, after living through two world wars and the Great Depression, I'm a great believer in grabbing love and happiness wherever you can." When Andy said nothing, she added, "I'm flattered that you feel comfortable enough to confide in me."

Andy sounded relieved. "It's something I've kept bottled up since Clark died twelve years ago. There have been so many times I've wanted to talk about it, but I never trusted anyone enough to keep my secret. No one else knows, except his family up in Jefferson City."

"Didn't you tell me Clark didn't get along with his father?"

Andy choked. "I'm sorry. I've not heard anyone else say his name in so many years that—"

"I understand."

After a moment, Andy said, "You remember correctly.

Clark's mom was a loving woman, but his father was a tyrant. He beat Clark regularly, and finally Clark fought back and told him about us. That was the last straw."

"What happened?"

"Mr. Foster ordered Clark out of the house and told him not to come back. Clark enlisted in the army right after that. I begged him not to, begged him to stay with me until he got drafted, but he had a stubborn streak I couldn't compete with."

"I'm so sorry."

"I found out he'd been killed by seeing his name in the newspaper among the war dead."

"Have mercy," Eulalie breathed.

"I didn't think things could get any worse until I drove up to Jefferson City to the funeral. His father stopped me at the church door and told me I wasn't welcome because I was a degenerate and had killed his son. I was so overwhelmed by grief and rage that for the first time in my life I wanted to hit someone."

"And?"

"I punched Mr. Foster so hard I knocked him through the door and into the sanctuary. I stayed long enough to look at the flag-draped casket and then I got in my car and drove home."

Andy wasn't aware that Eulalie's hand had stolen into his until she gave it a gentle squeeze.

"Good for you."

36

Fern was fuming. She and Junkin had had a knock-down-drag-out over breakfast about her not doing her part in spying on Anrita Harrington. They made peace only after Fern called Anrita on the pretext of choosing obituaries to read at the sesquicentennial. Fern's bad humor deepened, even when Anrita graciously invited her over that afternoon and said she would make sure Sylvianne was there too.

"Alright, Junkin. I'm seeing Little Miss Perfect at four," Fern sniped. "Satisfied?"

"Not until you find out what she and her husband are up to."

"What makes you think they're up to anything?"

"Just do as you're told and report back."

"It would help to know what I'm looking for."

"Good Lord, woman! Do I have to spell out everything? Gossip with those women like you always do and work your way around to asking how Calvin's doing. For all I know, he and his buddy at the newspaper are planning a smear campaign."

"Are you crazy? You think Anrita's going to tell me that?"

"You won't know unless you try, so just do it!"

Junkin stormed out of the kitchen, followed by slamming cabinet doors and crashing dishes.

Promptly at four, Fern glued her smile in place and knocked on Anrita's door. Her hostess welcomed her warmly and took her onto the screened-in porch where Sylvianne was waiting. Sylvianne returned the outsized smile and waved.

"Hey, Mrs. Mayor. How're you and how's hizzoner?"

"We're fine, thank you." Fern giggled in spite of her foul mood. "You're such a cut-up!"

"Heaven knows," Anrita said.

"Hold your applause," Sylvianne said wryly. Then, "You

know what, Fern? I've been thinking about that word hizzon-er and wondering why there's not one for the mayor's wife. Or what they call a woman mayor."

"Lady mayors are against the law, aren't they?"

"Heavens, no. Cincinnati has one."

Fern's eyes widened. "Is that right?"

"Yes, indeed. Why, the first American woman mayor was a Kansas gal named Susanna Salter, back in the eighteen eighties. Her name was put on the ballot as a joke by men hoping to humiliate her and discourage ladies from going into politics. Their prank backfired when she got elected. Not only that, but Susanna had one of her nine children while she was in office." Noting Anrita's disbelieving look, Sylvi-anne added, "Cassie's not the only one who knows things."

"I didn't say a word, but I admit I'm surprised."

"Still waters," Sylvianne slurred.

Anrita scooped up Sylvianne's empty cocktail and told Fern to help herself to a pitcher of iced tea. "It's unsweetened, but there's some saccharine in that little container."

"No, thanks. I've had so much iced tea my eyeballs are do-ing the back stroke. What's Sylvianne drinking? Is that an R.C.?"

"Why, yes," Anrita lied. "Would you like one?"

"Please."

"I could use another one too!" Sylvianne called as Anrita headed for the kitchen. She turned to Fern. "So how're tricks these days?"

"Fine, I guess. Everyone's working real hard and it looks like things are coming together for the Labor Day celebra-tion."

"Glad to hear it." Sylvianne rummaged through her tipsi-ness for something else to say. "I heard there was a little bit of excitement at the Baptist Church yesterday."

"I had a splitting headache and didn't make the service. What happened?"

"The way I heard it, Sonny Hull was introducing a new

family, the Huffakers, to the congregation."

"I've met the Huffakers. She's real nice."

"Mmm-hmm. Well, Mr. Hull got his tongue twisted when he asked everyone to 'Say hey to the Huffakers.' "

Fern still didn't see what was coming. "Oh, really?"

"Really." Sylvianne was struggling not to crack up when she said, "Apparently Mr. Hull's well-intentioned announcement came out, 'Say huff to the Hayfu—' "

"Drinks everyone!" Anrita called, deliberately stepping on Sylvianne's punch line. If Fern fathomed it was deliberate, she gave no indication, and before Sylvianne could complain, Anrita brandished a manila envelope. "Here are your obituaries."

"If only," Sylvianne muttered, barely sliding under Fern's radar.

Fern emptied the pages onto her lap and thumbed through them. "Don't think I'm questioning your work. I'm just one of these people who goes over every detail and leaves nothing to chance."

"We understand." Anrita ignored Sylvianne's murderous glare while Fern perused the changes.

"These look good, ladies. You've obviously worked very hard."

"Night and day," Sylvianne said.

"I especially like the one for Colonel Crockett. Why, I don't think Meander had a finer Confederate hero." Anrita was about to ask why there was so much emphasis on the Confederacy when Fern said, "How's Mr. Harrington?"

"Calvin? Oh, he's fine."

"I'm glad to hear that. I know he must've been upset by that business with his station wagon."

"Upset wasn't the word," Sylvianne said.

"You know our sheriff was only doing his job," Fern chirped. Anrita tensed, trying to decide whether or not to mention the night Calvin caught Junkin driving drunk and not letting Sheriff Kirkendol do his job. The chance was lost when Fern said, "Is Calvin working on any new projects?"

"As a matter of fact," Anrita said, thinking about the blistering editorial planned for a special Fourth of July edition of the Meander News-Sentinel. "There's been some talk about all those other people getting ticketed, so Calvin has been talking to—"

"That's such stale news," Sylvianne interrupted forcefully. "I'll bet Fern has fresher stuff, what with her being the mayor's wife and all. How about it, Fern?"

Fern knew she was supposed to keep digging about Calvin, but she couldn't resist the spotlight. Up until then, Anrita and Sylvianne had been borderline indifferent, and now here they were asking for her opinion.

"Well, there was that business down in Sweetwater last week," she said, swelling with self-importance. "Junkin told me about it and said all good citizens should be concerned."

"Do tell!" Sylvianne urged.

"A bunch of colored women went to the local white beauty salon to get their hair done. Can you imagine anything more ridiculous?"

"I can think of a couple of things," Sylvianne opined.

Anrita was frantically thinking of how to steer the conversation into safer waters when a familiar voice called from the front door. "Anybody home?"

Oh, no! Anrita thought. Not her. Not now!

Sylvianne cupped a hand and called back. "Come on in, Cassie! We're out here on the porch with Fern Abernathy!"

Dear Lord, Anrita prayed. Please help me get through this.

"Mrs. Abernathy!" Cassandra gushed. "It's so nice to meet you finally. I've heard so much about the new mayor's wife."

"Hi, there. I've heard a lot about you too."

"Is that right?"

"You're the high school English teacher, aren't you?"

"Guilty as charged," Cassandra confessed. "Although that might not be a wise choice of words these days."

"I beg your pardon?"

Cassandra ignored her. "Any chance I might have some of that iced tea?"

"I'll get another glass," Anrita sighed.

"You sound tired, honey," Cassandra said to Anrita.

Anrita shot her a look. "It came over me all of a sudden."

Anrita was still within earshot when Sylvianne got the conversational train back on track. "Fern was telling us about some colored women down in Sweetwater having the audacity to patronize a while beauty parlor. What do you think of that?"

"Why, I don't know." Cassandra turned an innocent face to Fern. "What exactly happened?"

"The way I heard it," Fern continued, believing she had a sympathetic audience, "these three coloreds went into the beauty parlor and demanded to have their hair done. Now we all know they need the kind of glop white beauticians don't have."

"Glop?" Cassandra queried. "I don't believe I know that word."

"And you call yourself an English teacher?" Sylvianne jibed. "You mean hair straighteners, don't you Fern, darlin'?"

"Why, yes. That's exactly what I mean. Can you imagine the audacity?"

"Audacity is exactly the word I was thinking of," Cassandra said.

"I'm so glad you agree, Miss Maddox. I swear those people never think things out, but of course we know their brains are smaller than ours."

"Hmmm," Cassandra mused. "I must've been absent the day they taught that in biology class."

"Oh, I didn't learn that in school. It's something you pick up as a kid."

"Like mumps?"

"Not exactly, but sort of I guess." Fern was foundering. "Anyway it's something I've heard all my life, so it must be true."

Hovering in the doorway, Anrita was a nervous wreck as she tried desperately to defuse the explosive situation. "Would anyone like cookies?"

"No, thank you," Cassandra and Sylvianne chorused.

"I'd like some," Fern said.

"Good." Anrita glared at Cassandra. "Would you mind helping me in the kitchen?"

Cassandra glared right back. "Not while I'm in the middle of such an interesting discussion with the mayor's wife. Whoever could've imagined she was such a font of knowledge?"

"Don't you mean fountain?" Fern asked.

Cassandra cleared her throat. "I stand corrected, my dear."

"I'll get the cookies," Anrita said, retreating as Cassandra mounted her attack.

"Tell me, Mrs. Abernathy. What are some of the other intellectual gems about colored folks that you've picked up along the way?"

"Well, I know that you can tell if someone has colored blood if they have bluish fingernails."

"What if someone hits their thumbnail with a hammer?" Sylvianne asked. "Wouldn't that throw you off the scent?"

Fern giggled. "There you go. Cutting up again."

"Sometimes I can't help myself."

"What else?" Cassandra pressed.

"Some people have little white crescents at the bottom of their eyes."

"Fascinating!"

"I guess so, but it's worrisome too."

"How so?"

"Sometimes those people can pass for white, you know. They can get into our churches and restaurants without us knowing about it. Schools too!"

"Would that be so bad? I mean if you can't tell the difference, who cares?"

"My husband says just one drop of nigger blood makes someone all nigger, and it's against the law for them to use our facilities." She shrugged airily, unaware of the revulsion blooming on three faces. "I don't know why they want to use ours anyway when they have their own."

Cassandra swallowed the bile burning her throat. "Perhaps because their facilities are inferior to ours."

"I never heard that."

"I guess it's something you didn't pick up along the way," Sylvianne offered.

"Not me. I've always known things how things are supposed to be, and if the colored facilities are not as nice as ours, they should give them a good cleaning."

Cassandra blanched. "Are you serious?"

"Of course, I am, silly," Fern said with a sickening simper. "Why wouldn't I be?"

"Damned if I know."

Fern took umbrage. "That's mighty strong language for a school teacher, isn't it, Miss Maddox?"

"Lady, you have no idea what strong language is, but you're about to find out."

"Cassie, please," Anrita pleaded. "We're all ladies here and—"

"Speak for yourself!" Cassie snapped, face flushing. "There are times when the white gloves have to come off, and if I were wearing any I'd be throwing them across the room."

Fern was bewildered. "You're awful red in the face, Miss Maddox."

"And you have no idea why?"

"Why, no, ma'am, I don't."

Sylvianne looked at Anrita. "Suddenly I need another R.C. and maybe a moon pie too."

"Help yourself," Anrita said resignedly, knowing moon pie was Sylvianne's code for bourbon. "You know where everything is."

"You sure you want to miss this?" Cassie asked.

"Something tells me I'll be able hear everything from the kitchen."

"Miss what?" Fern asked nervously. "And what did you mean about white gloves?"

"They're only a metaphor, for God's sake."

"But I thought—"

"You *thought?!*" Cassandra spat, outrage growing. "I doubt you've had a real thought in your entire life!"

Fern was stunned. "Wha … what?"

"Why else would you would vomit such ridiculous, unadulterated hogwash about colored people?"

Fern's confusion deepened. "Vomit?"

"Yes, vomit," Cassandra said, rising angrily. "Because that's exactly what it is, and all I can say is that with you and your crooked, equally ignorant hillbilly husband in charge of this town, Meander is going to hell in a hand basket!"

Fern was on her feet too, hands flying to her hips. "How can you talk to me like that?!"

"By moving my lips and telling the truth, that's how. How on God's green earth can you say colored people's brains are smaller than ours?"

"It wasn't my idea," Fern protested. "And it's true."

Trembling with outrage, Cassandra raised her hands and backed away. "I'd better get out of here before I say something I'll really regret."

"Good," Fern shot back, "because I've heard enough."

"No doubt about it." Cassandra looked the enemy hard in the face. "Although I suspect you've heard way more than you can process because when it comes to small brains, lady, you've cornered the damned market." She turned to her ashen hostess. "Sorry, Anrita. I just couldn't keep still one more minute."

"I'll see you out," Anrita said softly." When they got to the front porch, she threw her arms around Cassandra and hugged her tight. "Thanks, Cassie."

"For what? Acting like a lunatic and ruining your afternoon?"

"No, dear. For saying everything I should've said and

didn't." She sounded awestruck. "Where in the world did all that come from?"

"I guess it's been simmering a long time and the pot finally boiled over. And if you make a joke about the pot calling the kettle black, Anrita Harrington, I'll never speak to you again."

37

Fern was still shaking with indignation when she got home. Seeing Junkin's Eldorado in the driveway, she hurried inside to tell him what happened at Anrita's house. She found him changing clothes in the walk-in closet they told everyone was a dressing room.

"Hey, Little Bit. How'd the meeting go?"

"Awful, Junkin! Just awful! You won't believe what happened!" Fern turned around. "Help me with these darn buttons, Junkin. I need a long soak to calm my nerves."

"You're trembling, honey. What's wrong?" Fern undressed to her slip, anger reblooming as she re-enacted the scene on Anrita's side porch. She knew Junkin would be annoyed but didn't expect him to bellow so loudly that Zanna heard him over her vacuum cleaner three rooms away. "Who the hell does Anrita Harrington think she is?!"

"You're not listening!" Fern yelled back. "Anrita had nothing to do with it, and neither did Sylvianne McNeil. It was Cassandra Maddox who did all the talking, and she wasn't even supposed to be there. She barged right in and—"

"If it happened in Anrita's house, it's her fault! If anybody pulled that crap in front of me, I'd sure as hell make them sorry."

"Junkin, sometimes things happen so fast they can't be helped. Cassandra turned the conversation inside out, and next thing I knew she was up and out the door." Fern finished undressing and slipped into a turquoise chenille robe with tulips and hearts on the back. She risked ratcheting Junkin's temper up another notch when she continued. "Cassandra had a few choice things to say about you too."

When Junkin didn't answer, Fern knew he wasn't listening. Sure enough, she turned around and saw him, naked except for his boxers, preoccupied with the full-length mirror.

He squeezed a handful of belly flab. "Think I need to lose a few pounds, Little Bit?"

"I think if you can grab that much fat—"

Junkin pouted. "That's mean!"

"If you think that's mean, Mr. Hotshot Mayor, wait'll I tell you what Cassandra said."

"Go on," he muttered.

"I don't recall exactly, but I remember a few words like 'crooked' and 'ignorant hillbilly.' She also said thanks to you this town was going to hell in a handbasket."

Junkin looked like he was going to explode. "That bitch!"

"Calm down before you have a heart attack."

"Where's your little address book?"

"What do you need that for?"

"I need to call Laverne Richardson, that's what for."

"Why?"

"Just answer the damned question, Fern."

"It's in my purse."

"Bring it here."

Fern obeyed and sat on the edge of the bed, waiting anxiously as Junkin dialed the phone. She couldn't imagine what he was up to.

"Laverne? This is Junkin. How soon can you get over here with that photo? You know the one I mean. Fifteen minutes? Good. Bring Doyle and tell him to bring his trunks. He and I'll have a swim and a powwow." He hung up and looked at Fern. "Company's coming."

"Want me to tell Zanna to set up the Hooch Hut?"

"Nah, I'll do it myself. She'd probably take a few nips."

"I've never caught her drinking, and you know I keep an eye on your liquor."

"They all drink, Little Bit. She probably waters it down."

"Mmm. I didn't think of that."

"That's what I'm here for, honey. To think for you. Now hop in that tub and hurry up."

"Alright." Fern gave him a quick peck on the cheek. "I'm

sorry I had to tell you those nasty things."

"And I'm sorry you had to hear them, but don't you worry your pretty little head. You know I'll take care of things."

Junkin was finishing with the bar set-up when Zanna answered the doorbell and sent the Richardsons out to the pool. Junkin all but yanked a manila envelope from Laverne's hands and tore it open. He held it up to the light.

"This is even better than I remembered."

"Who is that?" Doyle asked. "Laverne wouldn't tell me."

"It's supposed to be a secret, honey," Laverne said. "You see, the mayor and I—"

"I'll tell him," Junkin interjected. He'd knew that the best way to deal with Laverne's interminable rambling was to talk over her. He handed the photo to Doyle. "Can you guess who this is?"

Doyle's eyes widened as he ogled the curvaceous beauty in the black swimsuit, curly black hair cascading over bare shoulders. "Va-va-voom! Wasn't for the dirty face she could be in Playboy!"

"Who you boys talking about?" The loud clack of heels announced Fern's approach, a vision in shocking pink toreador pants with turquoise blouse and matching mules. She sucked on a Mountain Dew. "Well?"

"Give her the photo, Doyle."

Fern sipped again and studied the image. Luckily, she was facing the pool because when she figured out it was Cassandra she spewed a mouthful of Mountain Dew into the water. Junkin grabbed the photo before it got wet.

"Little Bit, I've told you a thousand times not to drink and think at the same time!"

"I can't believe that's—"

"None of us could believe it neither, but Laverne took that picture at Anrita's party."

When Junkin paused to light a Lucky, Laverne seized her opportunity to talk. "Cassandra didn't know I took it though because she made me promise not to take any pictures but when she was cutting up and carrying on I just snuck behind Helen Highwater and took one. You know Helen's a right hefty gal and she used to be Helen Chesney before she married Tim Highwater and got that funny name. They say she can hit the highest note in hymn-dom when she sings How Great Thou Art, but I think—"

Junkin ignored her diatribe. "This photo is worth its weight in gold, and I plan to use it for all its worth."

"What've you got in mind?" Doyle asked.

"Running this bitch out of town, that's what. She was hateful to Fern this afternoon and besides that I hear she's been teaching filth to our kids."

Fern brightened. "So, you're going to show that picture to Dan Warren and demand that he fire her?"

Junkin had no intention of involving himself with more blackmail. He puffed out his chest and said, "No, I think the principal should make his decision without any undue influence from the mayor's office, but I'll arrange to have a copy of that photo delivered to the school."

"That's it?" Doyle asked. "No letter or nothing?"

"Nah. I think a photostat is enough to convince him the woman is unfit to teach in the Tennessee public school system."

Fern was dazzled as usual by her husband's brilliance. "That sounds wonderful, honey!"

"I don't see how Principal Warren can refuse to act," Doyle added.

"Me neither." Junkin gulped his beer and belched, obviously pleased with himself. "Honey, I need a private moment with Doyle, so why don't you sweet things fetch us some nibbles?"

"How about some potato chips and that new California dip?" Fern asked.

"That's fine." Junkin looked at Doyle. "Never thought I'd like anything named after those West Coast commies, but that stuff's pretty good."

"We'll be back in a jiffy."

"Take your time." Junkin motioned for Doyle to scoot his chair closer. "Speaking of Playboy, you got any new issues of Adam and Swank?"

"Yeah, but I ain't through with them yet." Doyle guffawed. "If you know what I mean."

"I know what you mean and I wish to hell you'd hurry up. I need 'em too."

"I'll drop them by your office sometime next week." When Junkin gave him a look, he added, "In the usual plain brown wrapper marked 'personal.' "

"Good man. Now I got something else I need to talk about. Can you get Laverne's key to the Harrington plant again?"

"Sure. She's got so much crap dangling from that damned chain, she never missed it the first time. I'm not sure she even remembers Anrita giving it to her."

"I was never clear on why Anrita did that." Junkin said.

"Gave it to her the day they dedicated the plant. Said it was because they're family."

"Thank God she did because you need to pay another visit to the plant."

"What for? I looked real good that last time and didn't find nothing."

"Maybe you didn't look as good as you think. That damned recipe's got to be there, and I wanna get my hands on it before Calvin Harrington corners every goddamned salad market in the South. I've already got people scouting for kitchen locations in Memphis and Birmingham."

"Doesn't Fern make chicken salad?"

"Yeah, and it tastes like owl shit. I asked her what Anrita puts in hers to make it so good and she said she couldn't figure it out. That's why we need to get our hands on the original recipe and change it just enough to dodge a lawsuit."

"I don't know, Junkin. After looking around myself, I decided that if that recipe's in the plant, it's in a safe somewhere. The one I saw on the kitchen wall didn't have any spices except salt and pepper."

Junkin was losing patience. "You sure you looked everywhere?"

Doyle thought a moment. "I didn't check the restrooms."

"Maybe there's a storage room or something in there. You got to consider every possibility."

"Alright. I'll take another look."

"And don't make such a damned mess this time."

"I told you I was rushed, Junkin. I kept hearing weird noises from that plastics plant next door and I got all jumpy."

"Alright. Alright. How soon can you get over there?"

"Laverne said Anrita and Calvin were taking John to the mountains this weekend. With them outta town, I can take as much time as I want."

"Perfect! Like I said before, if you find that recipe, we'll hit the Harringtons where they live and be millionaires before you know it."

"I'll do my best, boss."

Junkin downed his beer. "Let's get into our trunks, buddy. I need to cool off after all this talk."

Not ten feet away, Zanna watched through the venetian blinds in the pool house which doubled as a laundry room. While loading the washing machine, she overheard every word of the ugly conversation. Once the men were gone, she slipped back into the house unseen.

38

Fern climbed on top of a picnic table and told Myrna to hand her Sheriff Kirkendol's bullhorn. She aimed it toward the two-dozen bored, restless teen-agers assembled in Crockett Park. "Alright, everybody. Y'all listen up!"

Lurleen whispered in Dottisue's ear. "Something tells me this is going to be amateur night in Dixie."

"Literally," Dottisue whispered back.

"This is the first of two rehearsals," Fern continued. "The second is the Saturday night before the beauty pageant. The bleachers will be in place by then so everyone will learn their seat assignments. The queen and her escort will be the last to take their places, but since we don't know the winner yet, today will be a simple walk-through. Any questions?"

"No, Mrs. Abernathy!" everyone called back.

"Good." Fern pointed to the park entrance. "Line up in pairs on the other side of the stone arch. Alright, everybody. Let's hustle."

"Come along, your majesty," Dottisue said to Lurleen.

"What are you talking about?"

"Oh, you know you're going to win."

"Says who?"

"Everybody, that's who."

"That's news to me." Lurleen tossed her head as they fell in line and moved toward the gates. "I think the whole beauty pageant is ridiculous."

"Your mama sure doesn't."

"Don't remind me." Lurleen knew Dottisue was right, especially since she'd overheard her mother's endless bragging about how her daughter was the prettiest, most talented girl in town. If she became Queen of the Sesquicentennial, Lurleen knew people would think her father bribed the judges, but where her parents were involved she had no voice.

She took Rocky's arm as John and Dottisue fell in behind. "Let's get this stupid thing over with."

"The sooner, the better," Rocky said. "We're meeting the sheriff in an hour."

"Are you sure that's a good idea?" Lurleen asked.

"We don't have any choice. The whole town's up in arms about the Klan, and it's our civic duty to tell the sheriff what we saw."

"Rocky's right," John said.

Dottisue was scared. "I hope he'll keep our names secret."

"Sure, he will. I see that stuff on Dragnet all the time. You know. Witnesses going to the police and asking for anonymity."

Worried that someone might overhear, Lurleen changed the subject. "Dot, what are you doing in the talent competition?"

"I can't decide between rifle twirling and playing water glasses."

"At least you can do more than one thing. Singing is my only talent."

"That's what you think!" John whispered.

She gave him a playful swat. "Hush!"

John twirled an imaginary villain's his moustache. "You have hidden talents, my pretty."

"And if you don't pipe down you've seen the last of them!"

The walk-through of the Cavalcade of Cavaliers and their Beautiful Belles took over an hour because Fern fussed with endless details. She repeatedly changed the procession route and rearranged the twelve couples until Lurleen reminded her they were not human chess pieces. By the time Fern sent everyone home, John, Rocky, Lurleen and Dottisue barely made their appointment with Sheriff Kirkendol. Since he'd known all of them since they were kids, his manner was avuncular as he ushered them into his office. He turned to Rocky.

"Okay, young man. What's this urgent business you need

to discuss?"

Rocky steeled himself and expelled an answer. "It's about the Ku Klux Klan, sheriff."

"What about it?"

"We know who they are. A lot of them anyway."

Kirkendol closed his office door. "How did you come by this information?"

"Dottisue and I were in the hayloft of the barn out at the Boruff farm and—"

Kirkendol looked from one face to another. "Did you four switch partners or something?"

Rocky realized his mistake too late. "Damn!"

"Don't worry about it, son. I'm not your father. Who you kids date is your business. Now tell me what you saw."

"We saw a Klan meeting, sir."

"Were they in robes?"

"No, sir."

"Then how do you know it was the Klan?"

Dottisue piped up in a shaky voice. "Because they burned a cross and talked about being at the Tower Theater,"

"And discussed plans for disrupting the Labor Day celebration," Rocky added.

"Do you know these men?"

"Yes, sir. Almost every one of them."

Kirkendol handed Rocky a legal pad. "Would you write down their names please?"

"Yes, sir."

When the sheriff saw the first name on the list, he turned to Lurleen, who had not said a word. "Did you know this about your daddy, young lady?"

"No, sir, I didn't."

"Were you there too?" Lurleen shook her head no. "Then why are you here?"

"Mostly moral support," John interjected. "Plus we were the ones who dropped them off at the farm."

"Where were you and Miss Abernathy during this alleged

Klan gathering?"

Rocky didn't appreciate the implication. "We're not alleging anything, sheriff. We know what we saw."

Kirkendol ignored him and repeated his question to John.

"We were ... we were parked about a mile down the road."

"Why did you go your separate ways that night?"

"Privacy!" Lurleen's loud declaration triggered a brief smile from the taciturn sheriff. "Rocky and Dottisue told us what happened when we picked them up. If you'd seen how scared they were, you'd know they're telling the truth."

Kirkendol said nothing, and when Rocky finished writing names, the sheriff slipped the list inside a desk drawer.

"What're you going to do with that information?" Rocky asked.

"I'll go over it later. I have other business this afternoon."

John, who was still fuming over his father's mistreatment, challenged Kirkendol's cavalier response. "Those are dangerous men on that list, sheriff, and it took a lot of courage for Rocky and Dottisue to come forward."

Rocky jumped in. "Surely you're gonna stop those jerks from messing up this ... this Labor Day thing!" He had never been able to wrap his lips around the word "sesquicentennial."

Lurleen spoke up before Kirkendol could respond. "May I say something, sheriff?"

"Go ahead, Miss Abernathy."

"The whole town knows my father's done some underhanded things, and I hope you're not going to give him special treatment simply because he's the mayor."

If Kirkendol was surprised by the girl's disloyalty, he didn't show it. "Far as I know, those men didn't do anything illegal except trespass on someone else's land."

"Then arrest them for that!" Kirkendol's stare made Rocky recognize his second big mistake. "Oh. You'd have to arrest Dot and me for trespassing too, wouldn't you?"

The sheriff raised his hands when he saw the stricken

young faces. "Everybody calm down and stop jumping the gun. The Ku Klux Klan is a legal organization, and those men are completely within their rights to gather and discuss their business."

John was appalled. "So you're not going to do anything with Rocky's list?"

"I told you I'd look it over," Kirkendol replied coolly.

"Come on, y'all," Rocky groused. "We're wasting our time."

Lurleen hung back as her friends filed out of the office. "Is Rocky right, Sheriff Kirkendol? Were we wasting our time?"

"Don't believe everything you hear, Miss Abernathy."

"Believe me, I don't. Our teacher Miss Maddox taught us to believe half of what we see and hear, and even less of what we read."

"Is that right?"

"Yes, sir. And I have to say I'm very disappointed in what you've said and done today."

Kirkendol looked pained. "I'm sorry you feel that way, young lady."

"So am I." Lurleen turned to go, but he asked her to shut the door. "Something else, sheriff?"

"One more question. Did you tell your father that you know about him and the Klan?"

"Of course not. He'd badger me nonstop until I told him how I found out."

"Meaning he'd know you're secretly dating the Abernathy boy."

"Exactly." Lurleen was resigned. "I'm sure you know how demanding and persuasive my father can be."

"I think everyone would agree that he's a man who knows how to get what he wants." Lurleen saw the mask of caution drop for a second before slipping back into place. "I'm glad you're not going to say anything. In fact, the less said about this whole business the better."

"So you plan to hush everything up?"

"Yes, young lady. I do."

"But why?"

"I have my reasons, just as you have your reasons for making your father believe your boyfriend is Rocky Millsaps."

"You're right about that. Will you really keep my secret?"

"Yes, ma-am, I will."

Lurleen couldn't help smiling. "I think I got the better deal."

The sheriff's eyes drifted to the desk drawer and back. "Don't be so sure, Miss Abernathy."

39

By the end of June, Andy had finished landscaping the old slave cabin. Eulalie was so thrilled that she decided to show off his work at a Fourth of July barbecue. She invited forty of Meander's finer citizens and kept Lou busy in the kitchen for two days. She hired Zanna to help serve and a crew of men to set up canopies and tables covered with red, white and blue cloths. The American flag flew proudly on a pole by the bluff, and the grounds looked festive enough for the pages of Holiday magazine. Eulalie did a last-minute inspection, heaping praise on Lou and Zanna before dressing in a long sleeved white lace afternoon dress and her best pearls. She came downstairs to find Andy waiting in the foyer. She was pleased to see how handsome he looked in his seersucker suit.

"I do believe you're the most dashing gentleman in Meander!"

Andy's cheeks colored. "I still can't believe you've asked me to act as host."

"There's no one I'd rather have at my side. Besides, since you're half my age, we'll give folks something to talk about."

"My customers will sure be surprised since I've never socialized with them before."

"High time you did."

"Thank you, Eulalie."

"Whatever for?"

"Being my only real friend."

"Now don't start that or you'll ruin my maquillage."

"Your what?"

"A French word for make-up." She flicked an imaginary piece of lint from her lacy sleeve. "I'm sorry. I guess being all dressed up made me want to use fancy words. In any case, I'm the one who should thank you, for finding that old Bible

and that law book. What I've read so far is going to tu[ ]
town on its ear."

"You sure you don't want to share some of those findings?"

"Patience, young man. As Hercule Poiret says, 'All will be revealed.' " Eulalie slipped an arm through his when she heard cars on the circular gravel drive. "Our guests are here."

They spent a half hour receiving people and the next fifteen minutes giving an interview to Louise Sebby, the local society columnist. Louise took several photos of Eulalie and Andy before excusing herself to circulate.

"Soon as I get those flashbulb spots out of my eyes, we'll circulate too." Eulalie squinted toward the terrace. "If that's Zanna with the champagne, flag her down." Moments later Eulalie enjoyed her first sip of the day. "Ahhh. I do love the way this stuff buzzes right through me. Don't you want some, Andy?"

"I think I'll have a bourbon."

"Bar's over there. Help yourself." She waved as Anrita and Sylvianne headed in her direction. "Hello, there!"

"Hey, Miss Sugar!" Sylvianne called. "You look like you stepped off a bandbox!"

"You too, sugar." Eulalie offered her cheek for the ladies to peck and admired Sylvianne's peach silk blouse, white pleated skirt and picture hat. Anrita was equally sweet in a pale yellow sun dress and matching hat. "You both look fresh as daisies."

"I hope I can stay that way in this heat," Anrita said.

"I know what you mean." Eulalie heard a snap when the flag fluttered atop the pole. "Looks like a nice breeze is coming up off the river. Let's find some shade and enjoy it." She took their arms and strolled across the lawn. "Y'all tell me what's going on around town. I've been absolutely buried here at Blufftop, what with Andy landscaping the back and me helping Fern Abernathy with the sesquicentennial slide show."

"Fern had us editing the obituaries," Anrita reported.

"It was that or getting tangled up in chicken wire," Sylvianne said. When Eulalie gave her a blank look, she added, "She wanted us to work on floats."

"I swan! Where does that woman get her gall?"

"Heaven only knows, but isn't she an absolute treat to work with?"

"My dear, if your tongue were more firmly in your cheek you'd have an inverted dimple."

Sylvianne let out a whoop. "Score one for Miss Sugar!"

"We're all friends here, so I see no need to be coy," Eulalie said. "That woman is a royal pain, and when I think about her and her hateful husband running this sweet little town into the ground, I get apoplexy."

"Join the club," Sylvianne said.

"I don't know what can be done about them," Anrita lamented. "Calvin and I have talked about it, and as long as Junkin has the sheriff in his corner and keeps appointing his cronies to positions of power, we're helpless."

"I nearly fainted when he appointed Donald Watkins comptroller," Sylvianne said.

Eulalie looked pained. "That Watkins clan has been here almost as long as mine, and they've never amounted to a hill of beans. They've lived in those same ratty shacks by the railroad tracks and done nothing but burp out more babies for the welfare rolls. None of them ever finished grammar school and I can't think of a single one ever holding a job."

Sylvianne was aghast. "So now we have a dunce trying to balance the city books."

Anrita said, "I'm sure Junkin doesn't let Mr. Watkins anywhere near the books when he can do it himself with no one to answer to."

"At least we have history in our favor," Eulalie said as they slipped inside the food tent.

"What do you mean?"

"The last Russian tsar saw himself as an autocrat too, and

we all know how that turned out."

"Yes, indeed!" Sylvianne said.

"Now I say we stop talking politics or we're going to ruin the occasion." Eulalie gestured at an array of silver trays laden with hors d'oeuvres. "Lou and Zanna have worked their fingers to the bone for two days, so please help yourself." She glanced at her watch. "The barbecue should be ready in half an hour."

"What time are the fireworks?"

"Right after sunset, and we have the best view in town, if I do say so myself. Now if you'll excuse me, I'll help myself to a bit more bubbly."

Eulalie flagged Lou for another glass of champagne and headed for Andy when she spotted him under the terrace awning. "What are you doing up here by yourself?"

"You want the truth?"

"Please."

"I haven't been to a party since I was a little boy, and it was certainly nothing like this."

"So?"

"So I'm a bit nervous."

"Then finish that bourbon and have another."

"You know I'm not a big drinker."

"All the more reason to have a second belt." Eulalie patted his cheek as she scanned the gathering. "Why don't you go talk to Helen Highwater? She dropped by yesterday and said she loved how you landscaped the cabin. She's thinking about redoing her iris rock garden. Maybe she'll offer you a job."

"You always seem to be looking out for me."

"I'm just playing Auntie Mame, dear boy. Please indulge me."

Andy took Eulalie's advice and relaxed after a second bourbon. Not only did Helen offer him a landscaping job, but he soon found himself drifting easily from one conversational group to another. By the time everyone had feasted on Eulalie's splendid barbecue and dusk cast long shadows across the lawn, he realized he'd had more fun in the last two hours than in the last ten years.

"You're right," he told Eulalie as they settled into wicker lawn chairs and prepared to watch the fireworks. "That extra shot of bourbon did the trick."

"So I see. Everyone's talking about how charming you are, and I couldn't agree more."

"Sometimes I think you're more Henry Higgins than Auntie Mame."

"Maybe so, but as long as … what in the world is that?"

"What?"

"Through the trees over there. I was taught not to point, but this may be an emergency."

"It looks like smoke." Andy craned his neck. "Probably some kids setting off fireworks."

"I better take a look." Eulalie got to her feet, and, with Andy close behind, hurried to the edge of the bluff. Only thirty yards away, alongside a fence marking the end of the Saunders's property, was the source of the smoke. When Eulalie saw fire, she grabbed Andy's arm. "Dear Lord! Look at that!"

"Damn!"

Thrust between two enormous boulders was a burning cross twelve-feet tall. As the gasoline-soaked wood ignited, flames crackled and shot ever higher into the air. The ugly blaze was big enough to be seen by the holiday crowds gathered by the river down below, no doubt the Ku Klux Klan's intent.

"We can't let them get away with this!" Eulalie cried. By then everyone else had seen the blaze and gathered for a closer look. She turned to the crowd. "Do you men have any idea what to do about that monstrosity?"

"Do you have a hose that would reach that far?" Floyd Rochelle asked.

"No good," Calvin warned. "Water might spread those

flames to the woods."

Dave Mearns looked grim. "I think I've found my Sunday editorial."

"I hope you've got plenty of space," Andy said, "because your story's about to get a lot bigger."

"What do you mean?"

"Never mind. Come on, Miss Sugar!" Everyone watched as Andy and their surprisingly spry hostess loped toward the house. Once inside, Andy headed for the library. "Where's the key to the gun cabinet?"

"God in heaven! You're not going to shoot someone!"

"Not some *one*. Some *thing!* That damned cross to be exact."

"Don't be ridiculous, Andy. Firing bullets won't do anything."

"No, but firing the elephant gun sure will!"

"Darling boy!" she cried, rushing to her desk to extract keys. "You're brilliant!"

"Is it loaded?" Andy asked as she unlocked the cabinet.

"Of course not, but that drawer down there is full of ammunition." Andy rummaged noisily through a stack of boxes. "Find anything?"

"Here's one that says Nitro Express and has the silhouette of an elephant on it." Andy popped it open and pulled out a cartridge the size of his hand. "This has to be it!"

"Do you know how to load that thing?"

"My Uncle Ralph took me hunting a lot, so I ought to be able to figure it out."

"How's your aim?"

"I was so good on the firing range that the other boy scouts hated me." Eulalie watched anxiously as Andy popped a cartridge into the barrel and locked it in place. "Ready for an adventure, Auntie Mame?"

"Lead the way, Patrick!"

In the short time they were gone, flames from the cross had climbed high into the darkening skies. Everyone was still huddled by the edge of the bluff, but they parted like the Red Sea when they saw Andy coming their way.

"Good Lord, Andy!" Calvin called. "Is that an elephant gun?"

"The one and only!" Andy tossed his suit coat to Eulalie and cupped a hand to his mouth to make himself heard. "Everybody back away. This thing's gonna kick, and I have no idea how hard or where I might end up."

"Please be careful!" Eulalie called.

While everyone held their breaths, Andy took aim at the blazing target. It loomed large and bright through the cross-hairs, and for a moment he was hypnotized. Something told him if he hesitated he'd never shoot, so he planted his feet far apart, assumed a stance and pulled the trigger. The resulting crack was deafening, but Andy barely heard it as he catapult-ed backwards from the powerful recoil. As he landed on his back, he heard a distant cheer from the crowd. He lay un-moving with the wind knocked out of him until he felt a cool hand on his forehead.

"Lie still," Lou soothed. "You'll be alright in a minute."

"Did I hit the cross?"

"Glory be, child! You blew that sucker to kingdom come!"

A hundred feet below, an astonished crowd watched chunks of flaming wood explode from atop the bluff and fall sizzling into the waters of the Tennessee River. They'd barely had time to register that strange sight when the riverbank ignited with fireworks. Everyone cheered the display except Junkin Abernathy who raged with impotent anger when his blazing cross of hatred was blown to smithereens.

"Somebody's gonna pay for this!"

40

The embers of the cross had barely cooled when Junkin called an emergency Klan meeting at the Boruff farm. His outrage was reflected by the biggest turn-out since the Tower Theater demonstration, and it grew when he got a good look at Dub and Doyle. Neither had been seriously injured, but both had small burns on their arms and faces and were still picking splinters from their hair. Junkin took Doyle into the barn.

"You gonna be able to handle our business tomorrow night?"

"Hell, yeah. These marks ain't as bad as they look."

"What did you tell Laverne?"

"That I ran into some kid's fireworks. She didn't give it a second thought."

"So no one knew it was you and Dub up on the bluff?"

"No way. We got the cross set up the night before, and by the time we set it on fire it was almost dark."

"What the devil happened?"

"We were making sure the cross was lit good when the damned thing blew up. At first I thought we'd been struck by lightning."

"What the devil caused it?"

"I don't know but it sorta reminded me of the bazookas in the war. You better believe me and Dub had some serious puckering going on!"

"Could someone have done something from the Saunders property?"

"That explosion was so fierce it could've come from any-where."

"Alright now. Let's think this thing through. The only people who knew about this were you, me, Sonny and Dub. You didn't blab anything to Laverne, did you?"

"Hell, no. You know me better than that." Doyle bristled. "Why don't you ask Dub if he told one of the girls at the Kitty Korner?"

"Calm down, man. I'm trying to figure all the angles because it's like someone knew our plan and was lying in wait."

"So?"

"So I'm gonna get to the bottom of this if it's the last thing I do." Junkin slipped thumbs under his suspenders as he swelled his chest. "I figure if we've got invisible enemies, who better than to destroy them than the Invisible Empire?"

"I hear you."

"Hey, boss. You got a minute?"

Junkin saw Sonny Hull's skinny silhouette in the barn doorway. "What do you want?"

"I got some news."

"It'd better be good because I'm sure as shit in no mood for the other kind."

"Oh, it's good. Real good."

Junkin turned back to Doyle. "Go back outside and calm the troops 'til I get there. If we don't talk again, be sure to call me tomorrow night soon as you finish your job."

"Will do."

Junkin turned back to Sonny. "Okay, Skeezix. What's up?"

"I finally found that guy who lives out the Old Quarry Road."

"Yeah? What is he a hermit or something?"

"I reckon he's an 'or something.' "

"What're you talking about?"

"Hell, the man was naked as a jaybird!"

"What?!"

"Yes, siree. I was looking all over the place and finally found him washing himself in the creek."

"So what? That shack of his probably don't have indoor plumbing. A man's gotta take a bath somewhere."

"I thought that too, until he come right out and told me he was one of them nudists. You know. Like in your magazines."

Junkin ignored the reference. "Go on."

"He asked what I was doing on his property, so I told him I was hiking by myself and apologized for bothering him."

Junkin chuckled. Sonny had never had an original idea in his life, at least none he knew about. "Good thinking."

"Yeah, I was right proud of myself." Sonny preened a little. "Anyway, we talked for a while and when I was about to steer the conversation around to the fire, he brought it up himself."

"What did he say?"

"He said he wasn't there at the time, but that he was still pissed off that it burned several acres of his land."

"So he didn't see anything, huh? I reckon that's good news, but I still don't know where that damned Hickman got his information."

"I got something better than that, boss. Me and this guy, name's Jake Sawyer, talked some more, and he turned out to be real nice. At first, it was peculiar talking to somebody without no clothes on, but after a while it felt pretty natural. In fact, when Jake said it was okay if I went skinny dipping too, I did."

"You what?!"

"Aw, there wasn't nothing queer about it. It was hot as hell, and that cool water felt damned good. Besides, if I hadn't done it I wouldn't have found my other big news."

"Good Lord, man. I'm beginning to think I'm talking to Laverne Richardson. Finish your damned story."

"Okay. So Jake and me talked some more and he asked if I'd ever been to a nudist camp and when I told him no he said I should go if I like being naked outdoors with naked women. I told him that sounded damned good to me and that's when he said he was planning on turning his place into a nudist camp."

Junkin's jaw dropped. "Are you shitting me?!"

"No, siree. He says he's got himself a partner who's raising money, and pretty soon they'll start building things. You know. A swimming pool and a volleyball court and stuff like that. They're gonna call the place Sunny Side Up. Ain't that cute?"

Junkin wondered yet again if this moron was ever going to finish his story. "I don't give a rat's ass if they call it the Taj Mahal. What's your big news?"

Sonny looked crushed. "I thought you'd want some background info on the place, but I guess that's enough, huh?"

"More than enough."

"Okay, then. The big news is that his partner is Reverend Hickman."

For the first time in his life, Junkin felt like he was hallucinating. Surely, he hadn't heard right because things that appear too good to be true usually are.

"Are you absolutely sure?"

"I only know one Reverend Hickman, boss."

"I'll be double damned."

All Junkin could think about was that the money Hickman said was going toward a new church organ was slated to fund a camp for people to run around naked. It was so crazy and convoluted that he started laughing and couldn't stop. When he finally regained his self-control, he wiped away tears and put his arm around Sonny's thin shoulders.

"I apologize, old buddy. That long story was more than worth listening to. Hell, it even had a moral."

"It did?"

Junkin nodded. "The Lord works in strange and mysterious ways."

41

Doyle's night got off to a wretched start. In his haste to sneak off to the Harrington plant, he'd let Laverne catch him taking Anrita's plant key off her key chain. As if that weren't bad enough, not being one to think fast, he'd blurted out the reason he needed it. He was relieved when Laverne approved his plan, but relief turned to misery when she and her non-stop babble insisted on coming along.

"You just said you've been out there before and come up empty-handed, so maybe you just need a woman to show you where to look. We're just talking about a recipe for heaven's sake, but I suppose either way two heads are better than one, but I just can't understand a man keeping secrets like this from his wife and—" Laverne blathered on and on as usual, but nineteen years of marriage had taught Doyle to tune her out after the first sentence. It was the only one that ever had any remotely worthwhile information.

They got to the plant a little after nine. Doyle was thankful that the plastics plant was shut down for the holiday weekend, so noise from next door wouldn't give him the willies again. He parked the car and turned to Laverne.

"You're sure the Harringtons are in the Smokies?"

"Far as I know. I mean, she's been talking about this trip for weeks and how much she's looking forward to having dinner at the Blackstone and—"

"That's all I need to hear," he said, cutting off any burgeoning diatribes. He took a flashlight from the glove compartment and got out of the car. "Keep quiet and come on."

Once Anrita's master key let them into the plant, Doyle clicked on his flashlight and headed for the rest rooms. "You look in the ladies' room and I'll check the men's."

"Okay."

They explored the restrooms and found no storage cabinets or doors leading anywhere except to the stalls, but they did make a discovery when they returned to the hall. Someone flipped a light switch, and they found themselves facing Calvin and Anrita Harrington.

"What the hell—?!" Doyle gasped.

Calvin glared. "I was thinking the same thing. You want to tell us what you two are doing here?"

Laverne's usually sweet face went through a peculiar transformation making the Harringtons think they were talking to a stranger. The sensation was reinforced when they heard her icy reply.

"Because you don't deserve all that money, that's why."

Anrita was floored. "What are you talking about?"

"You know good and well that you stole that chicken salad recipe from our grandmother."

"What?!"

Doyle was equally surprised. "You never told me that!"

"I told you lots of times, but you never listened."

"Where in the world did you get that fool notion, Laverne? Sure, I use a little lemon juice and paprika like Mam-ma, but the rest is my own creation."

"Bull! I remember tasting the exact same thing at Mamma's when we were little."

"That's impossible. The ingredients are different."

"No, they're not!" Laverne snapped. "You're lying!"

"Laverne!" Anrita was so stupefied by her cousin's vitriol that she actually took a step backwards. "How can you say that?"

"Because it's true, and it's about time somebody knocked you off your high horse!"

"Is this my reward for showing you nothing but kindness all these years?" Anrita turned to Calvin. "Here's living proof that no good deed goes unpunished."

"Yup."

"Baloney!" Laverne shot back.

Anrita's sweet nature was fading fast. "If you truly believe

I stole Mam-ma's recipe, make up a batch of her chicken salad and we'll have a taste test. You can even pack the jury."

"If I had the recipe I wouldn't be here," Laverne snarled. "You stole it, and you know it."

"That's enough!" Calvin ordered. "The issue is not any damned recipe but the fact that you two are guilty of breaking and entering."

"Is that so?" Doyle drew himself up and looked at Anrita. "Did you or did you not give Laverne a key to the plant of your own free will?"

"Sure, I did, because I trusted her and because she knew she was to use it only for emergencies. I never imagined she'd use it to burglarize the place."

Doyle looked at Laverne. "When Anrita gave you that key, did she specify how you were to use it?"

"No," Laverne lied. "Never."

Calvin was about to lose his temper. "Forget about the damned key. Laverne confessed that she was after the recipe, and we caught you red-handed."

"You think that'll stand up in a court of law?" Doyle taunted. "It's your word against ours."

"I guess there's only one way to find out."

"You're right. Let's call the sheriff." Before Calvin could respond, Doyle smirked. "On second thought, maybe that's not such a good idea. I understand y'all aren't on the best of terms these days."

Calvin felt Anrita take his arm. "It's not all Doyle's fault, dear. We know he didn't dream this up by himself. He's never had any business sense, much less two nickels to rub together. Even with my recipe, there's no way he could finance a big operation like ours."

"Of course not, but there's someone else who could. Junkin Abernathy's behind it, like he's behind every other dirty deal in this town."

"You don't know what you're talking about!" Doyle growled.

Calvin was the picture of cool as he dropped the first bomb. "Come off it, man. We know you and Junkin planned this latest break-in by his swimming pool."

"You're crazy!"

"The same night you schemed to get Cassandra Maddox fired," Anrita weighed in. "Good heavens, Laverne! How could you betray Cassie? You not only broke your promise not to take photos at my party, but turned right around and used them at her expense. Cassie has never been anything but sweet to you and—"

Laverne didn't hear a word Anrita was saying. She was too busy exchanging bewildered looks with Doyle. As the truth dawned on them, they said the name at the same time.

"Zanna!"

"Yes, Zanna," Anrita confirmed. "She overheard the whole thing and thank goodness had the courage to tell us about it."

Laverne was seething. "When Fern hears this, she'll fire her black ass so fast it'll make Zanna's head swim!"

"Don't bother spreading your bad news. Zanna works for me now. In that kitchen right there in fact."

"That's colored loyalty for you," Laverne spat. "Ungrateful bitch!"

"My, my. What a sweet, Christian thing to say."

"Sounds like something she'd learn from Reverend Hickman," Calvin said.

"The preacher's got nothing to do with it," Laverne sputtered. "I learned about coloreds long before I met him."

"How charming," Anrita said when drool ran from both ends of Laverne's mouth. "I believe you could use a handkerchief."

"That's another reason I despise you, Anrita Harrington! You're so damned grand and condescending. You think you're better than everyone just because you made a few dollars off some damned chicken salad."

"Not everyone, cousin dear. Only you."

Calvin chortled. Laverne and Doyle seethed.

"That's exactly what I'm talking about, Anrita. Your way of twisting things around and using fancy words."

"You must be confusing me with Cassandra. She's the one with the exemplary vocabulary."

Laverne pointed a finger. "See there! It's big words like that I'm talking about because every time I turn around, you're—"

"That's enough!" Calvin wasn't about to endure another of Laverne's interminable run-on sentences. "You two get the hell out of here. Now!"

Anrita was shocked. "You're letting them get away scot-free?"

"Not exactly." Calvin grabbed Laverne's key ring, removed the key and tossed the ring to Doyle. "Now they can leave."

Doyle made no effort to regain the key. "C'mon, Laverne."

"Hold on a minute," Anrita said.

"What now?" Laverne griped.

"I could give you that recipe right now, and you could go into my kitchen and make a batch of chicken salad, but it would never taste as good as mine."

"What are you talking about?"

"My food is made with love and blessed before it's loaded onto the delivery trucks. The Bible says you reap what you sow, Laverne Richardson, and that's why your chicken salad would be bitter as gall."

Laverne's face blazed with rage as she hurled the word in Anrita's face. "Bullshit."

"Same to you, honey child." Anrita smiled sweetly. "And twice on Sunday."

42

"I have something for you, dear boy." Eulalie pointed to a large box on the coffee table. "I hope you like it because it's the first of several surprises you're getting tonight."

"What's the occasion?"

"The occasion is simply to make Miss Sugar happy." She waved a hand. "Now go ahead and open it."

Andy took the lid off the box from Rich's department store in Atlanta and peeled back the tissue paper. He knew what it was as soon as he glimpsed white linen. "Oh, no."

"Oh, yes!"

Andy lifted out a beautifully tailored suit and blinked when saw the label. "Made in Rome?!"

"Yes, Rome. Not too many townsfolks will appreciate it, but you and I certainly will."

Andy feigned shock. "Are you saying the local yokels are lacking in taste?"

"I'm saying whoever thinks we don't have peasants in this country has never been to a wrestling match or the Ramp Festival. Personally, I've never subscribed to the notion of visiting places you can smell before you see." She reconsidered. "That was tacky of me, wasn't it?"

"Sometimes tackiness and honesty go hand-in-hand."

"Indeed, they do." Eulalie waved a hand. "Try the jacket on."

Andy was embarrassed. "You know I can't accept something this expensive."

"Why in the world not? Really, Andrew. It's not as though I'm some crazy old lady splurging on her gigolo."

"Like in Sunset Boulevard?"

"You do love your movies, don't you?"

"They're my favorite escape mechanism," Andy confided. "After Clark's death, they're pretty much all that keep me going."

"Well, that suit is merely replacement for those seersucker trousers you ruined when you fired the elephant gun. You know, I still get upset thinking how badly you might have injured yourself."

"But—"

"No 'buts.' Now turn around and let me see how that jacket looks." Eulalie clapped her hands together when he obliged. "Perfect! You can get the trousers cuffed and hemmed here in town."

"You're much too generous, but of course you know I'm secretly thrilled."

"Good. Now leave that here, and let's go into the library. I have some important things to tell you."

Andy found the house oddly quiet. "Where's Lou tonight?"

"She's over at her friend Mary's house. They're making a special outfit for a dinner party I'm having in a couple of weeks."

"Special outfit? You mean like a new uniform?"

"You might say that. You'll see for yourself at the dinner. It will be dressy, so you can wear your new white suit."

"What's the date? Thanks to you I've got more work than I know what to do with, and I've been keeping some long hours."

"Saturday August tenth and don't you dare tell me your dance card is full."

Andy smiled. "I'll be there with bells on."

"Wonderful." Eulalie retrieved a folder from her desk and settled into her favorite chair. Andy sat opposite and watched her flip some papers. "Remember when I told you what I'd found in that family Bible is Meander's missing history link?"

"Yes, ma-am."

"You'll be happy to know I have tons more ammunition to make little Miss Fern squirm."

"In that case, I can't wait."

"For starters, Meander was primarily Unionist and abolitionist almost from the beginning. Slavery never had a good foothold in East Tennessee simply because of the lay of the land."

"Too mountainous for plantations?"

"Exactly. Slaves were a luxury in these parts, not an economic necessity. What's truly surprising is that at Tennessee's Constitutional Convention in seventeen ninety-six, delegates wanted to give free Negroes the right to vote if they met certain criteria, and an early movement to abolish slavery almost succeeded."

"Are you serious?!"

"Very serious. When secession came, East Tennessee tried to form a separate state loyal to the Union, but they failed."

"You mean they wanted to secede like West Virginie? That *is* a surprise."

"Indeed it is. What's more, according to these Bible entries, Meander was a hotbed of Unionist guerilla warfare. They spied, blew up bridges and cut telegraph lines to hamper the Confederacy. Control constantly shifted back and forth during the war which, by the way, is how the town of Seesaw got its name."

"I always wondered about that."

"To show you how divided things were, Tennessee provided more soldiers for the Confederate Army than any other state, but also more troops for the Union than any other Southern state. And of course more battles were fought here than anywhere except Virginia."

"Sounds like your script rewrite will be pretty extensive."

"We weren't exactly drenched in the moonlight and magnolias Fern described, but I can hardly replace Dixie with Yankee Doodle Dandy. There's no denying East Tennessee belonged to the Confederacy, and The Conquered Banner was written in Knoxville after all."

"The what?"

"It's the official requiem for the Lost Cause, and it certainly deserves mention."

"Did you find that in the family Bible too?"

"No. It's something I learned from Ida Turnbull, bless her heart. Miss Ida almost jumped out of her skin when I told her what you and I had uncovered. After I promised to donate the Bible to the library this fall, she was only too happy to help me put together a history slide show." When Andy looked worried, Eulalie said, "It's alright. She thinks it's just a hobby and has found beautiful public domain photos from the Bettmann Archive and Harper's Weekly. Earl Tipton is currently converting them to slides, and no doubt there will be a certain measure of surprise when I start the slide show."

"To put it mildly," Andy joked. "I'm wondering if you should get Sheriff Kirkendol to station a deputy between Miss Fern and the slide projector."

Eulalie turned serious. "The point is, Andy, that she wants a one-woman show promoting what she wants the citizens of Meander to believe. It's doubly wrong because she's not telling the truth."

"Like husband, like wife."

"Exactly. I may not be able to do anything about our corrupt mayor, but this opportunity is too golden to ignore." She gave him an impish look. "Don't you think there's something divinely providential about us getting the historical facts about our little hometown just in time for its one hundred fiftieth birthday?"

"Indeed, I do."

"Then you'll also agree that, for now, we need to keep that knowledge to ourselves."

"Absolutely."

"Alright then, but brace yourself because I'm about to tell you something personal that no other living soul knows, not even Lou."

Andy was taken aback. "I'm flattered since I know how close you two are."

"I'll tell her in time, but I believe you'll understand my decision once you hear me out. It's about those letters in the strong box. I read them that first night and haven't been able to stop thinking about them. They were love letters written by my grandfather, the Colonel, to a Knoxville woman named Bessie Winters. It turned out she was his mistress."

"Uh-oh."

"You have no idea how big an 'uh-oh' it is, my dear. Remember I told you that my grandmother, Rosalie, was addicted to laudanum? With her spending most of her time in a stupor, it's no real surprise that Granddaddy looked for female companionship elsewhere. The real surprise was finding out Bessie was an octoroon. Do you know what that is?"

"No idea."

"It's someone who is one eighth colored, and seven eighths white. I learned about them when Edward took me to New Orleans."

"I guess colored mistresses were pretty commonplace back then. Was this Bessie a slave?"

"Oh, no. She was a free woman of color. The Colonel was not only with her for many years, they even had a child together, a son born right in the middle of the Civil War. They couldn't marry of course because there were laws against miscegenation, but my grandfather saw to it that the child was taken care of. In fact, he was educated in London."

"Wow."

"Here's where it gets a little sticky, Andy, so please bear with me."

"Are you alright?" he asked. "You look a little peculiar."

"You'll know why in a minute." Eulalie cleared her throat. "Bessie died in eighteen-seventy-six, and my grandmother died a year later. The Colonel was left all alone, so he brought his son here and told everyone Randolph was his nephew. Because there were no other relatives, Randolph inherited Blufftop."

"What?!"

Eulalie reached inside her skirt pocket and pulled out a small envelope. "This was alongside the last letter my grandfather wrote Bessie. It's in his handwriting and is addressed To Whom It May Concern. You're free to read it."

As Eulalie expected, Andy's eyes widened and as he read that Randolph Lee Crockett, known publicly as the nephew of Colonel William Talmadge Crockett, was actually his son by Bessie Lee Winters, a free woman of color.

"Was Randolph your—?"

"Randolph was my father, which means that because my grandmother was a woman of color, I am one thirty-second black."

"I ... I don't know what to say."

"That makes two of us."

"When did Randolph stop being the Colonel's nephew and become his son?"

"I've no idea how he pulled that off. When I was growing up, I was told the Colonel was my grandfather, which is what I always called him. I don't know what people thought about that, any more than I know how many people knew the truth. They're all long dead, but who knows who said what to whom? For all I know, that little secret is still simmering somewhere in town. I suspect there's a record of Daddy's birth in the Knoxville Court House, although it's doubtful that the Colonel was listed as his father since his mother was a colored woman."

"Are you going to look for the record?"

"I don't know yet. I'm still overwhelmed."

"Forgive me for asking, but did you father look—?"

"Colored? You've seen photographs. He was actually lighter than me because Mama was Italian with deep olive skin. You know, I keep telling myself none of this matters because I'm the same person that I always was, but I'm not. I've taken a long hard look at who I am and what I believe where race is concerned. For obvious reasons I wasn't raised with racist ideals, but I'm still a product of time and place and can't shake some of the notions inside my head."

"Why do you have to do anything at all?"

"Because I want to understand myself better. I've started wondering about lots of things."

"Such as?"

"What prompted me to pull Lou out of that sharecropper's cabin and bring her here. I know lots of white Southern women played Lady Bountiful, but I'm no longer sure about my motives. Like many other so-called upstanding citizens, I've ignored this awful segregation system and the growing civil rights movement, but ever since the Ku Klux Klan came to town, it's bothered the hell out of me. "

"I'll bet it would help if you talked to Lou."

"I'm sure it would and it upsets me a little that I told you first."

"Because I'm white?"

"I'm ashamed to say so, but, yes."

"Don't be too hard on yourself, Eulalie. We live in a society with a long history of bigotry, and you can point fingers in a dozen directions. Whether it's the Europeans who brought over the first slaves or the Africans who sold their own people into slavery, there's more than enough blame to go around."

"I'm sure you're right, but—"

"It's going to take time."

Both turned toward a familiar voice.

"Eulalie!"

"In the library, Lou!"

Lou bustled into the room, a bolt of orange, green and yellow material tucked under one arm. "Oh! I thought you were alone."

"Hey, Lou." Andy noticed the bright fabric. "What in the world is that?"

"Something I need Miss Sugar's opinion on." She unrolled the exotic print and held it up to her neck. "Does this look African enough?"

"It's perfect! Where did you find it?"

"Watson's Basement in Knoxville." Lou looked at Andy.

"Have you told him what you're up to?"

"Not yet."

"Told me what?"

"In a minute, dear." Eulalie waved a hand at the fabric. "Do you have a pattern yet?"

"Mary got hold of some old National Geographic magazines about Africa and says she can copy an outfit from the photos. They're of the Gold Coast, but we hope it's close enough."

"I'm sure it will be fine, especially considering our audience."

Andy was totally lost. "Are you making some sort of tribal dress?"

"We're sure gonna try," Lou replied.

"Yes, indeed," Eulalie added.

Andy looked from one woman to another. "What are you two scamps up to?"

"You'll find out at the dinner party," Eulalie replied.

Andy watched Lou refold the gaudy fabric. "Are you going to wear that?"

"Not me. This is Mary's outfit."

"Who's Mary?"

"An old friend of mine from Knoxville. She recently moved here and is working for the Harringtons."

"I feel like I've walked in on the middle of a movie," Andy said.

"You have, my dear," Eulalie said. "One that's been running for centuries."

43

"Get in this house, man!" Calvin called from the front door as Grady got out of his car. "How the hell are you?"

"I'm fine." After dispensing with his usual bear hug, Grady said, "You sure you don't mind me dropping by at the last minute?"

"Not at all. I could use the company. I could also use some cheering up."

"What's wrong?"

"I'll tell you after I grab a couple of beers."

"Sounds good to me." Grady trailed Calvin into the kitchen. "Where's that pretty bride of yours?"

"Anrita's at the movies with one of her girlfriends. We'll go out to eat when she gets home. She's dying to meet you and said to say she's sorry she couldn't fix dinner tonight."

"I'll miss the home cooking, but that's what I get for coming on such short notice. I've got a couple days' break from filming, so I decided to treat myself to a drive through the Smokies. I was having lunch in Gatlinburg and thought I'd keep going and pay you folks a visit."

"You're spending the night of course."

"You know me, Cal. I hadn't thought that far."

"No need to. Anrita made up the guest room before she went to the movies."

"Man, she thinks of everything."

"Yup. Speaking of movies, how's Thunder Road coming along?"

"Fine. Just fine. Did some of my fanciest driving yet, if I do say so myself. Hey, it's only a B picture, but those things can hit it big when you've got a star like Bob Mitchum."

"I sure enjoyed talking to him that day I visited. He's real down to earth."

"He's the best. I've been in this crazy business a long time and worked with some real prima donnas. Believe me when I say some of these guys are nothing like what the publicity department churns out."

"You talking about anybody in particular?"

"Come on, buddy. You know I'm not one to kiss and tell."

"No, I reckon not." Calvin popped a cap and passed the bottle to Grady. "'Course that's not gonna make Anrita happy."

"If she likes Hollywood gossip, I've got a few clean stories stashed away." Out on the side porch, Grady said, "So, what's this about you needing to be cheered up?"

"Things are a mess around here lately, and I don't know what to do about it."

"You're not saying your marriage is in trouble."

"No, no. I don't think Anrita and I could be happier, but we might be if Meander ever got back to normal."

"What do you mean?"

"Aw, it's just small-town stuff that somebody living in a big city like Los Angeles would find stupid."

"Guess you've forgotten I grew up in Victoria, Kansas. I know all about small towns."

Calvin sipped his beer before delivering a quick summary of what had happened since Junkin Abernathy's ill-gotten election victory, including the ridiculous fines and ticketing and the invasion by the Ku Klux Klan. Grady proved to be a good listener. He even asked a few pertinent legal questions before commenting.

"I'd sure like to meet the fellow who blasted that burning cross with the elephant gun. Sounds like a special effects guy."

"I haven't seen an explosion like that since the war. It was pretty damned impressive."

"I'll bet. But on a serious note, your mayor sounds like a cut-rate Huey Long."

"I'm sorry to say those men breed like flies in the South."

"Yeah, but the South also produces beautiful, feisty belles and dashing gentlemen, riverboat gamblers and wild eccentrics. Hollywood loves 'em which is why they're in so many movies." Grady grinned. "Believe me I met some colorful folks over in North Carolina."

"I'm sure that's true, but right now Meander's a little too colorful to my way of thinking."

"So this Abernathy guy answers to nobody?"

"Nope. The City Council is supposed to provide balance, but that doesn't keep him from abusing his powers."

"You mean, like selling bootlegged booze while claiming it's against the law for you to drive a station wagon with a sign saying Moonshine Kills?"

"Yup."

"Is it against the law to advertise movies too?"

"Of course not. Why?"

"Just something I've been thinking about since we talked on the set."

"You've lost me."

"Stay right here!"

Calvin waited patiently while Grady hurried out to his car before returning with a long cardboard tube.

"I was saving this as a present for Anrita, but you may as well see it now. The movie's not set to open for months, so this is hot off the presses." Grady shook out the tube and unrolled a promotional poster for Thunder Road. "What do you think?"

Calvin took a closer look at a full color illustration of Robert Mitchum crouched with a gun in his hand and a flaming car crash behind him. The promotional copy screamed, "He ran moonshine and paid the devil!"

"Wow!"

"Are you thinking what I'm thinking?" Grady asked.

"That I should replace the Moonshine Kills sign on my station wagon with this poster?"

"But keep the corpse on top."

"So I'd only be promoting a movie, and there's no law against that."

"Bingo!"

"Yeah, but I'll bet Abernathy comes up with a way to get around it."

"Then you'll come up with something else. Screw the bastard!"

"I guess you're right."

"Damned right I am." Grady gave him a hard look. "You know something, Cal? I'm a little disappointed in you."

"What? Why?"

"Because when we were on Guadalcanal, you were one of the toughest soldiers I knew. It's not like you to give up without a fight."

"I appreciate you saying that, but that was a whole other ball game. I can't fight an enemy who's holding all the ammo."

"Then you've got to come up with your own ammo." Grady gestured at the poster. "This'll do for starters."

Calvin drew himself up. "You're right."

"Atta boy!" Grady clapped him on the back. "Now point me toward the little boy's room and get me another beer."

The combination of beer and an empathetic old friend lifted Calvin's spirits. He was rifling through the refrigerator when female voices came through the front door. Anrita and Sylvianne were back from the movies.

"I don't think Elizabeth Taylor ever looked more beautiful," Anrita said.

"Yeah, but did you notice how different Montgomery Clift looked in certain scenes?"

"Now that you mention it."

"They were in the middle of filming when he wrecked his car after leaving a party at Elizabeth's house. They had to rebuild one whole side of his face."

"How do you know all that?"

"Like you don't flip through my issues of Photoplay every

time you're next door."

"I might have glanced at one or two," Anrita confessed.

"You ladies must've seen Raintree County." Grady had been listening from the hallway.

"And you must be the famous stunt man and war hero, Grady Fletcher," Anrita said, holding out her hand. "I'm so happy to finally meet you after all these years."

"I'm the stunt man. Your husband is the war hero," Grady said. "And I sure was hoping for more than a handshake."

"Me too." Anrita gave him a warm hug. "This is my friend, Sylvianne McNeil."

Grady nodded politely. "Miss McNeil."

"It's Mrs. McNeil." Sylvianne's eyes scoured him like a searchlight. "Should I also be hoping for more than a hand-shake?"

"You can hope for anything you like, Mrs. McNeil."

"In that case, I'll hope for something more."

Anrita blushed. "Sylvianne!"

"If the man's from Hollywood, he doesn't shock easily, right, Mr. Fletcher?"

"You can call me Grady."

"And you can call me later, sir."

With a saucy toss of her head, Sylvianne headed out the back door, leaving Calvin and Anrita staring in disbelief.

"I have to apologize for Sylvianne's behavior," Anrita said. "She's my dearest friend and would do anything for me, but sometimes she—"

"Sometimes she knows exactly what she's doing," Grady finished. "Hey, I don't need an apology, but I do have a favor to ask."

"What's that?"

"I'm betting you want her phone number," Calvin said.

"And I'm betting you're right!" Grady pulled out an address book and jotted down the number. "Hey, Calvin. Remember those feisty Southern belles I was talking about earlier?"

"What about them?"

"I do believe I just met myself one."

44

Cassandra poured herself a bourbon and retreated to the screened porch at the back of her house. She settled onto the glider and rocked gently back and forth as a soft twilight rain blurred the flashing lightning bugs. What should have been a peaceful moment unraveled when she recalled what happened that afternoon when Principal Daniel Warren summoned her to his office. He said nothing was wrong, but his nervousness warned otherwise. Cassandra had been on the Meander High school faculty twenty-two years, twelve of them with Warren as principal. She knew him to be a milquetoast and was surprised when he got right to the point. She sipped the bourbon and replayed the scene in her mind.

"This arrived in a plain brown wrapper, Miss Maddox. Would you please explain it?" He pulled the provocative photostat from his desk and handed it to her. "Well?"

"It's very simple, Mr. Warren. I went to a party dressed as the Lil' Abner character, Moonbeam McSwine."

"Would you say your costume was a bit revealing?"

"I'd say it was a lot revealing, but since there were only church ladies present, what difference does it make?"

"It makes a difference because you're on the faculty of this school. As such, you are expected to conduct yourself with a certain amount of decorum. Especially in public."

"It was a private party at Anrita Harrington's house, and I specifically asked that no pictures be taken of me."

"Clearly that request was ignored."

"And clearly I learned who not to trust."

Warren's eyebrows rose. "So you know who took the picture?"

"Laverne Richardson was the only one with a camera."

"You were unaware that she took this photo?"

"It's obviously candid and un-posed, Mr. Warren. I was

cutting up for some other ladies when she snapped it."

"I see." Warren studied the photograph for such a long time that Cassandra grew uncomfortable. "Why would Mrs. Richardson want to … expose you in such a manner?"

"I've no idea."

"Surely there must be some explanation. Aren't you friends? Don't I remember something about a canasta club?"

"We play cards on occasion, but we were never what I would call friends."

Warren was silent a few long moments. "You've put me in a very difficult position, Miss Maddox. If this photo ever surfaced and it was revealed that I had prior knowledge of its existence, I could also be terminated."

"Terminated?!" Cassandra half rose from her chair before sitting again. "You're going to fire me over a photograph?"

"Miss Maddox, please try to understand my position."

"I've been at this school over twenty years, during which time my record has been exemplary. No teacher has a higher rate of students who went on to college, and—"

"Be that as it may," Warren interrupted, "there have been other questions raised about your teaching techniques and lesson plans."

"Such as?"

"Your recommended reading material is not consistent with that of the school."

"No, it's not, because the students in my advanced class are smarter, and when I encounter young people eager to learn, I see no point in limiting them to tired, old-fashioned curricula."

"You don't deny recommending Catcher in the Rye?"

"Oh, but I do. In fact, I told my students I was not allowed to recommend it, but that they could expect to find it on the final exam."

"You're walking a dangerous tightrope, Miss Maddox."

"I've been on that tightrope ever since I started here," Cassandra declared, "and I have no regrets. Those children were famished for knowledge, and I was only too happy to feed them."

"Have you read Catcher in the Rye?"

"Of course I have."

"And you didn't find it obscene?"

"To the contrary, I found it brilliant, especially in its handling of teen-aged angst and alienation. Holden Caulfield is a great hero of American literature."

"You don't find his smoking and drinking and lying objectionable?"

"Put into context, I find them admirable." When Warren looked pained, Cassandra's anger surged. "Why don't we stop beating around the bush and get right to the $64,000 question?"

"What might that be?"

"The book contains the word 'fuck.' "

"Miss Maddox!"

"Calm down, Mr. Warren. I'm merely quoting the author."

"Nevertheless—"

"What's more, I don't believe J. D. Salinger was being gratuitous or salacious in using that word, and I applaud his courage."

"I suppose you also liked Lady Chatterly's Lover."

"Actually, I found it boring, but what's that got to do with anything?"

"I'm trying to put things into perspective before I make a decision."

"About firing me?"

"Yes. After our conversation, I've decided I may have been a little hasty." Warren stood and walked around his desk, perching on the edge so he was facing Cassandra. He dropped a hand casually to his thigh and began drumming his fingers. "Under extreme circumstances such as this, extreme actions are sometimes required."

"What sort of extreme actions?"

"I'm sure you're familiar with the Latin phrase, *quid pro*

quo."

"Of course," she replied cautiously.

"I think it might serve us well in this situation." Warren picked up the photo and studied it again. Cassandra knew exactly where he was looking, and it gave her the heebie-jeebies. "I must say I had no idea what you've been hiding."

Cassandra's stomach turned over. "Please, Mr. Warren. I hope you don't think—"

"It would make things so much easier for both of us if I pretended I never saw this photograph."

"Yes, I suppose it would."

"And how do you suppose we might arrange that?"

"I … I don't know, sir. You're the one in charge."

"Yes, I am."

"So what would you suggest?"

"You're a clever girl, Cassie." Warren's eyes lingered on her breasts while his lips parted in a saurian smile. "I'm sure you can figure it out."

Cassandra sprang to her feet, outrage boiling over. Her slap was more sudden than strong, but caught the principal off-guard and sent him sprawling.

"That's half your answer, Mr. Warren!" she yelled. "The other half is a quote from J. D. Salinger." She took a deep breath and spat the words. "Fuck you!"

All that came roaring back as Cassandra listened to some distant thunder when the rain intensified. She sipped again.

"What was I thinking?" she muttered. Then, "Bullshit! What was *he* thinking?!"

"Cassie! Is anybody home?"

She looked toward the driveway and the sound of a male voice. "Who's there?"

"Chuck Kirkendol!"

"I'm back here!" Cassandra watched Chuck stride across the wet lawn and hurry toward the shelter of the porch. She was in no mood to be polite. "What're you doing here?"

"Just wanted to talk a minute." He took off his Stetson and

ran fingers through curly red hair damp with sweat. "Are you busy?"

"The truth is, Mr. Lawman, that I'm in a glider swilling bourbon all alone and watching the damned rain and feeling sorry for myself. Does that sound busy to you?"

"Look, Cassie. If I've come at a bad time—"

"Since I don't see any good times on the horizon, you'd better speak your piece right now. Unless you've come to gloat of course."

"Gloat? About what?"

Cassandra looked at his watch. "Let's see. It happened four hours ago. Surely that's enough time for it to be all over town."

"I honestly don't know what you're talking about."

"I suppose that's possible." She sipped again, more heavily this time. "Unlikely, but possible."

"You want to tell me what put that big chip on your shoulder?"

"Sure. I'm about to get fired."

"What?!"

"Yes, indeed. The principal thinks I'm unsuitable to teach the innocent young people of our fair community. At first, I thought Mr. Warren and I might work something out, but I couldn't agree to his terms."

"What did he ask you to do?"

"Let's just say our squeaky-clean principal has a very dirty mind." Cassandra lofted her glass. "So I knocked him on his behind and told him to go fuck himself. Or more accurately, J.D. Salinger did."

"You're not making a lot of sense."

"You're the rough, tough lawman. You figure it out."

When she slurred those last words, Chuck said, "How much have you had to drink?"

"Not nearly enough, I can tell you, and what I do in the privacy of my home is nobody's business but my own. Unless of course you start sending your damned storm troopers into people's houses, which wouldn't surprise me one bit, considering those ridiculous fines and citations and your ticketing Calvin Harrington for no good reason."

Chuck passed his hat nervously from one hand to another. "That's something I want to talk to you about."

His soft tone calmed Cassandra, and she put her temper on hold. "I haven't heard that voice since high school."

"I want to talk to you about that, too."

Cassandra smiled in spite of herself. "Don't tell me we're about to have a little trip down memory lane."

"Unless you have any objections."

"I'm not sure what you're up to, sheriff, but the bourbon's sitting on the kitchen counter if you want some."

"Thanks, but I'm still on duty."

"Suit yourself." Cassandra patted the seat of the glider. "Have a seat then, but don't rock the boat."

"I'd better sit over here." Chuck sat opposite her and said, "I'd like to speak frankly if you don't mind."

"High time."

"I guess I deserve that."

"Yeah, I guess you do."

45

Fuzzy from the liquor and still unsettled by the events in the principal's office, Cassandra had trouble following Chuck's conversation. His sincerity eventually prompted her to set the bourbon aside and force herself to concentrate.

"I've tried to keep a lid on this since Evie got herself killed, but I can't do it anymore. I regretted marrying her from day one, but I never had a choice."

"You had a choice not to get her pregnant," Cassandra said evenly.

"Yes, I did, but there was no getting around the guns our parents held to our heads once they found out. Things were never good, even after Coralee was born. In fact, they got steadily worse."

"You don't have to go into all that, Chuck. The whole town knows Evie was a wild child."

"It was a lot worse than people think, except for our neighbors who heard all the knock-down-drag-out fights. I put up with her drinking and affairs with other men because of Coralee. I know that's not a good reason for staying in a bad marriage, but it was my choice." Chuck sighed. "The hardest thing I ever did was breaking up with you and telling you I was marrying Evie."

"It was pretty hard on this end too," Cassandra confessed, "but I knew I had to move on or die. To paraphrase Tennessee Williams, 'You used to be so good-looking I couldn't stand it. But now I can.'"

Chuck had a strange look, as though recognizing a stranger. "May I ask you something personal?"

"I may not answer."

"Fair enough. Why haven't you married?"

"Maybe because I never fell in love again." Cassandra swallowed hard. "Dear Lord, Chuck. That was twenty-five years ago."

"Twenty-six to be exact, and when I think I could've spent them all with you, it makes me sick to my stomach."

"Why are you dredging all this up?"

"Because I love you, Cassie. I always have and I always will. And if there's any way in the world for us to start over, I'd sure like to try. Hell, I'll agree to any terms you want if you'll let me take you to the Blue Circle for hamburgers without pickles and onion."

"You remembered."

"That and a whole lot more."

"I suppose I do too. Do you still like the broasted chicken at Archie's Drive-In?"

"Yeah." He took her hand and she surprised herself by not pulling away. "Can I call you sometime next week?"

"Don't you mean 'may' I call you?"

"Ever the English teacher, huh?"

"For the time being anyway."

"So may I call you?" he persisted.

"Not until you answer a personal question."

"Shoot."

"Why should I involve myself with the second most hated man in town? The mayor, of course, wins first place by a landslide."

Chuck grinned. "Still sassy as ever. I love that about you."

"A little too sassy according to Principal Warren."

Chuck released her hand and sat back. "Please tell me what happened with him."

"Alright, but I'm not letting you off the hook about your nasty behavior these past few weeks."

"Fair enough."

Cassandra gave him a brief rundown of Laverne's photograph and Warren's lewd proposition. Chuck tried to remain professional, but he cracked up when she described decking the principal and repeated her parting shot.

"Good for you! That guy deserves everything he got and

then some. You're going to file an official complaint if he fires you, aren't you?"

"As far as I'm concerned, it's a done deal. Besides, what good would a complaint do? As far as I can tell, justice and fair play went out the window the minute Junkin Abernathy was elected mayor. Which brings us back to your part in all this."

"Interesting choice of words, because a 'part' is exactly what it is."

"Come again?"

"Before I say more, I have to swear you to silence. What I'm going to say is in absolute confidence and must not be repeated to anyone. Well, maybe Anrita and Sylvianne because I know y'all are the three musketeers."

"I promise we can keep a secret, but what's with the cloak and dagger stuff?"

"I know I've behaved like a bully and that people think I'm Abernathy's toady, but nothing could be further from the truth. I've only been play-acting because it's the only way I know to nail him."

"I'm not following."

"You may think he's only another ignorant redneck, but Junkin Abernathy is as slick as they come. I've been sheriff a lot of years and I know about each and every one of his little scams, schemes and shenanigans. No matter how hard I've tried to catch him, he stays one step ahead. For example, everyone thinks he owns all that property behind Big Shots, but in fact it's owned by some made-up consortium I've never been able to pinpoint. That's where he stores his moonshine."

"What about the bar? There's no question that he's selling illegal liquor in a dry county."

"He used to sell memberships to a fake private club, but when I found a way to bust that, he changed tactics. Now he sells tickets to people which can be redeemed for drinks. There's no alcohol involved when money changes hands, so that's also a dead end."

"Then what about the Kitty Korner?" Cassandra pressed.

"It's legally owned by Lola Rodgers, the madam who runs it. There's no point in busting her because Junkin would simply replace her. Besides, she's an honest whore, pardon my French, and makes regular contribution to the department's widows and orphans' fund. She and I let Junkin think she's paying me hush money, so he thinks I'm as crooked as he is."

"Then you're actually doing undercover work?"

"Exactly. I'm playing along with everything Junkin wants and keeping my eye peeled for the least infraction. I've even got Coralee on the alert."

"I'd forgotten she was Junkin's secretary."

"Something she hates with a passion I'm happy to say, but so far we're not having much luck."

"And you're willing to let everyone to think you're a bad guy, while in fact you're the one in the white hat?"

"That's one way to put it."

"And you're going to keep this up until—?"

"Until I find a way to put that crook behind bars." He looked at his watch. "I'm officially off-duty now. Does that drink offer still stand?"

"Sure thing. And you don't even need to buy a ticket."

She took his arm as they walked into the kitchen. "It's a shame people don't know the truth. If they did, maybe somebody would come forward with something on Abernathy."

"I suspect half the people in Meander have something on him, but the problem is, one, getting them to talk and, two, making the accusations stick once they do. I recently stumbled onto a couple of things that look promising though."

Cassandra poured bourbons for both and clinked their glasses together. "Do tell."

"There's a new lover's lane out Thunder Road at the old Boruff place. Turns out some kids were out there when they had some very unexpected visitors." Chuck tool a healthy slug of whiskey. "Whew. I've needed that all day."

"You've probably needed it since Abernathy got elected, but finish your story."

"Rocky Millsaps and Dottisue Davis were hiding in the hay loft when none other than the Ku Klux Klan held a meeting, complete with a burning cross."

"Oh, my God! Did the kids get caught?"

"No. Thank goodness they had the good sense to keep quiet and out of sight, but they saw enough to give me a list of names."

"Don't tell me our illustrious Junkin Abernathy is—"

"The Exalted Cyclops himself!"

"What does that mean? President?"

"According to Eugene Proctor."

"Please don't tell me he belongs to the KKK too!"

"No, no. But he sees all and knows all when it comes to Meander."

"And its windows."

"Exactly. He came over to my house one night to say he'd seen Junkin trying on his Klan get-up. Apparently the Exalted Cyclops's robe has special markings so lesser members can identify him." Chuck locked his fingers together and turned his palms out to pop his knuckles. It was a boyhood habit that made Cassandra nostalgic. "So next time I see another Klan gathering, I'll know which one's Junkin."

Cassandra feigned astonishment. "What more can you say about a mayor who's a bootlegger, a whoremaster and an Exalted Cyclops?"

Chuck considered telling Cassandra what else Eugene had seen Junkin do, but decided to save it for another time.

"Welcome to Calhoun County, I guess."

46

Word of Cassandra's firing and rumors of a naughty photo inspired one of Reverend Hickman's more spiteful sermons on pornography and immorality, but since he didn't
dare mention her by name, not everyone realized she was the
target of his tirade. The preacher took his usual perverse
pleasure as fans swished faster and the usual suspects began
squirming and sweating, reactions that had nothing to do
with the sweltering sanctuary. Afterwards, while chatting
with his congregation outside, he basked in his own glory as
Abernathy loudly praised his fire-and-brimstone homily.

"Why, thank you, mayor. You know, when it comes to
morality, we must be eternally vigilant and—"

Abernathy leaned in to whisper. "Cut the crap, preacher.
We need to talk private, and I don't mean maybe."

Such insistence struck fear in Hickman's heart as he
hissed back. "It'll have to wait, Junkin. I'm guest of honor at a
luncheon hosted by the Ladies' Uplift League."

"You and the League can suck my lollipop, reverend, and
I ain't just whistling Dixie! I'll wait under that shade tree
there, so hurry up!"

In a much louder voice, Hickman said, "Mighty fine to
see you, Mister Mayor." He turned to the next person in line.
"Good morning, Mrs. Gryder. My, what a pretty hat!" With
Junkin glowering a short distance away, the next fifteen
minutes were agony for the minister. Hickman had barely
said good-bye to his last parishioner when Junkin barreled
over and ushered him back into the church.

"What on earth is wrong with you?" Hickman demanded.
"People are still watching."

"I don't give a shit if all twelve disciples are watching. We
gotta talk."

"About what?"

"About those substantial deposits I've been dropping in your collection plate the past few months." "I can't tell you how much I appreciate them." Hickman cried out when he was strong-armed into the coat room. "What're you doing? That hurts!"

"I'll do lots more than that if you don't explain why you're trying to blackmail me."

"How can you use such a word here in the house of the Lord? I think we should get down on our knees right this minute and pray for forgiveness."

Junkin was staggered by the man's audacity. "Are you for real?"

Hickman dropped to his knees. "Surely if we both pray together, the good Lord will find a way to—"

"Stand up, you self-righteous phony!" Junkin yanked him back to his feet. "I finally figured out why you needed to bilk me over that damned fire. I kept asking myself why it mattered to you and how you found out I was involved."

"Before you go any further," Hickman said, "I think you need to consider that it isn't only your part in that destructive fire that I'm keeping a secret. There's also your involvement in that ... oh, let me see. How shall I put it? Your little hooded fraternity?"

Junkin grabbed the preacher's lapels and yanked him closer. "Listen to me, you lying hypocrite. I not only know that you're the co-owner of some of the property that got burned. I also know what you plan to do with it."

"I've no idea what you're talking about."

"I sent my man, Sonny Hull, out there to see what he could uncover, and he had a long talk with a gentleman named Jake Sawyer. Mr. Sawyer had some mighty interesting things to say about you and your little enterprise."

The preacher paled. "I've never heard of this man."

"No? Well, he's sure as hell heard of you, reverend, and I know you plan on turning that empty land into the Sunny-side Up Nudist Camp. Now I suggest you close your mouth before a bug flies in."

"Mayor Abernathy! How do you come up with these pre-
posterous, outrageous and completely unfounded—?"

"Bullshit!" Junkin released Hickman's lapels so suddenly
the minister reeled backward, nearly impaling impaled himself on a coat hook. "I figured you might deny everything, so
I have a little something I want you to look at." He reached
inside his jacket and pulled out a digest-sized envelope.
"Here."

Hickman's eyes narrowed. "What's that?"

"Your mail, that's what."

"What are you doing with it?"

"While Sonny was telling me about the nudist camp, he
remembered you had a private post office box and got a lot
of mail in plain brown wrappers. I got mighty curious about
it, so why don't we take a look together and—"

"It's a federal offense to—"

"Go on. Open it!"

Hickman's forehead was glossy with sweat. "I don't want
to."

"I don't see that you have much choice."

"I said no!"

"Hmmm. I figured you might say that, so I've got another
back-up plan." The mayor was obviously enjoying himself, a
cat toying with helpless prey. "We'll let your wife open it. I'm
sure Mrs. Hickman would like to know about your extracur-
ricular reading material."

"You wouldn't dare!"

"I reckon there's only one way to find out." He leaned out
of the coat room and waved. "She's waiting for you right outside with the rest of the Uplift League ladies."

"Give me that!"

Reverend Hickman grabbed the envelope and clawed it
open, earning a nasty paper cut in the process He sucked his
thumb before continuing.

"I wish you could see yourself," Junkin said.

Hickman muttered something incoherent when he peeked inside. "Alright, Abernathy. You've made your point." He tried to tuck the envelope inside his coat, but Junkin snatched it back.

"Oh, no you don't! Didn't Jesus teach you how to share?"

Junkin shook the envelope until two digest-sized magazines slid into his hand. One cover pictured two naked busty ladies playing volleyball, and the other showed a half dozen nude couples in a swimming pool, the women straddling the men's shoulders for a spirited game of war horse. The titles were, respectively, Sun Worshippers International and Sunshine & Health.

"Well, whaddya know. Looky here!"

"I said you've made your point," Hickman muttered. "What more do you want?"

"I want an end to the blackmailing once and for all."

"Alright."

"Your word's not good enough."

"Surely you don't want it in writing?"

"Hell, no. But I want something better than a nervous promise made in a coat room."

"I'm a minister, for God's sake. What more do you need?"

"C'mon, and I'll show you."

A much bigger man, Junkin had no trouble grabbing the preacher by the back of his coat and propelling him into the sanctuary and down the aisle. His destination was the pulpit.

"I want you to stand here and put your hand on the Bible and swear under that big cross that you'll never mess in my business again."

"This is ridiculous," the preacher said, squirming uselessly.

Junkin reveled in the moment. His long-held suspicions that Hickman was a greedy, duplicitous charlatan were borne out by plans for a nudist camp of all things, and he couldn't help gloating.

"What's the matter, reverend? Scared you'll be struck by

lightning? With your crooked history it wouldn't be no surprise."

"I've already sworn once," Hickman said, struggling to pull free. "Now let go of me and get out of my church."

"Put your hand on the Bible and swear!"

"I refuse to be bullied in the house of the Lord!" Hickman insisted. "Now let go of me."

Junkin saw an opportunity too rich to pass up. "Okay. Whatever you say."

The struggling minister was freed so abruptly that he lost his balance, reeled away from the pulpit and toppled into the baptismal pool. The resultant splash sent water cascading all over the altar, prompting Junkin to jump out of the way to keep his shoes dry. When Hickman finally surfaced and regained his balance, he scrambled from the water like a drunken walrus. He perched on the edge of the pool, face blazing with humiliation, but he realized the worst wasn't over when Junkin howled with laughter.

Bobbing in the baptismal pool, a pathetic island of hostess black, was the minister's cheap toupee.

"Holy shit, preacher. Your hair's as fake as you are!"

47

"Hello, dear boy." Eulalie turned her head so Andy could buss her cheek. "I have a surprise for you."

"Another one? You say that every time I come over here."

"Don't begrudge an old lady a little fun." She took his arm as they walked into the living room. "Look in the box on the coffee table."

"The dinner party invitations?"

"I hope you like them."

Andy picked up a cream-colored envelope and pulled out an engraved invitation. "You sure went all out."

"Not yet, but I will when I use wax and the family crest to seal the envelopes. Do you think that'll be too much?"

"For Meander? Absolutely."

"Oh, goody!" She watched his face as he read the invitation. "Surprised at the guest of honor?"

"Who in the world is Madame Marie Reynard de la Noir?"

"Who do you think?"

"I haven't the faintest … oh, no. You wouldn't!"

"Of course, I would!"

"This bash is for Mary!"

"Mais oui, mon cherie."

"I think I'd better sit down."

Eulalie picked up a fan and waved it languidly. "Roughly translated, the name means Mary Black Fox which she thought would be a cute inside joke, but now that I think about it, the name sounds more Cherokee than African."

"Isn't she supposed to be from Ghana?"

"Yes, but I decided to fancy things up a bit when I learned Mary took French in high school. She's not fluent but she does a very credible French accent."

"Was Ghana a French colony when it was called the Gold Coast?"

"British."

"So why would she be French?"

"Because she's originally from Dahomey, a French colony next door to Ghana."

"So are we to assume the Madame moved to the country next door?"

"Correct," she replied, as she continued spinning her outrageous tale. "So she could be with her husband, Roland, an engineer who's here studying T.V.A.. He's Ghanian, you see."

"Why isn't he one of the honorees?"

"Unfortunately he'll be unable to attend because he has a prior engagement in the Oak Ridge labs."

Andy was dubious. "You don't think this crazy tale is too far-fetched?"

"Not for a couple of cretins like the Abernathys."

"What about the rest of your guests?"

"They're all onto my little scheme." She stopped fanning and narrowed her eyes. "Have you any idea how hard it was to find people willing to socialize with the Abernathys?"

"I'm sure it was a challenge."

"It's the most difficult guest list I've ever put together. All I could come up with were the Earl Tiptons, Helen and Frank Highwater, and the Mearnses."

"You invited Dave Mearns after he wrote all those scathing editorials about the tickets and fines?! Everyone knows the mayor's behind them, and he'll probably blow a gasket when he sees Dave!"

"But don't you think colorful guest lists make for the most interesting parties?"

"Not to mention fireworks."

"It's anyone's guess how Junkin will behave, but we'll have a story either way. Two stories actually."

"What do you mean?"

"I've also invited Anne Jernigan. She's a reporter for the Knoxville paper, but the Abernathys won't know who she is. Just like they won't know our honored African guest is a

Knoxville gal who now works for Anrita."

"You sure live dangerously."

"I don't know about that, my dear. It took tear gas and the National Guard to get those poor colored students into high school over in Clinton. Hosting a small interracial dinner party pales by comparison, don't you think?"

"What I think is that I admire your courage."

Eulalie set the fan aside. "I'm so pleased, especially since I don't know your views on segregation."

Andy took a minute. "It's what I grew up with and ... oh, I don't know. It was just *there*."

"I understand."

"The truth is that I've never mixed with colored folks socially because I don't have any colored friends."

"You've got at least one," Lou said as she carried in a tray of petits fours. She winked at Eulalie. "Maybe more."

Andy turned to Eulalie. "You told Lou about your heritage, huh?"

Lou chuckled. "She told me alright, and it's the closest I've ever come to fainting dead away."

"I always thought the Old South was as much illusion as reality," Eulalie said. "I'm a walking, talking illustration of that very thing."

"Black and white, or colored?" Lou teased.

"All the above!" The two dissolved in laughter but Andy remained serious. "Didn't you think that was funny, dear?"

"I guess so, but I'm still wondering why I never thought much about discrimination. I read the papers and watch the news and I know colored people are treated unfairly, and I of all people should understand bigotry because ... uh, never mind."

Eulalie patted his knee. "I hope you'll forgive me, Andrew, but I told Lou about Clark. I know I should've asked you first, but the three of us have grown so close after all that's happened these past few months that I see no call for secrets."

"I agree."

"I promise your secret is safe," Lou insisted. "Eulalie will tell you I'm like that old sphinx when it comes to keeping my mouth shut."

"I believe you, Lou. It's just that I'm not used to anybody knowing the truth, and it'll take some getting used to."

Eulalie said, "Believe me. I'm struggling with old secrets too."

"You know what this whole thing reminds me of?" Lou asked.

"Why don't you sit down and have some sweets and tell us."

"Don't mind if I do." Lou chose a candy and chewed thoughtfully. "It's a good thing these things are store-bought. If I knew how to make 'em I'd weigh a ton."

"Finish your story," Eulalie said.

"I'm thinking this is like that old tale about water lilies growing in the mud. Their faces are beautiful but their feet are dirty."

"I don't follow you."

"Those Abernathys are the dirt that made us pretty water lilies bloom together."

"That's a very sweet sentiment," Andy said.

"Lou comes up with these little gems all the time," Eulalie said. "I've often wondered how far she might have gone if she'd had a real education."

"Sometimes it's good not knowing too much." Lou scooped up another sweet. "Now I better finish my work if I'm gonna to get to Zanna's house in time for dinner."

"Alright, dear." When she and Andy were alone again, Eulalie said. "There's a reason why I told her about Clark, Andy. You know I don't like driving on those busy highways, and last week I needed Lou for a very special errand that involved you."

"What do you mean?"

"She drove me up to Jefferson City."

A frisson rippled down Andy's neck. "Why?"

"Because I haven't been able to stop thinking about Clark's father keeping you from Clark's funeral. I did a little homework, and after discovering he died two years ago, I decided to pay his widow a visit."

"Eulalie, please don't tell me you—"

"Let me finish, and if you're mad at me for meddling, you have every right to curse and yell and stomp out the door."

"I have to admit I'm pretty upset right now."

"You're certainly entitled." Eulalie retrieved a small box from a side table and set it in her lap. "I spoke with Mrs. Foster on the phone before I drove up. I had all sorts of notions of what she might be like. After all, I'd never met a woman who let her own son get thrown out of the house. I had my suspicions of course, and they turned out to be true."

"That Foster beat his wife?"

"You knew?"

"Clark told me. Said his home was a house of horrors."

"Apparently Mr. Foster's death changed everything. Mrs. Foster, Gloria, sounded very shy when she answered the phone but she was happy to talk when I explained I was another Tennessee mother who lost a son on Iwo Jima."

"So she invited you to the house?"

"She has a small apartment above a pet shop. In fact, every so often our conversation would be interrupted by a squawking macaw. Anyway, after we'd chatted over coffee, I told her I had a dear friend who'd known her son and when I mentioned your name she burst into tears."

"Eulalie, I'm not sure if I want to hear any more."

"It's not what you think. She remembered your name because Clark had told her about you, and she was upset because she hadn't tried to stop her husband when he barred you from the funeral."

"Did she remember me punching him in the face?"

"She not only remembered, young man. She said it was one of her favorite memories." Eulalie gave Andy a moment to digest that. "I have to be honest here, Andy. I didn't call on Gloria Foster solely to learn about Clark. I've always wondered about Geoffrey's final days on Iwo Jima and thought meeting another woman whose son died there might help. Gloria said Clark distinguished himself in the assault on Mount Suribachi, and, after being wounded, he pulled three men to safety. They survived, but Clark didn't. Did you know about that?"

"No."

"Look inside the package, Andrew."

Andy's hands trembled as he opened the box and a lump seared his throat when he saw the Purple Heart inside.

"My God!"

"Mrs. Foster insisted that I give it to you, on the condition that you come visit and take her to the cemetery some time."

Andy shook his head, as though clearing old cobwebs. "This means more to me than you could ever imagine. I'm ... I'm beyond grateful."

"I'm the one who's grateful, my dear. I didn't realize until I shared my grief with another mother who'd lost a son how much unfinished business I had with Geoffrey."

Andy took the medal from the box and hefted it in his hand. "It's heavy."

"Is it?"

"Yes." He lowered his head and pressed the medal to his heart. "Will ... will you excuse me a minute?"

"Of course." Eulalie watched Andy slip outside through the French doors and lose himself in the growing dusk. A moment later, Lou called from the hall.

"Y'all alright in there?"

Eulalie blinked away tears. "Yes, Lou. I believe we are."

48

As Knoxville vanished in his rear-view mirror, Junkin felt on top of the world. His semi-annual morning powwow with fellow Exalted Cyclopses from nine Klaverns renewed old friendships and produced a solid six-month plan to recruit more members. Afterwards he lunched at Regas' Restaurant with Roy McCampbell, his best moonshine customer, and marveled at a recent article in the Washington Post naming Knoxville the Bootleg Capital of the World. Roy added credence to the story by placing his biggest order yet. Junkin was so pleased with his achievements in bigotry and crime that he began humming on the drive back to Meander.

He had been inside the city limits exactly two minutes when he saw something that erased his high spirits. "What the hell?!"

Driving in the opposite direction on River Road was Calvin Harrington's station wagon, complete with dummy corpse. As if that weren't bad enough, Calvin recognized the mayor's Eldorado and had the gall to wave and honk his horn. Junkin slammed on the brakes and did a U-turn, but to his disgust Calvin did the same thing. They passed each other again, but this time Calvin thumbed his nose. Determined to get to the bottom of this display, Junkin turned around again only to get trapped behind a slow-moving tractor. By the time he caught up, Calvin was parked in front of Belle Fleur chatting with Andy. Junkin screeched to a halt and hung out the window.

"Didn't the sheriff tell you to stop driving that piece of junk around town?"

"Good afternoon to you too, Mr. Mayor," Calvin called cheerily. "Why, yes, I believe he did."

"What the hell do you think you doing?"

"I think I'm having a nice conversation with Mr. Jenkins,

that's what."

"Howdy, Mr. Mayor!" Andy called.

Junkin ignored him. "You know damned well that's not what I meant!"

"Then you must be talking about my Moonshine Kills sign." When Junkin continued to glower, Calvin said, "I took that off as soon as Chuck Kirkendol explained the law."

"Then what's that on the side of the station wagon?"

Calvin turned to Andy. "Can you beat that? A mayor who can't read."

Junkin was so focused on the dummy, he hadn't noticed that the Moonshine Kills signs had been replaced with movie posters for Thunder Road.

"What the hell are you trying to prove?"

"Nothing. I'm just helping my old friend Robert Mitchum promote his new film."

"You expect me to believe you know a big movie star like Mitchum?"

"Yes, sir, he does," Andy said, deciding to join the fun. "In fact, Mr. Harrington was over in Asheville not long ago where Mr. Mitchum was filming the movie. It doesn't open until next year, so how else would Mr. Harrington get these posters ahead of everyone else?"

"I don't know and I don't care," Junkin spat, "but soon as I get home I'm gonna call Kirkendol and have that damned station wagon impounded and you thrown in jail."

"Don't think I'd do that if I were you, Mr. Mayor. I went down to the station house and talked to the sheriff, and he said there's nothing illegal about advertising a movie or toting around dummy corpses."

"Bullshit. That corpse is what you're advertising and you're not gonna get away with it."

"I think I already have."

While Junkin fumed, Calvin got in his Thunder Road station wagon and drove away. Junkin was so angry he didn't realize anyone was talking to him until Andy walked over to the Eldorado window.

"Didn't you hear me, mayor?"

"What?"

"I said you might want to move on because you've got traffic backed up all the way to the Tower Theater."

Andy barely had time to step back before Junkin stomped on the accelerator and the car shot down Main Street. Everyone within forty feet was treated to a burst of exhaust fumes and a thunderous, "Son of a bitch!"

Junkin was still steaming when he pulled into his driveway. He barely noticed the new bent-over butts in the side yard since Fern had replaced the sign she'd kicked to smithereens. She stood up and waved when she heard his car.

"Hi, honey!"

Her chirpy greeting didn't help his mood. "What're you so damned happy about?"

Fern planted fists on her ample hips. "I'm not going to tell you a thing until you change that nasty tone."

When Junkin ignored her and stomped into the house, Fern tossed her trowel aside and went after him. She usually left him alone when he was in one of his ugly moods, but today she decided to confront him.

"All I did was say hello, Junkin. I don't know what happened up in Knoxville, but you got no business taking it out on me."

"I'll do anything I please." Junkin headed straight to the bar and poured a stiff shot of bourbon. He threw it down and poured another one. "You hear me?"

"I hear you alright and getting loaded isn't going to help anything."

"If I wanna chugalug a Ball jar of bourbon, it's none of your goddamned business, woman. I'm the mayor of this town and nobody tells me what to do."

Fern's good mood soured fast. She had been on cloud nine ever since Sonny Hull delivered the beautiful invitation to Eulalie's party. She could scarcely believe that she, little

Miss Fern Myrtle Grimes Abernathy of Seesaw, Tennessee, had been asked to a formal dinner hosted by none other than Eulalie Saunders. Invitations to Blufftop were the most sought-after in town, and she couldn't wait to tell Junkin they'd made it to the top tier of Meander's elite. At least she thought so until he came home growling like a bear and swilling bourbon like there was no tomorrow.

"Is that so?"

"Yes, that's so!" Junkin snarled. He looked around the living room with disgust. "And I'll tell you something else, missy. This place looks like a pig sty. Where the hell is Zanna?"

"I'll tell you exactly where she is, Mr. Smarty Pants. She's working in Anrita Harrington's salad kitchen, that's where. And if it hadn't been for you telling Doyle Richardson to break into the Harringtons' plant, right there in front of God and everybody, that girl would still be working here."

Junkin poured another shot as Fern warmed to the fight.

"You've done stupid things in your life, Junkin Abernathy, and, since you became mayor,

I've turned a blind eye, but these stunts really take the cake. It won't be long before the whole town knows you and Doyle were trying to steal Anrita's chicken salad recipe and get Cassandra Maddox fired."

"Says who?"

"Bad news travel fast in this town, and yours breaks some kind of speed record."

"I don't reckon that it ever occurred to you that you were the main reason I did those things."

Fern hadn't anticipated this about-face. "What're you talking about?"

"You never said so, but I always thought you were jealous of Anrita's success. Was I mistaken?"

"Well, I—"

"That's why I wanted to take her down a peg or two. Same thing with the Maddox woman after she insulted you. I have to take care of my Little Bit, don't I?"

As usual, Fern melted under his flattery, especially when he used her pet name. "Aw, thank you, honey." She blinked away a tear when he opened his arms, making her hurry to get a hug. "I'm sorry I was so mean."

"Nah, I was the one who was mean," Junkin admitted in a rare moment of self-effacement. "It's that damned Calvin Harrington. Did you know he's driving his station wagon again?"

"Are you kidding?" Fern tut-tutted when Junkin described his confrontation with Calvin. "I swear those Harringtons were put on this earth simply to make our lives miserable."

"Meander's life too. I'm telling you they have to be stopped."

"What're you going to do now?"

"I don't know yet but whatever it is it's gonna be a dilly."

"I'm sure you'll think of something." She pecked his cheek. "Now can I tell you my good news?"

"Sure."

"Don't go away!" Fern ran into the kitchen and grabbed Eulalie's invitation from the kitchen table. "Here!"

Junkin's eyes narrowed when he read the engraved script. "Who the hell is this Madame Whatchamacallit?"

"Some French lady I guess. The invitation says she's the guest of honor, so she must be pretty darned important."

"I reckon so," Junkin considered. "It makes you happy, don't it?"

"It sure does, and I have you to thank. If you hadn't gotten yourself elected mayor, I don't think we'd ever have been invited to one of Miss Sugar's parties. They're always the talk of the town."

"I guess we're about to figure out why everybody's talking, huh?"

"We sure are, but I'm worried."

"About what?"

"I don't have anything to wear."

"What are you talking about? You've got three closets full of clothes, not to mention what's in winter storage."

"But everybody's seen that old stuff."

"I'll bet Miss Sugar hasn't," he teased.

"Don't be silly, Junkin. Now you know I have to have a new dress for the occasion, so can I go into Knoxville and see what Miller's has?"

Junkin reached into his pants pocket for a roll of bills. He peeled off a few and held them out. "Little Bit, if it'll make you happy, drive down to Atlanta and get yourself something extra special at Rich's."

"Promise?"

"Promise!"

"You're the most darlin' husband ever!" Fern tucked the money in her bra and smothered Junkin's face with kisses. "I'll get Myrna to ride down with me. Oh, Junkin! I'm so excited. I bet you this party's gonna be something we'll never forget."

"Me too."

49

"You want some iced tea, Cassie?" Sylvianne asked. "I picked some fresh mint."

"Love some." She followed Sylvianne into the kitchen. "Anrita not here yet? She's usually so punctual."

"I told her to come later because I wanted a few minutes alone with you. I have big news."

"About your mystery date?"

Sylvianne was crushed. "Did Anrita blab?"

"She didn't say a word. I saw y'all myself."

"When?"

"Coming out of the Rivoli Restaurant as I was driving by. And I must say you two looked pretty chummy."

"Isn't he dreamy?"

"I didn't get a very good look but he looked more rugged than dreamy."

"Believe me, a man can be both rugged and dreamy, honey child, and you'll never guess in a million years what he does for a living."

"Do tell."

She handed Cassandra a glass of tea. "He's a stunt man in the movies!"

"Then he must be Calvin's old army buddy. I've heard about him for years. What's his name? Grady—?"

"Grady Fletcher."

"And how did you get your hooks into him?"

"I'll ignore that rude remark, accurate though it may be." Sylvianne fixed herself a bourbon and Coke and headed for the patio. "Grabbing Grady's attention wasn't easy because I didn't have much time. He's working on a movie over in Asheville and decided to visit Calvin and Anrita before heading back the next day. When she and I came back from the movies and I saw Grady right there in her kitchen ... well, it gave me the shivers."

"So what did you do?"

"I let him know I was more than a little interested, wiggled my behind like Marilyn in Niagara and slithered right out of there."

"Poor man never had a chance."

"Say what you please, but he got my number from Calvin and—"

"Oh, I'd say he got your number without asking Calvin."

Sylvianne feigned indignation. "Do you want to hear this or not?"

"Sorry. I'll keep still if it kills me."

"The fact is, I had changed into a cocktail dress and was looking for my long black gloves when Grady called to ask me to dinner."

"You were pretty sure of yourself."

"You can't ignore death, taxes and tight skirts."

"And Yankees say we Southern girls are slow."

"Not this one, and I was taking no chances with this gentleman. We had a lovely dinner and an even lovelier nightcap, sweet man. I wish I could've fixed him breakfast, but I hadn't been to the Pig and didn't have anything in the fridge." Sylvianne fluttered her eyelashes. "I must say the man wakes up with a ferocious appetite, among other things."

"Sylvianne McNeal! You're a scandal to the jaybirds!"

"I sure as hell hope so. Face it, Cassie. You and I have lived in this one-horse town all our lives, and I'm sure people gossip about my four divorces and my clothes and my fondness for bourbon but you know what?"

"What?"

"Frankly, Miss Scarlett, I don't give a rat's patootie!"

"I wish I could say the same," Cassandra lamented. "I know people talk about me too. The old maid school teacher who gets her jollies making her students read dirty books. Unfortunately, it's probably cost me my job."

Sylvianne waved a hand. "We can talk about that later. I want to talk about Grady some more."

Cassandra whooped. "Honey, you are nothing if not to the point!"

"I want to tell you what happened at breakfast."

"You sure you don't want to tell me what happened *before* breakfast?"

"I most certainly do not, and you will kindly stop interrupting. As you already know, we went to the Rivoli where I grabbed my favorite booth, the one way in the back where nobody can see you except the waitresses. Anyway, Grady started flipping pages on the Wall-o-Matic and asked what I wanted to hear. I told him to pick whatever he liked and couldn't believe he chose my personal top three from Your Hit Parade."

"Is that right?"

"Yes, indeed. Fascination and Shangri-La and So Rare. For heaven's sake, Cassie! What are the chances of that happening?"

"Slim and none I guess."

"Oh, I know it's not what one builds a relationship on, but at least our taste in music is the same."

"So where do you go from here?"

"If you weren't already sitting down, I'd sure tell you to."

"Uh-oh."

"He's invited me out to Los Angeles!"

"After one date?"

Sylvianne looked miffed. "You act surprised."

"Because that kind of thing would never happen to me."

"It might if you'd let your hair down once in a while, and I mean that literally." Sylvianne reached over and tapped the pins holding Cassandra's bun in place. "I remember how good you looked as Moonbeam McSwine. Everyone was floored when they saw the transformation, including me."

"I appreciate that, Sylvianne, but playing the sexpot isn't my calling."

"Sister, at my age it's not mine either but I believe in doing the best I can with what the good Lord gave me. Grady's a man of the world with a couple of divorces under his belt too, so I knew he wasn't going to wait around for me to take the lid off the cookie jar. Oh, I don't know. Maybe he's as full of baloney as the next men, but he said he likes mature women who know who they are and what they want, and I like to think I fit that category."

"So are you going to California?"

"Heavens, yes! Chances like this don't come along every day, and I aim to make hay before there's a damned solar eclipse." Sylvianne sipped. "May I ask you something personal?"

"Sure."

"How long has it been since you've had a date? Eight, nine years?"

"Why would you ask that of all things?"

"Because Grady was telling me about his brother Hart who was widowed a couple of years back, and I was thinking since you might have some free time now that—"

"Thanks, but I've no intention of going to Los Angeles for a blind date."

"When you put it that way I guess it sounds a little far-fetched."

"No pun intended."

"Anrita and I worry about you being alone," Sylvianne insisted. "I know I'm alone too, but for better or worse I have my boys Jack and Jim to keep me company."

"As in Daniels and Beam?"

"The same."

"I appreciate your concern, Sylvianne. I truly do. But let's get back to the last time I had a date."

"Go on."

"What would you say if I told you it was last night?"

Sylvianne looked at her cocktail. "I'd say this is the fastest I've ever gotten buzzed."

"I'm serious."

"Now that I know I'm not hallucinating, tell me more. Anyone I know?"

"I'll say."

"That's a peculiar answer."

"You know him and so does Anrita. Calvin knows him especially well."

"Then tell me, or heaven's sake!"

"Alright, but before I do, you have to swear on a stack of Bibles that you'll never tell another living soul. I'm not being coy either. There's a good reason why secrecy is so important."

"Does Anrita know?"

"No. I'll tell her when she gets here."

Sylvianne clapped her hands. "Oh, boy! For once I get to scoop Anrita Harrington. I thought I had her beat when I saw John and Lurleen smooching, but never mind about that. Hurry up and tell me!"

"Swear?"

Sylvianne crossed her heart. "Scout's honor. Now who's the mystery man?"

"Chuck Kirkendol."

"No!"

"Yes!"

"Good lord! Didn't you two go together in high school?"

"Yes, but he got Evie Lofton preggers and had to make her an honest woman."

"And ruined his life in the process. I remember when Evie and Showboat Owens died in that car wreck, both drunk as fiddler's bitches. The way that girl carried on, I knew she'd come to no good."

"I'm ashamed to say I secretly prayed for something like that to happen, in the beginning anyway. God forgive me."

"That's a perfectly natural response when you're young and in love." Sylvianne offered. "So you and Chuck are thinking about rekindling those old embers, eh?"

"We'll see." Cassandra pulled pins from her bun and shook her hair free. "Better?"

"Much better, and I'm all for it, but, c'mon, Cassie. Chuck Kirkendol is an a-number-one asshole. Why would you want to mess with him after all this time?"

"Because I never stopped loving the guy." After letting that bombshell register, she said, "But forget that for now. There's something else top secret I want to tell you."

"Okay." Sylvianne listened incredulously as Cassandra explained Chuck's undercover work to put Junkin Abernathy behind bars. "Damn! I have to say he's playing his part to the hilt. I mean, giving Calvin a ticket for that silly station wagon. Good grief!"

"We talked about that. He said he hated doing it to an old friend, but that he can't raise the slightest suspicion with Abernathy or he'll blow the whole operation."

"It all makes sense now, but how long does this charade have to go on? Is he anywhere close to nailing Abernathy?"

"He didn't say." Cassandra didn't mention Chuck's enthusiasm over learning Abernathy was head of the local Klan. "The poor guy's miserable with all his old high school friends mad at him, but he's just doing his job as a lawman."

"Well, I, for one, have all new respect for the man."

"I was hoping you'd say that." She paused a beat. "There's one more thing I want to tell you about Chuck Kirkendol, but you can't tell Anrita."

Sylvianne crossed her heart again. "Go ahead."

"Grady's not the only man who wakes up in the morning with a fierce appetite, and I don't mean for grits!"

50

Eulalie was studying her pearl earrings in the dressing table mirror when Lou's image appeared over her shoulder. "I'll swan, Lou. You look like you're about to face a firing squad."

"Is that right?" Lou grunted as she draped a pearl necklace around Eulalie's throat and snapped the clasp. "And how come you look all cool, calm and collected?"

"Because I'm a big phony. When I think about tonight, my insides turn to jelly. How's Mary doing?"

"Last time I checked, she was cool as a cucumber. Zanna's helping her put the finishing touches on that Halloween costume."

"I wish you'd stop calling it that," Eulalie said, secretly amused. "You two did an excellent job copying Ghanaian fashions. I'll bet she looks wonderful."

"She said that head wrap thing is too tight."

"Then go fix it or she'll get a headache before this charade is over."

"Alright."

While Lou was gone, Eulalie looked back at the mirror and, as she sometimes did, talked to her reflection.

"I sure hope you know what you're doing, Eulalie Saunders. Lord knows, you've done some wild things in your day, but this has to be the wildest yet." She closed her eyes and whispered a quick prayer for a peaceful and productive evening. Then she looked at herself again and basked in her own audacity. "Only one way to find out, old girl. On with the show!"

Eulalie stood and smoothed her Chanel dinner dress, a pale blue sheath that emphasized her svelte figure and complimented her silver hair. After a final check in the mirror, she decided she was as ready as she'd ever be and went to the guest bedroom where Mary was dressing. She tapped on the door.

"May I come in?"

"Yes!" three voices chorused.

Standing in the middle of the room, Mary was an African vision in a brilliant array of oranges, yellows and lime green batik. Her ankle-length skirt was topped with an over-blouse worn off one shoulder. She wore a matching head wrap, sandals, scads of metal bracelets and huge gold hoop earrings almost brushing her shoulders.

"Does I look alright?"

"Kwame Nkrumah himself would be dazzled."

"Who's that?" Zanna asked.

"The President of Ghana," Mary replied.

"Goodness me. You've certainly been doing your home-work," Eulalie walked around Mary, smiling with approval as she appraised the costume from every angle. "Alright, young lady. All you have to do now is wait for Lou to come get you once everyone's assembled on the terrace. She'll signal me so I can announce your arrival. Any questions?"

"Only how I can keep my knees from shaking."

"How about something to drink?"

"An Orange Crush would hit the spot."

"I'll get it," Zanna said, bustling away.

Eulalie grew concerned when Mary began pacing, pausing now and then to fuss with a bracelet or fiddle with her head wrap. "You look absolutely convincing, Mary."

"I appreciate that, but the more I look at myself in that mirror, the more I think what we're doing is a little crazy."

"Actually, my dear, it's a *lot* crazy, which is why I will now wish you good luck and leave you alone with your thoughts."

After making her routine inspection downstairs, Eulalie sat in the living room to wait. Andy arrived first, followed by everyone except the Abernathys. As the minutes crept by, Eulalie fretted that word of her scheme had leaked when she heard the blare of a car horn. She took Andy's arm as they walked to the foyer, and when Lou opened the front door they saw Junkin slide unsteadily from the Eldorado.

Her fingers dug into Andy's arm. "Uh-oh."

There was no doubt Junkin had been drinking, but their attention was drawn elsewhere when Fern struggled free of the Cadillac and sashayed toward the house.

"Dear God in heaven!" Eulalie cried. "What on earth is all that?"

Andy chuckled softly. "Looks like Frankenstein brought his bride."

"I told y'all Halloween was comin' early this year," Lou whispered. "What has that woman done to her hair?"

"I don't know," Andy whispered back. "I can't get past the godawful dress."

"Shush you two!" Eulalie said, struggling to maintain her composure as the Abernathys weaved and wobbled toward her front door.

"Yoo-hoo!" Fern chirped. "We're here."

"I'll say," Andy whispered.

Fern wore a strapless yellow satin dress with a mountain of crinolines that sitting in the car had flattened into a lop-sided bell. Her bare shoulders were barely visible in a tangle of organdy that looked about to devour her, and perched atop her freshly bleached beehive was a rhinestone tiara. Enormous silk cabbage roses cascaded from bustline to hemline, and, fighting for survival was an orchid corsage at her bosom. Eulalie struggled not to blanch as the woman rustled closer.

"Mrs. Abernathy," she managed. "That dress is … well, you simply take my breath away."

Fern flipped her wrist. "This old thing? I've had it forever."

"Little Bit's pulling your leg," Junkin announced, swaying close enough to envelope everyone in the stink of bourbon. "She went all the way to Atlanta for that thing, and I told her she was going to be the belle of the ball."

"No doubt about it," Eulalie said graciously. "She may even upstage our guest of honor."

"Oh, heavens, I hope not!" Fern gushed, giggling like a schoolgirl.

Eulalie extended her hand. "Welcome, Mr. Mayor. I'm so glad you and Mrs. Abernathy could join us this evening."

"Wouldn't have missed it for the world. I'm gonna let you in on a little secret, Miss Sugar. I been eyeing this place since I was a kid and wanting to see inside. Looks like I had to get myself elected mayor to do it, but better late than never I always say! Ain't that right, Little Bit?"

Fern stopped giggling and squealed when Junkin clapped her on her back, grinding the stiff organdy into her bare skin.

"Are you alright, my dear?" Eulalie asked.

"I'm fine. Junkin just don't know his own strength sometimes, especially when he's had a couple of belts."

"Yeah, I reckon I got a jump on everybody tonight. Had a business meeting over to the Big Shots that ran a little long."

"I beg your pardon," Eulalie said.

"Junkin owns a little cocktail lounge out on the River Road." Fern leaned closer, enveloping Eulalie in a putrid fog of Joy and residual hair spray. "It's not a place real ladies go, if you know what I mean."

"I'm not sure I do, but we'll leave it at that." Eulalie took Andy's arm. "Shall we go inside? The other guests are on the terrace."

"Right behind you," Junkin said. "Sorry we're late but Fern here had girdle problems."

"Junkin!" Fern giggled. "You hush now!"

Junkin guffawed, pleased with himself, and as, Eulalie feared, headed straight for the bartender. She turned to Lou. "You'd better get Mary down here before that fool passes out."

"Right away."

Luckily, Junkin went into in full mayoral mood on the

terrace, smiling and glad-handing everyone, even Dave Mearns, until Eulalie held up her hands for silence. "As you all know, tonight's soiree is to welcome and honor our guest from overseas. Unfortunately, her husband is up in Oak Ridge on engineering business, but I'm thrilled that she agreed to come alone." Eulalie braced herself when she saw Mary approach from the living room. "Ladies and gentlemen, may I present Madame Marie Reynard de la Noir, who comes all the way from the brand-new nation of Ghana!" She began applauding and everyone followed suit until Mary stepped onto the terrace. Junkin abruptly stopped when he got a good look at her.

"What the hell—?"

Eulalie's hand fluttered to her pearls and she braced herself, relieved after a deathly long pause when she heard Fern's none-too-subtle aside.

"It's alright, honey. She's a *foreign* colored."

It took Junkin a moment to grasp what his wife said, and he watched closely as Mary bowed to each guest as she was introduced. Coached by Eulalie, Andy took Mary's extended hand and brushed it with his lips.

"Bienvenue, Madame de la Noir."

"Merci, monsieur," Mary said. "It's a great pleasure to be in your country."

"I assure you the pleasure is ours," Andy replied.

"I'm the mayor here," Junkin said as Mary approached, "but I'm afraid I don't speak no French."

Mary replied with her best French accent. "No matter, M'sieur Mayor. I speak English."

"Now, ain't that something!"

Eulalie held her breath when Mary extended her hand. This was the moment she feared most, but, to her utter amazement, Junkin not only took the hand but followed Andy's lead and kissed it. Eulalie was still reeling when Fern took things even further by dropping a little curtsy when she was introduced.

"It's real nice to meet you, madam."

"And you as well, Madame Mayor."

"Madame Mayor," Junkin grinned. "Ain't that cute, Little Bit?"

Andy whispered in Lou's ear. "If I hadn't seen this, I'd never have believed it."

"I saw it and I still don't believe it!" Lou whispered back. "I better get some more hors d'oeuvres while I got something left of my sanity."

Cocktail hour went smoothly, but dinner was an even greater success as Junkin plied Mary with questions and hung on her every word. Thoroughly rehearsed and caught up in the moment, Mary's answers were letter-perfect, and by the end of the evening Junkin was charmed. The only person who wasn't pleased was Fern. As Junkin continued to drink, he got chummier and chummier, and by the time coffee was served he was all but flirting with Mary.

"You know, it's getting late," Fern announced. "Junkin and I need to be getting along home."

"Aw, the night's still young, Little Bit," he slurred. "I was thinking we should all go over to the Big Shots and have a drink. Everything's on the house!"

"Junkin!" Fern was apoplectic. "Get a hold of yourself. We can't just go traipsing—"

"Oh, I know you're all worried about Miz Marie here, but nobody's gonna say nothing. I own the place, and that means I make the rules."

"What is this Big Shots?" Mary asked, feigning ignorance.

"No place you'd want to go, madame," Fern said quickly. "It's real loud and smoky and … well, it's not your sort of club."

If only she realized what she was saying, Eulalie thought.

"Is it … how you say? A typical American night club?"

"Typical is the word," Dave Mearns offered.

Deciding things were drifting into dangerous waters, Eulalie said, "I'm afraid Madame de la Noir has a full schedule tomorrow, so we'd best call it a night."

"That's too bad," Junkin said. "I was kinda hopin'—"

"Thank you so much for a nice evening," Fern said, rising in a cloud of noisy organdy. "Come along, Junkin."

He rose unsteadily and, to Eulalie's shock, gave Mary a broad wink before wobbling after his wife. Lou hurried to open the front door, and Eulalie reached it just as Fern pushed a disgruntled Junkin into the passenger seat and shouted that he was too drunk to drive.

"Good-night!" Eulalie called cheerily. "We must do this again!"

"God will punish you for such a big lie," Lou chuckled.

"Why, yes!" Fern called back. "We'll have you down to the house real soon."

Eulalie waved good-night and went back inside. Lou was about to close the front door when Fern's shrill tones rose above the car ignition. Eulalie and Lou heard only snippets as Fern revved the engine, but all of them were juicy.

"Making a big fool of yourself over that colored girl ... talking crazy about going to Big Shots ... ruining my big chance!"

Lou turned to Eulalie as the Eldorado roared into the velvety night. "Well, now. I do believe your dinner party was a success."

"I guess so, but it sure didn't turn out like I expected. I'm still in a bit of a shock."

"Me too," Dave said as he and the others joined them in the foyer. "I can't believe I'll be writing something nice about Junkin Abernathy."

"So will I," Anne Jernigan said. "Your mayor may have been soused, but he was certainly polite to Mary."

Helen chuckled. "A little too polite if you ask me. The old fool was practically drooling."

"I think everyone will agree Mary did an incredible job," Andy offered.

"Indeed, she did." Eulalie looked at Dave and Anne. "I

can't wait to read the stories, and while we're on the subject of publicity, be prepared for some surprises at the Sesquicentennial celebration."

"What kind of surprises?" Dave asked.

"Let's say compared to what I have planned, tonight will look like child's play."

"I think I'm smelling another story," Anne said. "Shall I come back down for the celebration?"

"By all means."

Eulalie finished her good-nights and thanked everyone for their help. She hugged Andy and sent him home before going back to the living room where she planned to congratulate Mary on a superb performance. She found her actually trembling with excitement.

"Good heavens, Mary! Are you alright? You look like you're about to explode."

"I am!" Mary cried. "Where's Lou?"

"Coming!" Lou cried as she closed and bolted the big front door. She was also surprised by Mary's agitation. "What's going on?"

"You're not going to believe this!" Mary cried. She peeled off her turban and tossed it gleefully into the air. "You're simply not going to believe it."

"Believe what, for heaven's sake?" Lou asked.

"The mayor! That Junkin Abernathy!"

"What about him?"

"That's Bubbles!"

"No!" Lou and Zanna gasped together.

"May God strike me dead if I ain't telling the truth!" Mary cried. "I knew it the minute I saw him because Lorraine showed me his picture!"

Mary, Lou and Zanna whooped and hollered until tears streamed down their faces. After a while they flopped onto the couch where they collected themselves only for the laughter to start all over again.

"Alright, you three hyenas," Eulalie teased. "Who in the world are Bubbles and Lorraine?"

51

Dave Mearns's editorial about Eulalie's party in Sunday's special Sesquicentennial Edition of the Meander News-Sentinel was the talk of the town. Locals hadn't been this divided since the Monkey Trial, and not even excitement over that night's beauty pageant and the next day's celebration kept folks from taking sides. Most considered it a tempest in a julep cup and congratulated Miss Sugar for daring to invite a colored woman to dinner, and some even praised Mayor and Mrs. Abernathy for attending. The minority camp, opposing any and all forms of integration, said Eulalie should be ashamed of herself. Junkin was caught squarely in the middle, and, after a flood of angry phone calls from his fellow Klansmen, he ordered an emergency Klavern meeting at the Boruff farm. When he found himself facing furious condemnation, he rushed to defend himself.

"Calm down, boys!" he called, taking his usual position on the farmhouse porch. "I know you're upset about that newspaper article but you got to hear my side of things."

"Just tell us one thing, chief," Doyle Richardson called. "Is that story in the newspaper true? Did you eat dinner with a nigger?"

Junkin raised his hands for quiet when the mutterings grew loud. "Alright, alright. Now hear me out. To begin with, when my wife and I accepted Mrs. Saunders' dinner invitation, we didn't know that colored woman would be there. You can imagine what a shock it was."

"So why didn't you get the hell out soon as you saw her?" Sonny Hull demanded.

"Believe me that was my first impulse, and Fern's too, but this situation was different. This woman wasn't some home-grown pickaninny. She was an honest-to-God African, and her husband is a big-time engineer come here to study T.V.A.

I've never seen a colored behave like that. She spoke French, and—"

"Colored's colored!" someone shouted.

"You're making excuses, Junkin!"

"No, I'm not," he insisted. "I wanted you to know what the situation was and that the reason I went through with it is because I was protecting myself. Did it occur to any of you that this might have been a set-up? Yeah, that's right. A set-up by Mrs. Saunders with help from Dave Mearns."

"How do you figure?" Doyle called.

"I don't think it was no coincidence that the local newspaper editor was there, what with all the nasty dirt he's written about us. Considering he all but accused me of belonging to the Klan, I think Mrs. Saunders concocted this party to see what I'd do and he was waiting to write about it. Y'all know City Council is working to ban the Klan, and if they succeed and confirm that I'm your president, they'll get rid of me as mayor too. I need, we *all* need, for me to stay behind the scenes to protect us and the true cause." The men quieted down in the face of such dazzling logic. "By playing along with their little scheme, I let 'em think I believe that whites and coloreds socializing was okay, because confusing them is what we need. You know what they say, boys. Divide and conquer!" He threw his arms wide, as though to embrace everyone in that dusty farmyard. "My goal, first and foremost, is to protect the Brotherhood."

Pleased by mutterings of approval, Junkin moved in for the kill. "To further prove my devotion and dedication as Exalted Cyclops, come hell or high water, I'm going to march with you tomorrow night at this centennial thing! Soon as Fern and I arrive at the end of the parade, I'll slip away and change into my robe. My place is with you men, not on some platform with a bunch of hotshot citizens and beauty queens. You boys hear me?" Junkin basked in whistles and cheers before continuing. "Now, speaking of beauty queens, I gotta get back to town 'cause I'm one of the judges at that damned pageant. I'd sure like to help make more plans for tomorrow, but Fern would kill me if I backed out of two events in as many nights." He turned to Sonny. "You take charge and let me know when and where we're assembling, and I'll be there, brother!"

After making a big show of retrieving his robe from the farmhouse chimney, Junkin waved it in the air, climbed back into his Eldorado and blasted off in a cloud of dust. He congratulated himself on defusing a potential powder keg and his ability to maintain a poker face while lying to his fellow Klansmen. The truth was, he'd been mulling over his reasons for not bolting in disgust as soon as he saw Marie. He told himself it was because Mrs. Saunders was trying to make a fool of him and that he had outsmarted her by beating her at her own game, but his gut told him it was something else. He had simply never seen a black woman as beautiful and desirable as Marie de la Noir. Hell, she was nothing at all like Lorraine. Her exotic clothing and foreign manners and French accent only enhanced her fine looks, and the more bourbon he drank, the more irresistible she became. He thanked his lucky stars that his wife, of all people, got him out of there before he embarrassed himself.

"Close one," he muttered.

Junkin forgot about Marie as he sped down the River Road and thought of more pressing issues. He'd get home with barely enough time to change clothes, scoop Fern and get to the pageant. There was also the disagreeable chore of telling her that unexpected business meant he'd have to bow out of tomorrow night's closing ceremonies. It was scarcely the first time his dirty doings disrupted their plans, but considering how hard Fern had worked on the celebration, Junkin knew this last-minute change would trigger an especially nasty explosion of slammed drawers and cabinet doors, but dread evaporated when he remembered his trump card.

"The car!"

Junkin was fond of playing harmless little tricks on Fern.

Yesterday he told her the yellow convertible he ordered for her to ride in the parade was indefinitely delayed, when in fact it was stashed out at Big Shots. He figured his best strategy was to let her blow up and then give her the good news that they were the first family in Tennessee to take delivery of Detroit's newest brainchild. He knew she'd be all mushy and forgiving, but he braced himself when he turned into the driveway and saw her on the front porch, dressed to the nines but with a scowl visible from the street. She was actually tapping her foot as he hopped out of the Eldorado and strode toward the house.

"Hey Little Bit!" he called. "Sorry I'm late."

"Don't you 'Little Bit' me, Junkin Abernathy! You've got exactly fifteen minutes to change into a suit and tie and get us to the auditorium. I only hope we get there in time for the parade of contestants." She fussed with the enormous purple orchid corsage on her left wrist. "I'm so put out with you I could spit!"

Junkin knew to keep his mouth shut, ducking into the house and waddling quickly down the hall to his bedroom with Fern close behind. She had laid out a fresh shirt alongside his seersucker suit and continued tapping her foot while he changed clothes. "I don't suppose you can tell me where you've been, and don't say the office or Big Shots because I already called there."

"An emergency political meeting," Junkin answered as he struggled with his clip-on bow tie. "We're expecting trouble from the coloreds."

Fern was instantly diverted. "Not at the celebration tomorrow I hope!"

Junkin deepened his emergency lie. "We don't know yet, but I had to take precautionary measures and put some plans in place."

"So you were at the sheriff's office. Hmmm. I didn't think to call there."

"In the parking lot actually," Junkin said, embellishing

this unexpected alibi. "If those baboons try anything, we'll be ready for them."

Fern's face fell as she sat on the edge of the bed. "I sure hate to think about a bunch of coloreds ruining something I've worked on so hard."

"Don't you worry about it, Little Bit. If they try anything, we'll nip it in the bud." When he saw her dab away tears, he decided to play his trump card early. "But never mind about them. I've got wonderful news."

"What?" she sniveled.

"Your new car is here after all!"

"Really?"

"It arrived this afternoon. I thought I'd surprise you with it tomorrow, so I had them deliver it to Big Shots."

"Oh, Junkin! I'm so relieved." As he hoped, Fern hugged him when instant gratification eclipsed more serious concerns. "I can't wait to ride in it. I want everybody to be pea green with envy."

"I'm sure they will be, honey. Remember, no one else in the whole state of Tennessee can get one of these cars until next year." He pecked her cheek while she adjusted his crooked tie. "Now we'd better get going."

As they drove downtown, Junkin decided telling her about his disappearing act tomorrow night had better wait and let Fern babble about how she hoped her new yellow dress would match the yellow of the new car. They arrived at the high school auditorium and hurried to take their seats beside Myrna Riddick at the judges' table. When Junkin finished smiling and waving at the crowd, he scanned the program. "I don't see no swimsuit competition listed."

Fern giggled. "It was this afternoon, you dirty old man. Tonight's the talent competition and the crowning of the winner."

"Oh. How'd Lurleen do?"

"She won, of course. None of those other girls can hold a candle to our little peach blossom." Fern leaned closer. "But to be on the safe side I've given the other judges some very encouraging words."

"That's my girl!"

"Lurleen's only talent competition is Charm Copenhaver, but the three Tammys are no problem." Fern shushed everyone when the house lights began to dim. "Here we go!"

Fern's intuition, prejudicial, maternal and otherwise, was correct about the talent competition. Tammy Lou Wilcox's birdcalls were mediocre at best, and Tammy Fay Lumpkin put most of the audience to sleep with her speech on the importance of the Golden Rule.

"Shame on her," Fern said, stifling a yawn. "That's the same speech she gave at the 4-H competition last spring."

The audience paid more attention when Tammy Kate Ogle recited Joyce Kilmer's Trees while twirling a baton, but only because she dropped the thing half a dozen times before relating the famous last line. Charm was up next, and Fern couldn't help nudging Myrna and commenting on the girl's makeshift gown.

"I know the Copenhavers are poor as church mice, but you'd think they could've come up with a decent dress. I wouldn't even let Lurleen try on something that tacky, much less go out in public."

"I dropped my program," Myrna whispered back. "What's Charm gonna do?"

"She's singing something from some opera."

With Revé Privette accompanying her on piano, Charm blew the roof off with a stunning performance of Un Bel Di, from Madame Butterfly. Fern barely hid her disgust when the audience sprang to its feet and rocked the auditorium with applause.

"Lurleen better be in good voice tonight," Junkin said. "That little Copenhaver gal was pretty darn good."

"Hush up!" Fern snapped.

Lurleen was easily the prettiest contestant, and since she had already won the swimsuit competition as well as Miss

Congeniality, she went into the talent competition with a solid lead. She had chosen Love Is Where You Find It and was sounding like Katheryn Grayson in The Kissing Bandit until she reached the dangerously high trill midway through the song. Her voice soared smoothly until, to everyone's horror, it quavered, cracked and stopped in a hoarse cough. For a long agonizing moment, Lurleen froze before bursting into tears and rushing offstage. Fern started to rise, but Junkin grabbed her arm.

"Leave her alone!" he whispered.

"But she needs her mother!" Fern insisted.

"What she needs is to act like a grown-up," Junkin griped. "I'm ashamed of a daughter who's a quitter."

"It was some kind of accident, Junkin. Her voice—"

"You're a judge, Fern. Now act like it!"

Fern reluctantly stayed put, even during the awkward wait before the emcee announced that Miss Lurleen Abernathy had voluntarily withdrawn from the pageant. That left no doubt as to the winner, and a few minutes later the entire auditorium was on its feet again when a teary Charm Copenhaver was crowned Miss Meander Sesquicentennial. Fern was humiliated, but Junkin was pragmatic.

"I reckon one good thing came out of this ugly business," he announced as they climbed back into the Eldorado.

"What's that?"

"No one can claim we rigged the damned thing."

52

Labor Day, September 2, 1957, dawned bright and beautiful over Calhoun County. The excitement in Meander was almost tangible as Fern's exhausted but eager volunteers put the finishing touches on decorations for the Sesquicentennial. American, Tennessee and Confederate flags flew from every house, store front and gas station, and Main Street was festooned with so much patriotic bunting that the place looked like a nesting ground for American eagles. Crockett Park was an explosion of red, white and blue crepe paper streamers, from the riverside bandstand to the VIP bleachers and speaker's dais. By the time the parade ended at the park and people settled in to watch Fern's gaudy line-up of events, a mysterious tingle was in the air. Everyone felt it but no one knew the source. Because Fern's top volunteers were allotted choice spots near the dais, the Harringtons had ringside seats along with Cassandra, Sylvianne and her new beau, Grady Fletcher.

Grady turned to Calvin. "Tell me something, old buddy. How did your mayor get his hands on that car he was riding in? Those things are barely off the assembly line."

"Who knows? All I can say is that it's one peculiar-looking automobile, especially with that grill."

"It looks like a Buick sucking a lemon."

"What did you say it's called, Grady?" Anrita asked.

"An Edsel."

Cassandra piped up. "What I really want to know is how Meander's First Lady found a dress and hair bleach in that same bilious yellow as the car. Not to mention matching opera gloves and football mum corsage." She gestured at Fern's Mistress of Ceremonies get-up, a body-hugging lace sheathe with exaggerated tulle ruching at the bosom and perilously high heels. She sported the same tiara she'd worn to Eulalie's soiree, this time with matching rhinestone choker. "Poor thing's got up like the Royal Trollop."

"I can just hear my farmer daddy now," Grady said.

"What would he be saying?" Sylvianne asked.

"That the woman looks like a bale of hay with the middle stave busted."

"On a serious note," Anrita said, pointing at the empty VIP dais, "where do you suppose the mayor is? He disappeared right after the parade ended."

"He's not the only one." Sylvianne took inventory as the last of the belles sat in a flurry of noisy crinolines. "Where's Lurleen? Did she drop out of this event too?"

"Uh, sort of." Anrita turned to Calvin. "I have something to tell you, and I hope you won't be mad at me."

"What is it, honey?"

"First, promise you'll stay here at my side."

He started to smile but stopped. "Alright."

Anrita was suspicious. "Do you know something?"

The smile bloomed. "Maybe."

"About John?"

"And Lurleen."

"You know?!"

"Of course I do. Our boy has never played favorites."

"Are you upset?"

"Not once I got over the shock of learning they were dating, but after John explained things and promised to stay in school before starting a family, I calmed down. Lurleen's a sweet girl. It would be un-Christian for us to shun her because of her family."

Anrita hugged him tight and blinked away tears. "I feel the same way."

"For heaven's sake!" Cassandra laughed. "Will someone please confirm what I've been waiting to hear since June?"

"You knew?!"

"Yes, indeed, and I can't tell you how flattered I was when those kids shared their secret. I swear they're an ideal match."

"What are y'all saying?" Sylvianne cried. "Did John and Lurleen get married?!"

"They're eloping to Ringgold this very minute," Anrita reported.

"Good for them, although God knows what the Abernathys will say when they find out."

Anrita scanned the bleachers. "Surely Fern's noticed that Lurleen's not up there with the rest of the belles."

"I suspect she hasn't noticed anything except all the attention she's getting."

Calvin indicated the nearby crowd. "If we don't keep our voices down, the whole town's going to know about John and Lurleen."

"You're right. We need to quit talking anyway. Looks like Fern's about to get this show on the road."

Fern signaled the high school band leader for a fanfare before raising her gloved hands for quiet. As she leaned into the microphone, her first words triggered a screeching reverb that had everyone covering their ears.

"Not so close!" Andy hissed. He was sitting nearby as Eulalie's slide show assistant. "Step back a little."

Fern did as she was told and continued cautiously. "As Chairman of the Meander Sequincentennial, I want to welcome everyone to this party for our town's one hundred and fiftieth birthday. Did y'all enjoy the parade?" She paused for applause, relieved that she was no longer deafening her audience. She thanked the Meander High School band for the music accompanying the Cavalcade of Cavaliers and Beautiful Belles and grudgingly congratulated Charm Copenhaver on being crowned queen of the festivities. "I think everyone will agree Charm is living proof that miracles can happen."

"That hateful witch," Cassandra said. "Makes me want to put a lily in her hand."

"What does that mean?" Grady asked.

"Cassie would like to kill her," Sylvianne explained.

Grady guffawed. "You Southerners sure have a colorful

way with words."

"And we never believe in using just one when fifteen will do."

"Now then," Fern continued grandly. "To start our program, I'd like to introduce a re-enactment of the inauguration speech of Jefferson Davis, the President of our beloved Confederacy. My husband the mayor was to have played President Davis but he was unfortunately called away on emergency official business. I'm sure we all appreciate his selfless dedication." After pausing for applause that didn't come, she flushed and cut her speech short. "I want to thank Principal Daniel Warren for filling in for the mayor on such short notice. The other actors are listed in your program."

"Ye Gods and little fishes!" Cassandra moaned. "I don't know if I'll make it through this freak show."

"You and me and a few hundred other people," Sylvianne sighed.

Grady leaned closer. "Want a hit on my flask?"

Sylvianne patted his cheek. "Grady, my boy. You are proof positive that there is such a thing as Western charm."

For everyone within earshot, the next half hour was excruciating as Principal Warren fought a losing thespian battle in a bad wig, fake goatee and a period costume designed for the much-bigger Junkin. Even with the belt cinched to its smallest, Warren was constantly tugging his trousers into place.

Calvin couldn't resist a dig. "Looks like poor old Jeff Davis is about to lose his pants along with the war."

"I may be a rebel at heart," Sylvianne said, "but I'm about ready to shoot that old gray head myself."

Cassandra pointed to the dais when Eulalie closed her eyes and her chin drooped to her chest. Andy gave her a gentle nudge. "Miss Sugar's so bored she fell asleep." She scanned the thoroughly bored crowd. "She's not the only one."

"Maybe our surprise guest will win everyone back," Grady

said.

"What surprise guest?" Cassandra asked.

"You'll find out."

Yawns and restless fidgeting continued until Warren completed his dreary recitation and the band struck up a half-hearted Dixie. Most of the musicians had also fallen asleep, and it wasn't until the final bars that all the instruments chimed in. Fern put on a game face when she didn't need to raise her hands to stop any applause.

"Now I'd like to introduce Miz Eulalie Saunders who will narrate a slide presentation on the history of Meander. She'll be assisted on the slide projector by Andrew Jenkins."

Eulalie acknowledged the applause as she took the podium and waved to some familiar faces before holding up two books. "A few months ago, my good friend Andy here made a remarkable discovery in the old slave cabin on my property. This old family bible contains the history that went missing when the courthouse burned in eighteen-sixty-two, and this law book explains how our forefathers chose to govern in the early days. I have since checked with an attorney in Nashville who assures me that this book is not only authentic, but that its laws are still officially on the books. And some of them are real humdingers!"

Fern was seething. "Miz Saunders!" she hissed. "What are you doing? Stick to the script!"

Eulalie continued facing the microphone to ensure her response would be heard throughout the park. "For those of you who didn't hear the question, Mrs. Abernathy wants to know why I'm changing from her speech to my own. With all due respect, her Southern-fried facts are as fictional as Tara plantation. You good people deserve the truth about our hometown, and with a little help from someone you'll all recognize, I'm going to give it to you."

"Over my dead body, you sabotaging Judas!" Fern was halfway out of her seat when a tall figure slipped onto the dais and blocked her path. "Who the devil are you?"

Whatever the man replied was lost in wild whoops and applause as the crowd recognized Robert Mitchum.

"Ladies and gentlemen!" Eulalie called. "Please give a warm welcome to one of Hollywood's biggest stars, Mr. Robert Mitchum."

Mitchum politely waited for enormous applause to die down before saying a few words about the beauty of east Tennessee and western North Carolina where he shot his latest film, Thunder Road.

"This afternoon, Miss Sugar here took me out to see the real Thunder Road, and I'm mighty glad I didn't have to drive it myself. That's one helluva highway." After more cheers and whistles, he said, "But tonight is about you folks so let's get back to the program. I'm only here to turn the pages for this pretty lady." The crowd went wild when he leaned down and bussed Eulalie's cheek. Fern verged on apoplexy.

"Alright, everyone," Eulalie continued, "Please direct your attention to the big screen by the bandstand. It's show time!"

Eulalie's anecdote-packed history lesson combined with carefully chosen slides captivated everyone but the disgruntled Fern and a host of shadowy figures that began slithering into the crowd from all sides of the park. Because Meander's history archives had burned, no one knew what had transpired on this hallowed ground, and there was audible response when Eulalie described the heavy guerilla warfare inflicted on the Confederate army by the local citizenry and announced that East Tennessee had tried to secede from Tennessee and rejoin the Union.

"Not only that," she declared, "but you should be proud to know Tennesseans tried to give colored people the right to vote at their seventeen-ninety-six Constitutional Convention." She was waiting for Mitchum to turn the page when a deep voice boomed through the park.

"Lies! All lies!"

Eulalie's heart clutched when she looked up from her

speech and saw that the crowd in colorful summer clothes was now dotted with peaked white hoods. "Sweet Jesus, no!"

"What the hell?!!" Mitchum growled. "Is that the Ku Klux Klan?"

"I'm afraid so."

Eulalie gave up hope of continuing her narrative when shouting flared between the citizens of Meander and the intruders. The taunting quickly grew heated as two very different, long-simmering pots finally boiled over. No one knew who started the shoving or threw the first punch, but things escalated at a dizzying pace until the park exploded in chaos. As Eulalie watched in horror, a large robed figure pushed people aside and headed straight for the dais.

Mitchum draped a protective arm around Eulalie's shoulders. "Want me to get you out of here, ma-am?"

"Thank you, no. I'll be fine, but you're a big movie star, Mr. Mitchum, and you should get out of here."

"No way!"

Both looked down as the hooded figure reached the dais and shook a fist in Eulalie's direction. "You lying, nigger-loving bitch! You're a disgrace to Southern womanhood!"

There was no mistaking Junkin Abernathy's voice.

Calvin's years as a college halfback came into play as he leapt from his front row seat and tackled the mayor. Not only did he send Junkin sprawling but he ripped off the mayor's hood and tore his brand new Exalted Cyclops robe right up the back, exposing what was underneath his long robe. Those close enough to see pointed, yelled and exploded with laughter.

Junkin Abernathy was wearing a woman's pink panties, a lacy half-slip and a brassiere stuffed with wads of toilet paper.

"What in heaven's name?!" Anrita gasped.

"Jesus Christ!" cried Sylvianne.

"Talk about show time!" Cassandra cackled.

"And I thought I'd seen everything in Hollywood!" Robert Mitchum shouted.

Eulalie was focused elsewhere. "Time for that special slide!" she called to Andy.

"Coming right up!"

Andy deftly switched the slide of a Harper's Weekly lithograph of the Tennessee River to one of Junkin Abernathy locking lips with Lorraine Jones. When she saw the screen, Fern's hysterical screams traveled halfway to Knoxville as she leapt from the dais and rushed at her philandering husband. The double whammy of what was under Junkin's robes and the Kodachrome slide of him with his black mistress drove the disgraced Klansmen into chaotic retreat while Meander's townsfolk roared with laughter. But the best was yet to come as Fern straddled Junkin's midsection, skirt hiked high enough to reveal her daffodil-hued panties as she pounded her husband's chest and face. Her tiara swung alongside her head, snagged by a lock of bleached hair, as petals from her shattered mum corsage covered Junkin's body like so much yellow confetti.

"Looks like Miss Fern wants to put a lily in the mayor's hand," Cassie said.

While Mitchum remained transfixed by the melee, Eulalie flipped the pages of her law book to a particular page. She shoved it toward Andy. "Do you remember this?"

"Oh, my Lord! Of course, I do." Both turned as Chuck Kirkendol burst onto the dais and looked down at the flailing, wailing Abernathys.

"What the hell's going on down there?" he shouted.

"Sheriff Kirkendol!" Andy shoved the book at him. "You need to see this!"

Chuck pushed past him. "Later, buddy. I gotta get down there!"

Eulalie grabbed his arm. "It's important, Chuck. Please take a look."

Her commanding tone and the use of his first name gave the sheriff pause, and he bent over the book. As he read the passage Andy indicated, Kirkendol's annoyance turned to disbelief.

"Is this for real, Miss Sugar?"

"As real as it gets, young man."

"I'll be damned!" To her surprise, Chuck gave her a quick hug before leaping to the ground. With considerable difficulty, he grabbed Fern around the waist and pulled her off Junkin. She was still cursing and fighting like a wildcat, but Calvin and Grady managed to restrain her while the sheriff got Junkin to his feet amid a sea of toilet paper wads.

"Mayor Abernathy, you are under arrest!"

"For what?" Junkin sputtered.

"Help me out, Andy!" Kirkendol yelled.

"For violating Law 32, Statute 4-A, Section B of the Meander penal code!" Andy shouted back.

"What the hell are you fools talking about?" Junkin demanded, turning to confront the sheriff and unwittingly giving the crowd a rear view of his ladies' unmentionables. He ignored a wave of fresh catcalls. "Well?!"

Kirkendol turned back toward the dais. "Miss Sugar, would you be kind enough to take the microphone and respond to the mayor's question?"

"With pleasure, sheriff!" Eulalie's clear voice sailed to the farthest reaches of the park. "It is against the law in Meander, Calhoun County, Tennessee, for a male to appear in public wearing more than two items of female clothing." Over the roar of laughter, she said, "How many items can you identify, sheriff?"

"I count three, Miss Sugar," he replied as more laughter and whistles erupted. "And I sure ain't gonna look for more!"

"Jackpot!" Eulalie cried as Andy grabbed her and waltzed around the dais.

Scowling and red-faced, Junkin was hauled off to jail with his tattered Klansman robe and dirty lingerie displayed for all the world to see. His humiliation was complete when Robert Mitchum stepped up to the microphone and delivered the coup de grace.

"Hey, Mr. Mayor! Your slip's showing!"

* * *

"I feel like singing 'Ding-dong, the witch is dead," Andy said as Eulalie took his arm and headed for the park's stone gate.

"Me too. Who could imagine our sesquicentennial would end with bigger fireworks in the park than over the river." They had waited on the dais until the park was empty, enjoying the lightning bugs and chirruping crickets and the calm after the storm. As they walked to Andy's car, a flash of yellow caught Eulalie's eye when they reached the street. "Isn't that the Abernathys' new car over there?"

Andy squinted in the dim street lights. "It sure is. It must've gotten left behind, what with Junkin in the hoosegow and Fern in hysterics."

"Didn't she follow him to the jail?"

"Who knows? I was too busy watching Cassandra smooching with the sheriff."

"Another surprise on a day brimming with them. If someone had told me this morning everything that was going to happen tonight, I'd never have believed them."

"It's the kind of thing you can't make up," Andy said. "Did you have a favorite moment?"

"I lost count." Eulalie confessed. "How about you?"

"I guess when the townsfolk chased those cowards out of the park. I've never been so proud of this little burg."

"I couldn't agree more." As they walked on, Eulalie abruptly stopped. "Did you hear something?"

"Like what?"

"I'm not sure. Whimpering maybe." Andy gave her a blank look. "Stay here a minute." Eulalie walked over to the open convertible and leaned into the back seat. Andy heard low voices before she straightened up and motioned him over. She met him halfway to the car. "Fern's in the back seat, all curled up in the fetal position. She's in pretty bad shape."

"Should I call a doctor?"

"No, no. I think she's seen enough people for one day."
She looked a bit stricken. "I'm going to stay with her awhile."

"After she publicly insulted you on the dais?" He marveled. "You're a lot more forgiving than I am."

"Oh, I don't know about that." Eulalie looked sad. "Besides, I'm partly responsible for what happened tonight."

"Even so, I wouldn't feel right leaving you here."

"I promise I'll be fine, sugar. There's a phone booth right across the street. I'll call a cab when I'm ready to go home."

"You're sure?"

"Absolutely. Run on now." Eulalie pecked his cheek and went back to the Edsel where Fern hadn't moved. "Mrs. Abernathy? It's Eulalie Saunders again." Fern scrunched up even tighter. "Are you alright?"

"Go away and leave me alone."

"I'm not leaving you alone in this wide-open car. If you need someone to drive you home—"

"I don't need nobody," Fern said in a choked voice.

"Sure, you do, sugar. We all do. And we've all had bad days before."

"Bad day?!" Fern sniffled and snorted. "My husband made a giant fool of himself before the whole town and got himself thrown in jail and everything I worked on so hard blew up in my face, and my knee is banged up and I've lost a shoe, and on top of that my daughter's disappeared and I'm worried sick because I've no idea where she is." She shook so badly that her tiara, snagged in her hair, swung down and scraped her cheek. "Ouch!"

"Be careful or you'll put your eye out with that thing."

Fern groaned and sat up. Her elaborate beehive had unraveled into a lopsided rat's nest, and her gown was torn and dirty from her scuffle with Junkin. Thick mascara ran in teary black rivulets down her cheeks, and she was missing a yellow glove. She didn't flinch when Eulalie leaned down to gently unsnarl the tiara from her hair and hand it to her.

"Thank you."

"You're welcome. Now may I keep you company a few minutes?"

"What for?"

"Because we need to talk. For starters, I know where Lurleen is."

53

Lurleen's giddy mood plummeted when John parked in front of Ringgold's Chapel of Eternal Love and opened her car door. Hovering atop a sign flashing "Where Over 4,000 Love Doves Began Their Flight to Happiness!" were a couple of obese, badly painted doves, touching beaks and forming a crude heart with their wings.

"Good Lord," she murmured. "Could this place be tackier?"

John feigned disappointment. "Don't you want to be my little love dove?"

"Only if it's our lovey-dovey little secret." She took his arm as they walked toward a front door splattered with more hearts and doves. "But judging from the looks of this place, the faster we make it legal and get to the motel, the better."

Haste, however, was not on the agenda. Lurleen's hopes for a quick ceremony were undone by a justice of the peace reeking of cheap whiskey and yawning so often that the four other waiting couples yawned too. Nor had Lurleen expected half the brides-to-be to be in an advance state of pregnancy or to hear an LP of "Oh Promise Me" so badly scratched that it repeatedly stuck. Between yawns, the justice's frowsy wife, doing double duty as witness and musical director, gave the record player so many swats that the needle mercifully skipped to the end.

Lurleen was numbed by the tasteless scenario, barely recalling anything between "dearly beloved" and "Kiss the bride, son." John's kiss brought her back to reality, as did the minister's loud belch and instructions to pay his wife on the way out. John apologized as he and his new wife walked back to the car.

"I'm sorry that was so awful, honey. I hope you'll agree that the end justified the means."

"Of course, it does, and it's not your fault." She fanned her face. "I just want to take a bath and wash off that man's whiskey breath. All that yawning! If I'd seen his uvula one more time I think I would've screamed."

"At least he gave us stories for our future kids, right, Mrs. Harrington?"

"Right, Mr. Harrington." Lurleen snuggled close as John started the engine. She was fighting a residual yawn when he drove a mere hundred yards to Honeybee's Honey of a Honeymoon Hotel. "What are we doing here?"

"What do couples usually do at honeymoon hotels?"

Lurleen ignored the joke and peered through the windshield. "This place is way too fancy. We agreed to find a cheap tourist court somewhere, remember?"

"I didn't agree to any such thing. If you think back, I only nodded."

"What're you up to, boy?"

"Giving you a night of unbridled passion in the best honeymoon suite Ringgold, Georgia has to offer," John said, wiggling his eyebrows like Groucho Marx.

"That's very sweet, and I appreciate the thought, but what about saving money for school this fall? You know we're going to have a lot of expenses, and—"

John held out his hands, palms up. "It's not my idea."

"What do you mean?"

"It's a wedding gift from my parents. I told them separately that we were going to elope and they both slipped me money for the honeymoon. Mother pretended it was because we were saving her the expense of buying a new dress, and Daddy said it was because I was marrying the 'most precious little gal in Tennessee.' That's exactly what they said. Promise."

"I love your parents."

"You may have second thoughts when you get a load of our honeymoon suite."

"What do you mean?"

"I mean that Honeybee's Honey of a Honeymoon Hotel sent me a brochure."

"And?"

"You'll see."

"Whatever it is, it can't be worse than that horror back down the road."

"This is a different sort of horror, sweetheart. You better stay in the car while I get us checked in."

Lurleen reacted with a mix of dread and delight when John swept her into his arms and carried her into the suite. For a moment, neither could speak, overwhelmed by a sea of bad gold-and-white French provincial furniture and whore-red velvet draperies. The bed was, naturally, heart-shaped and smothered by a gold silk canopy wrangled by a herd of bare-bottomed plaster-of-Paris cherubs. The bedspread was such an intense puce it bore an unfortunate resemblance to bloodstains. Overhead, Muzak ceiling speakers hummed softly as Pat Boone sang "Love Letters in the Sand."

John didn't realize he was still holding Lurleen until she told him to put her down. "I'm afraid you'll drown," he said.

He referred to royal blue shag carpeting so deep Lurleen's toes disappeared as she waded across the room to inspect the hideous bed. To her relief, the spread and sheets were freshly laundered.

"Super clean and super tacky," she pronounced. "Makes me feel right at home."

"It'll look better with the lights out."

John reached for her but Lurleen backed away. "Down boy! I still want that bath, although Lord knows what that bathroom will be like."

"If you're not out in fifteen minutes, I'm coming in after you."

Lurleen grabbed her ivory-colored overnight bag. "Promise?"

"Promise."

John stretched out on the bed and, lulled by Lurleen's soft

singing, began to doze. He awoke to find her beside him in a filmy negligee secretly ordered from the Marshall Field's catalogue, and within minutes, they were basking in the afterglow of being husband and wife.

"I've never been happier than at this very moment," John confessed.

"Me either."

"I'm so happy I want to call the folks and tell them everything's alright." He eyed a frilly French telephone. "Do you think that stupid-looking thing works?"

"Pick it up and see. I'm going to change for dinner. I spotted a Stuckey's this side of Chattanooga."

"Sounds good. I could go for some of their divinity."

"Or maybe a pecan praline."

Lurleen blew him a kiss before disappearing into the bathroom. He pretended to catch her kiss before grabbing the phone and asking the front desk to connect him with long distance. His mother answered, and although Anrita was thrilled to hear that he and Lurleen were alright, her tone told John something was wrong.

"Is everything okay, Mama?"

"Your dad and I are fine, but ... oh, dear! I don't want to ruin your special day."

"Uh-oh. Did something bad happen at the sesquicentennial?"

"Not something, darling. *Everything!* For starters, your brand-new father-in-law is in jail."

"What?!"

John was alternately tickled and appalled at his mother's account of Meander's disastrous birthday party. He especially enjoyed her description of the Klan being chased from Crockett Park. "Sounds like the angry townspeople in that Frankenstein movie."

"And we're all hoping the monster's been run out of town for good."

"What a mess." John looked toward the bathroom door,

wondering how to break the news to Lurleen. "How's Mrs. Abernathy holding up?"

"To tell you the truth I don't know. After they pulled her and Junkin apart, she disappeared. She's a difficult woman for sure, but nobody deserves to be publicly humiliated like that, and I feel sorry for her. I'm sure she was terribly embarrassed, and I imagine she went home to lick her wounds."

"I guess we'll find out soon enough, but I'm not sure what to do now."

"About what?"

"How much I should tell Lurleen."

"You may as well go ahead and tell her the truth, son. She'll hear all the gory details as soon as y'all get back to Meander, and it'll be easier coming from you. Hold on a minute." John listened as his mother's hand muffled the receiver a few seconds. "Your dad says Dave Mearns is setting headlines in Second Coming type for tomorrow's paper, so you'd better prepare Lurleen as best you can." When John didn't respond, she added, "Oh, son, I hope this doesn't ruin your honeymoon.

"It won't. I'm going to wait and tell her on the drive home tomorrow."

"That's my boy. You can also tell her we send our love and best wishes and can't wait to welcome her into the family."

"Okay."

"Y'all drive safe now."

"We will, Mama. G'night."

"Good-night, John."

"What're you going to tell me on the drive home?" Lurleen stood in the bathroom doorway, brushing her hair.

"I guess you heard—"

"Only that last part."

He hung up the telephone and patted the bed beside him. "Come sit for a minute."

Lurleen paled a bit. "Is it serious?"

"If you mean is anybody hurt, the answer is no, but Mama said a lot of crazy stuff happened at the celebration tonight."

"What kind of crazy stuff?"

"Come here and I'll tell you."

Lurleen listened with shock and disbelief when he repeated Anrita's story. When he finished with the description of her parents rolling around on the ground, she pulled away and reached for the telephone.

"I have to call home."

"I understand." John watched with concern while Lurleen placed the call and hung up in frustration when the operator said there was no answer. "Are you alright?"

"No, I'm not, John. I need to get home. I know my mother as well as I know myself, and it's absolutely not like her to disappear."

"Maybe she's not answering the phone."

"She's never been able to ignore a ringing telephone, not even when Daddy got all those crank calls during the election."

"Maybe she went to see your father and is trying to raise bail."

Lurleen sniffed. "After what Daddy did, he'd better stay in jail where she can't get at him." She stood. "I need to find her and make sure she's okay. Fern Myrtle Grimes Abernathy may be a lot of things I don't like, but she's still my mama."

"Whatever you say, honey. Let's pack."

54

Meander couldn't stop talking about what happened that fateful night, but if it had known what was unfolding at Blufftop, the gossip machine would've gone into overdrive.

Eulalie and Fern were in the library, sipping coffee and munching Lou's cookies. Fern's hair was still wet after a long soak in Eulalie's old claw-foot tub, and she was wrapped in a luxurious terrycloth robe reserved for overnight guests. When Eulalie changed into a silk kimono, Lou quipped that it looked like a slumber party for old folks. The remark, albeit good-natured, got her banished to the kitchen to rustle up more cookies. Fern had lost many things that night, but her appetite was not one of them.

"Feeling better, my dear?" Eulalie asked.

"Yes, thanks, but I'd feel a whole lot better if I could figure out what the heck I'm doing here. I mean, everything that happened has me wondering if I've lost my marbles, and being here with you isn't helping."

"Please don't think me patronizing, but helping is exactly what I want to do."

Ever since finding Fern helplessly hunkered in the back seat of the Edsel, Eulalie had done her best to pull the woman from the brink of hysteria. She got off to a rough start by breaking the news that Lurleen had eloped with John Harrington, which triggered a ferocious hissy fit. That was the situation when Sheriff Kirkendol and his deputy came to investigate the screams. Chuck agreed when Eulalie asked him to drive them to Blufftop where she finally calmed Fern by insisting she get out of her tattered gown, take a hot bath and wash her hair. Only afterwards was Fern collected enough to listen as Eulalie extolled John's character and fine family and insisted that Lurleen had done very well for herself.

"I suspect you're right, Miss Sugar. Heaven knows my

Lurleen couldn't do worse than her stupid old mama."

"Don't be so hard on yourself. You and Mr. Abernathy were practically children when you married, and surely he wasn't such a bad egg back then."

"I'm not so sure. In fact, I'm not sure of a lot of things and keep asking myself how I could have been so dumb. How could I have ignored all those ugly things about the election and a lot of other nasty stuff too? Junkin was forever using the extension for phone calls and telling me to leave when one of his buddies came over. I wondered what they were talking about. Now I know it was women and the Ku Klux Klan, and heaven knows what else." She sipped her coffee with a trembling hand. "I've got to be one of the stupidest wives in history."

"No, you're not. I'm sure a day doesn't go by that some woman doesn't learn her husband is cheating or is involved in some form of nefarious behavior."

"Lucky me, I got the double whammy, although I'm not sure what your big word means."

"Nefarious is another way of saying Ku Klux Klan."

"Oh."

"And you never had a clue about either one?"

"No, ma-am. Can you blame me for going so crazy?"

"Not at all. If I'd been in your shoes I'd probably have grabbed my husband's elephant gun and gelded him on the spot."

Fern's eyebrows shot up. "Was that what blew the burning cross into the river?"

"Yes, indeedy. Andy Jenkins is a wicked shot with that thing."

"Good for him. I wish I'd had the courage to do something like that."

"You have more courage than you think."

"What makes you say that?"

"The way you behaved at my dinner party."

"What do you mean?"

"I had no idea what you would do when you met the guest of honor."

"I admit I started to storm out, but then I thought about how flattered I was that you'd invited somebody like me to dinner and how much I'd looked forward to it, and I decided I wasn't gonna let some African woman ruin it for me."

"I suppose now's the time to confess that the 'African woman' is Anrita's plant manager. Her name is Mary Fox and she's from Knoxville."

Fern was incredulous. "You don't mean that!"

"Oh, but I do, my dear."

"But why would you go to all the trouble to—?"

"It was my way of proving that no one's the worse for wear after socializing with black folks."

"I'll be damned!" To Eulalie's surprise, Fern burst out laughing. After a moment she said, "I gotta say you sure put one over on me, but you're right. Breaking bread with a colored didn't hurt me one bit."

Fern's admission gave Eulalie genuine hope for Meander's future.

"I'm happy to hear you say that." She looked toward the door when Lou reappeared empty-handed. "What happened to the cookies?"

"You've got company," Lou said.

Eulalie glanced at the grandfather clock and saw it was almost midnight. "Who in the world—?"

"Miz Abernathy's daughter and the Harrington boy." Lou turned and motioned toward the parlor. "Y'all come on in."

Lurleen rushed to embrace Fern. "Are you alright, Mama?"

"I'm fine, baby girl." Fern kissed her daughter's cheek. "I guess you know what happened."

"Mrs. Harrington told us everything. John and I were down in Ringgold, and when you didn't answer the phone we came home to look for you."

"How'd you find me?"

"I called Chuck Kirkendol," John explained. "He said he found you two outside Crockett Park and brought you up here."

Lurleen remembered her manners and looked at Eulalie. "Miss Sugar, I'm sorry to barge in like this, but we were so worried and all."

"I understand, sugar." Eulalie said. "Would you newlyweds like some coffee?"

John looked sheepish. "So you know we eloped, huh?"

"We know, and we think it's wonderful, don't we, Fern?"

"Indeed, we do," Fern replied.

"Oh, Mama!" Lurleen cried. "Really?"

"Really."

Lurleen remained astonished. She couldn't believe how pretty her mother looked without the caked-on make-up, lacquered beehive and loud clothes. In Eulalie's white robe, face scrubbed clean and an air of peace about her, Fern looked like a different woman.

"There's something I don't understand though," Lurleen said. "Since when did you two get so chummy?"

Fern tossed her damp curls. "Since we decided to let our hair down and get acquainted."

"And we've discovered we have lots more in common than we thought," Eulalie added.

Lurleen remained mystified "Like what?"

"Oh, like wanting to rescue and rejuvenate our beloved but ignorant, bigoted, white trashy, mayonnaise-slathering, moonshine-swilling, kudzu-swarming, cotton-picking, deep-frying, Bible-beatin' South."

Fern leaned over and clinked her coffee cup against Eulalie's. "Amen to that, sister."

Lurleen looked at John. "Now I've heard everything."

Eulalie waved at Lou, still in the doorway where she'd been watching the goings-on with a bemused stare. "This definitely calls for a celebration. How about pouring shots of bourbon for everyone, yourself included."

Lou grinned. "Coming up!"

John said, "That sounds mighty good to me, only—"

"Only what, young man?"

"I'm just surprised, that's all."

"About what?"

"My mama's always saying what a fine lady you are, and so I figured you for the refined, sherry type."

"Well, tonight's so very special that I feel like being a little unrefined." She winked at Lou and added, "Sugar."

Epilogue

Ida Turnbull says that what happened on Labor Day will go down as the most important moment in Meander history. She likens it to the assassination of Huey Long which freed Louisiana from the grip of a tyrant. As things turned out, Junkin Abernathy spent only one night in jail and was released the next morning after promising to leave Calhoun County for good. Sheriff Kirkendol was understandably skeptical of a villain's promise, but sure enough the mayor packed his torn robe and muddied undies and disappeared. Nobody, including his estranged wife and daughter, knows where he went, nor has anybody seen or heard of the Ku Klux Klan since their Exalted Cyclops flew the coop.

Chuck Kirkendol was appointed mayor following an emergency meeting of the city council and reaped an even greater honor when Cassandra Maddox accepted his proposal of marriage. When Cassie, as Meander's new First Lady, reminded Daniel Warren that both the school board and his wife Gayle would be interested to know why she slapped him, Warren promptly forgot any plans to fire her.

Mr. and Mrs. John Harrington now live in married students housing at the University of Tennessee in Knoxville, and Sylvianne McNeil writes that Hollywood isn't the cesspool everyone claims. Mary Fox operates a branch of the N.A.A.C.P. from a small storefront on Vine Street, and Anrita and Calvin are opening more salad plants in Memphis and Richmond, while Andy Jenkins shares both home and a thriving landscape business with Jack Freels, Sylvianne's prodigal brother. The biggest surprise in Meander was Fern's about-face as a human being and her friendship with Eulalie. Lou jokes that the two are thick as thieves, and Miss Ida says they give her new hope that peaceful coexistence between America and the Soviet Union is possible.

The End

If you enjoyed *Unrefined, Sugar,* I would be honored if you would tell others by writing a review on the retailer's website where you purchased this title.

Thank you!
Michael Llewellyn

Author's Notes

Others growing up in Fountain City, Tennessee, will likely guess that Anrita Harrington's character is based on the late Grace Kinser whose "Home-Style Salads" empire stretched from Knoxville to Miami. Gracie was a long-time friend of my parents, and, after moving to Atlanta, she kept me supplied with chicken salad when I was a student at Georgia Tech. She was a great lady and a celebrated philanthropist. I based no other characters on real personages, although fellow Central High School classmates will find their names intentionally mismatched. It's my way of acknowledging friendships spanning over half a century.

I hope everyone enjoys the ride.

"That marvelous train no longer runs, but my memories scream, 'All aboard!' It's all so changed I could loudly weep. I see that little boy—dime in hand—waiting for the movie house to open more than doors." —Page Johnson

Acknowledgments

Thanks are due to artist Bob Bush for another handsome cover design, and to A Thirsty Mind Book Design for their fine formatting. Special thanks to Jane Smith Patterson for her keen editing skills. I could not have produced this book without them.

About the Author

Michael Llewellyn is the author of twenty-two published books under various pen names in historical fiction, adventure, contemporary fiction, mystery and nonfiction travel. He is married and lives in Fredericksburg, Virginia. Visit him at http://michael-llewellyn.net/

Made in the USA
Middletown, DE
07 June 2018